I0788155

Dragon Tide: Episodes 1-5

Dragon Tide Omnibuses, Volume 1

Sarah K. L. Wilson

Published by Sarah K. L. Wilson, 2020.

DRAGON TIDE: EPISODES 1-5

First edition. March 21, 2020.

Written by Sarah K. L. Wilson.

For my little adventurers, Nev & Leif.

Other Books by Sarah K. L. Wilson

Dragon School Series
First Flight
Initiate
The Dark Prince
The Ruby Isles
Sworn
Dusk Covenant
First Message
Warring Promises
Prince of Dragons
Dark Night
Bright Hopes
Mark of Loyalty
Dire Quest
Ancient Allies
Pipe of Wings
Dragon Piper
Dust of Death
Troubled War
Starie Night
Ascendant Light
Dragon Chameleon Series
Rogue's Quest
Paths of Deception
City of Ice
Mist of Power
Silver Eyes
World of Legends
Chase the Moon
Shadow Quest

Creeping Darkness
Golem Siege
Memory of Mountains
Color of Victory
The Unweaving Chronicles Series
Teeth of the Gods
Lightning Strikes Twice
Thunder Rattles High
Bridge of Legends (ongoing)
Summernight
Dawnspell

*I wrote a story for my fans called WORTH A DRAGON[1].
This story became so powerful and real to me, that it inspired the Dragon Tide
series. You can read this series without reading the short story first, but it's
available for free to anyone who wants to read it. Find it on my website.
www.sarahklwilson.com.
Keep your tissues handy! It's a tear-jerker!*

---

1. https://dl.bookfunnel.com/ole7umzcrt

Episode One: Dragonlet

Chapter One

When your strongest memory is of a magnificent dragon, you think you see dragons everywhere.

Or at least, I always did.

I was standing on the ragged coast of our island looking out over a turquoise sea and dreaming that I saw dragons just under the surface of the water, their scales flickering in the light. I'd seen them there once when they saved me, rescuing me and my protector – Ramariri – when we thought we would both drown. He'd been so brave that day and so strong. I hadn't even realized that the golden dragon was really dying even as he fought to bring me to safety.

And every year on my birthday, I came out to the coast like I was doing right then and I looked out over the vast sea and thought of Ramariri and re-membered what he did for me – how he'd given his life to keep a six-year-old orphan safe.

Somehow, I would make his sacrifice worth it.

The waves lapped against the shore and I walked on the rocks and patch-es of sand in my favorite heeled boots – completely impractical for the beach. What would Ramariri have thought of those? I still thought I heard echoes of his voice in my mind sometimes.

Gulls screamed overhead, breaking my reverie and I sighed. I should get back to town before dinner. My adoptive parents were planning a surprise party for me.

I hate surprises because I like to know everything. I'd guessed that they were planning one ages ago. I was even practicing my surprised face so that I would be ready when I arrived. I tried it again. Could I fool them? I tried it again a little more subdued.

A sound almost like a song called to me and I looked wistfully out to the sea. Sometimes, when I was alone, I thought I could hear the ocean call me with a siren sound so beautiful that it was almost impossible to ignore. It was calling now.

And so was something else.

I tilted my head to the side, listening. What was that?

A sound like a cat's purr mixed with the squawk of a raven came from between the rocks up ahead. With a frown, I followed it.

I really should be heading back. But then I'd wonder what I'd missed here on the beach. I wouldn't want to miss out on investigating, would I?

The rocks were jagged here, and my heeled boots really were impractical – but so pretty! – as I worked my way carefully between them, trying not to twist an ankle.

There it was – the same sound again!

I followed the sound, but there was nothing here but rocks. Maybe some poor bird was injured and making that strange sound. I looked behind the nearest large rock, but there was nothing there. The sound came again.

And now it sounded almost as if it were mixing with that faint singing that I always heard when I was near the sea.

How strange.

I looked behind the next large rock. There was nothing there either. I should go back.

But maybe it would be around the next rock. One more couldn't hurt, right? It didn't make sense to give up without looking.

I picked my way to the next human-sized rock, looking behind it.

Shards of glass lay among the rocks. But they weren't the bottle-green I was used to. They were large, curved shards of smoky blue glass.

What could that be from? Glass was rare enough on the Havenwind Islands that no one would break it and then just leave it in the sand. I leaned down, picking up a shard of glass and holding it up to the light.

Transparent rainbows ran along the curve of the glass in an opalescent dance. The soft-blue glass made everything I saw through it look peaceful, as if I was swimming beneath the waves of the sea.

The sound came again.

That was close! Was it on the other side of the rock now? The side I'd just been on?

Quickly, I hurried around the rock, but now the sound was on the side with the glass again. I frowned, changing directions quickly and speeding around the rock again.

There!

A tiny creature, no bigger than a kitten, was sitting in the shards of glass looking up at me with huge pearly eyes. His tiny wings were tucked in close and small frills on his cheeks made him look surprised as he stared at me. He was blue as the sea and his tail tucked around his feet protectively.

He was a dragon.

A tiny, baby dragon.

I gasped with delight, dropping into a crouch.

"Well hello, little guy!" I said, reaching for him slowly, like I was going to pet a stray dog.

He flamed at my fingers and I flinched, but the flame wasn't hot enough to burn them. With a chuckle, I reached forward again, meaning to stroke his head but he leapt forward, landing on my arm and scrambling up to my shoulder.

I laughed, delight and surprise filling me in equal measure.

"Now, you're a surprise!" I said, running a finger over his small head. "Where are your parents? Are there more Blue Dragons here?"

But it would be hard to hide a full-grown dragon in these rocks.

I stood on tiptoes, looking at the ocean and the rocky shore and the tree-line, but there were no snuffling snouts or folded wings. No jets of flame or hisses of steam. No mental voices speaking to me.

"Dragons?" I called. "Are there any dragons here?"

There was nothing but silence. Just me and a helpless little dragon who was chewing on my ear.

In the distance, I saw the big flag unfurl on the high flagpole at the center of the village.

My party. If I didn't go to it, everyone would be worried. I'd better hurry. And I'd better think of something to do with the baby dragon.

"Go on, then," I urged. "Back to your momma."

I set him down on the sand, but he darted right back up to my shoulder, hiding under my hair.

"It's better if you're with your own kind," I said. "Safer."

I tried again to disentangle him from my shoulder, but he held on firmly, tiny claws biting into my shoulder and tail curled around my neck.

There were no parents nearby. No one to take care of him except for me, and he seemed determined to stay with me. With a sigh, I made a decision. No baby dragons would be abandoned on my watch!

"What should I call you?" I asked, flipping my long blonde hair over my shoulder and away from his chewing little teeth. His tail tangled around my neck and he hunkered down on my shoulder with a whine. "And where in the world, am I going to hide you?"

Because I definitely couldn't bring him to the village.

Not a Blue Dragon.

Not if I wanted him to live.

Chapter Two

There was already laughter and song when I reached the edge of our village. My father's fishing buoys hung in a line where he'd repaired them earlier today, their glass bulbs flashing in the afternoon light. He wouldn't lose as many days fishing as he feared.

Nets were strung between the trees where I'd spent my morning repairing holes and sorting out tangles. The smell of baking fish and vegetables filled the air, making my mouth water and making the baby dragon's belly rumble against my shoulder. Lanterns had been strung up in preparation for the party and a fire lit, and as I peered around the edge of our cottage, I could see that most of the village was already assembled even though it wasn't dark yet.

Now, where to hide the little dragon? He'd fallen asleep on my shoulder, his little sighs and snorts – while adorable – were definitely going to be noticed even if I covered him with my hair. And his rumbling purrs were putting me to sleep.

"Seleska!"

I jumped at the whispered voice.

Who –?

I whirled to look behind me, but it was only Heron, the blacksmith's apprentice. He was grinning, his white teeth gleaming in the afternoon light looking so pale next to his dark skin and warm brown eyes.

"Peeking at your own party?" he asked, teasingly. He stepped forward, always careful with his movements. His arms and back had thickened with muscle in the past few years of his apprenticeship and I'd watched him bend steel bars with his bare hands. But he was always gentle near me like he was afraid to break me.

"Maybe," I said, pulling my hair further forward to hide the dragon. He needed a name. I couldn't just keep thinking of him as 'dragon.'

"You know it's supposed to be a surprise," he teased. "But no one can surprise Seleska because she always finds out first."

"The boots were a surprise," I said. I'd probably mentioned a thousand times that I would like boots with a tall heel like the ones I'd seen a lady wearing in Abergande, but no one ever listened – until this morning when I found a pair of boots with iron-spiked heels on my doorstep. I knew exactly who had given them to me. There was only one person in the village who would indulge me that far. I gave him my most innocent look. "Do you think dragons brought them?"

"I think you have friends you don't even realize that you have," he teased, but then his face fell a little.

"Are you okay?" I asked, stepping forward and reaching out to touch his arm comfortingly. "Heron?"

He froze, his face filled with sudden fear. "Seleska!"

"What? Are you okay?"

"Seleska," he repeated, his voice hoarse. "What is that on your shoulder?"

I felt my cheeks heating. I bit my lip before replying.

"Wait! Don't get upset, Heron."

"Seleska," he looked around us before coming in so close that his forehead almost touched mine. Shock and worry filled his features, but he was still gentle as he whispered, "is that a dragon on your shoulder?"

"It might be," I said, admitting nothing despite the small snores coming from under my thick blonde hair.

"A Blue Dragon? The kind that pulls fishing boats under and kills sailors? The reason that we receive so few visitors from beyond? The reason that we do not sail the sea? *That* kind of dragon?"

"A dragon saved me," I protested in a small voice.

"A gold dragon, Seleska, and that is different! We've all heard that tale. He was kind and generous and he saved a little girl – you – and brought her to Renny and Halana who were broken-hearted over the loss of their little girl Adrina. But that's not Blue Dragons, Seleska! Blue Dragons sing sailors to their deaths, singing a song so sweet that they plunge into the water to hear more. You know that they are after your soul when you begin to hear their song. Have you been hearing dragon songs, Seleska?"

His manly face was knotted up in worry. It was utterly adorable to see all his hard edges softened with concern for me.

But he didn't need to be worried. This was only a baby dragon. What harm could he cause? Besides, I didn't want to answer the question about the dragons singing to me. I didn't want to admit that they had *always* sung to me.

"Blue Dragons helped keep Ramariri in the air when he was saving me. They pushed his belly up so he didn't fall into the water when he was running out of strength. I saw them, Heron!"

"I don't know what you saw, Seleska, but you have to report this little dragon."

"If I report him to the village elders, they will take him to Abergande," I said. I didn't want that. I was the one who found him. And he clearly liked me. I needed to help him just like Ramariri helped me. I owed this little Blue Dragon help. Because when I needed help, and when Ramariri knew it would cost his life to help me, he hadn't turned away. Besides, this little guy was a baby and alone. He needed me.

"And would that be so bad?" Heron asked, pulling away from me, his eyes locked on the little Blue Dragon.

"Just help me hide him for tonight, Heron. Please?" I begged.

"And then what?" he asked, warily.

"And then we'll talk about what to do," I promised. And I would find a way to convince him that we needed to help this baby, not hurt him.

He sighed. "It would be better if we just reported him."

I tried a small pout. "It's my birthday. Please?"

He sighed, rolling his eyes at my pouting. "Just for tonight. Come on."

My smile was probably brighter than the bonfire they were stoking in the village square. I felt like I could walk on top of the ocean I was feeling so light. By tomorrow, I'd have the perfect argument for Heron to make sure that the dragon could stay.

And I had the perfect name for him.

I'd call him Fireball.

Nasataa. A small voice whispered in my mind. Was that a masculine voice? It sounded like it. My eyes went wide when I realized it was this little purring ball of dragon. And he already had a name.

Nasataa.

Chapter Three

"Sixteen! So hard to believe that you've been with us for ten years!" my adoptive mother said as she kissed my forehead, her sun-darkened face spreading into a smile. She'd never been anything but loving and kind to me since the day they found me on the beach.

"We're proud of you," my adoptive father said. Renny was a man of few words, but the ones he said always counted. He leaned back into his chair, happiness radiating off of him like heat from the bonfire.

The fun of the party was fading as night descended and we sat around tables or the big bonfire, bellies full of fish and fruit, and hearts full of happiness. It was like nothing could ever go wrong, like life would always be happy and full of firelight flickering between the trees. Even the wind was warm and balmy, and the trees swayed gently, dancing with it.

Home, home, home the wind sang to me and my heart sang with it.

A smile filled my face and I hugged them close.

"Tomorrow, you'll be coming with me to Abergande," my father said.

"Abergande?" my eyes went wide. Going to the port was a rare treat. I loved the excitement of the town. There would be stalls selling jewelry and ribbons and bright cloth. There would be music and dancing and people from all over the Havenwind Isles. There might even be a boat! I'd seen one once. And though the people here feared them, I still longed for news of a home far away in a place full of trees and the smell of cinnamon – a place I still dreamed of most nights. This was my new home, but that place still mattered to me.

"You need to sell those shell necklaces you've been making all summer and purchase new supplies," my mother said. "And your father has agreed to take Heron there to continue his training."

"He's leaving?" my eyes shot to where Heron was joking with two other boys from the village. His eyes sparkled in the firelight when they looked up and saw me. Feeling my cheeks grow hot, I turned back to my mother.

My mother smiled kindly, but she only shrugged as she answered. "Old Dapnee doesn't have the work for another blacksmith, and Heron's apprenticeship is almost over. He'll need to leave eventually. He'll be a blacksmith somewhere else – somewhere where there is enough work for two smithies, or where they've lost their smith."

Why did the wind suddenly feel cold? I shivered, wrapping my arms around myself and glancing one more time at Heron, towering over the other boys, his thick muscles gleaming in the firelight. He was leaving. Leaving for Abergande while I stayed here. Who would I joke with now? Who would hunt shells with me along the beach? Who would help me hide baby dragons?

I chewed the inside of my cheek.

My mother caught my arm.

"Don't fret, Seleska. Enjoy the rest of the party. There will be time to miss your friend when he is gone."

I smiled, but I didn't feel happy inside. The village would feel dull and hollow without Heron.

"I think I'll take a walk," I said, scooting off my bench.

"Just make sure you are in your bed within the hour," my mother reminded me. "Tomorrow will be a long day of travel!"

I nodded, still smiling at them reassuringly, but my eyes felt glassy. Was Heron really going to leave?

I snuck off into the night, my feet taking me almost without thinking to the smithy. We'd hidden Nasataa there, and really, someone ought to check on him. I hoped no one noticed as I palmed a large piece of fruit and grabbed a wooden cup of water and a slab of fish.

I brushed away hot tears as I snuck inside the small building. What was Heron thinking? Leaving me without even saying a word about it!

Even now, in the forge, the embers were banked, staying hot for the work the next day. I snuck around to where we'd hidden Nasataa behind the furnace. His little chest rose and fell as he slept curled against the hot metal.

He was okay. And he was still here. I reached into my belt pouch and pulled out the scraps of fish and fruit I'd hidden, placing them in front of his sleeping snout. I put the cup of water beside them. When he woke up, he'd be hungry. And he'd be lonely. I'd have to make sure I was here first thing in the morning to get him. I'd need to hide him somehow in my things or he'd be discovered for sure.

"Seleska?" Heron's throaty whisper cut through the tranquil moment and I hurriedly brushed away the last of my tears.

"Yes?" I replied, trying not to sound hurt. He should have told me.

"I meant to tell you that I was leaving."

"And what? Your tongue fell out? You forgot what words mean?"

I could barely see him across the room with only the embers of the forge lighting the room. He was mostly just shadow there, but his voice was husky and laced with emotion.

"It was just so hard to say."

"How long have you known?"

"Months, I guess."

Months! He'd known for months!

The silence dragged out between us until eventually, he broke it again, this time with a lighter note to his voice.

"Maybe you should let that little guy go free. You can't take him with us tomorrow."

It was probably a good idea. But what if he didn't know how to take care of himself? What if he just wandered on the beach and got lost or starved? What if he thought no one loved him? What if he felt abandoned? Like he'd had a friend and then just been dumped when his friend went off to go have adventures? My heart felt tight in my chest and my breathing hitched.

"He is free. He chose to stay with me."

I'd take him to the beach tomorrow and see if he wanted to leave, but if he didn't, I wouldn't abandon him. There would be a way to hide him in my things. And he wasn't that heavy. I would just have to carry him with me to Abergande. *I* wasn't the one who abandoned my friends without warning.

"I'm sorry I didn't tell you," Heron said, sounding dejected.

"I'm sorry that you didn't, too," I said, petting Nasataa gently on his sleeping head before standing up and walking past Heron to the door. I opened it, trying to think of the right way to put the hurt in my heart. "I wish you'd trusted me enough to tell me."

I heard Heron's breath hitch in his throat, but I didn't want to hear what he might say. It was all just too painful and emotional. I needed some sleep and some time to sort out how I felt. I slipped into the velvet night, following the candlelight glow in the windows of my family's cottage.

Chapter Four

"Stay in there!" I hissed at Nasataa.

The little dragon was moving way too much. And he was growing heavier by the mile. The only way to get from our little village to the town of Abergande was on foot. All the village horses – and by all I meant the two owned by Jamrie and Esconse – were busy hauling cane and the donkey was just as busy with the sugarapple harvest. And that meant walking.

The path ran just inside the treeline along the beach, providing shade and shelter to travelers, but easy to follow with the ocean not far off. Any other day, I would have been absorbed in how beautiful the path was – how the brightly colored flowers hung from vines and filled the air with scents, how the waves of the ocean beat the shore in a way that lulled my spirit and made my heart soar, how the gentle breezes smelled of salt.

Today, I was distracted.

I had stuffed Nasataa in my bag of shell necklaces and armbands after he'd refused to return to the sea – again!

"Please," I'd begged. "It's safer for you with other dragons!"

But he'd climbed up my arm and dug his claws into my shoulder, absolutely refusing to budge. And his huge eyes were so cute that they just melted my heart. How could I say no to those eyes?

The shell necklaces were mine to sell and mine to carry to Abergande. No one else would look in the bag or notice that it was heavier than it should be, so it was a foolproof plan. Or at least, it had seemed like it when I put him in the bag that morning. Now, hours later, the bag was growing heavier by the hour and Nasataa just would not stay still!

I huffed, adjusting the bag and almost turning a heel in my boots. Pretty, they might be. But practical, they were not.

"When we get to Abergande, I have business in the *Leaping Dolphin Inn*," my father said. He'd been silent all morning, seemingly oblivious to the tension between me and Heron. "I trust that you can find the market and handle the sale of your shells?"

"Of course," I said, smiling.

Excellent! I was going to get to roam the town free of any oversight. I could sell my shell jewelry and buy whatever I needed on my own. I couldn't wait! I'd never had the chance to wander Abergande on my own before! And it would give me a chance to feed Nasataa and let him out to do whatever little dragons needed to do without prying eyes watching.

"We'll take a room there, so come and find me when you're done," my father said. He was pulling a handcart with his own goods brought to market. He mostly spent his time fishing, but he also made musical instruments from reeds, and it was these instruments that he was bringing to market today. If we were fortunate, we would both get good prices and have enough to stock up on essentials that our village couldn't make.

"I can walk with you to the market," Heron suggested, trying to act as if I wasn't furious with him. "It's on the way to Whitehead Smithy where I'll be finishing my apprenticeship."

Those words felt like a brand laid against my skin. White hot and painful. I blinked away tears, refusing to look at him. He hadn't told me. Everyone else knew, but he hadn't told me.

When we'd left the village Heron's family and other friends had been there to wish him the best with presents and hugs. His departure hadn't been a surprise to any of them.

I fell back behind my father's cart ignoring him. It hurt too much to talk to him. It hurt because I knew that this was my last chance and there was so much to say but my tongue just couldn't form the words. Instead, I reached into my bag, stroking Nasataa's head with a finger. He bit it and I flinched, looking around quickly to make sure no one had seen.

"Seleska," Heron whispered falling back to where I was. "Don't be mad, okay?"

"I'm not mad," I muttered. Adjusting my bag and pushing Nasataa's snout back in furtively.

"I'll come home every few months and see everyone."

Months!

He sighed. "What did you expect me to do? Stop working as a blacksmith? I've spent years training for it!"

"Of course not."

"Then what did you think? Did you think I'd always be in our village?"

"No."

"What, then?"

I stumbled over a root and he caught my arm, stabilizing me. My eyes were too watery to make out the path properly.

"I guess," I said as I caught my balance again. "I guess I just hoped that if you were going on an adventure that you'd take me, too." I sniffed, wiping my eyes harshly. "But I guess I'll just have to make my own adventures. And I'll have to go on them myself."

I patted my bag where Nasataa was snuffling against my hip. Maybe I had a new friend to go on adventures with. Maybe *he* would stick around.

"Don't be like that, Seleska," Heron said, lifting my chin to look at him with one finger. "I'll be back. We'll go on adventures someday."

"Sure," I said. But I knew it was a silly promise. He'd make other friends in Abergande. He'd have adventures all his own. And I would live in our little village and make shell ornaments and wish for more for the rest of my life.

Or maybe not. Maybe Nasataa and I would dive into the water and figure out exactly who or what was singing to me.

And with that thought, the song began again, louder than ever, pulling me toward the water.

Chapter Five

Abergande always took my breath away.

When we emerged from the path into the little cove along the sea, the sheer size of the place made me want to look and look and look. Houses and inns and taverns and shops hunkered so close to one another that you could hardly step between them. They stood on tall wooden stilts to keep them safe when storms and floods came, and to keep out the slithering, scurrying, creatures in this area of the island. Boardwalks wove from one shop to the next, serving as streets on which the citizens could walk or push laden carts. I was already beginning to smile at the sight when my father's gasp startled me.

There was very little that bothered Renny. I followed his gaze to a ship with white sails bobbing out from the cove in the deeper water and my own breath caught in my throat. A ship? Here?

Everyone knew that the Havenwind Isles didn't receive ships. Everyone knew that we didn't take in outsiders – though they'd taken me in ten years ago when I'd arrived on their shores an orphan child, hunted by enemies she didn't know.

But this was different. This was a real ship. This was news.

I hadn't seen a ship since I was a little child and the sheer size of it – even so far away – took my breath away. Our entire village could live on that ship.

My father and Heron both stiffened, exchanging an unreadable look.

"It's only one ship," Heron said.

My father shook his head, pursing his lips with worry, but he didn't say anything else as we followed the path into town.

"Be careful in the market," he said quietly to me as we arrived at the inn. "Don't take too long, or I will worry."

"I'll be careful," I assured him.

I followed Heron as we carefully worked our way onto the boardwalks and into the market. Abergande was such an exciting place to visit. On one corner, a fire-thrower was practicing his tricks, breathing fire out into the crowd for pennies. I laughed as we passed.

"I bet you could use him in the forge!" I joked to Heron.

"The fire isn't hot enough," Heron said, but his voice was distracted.

"Are you okay?"

"Just getting nervous." He smiled wryly at me. "I've never lived away from our village. No one here really knows me. I'm going to miss my family and friends."

"You could just stay," I said, throwing a coin to a smiling woman in the fruit stall and grabbing two mangoes from the stall. I shoved one into my bag, hoping it would settle Nasataa, before biting into the other one. What would it be like to live on an island without mangoes? They said that some of the Isles didn't have them. The food must be very bland.

"I can't, Seleska," he said as he stopped, grabbing both my hands in his so suddenly that I thought he was about to say something significant. He bit his lip, his eyes suddenly nervous. He didn't get the chance to speak.

A big burly man stepped out from the crowd with a grin on his face. He was a head taller than anyone there except for Heron and even wider across the shoulders. His scruffy face gleamed with sweat and when he clapped Heron on the shoulder, Heron swayed from the weight of the blow.

"There you are, apprentice! Excellent! Let's get you settled. I'm very happy to have the help. That ship arrived this morning and with it, orders for all kinds of repairs they can't do on board."

"Is that allowed?" I asked. "I thought ships weren't allowed to come to the Havenwind Isles."

He snorted. "Allowed or not allowed is not for me to say, but I don't turn away business. Say goodbye to your friend, Heron, and let's get you to work!"

Heron leaned down, kissed my cheek so quickly that my breath caught in my throat and then with a last smile he was gone, pushing through the crowds with the master blacksmith.

I wasn't crying. Really. I just had dust in my eyes. That happened sometimes when you were on the road.

It took a moment for me to gather myself and shake off the sadness and frustration that filled me. Heron was making his own choices. That was his right. I wasn't going to hang off him like an unwanted barnacle. Besides, I had my own adventures waiting for me, too. I just needed to figure out what they were.

An image formed in my mind of me and Nasataa swimming beneath the waves toward a treasure chest. Where had that come from? I had the strangest feeling that the thought was not my own at all.

I nearly gasped, a delighted smile spreading across my face. That was Nasataa! Wasn't it? Had he put that picture in my mind?

Was that normal for dragons? Maybe he was advanced.

With a smile, I pushed along the boardwalk to the little jewelry stand that always bought my wares – Lady Zeldar's.

"More necklaces for me, Seleska?" she asked smiling as she adjusted the colorful wrap-dress she always wore.

"Of course, Lady Zeldar!" I said, carefully reaching in to pull them from the bag without irritating Nasataa. A tiny nip at my hand made me flinch, but I tried not to let it show on my face and before I knew it, all the work I'd done for the past two months were spread out across the table while Lady Zeldar counted and graded and tallied what she was willing to pay.

There was a cheer a little further up the boardwalk toward where three branches met in a kind of a square. My gaze drifted to where a crowd was gathering there. I could almost make out what they were saying. Someone in a white, billowing shirt and tight breeches was standing up on the bench at the center of the square, gesturing broadly as he spoke.

"Who is that?" I asked Lady Zeldar.

She paled as she answered. "A ship came in this morning. That is the leader of the people who came to shore."

I felt something move at my side.

"Why is he making such a big fuss in the square? Do the Elders know he's doing that?" I asked, but before she could answer I heard my name called out from down the boardwalk.

"Seleska!" My father was running toward me, a look of fear on his face. I looked around. Where was the threat coming from? He wasn't being chased.

"Dragon!" a voice said from behind me and I spun to see Nasataa racing down the boardwalk.

Oh no! He was going to get hurt or caught by someone else.

I left my wares behind, running down the boardwalk toward the little dragon. He was at the edges of the crowd and I had to squeeze between people to chase him through their ranks.

"Nasataa!" I called quietly, trying not to draw attention while I squeezed between people in the crowd. No one had noticed him yet – what a relief! But I felt bad about ignoring my father's calls.

"Seleska!" He sounded worried.

I'd just grab Nasataa and then I'd answer my father.

There he was! The little scamp had climbed up a barrel and was standing on it on his hind legs. How had no one noticed him? I grabbed him quickly, fighting his bucking kicks, and stuffed him back into the bag before cinching the leather straps tight. If he wanted to go free he could – on a safe beach somewhere. Here, someone would grab him and probably kill him.

"Stay in there!" I hissed. He was going to get us both in trouble.

"Seleska!"

I turned, searching for my father now that I had the dragon in hand, but before I could even call out, I was being dragged backward by my long hair.

"Oww!" I said as I stumbled back and then someone grabbed my arm, spinning me around and marching me forward toward the square. I clutched at my bag. Was Nasataa okay in there?

I received a mental image of the little dragon unhurt but irritated as he flamed at the sides of my leather bag.

I could still hear my father yelling in the distance as hands shoved me forward.

"This is the one – the outlander who came here years ago!" someone in the crowd called out.

"Wha – " I began, but I was interrupted as more hands shoved me forward.

"If she's what you came for, then take her and be gone!"

"Excuse me," I tried again. "I'm not going anywhere!"

I didn't recognize these faces. These weren't people from my village. So how did they know about me? Why were they shoving me toward the grim-faced strangers?

One of the strangers grabbed my arm. I pulled against his grip, but he didn't even seem to notice.

The leader of the group leapt down from his perch. His face was darkened from the sun, but his coloring was light – just like mine. And beneath the scar that ran from eyebrow to chin, was a face that was triumphant as he looked at me.

"Perfect. We'll be taking her with us."

Chapter Six

"You can't take her!" my father bellowed, rushing through the crowd.

Acid swirled through my belly and I thought I might be sick. First, I was singled out and seized, now my father was putting himself in danger for me. And if anyone found the dragon, I would be in so much trouble!

"I'm afraid you are wrong about that," the leader said. "This is Princess Seleska of Tambrel and she is coming with us."

"I'm afraid you are mistaken," my father said. "This is my daughter. And yes, her name is Seleska – a strange coincidence, I'm sure. But she isn't going anywhere."

His jaw clenched firm and he crossed his arms over his chest. He knew full well that I used to be a princess. But that didn't mean that we needed to tell anyone else.

I bit my lip, looking around us. The crowd was drawing back. No one was going to side with my dad. And there were eight of these sailors in loose white shirts. Six strapping men and two bulky women, all with tattooed hands and wind-burned cheeks. They wore the same hardened expressions on their faces, like they had seen everything there was to see and weren't impressed with any of it.

And they were all armed.

"It's okay, Renny," I said in a small voice. I didn't want to see him hurt. This many strong men and women could kill him. And that would break my mama. She was already stained with sadness over the loss of her only daughter just before she adopted me. Losing my father, too, would break her. "I'll be okay."

"What are you going to do with her?" my father asked, fear tinging his words, so his voice came out husky and rough.

"Well," the light-haired man said, "for starters, we're going to be sure that we're right about her. Haul that barrel over here!"

Two of the sailors grabbed one of the rain barrels along the boardwalk, hauling it to where we were. What did they think they could do with that?

"You'll have to go through me first!" My father yelled, launching himself forward.

It was a crazy thing to do.

Amazing.

Loving.

Crazy as staring at the sun at noon. I loved him for it even as my heart ached when one of the sailors planted a fist in his belly and another one cracked him on the head.

"Dad!" I gasped. I almost never called my father that, but the shock of seeing him pummeled jarred it loose from my mouth.

He stumbled forward and a third sailor caught him, grabbing his arm and twisting it into a lock behind his back.

"Why don't you watch with us, hmm? You might find this educational," the sailor laughed.

The ones holding me jerked me forward toward the barrel. What were they going to do, give me a bath? Around us, the crowd was silent. No one had come forward to help my father. No one had said a word.

They were all silent spectators, waiting to see what would happen. How would they feel if I was their daughter or sister or friend? Would they still be so silent?

"Stop hurting my father!" I demanded, but no one even looked at me when I spoke.

"Now we see," the leader said, as they shoved me to the edge of the barrel and leaned me over the water. He shrugged at me as I was pressed toward the water. "And we hope that we're right and that this really is Princess Seleska. Because otherwise, she's about to drown."

I started to scream and then I realized I should be saving my breath. I gulped down as much as I could before a strong hand plunged my head beneath the surface, holding me there as I thrashed against the edge of the barrel.

Blind panic seized me, pushing all else from my mind. What were they trying to prove? That they could drown me in front of everyone? Well, they could! Good for them! They were bigger and stronger and oh – Skies and Stars!

My lungs were on fire, begging me to take a breath. Red danced across my closed eyelids. Please, please let me up!

I pushed against the hands, growing weak as I struggled. I tried to twist and jerk in unexpected ways to surprise them, but my head was spinning, my vision darkening.

I was going to die.

The pain was too much. I couldn't fight anymore.

An image of swimming with Nasataa deep under the waves filled my mind, almost as if the little dragon was begging me to let go and just breathe the water.

If only I could do that! But that was madness.

I fought harder, the pain so intense now – the longing for oxygen so all-consuming – that thoughts were driven from my mind. I was about to die.

I couldn't hold on any longer.

I sucked in a huge breath of water.

The blackness fled and the pain began to seep away.

Whoa. What? Was I really breathing *water?* My eyes were growing so big that I thought they might pop out of my head – but hey, maybe that was normal for me. After all, I was apparently half-fish.

And Nasataa knew that. How had he known?

Before I could think anymore, strong hands pulled me out of the barrel, jerking my arm to make me stand up straight, water streaming from my hair and down my face.

Around me, gasps filled the air. How long had he held me under? Long enough that these people thought I was dead. I looked for my father's face in the crowd. He was still held by sailors, but the shock on his face was the same as everyone else's. He hadn't known about this, either.

"As we suspected," the leader said. "She has her family's little gift. You're coming with us, Princess."

"I'm not a princess," I said, stepping with my metal-spiked boot as hard as I could on the instep of the man holding me.

Why hadn't I thought of that before?

He cried out in pain and I leapt forward, climbing the railing of the boardwalk in one quick motion and leaping into the sea.

If they wanted me, they were going to have to breathe under water, too.

Chapter Seven

The water closed around me and I sunk into the murky waves around the boardwalk. There sure wasn't much to see here. Seaweed climbed in patches around the supports of the boardwalk and shoals of small baitfish swam out from the shadows. Heaps of rock held crabs and other crawling creatures and rusty metal hooks, shards of pottery, and rotting rope lay in tangles on the bottom of the sea here.

Great. My first time underwater and I was swimming through a wet garbage heap. I shivered. This was so strange! Amazing and exciting, but strange.

I wanted to go back and save Renny, but wasn't I the reason they'd grabbed him? Maybe with me gone, they'd just let him go?

I swam away from Abergande, those spiky heels doing nothing to help at all. Good thing I could breathe under water, because I was pretty sure I wouldn't be able to kick up high enough to get a breath otherwise!

There was a splash and then a body dove into the water behind me.

I whirled to see the sailor who had grabbed me from the ground diving through the water, bubbles streaking all around him as he kicked toward me.

Oh no! If he caught me, it wouldn't matter how well I could breathe under water. I still wouldn't be able to fight him off! I needed to get somewhere where it would be tough for him to fish me out easily. But where? Going further out to sea would be best, but he could just keep following, dipping under the water whenever he needed to. I needed to get somewhere deep – too deep for them to swim to. But where would that be?

Singing filled my mind, almost blocking out my thoughts.

Deep, deep, deep, it seemed to say through the wordless tune and my head whirled at the sound of it.

With difficulty, I kicked off my special spike-heeled boots, sad to see them drop to the floor of the sea. I couldn't keep them – not when I had to swim to get away from these men – but I hated to lose them when Heron had gone to so much trouble to make them for me.

I leaned down and grabbed them, uncinching the leather strap on my bag so that I could stuff them inside.

The moment the cinch was opened, Nasataa leapt from the bag, scooting forward through the water.

Oh no! I'd never even thought to make sure he could breathe under water. Was he okay?

He seemed to be. He shot from the bag like lightning from the sky, but he didn't shoot to the surface. Instead, he shot forward toward the open ocean, sending me mental images of me following him as we plunged out to sea.

The first sailor bobbed back up to the surface for air at the same moment as a second one plunged into the sea, bubbles boiling up all around him. There were too many of them for me to wait here and see how long it took them to catch me. I had to flee. And fast.

I felt a tug on my hand and looked down to see Nasataa pulling at it, his little wings flapping energetically in the water.

Okay, okay, little guy. I'll follow you.

Hopefully, Renny would be okay up there. Hopefully, he wouldn't be hurt.

I swam forward through the water, following Nasataa as he raced in front of me. Every time I looked over my shoulder, more sailors were in the water. They were gaining distance as they swam. They were faster than me. But I had an advantage. I just had to use it.

I sunk to the bottom of the bay. The water was growing clearer here, the plants fewer, and the garbage less plentiful. I swam along the bottom, trying to swim as fast as I could. I wasn't a very fast swimmer. I'd never wanted to do more than just bob around on the top of the water and enjoy myself and this swim was not about enjoyment or slowly feeling the ripples of the water around you.

After a moment, I found a rhythm. If only Nasataa would wait for me! He was going too fast. He could swim more easily than I could walk. He stopped every few seconds, waiting for me, but never stopping long enough for me to catch up. He should go on without me and stop waiting for me. He'd be safer that way. He'd be protected from the people who were chasing me.

But no. He sent a picture in my mind of the two of us swimming and as I watched he grew larger and larger until he was the size of Ramariri, the golden dragon who had saved my life. Did that mean he meant that we should stay together forever? Did he realize that I was a terrible choice as a dragon mother?

But he didn't seem to care. He'd chosen me – for whatever reason – and there was no way I was going to let him down. Not if I could help it.

The sailors were still too far away to catch me, but they were gaining fast. How could they catch up when they kept having to go up for air, but I didn't?

Oh! A little way back, the hull of a small boat dipped into the water. This was not a fair chase!

I needed to dip down into some low place, and I needed to get there fast. But first, I had to check on my father. I couldn't run away if he was still in trouble.

I swam upward to the surface and broke through into the air, surprised at how cold my face felt and how bright the sun was, as it popped up into the sunlight.

"There she is!" someone yelled from the nearby boat. It looked closer from above the surface. Three bodies leapt from the boat back into the water. I had only seconds before they'd be on top of me. Desperate, I looked toward the town beyond.

There! I saw my father on the boardwalk looking worriedly out to sea. Behind him, the blacksmith and Heron stood with big hammers in their hands and there was not a sailor to be seen still on the boardwalk. I risked a wave to him – a sign that I was alright – and then I plunged back under the waves.

All the sailors were chasing me. He should be safe from them as long I was distracting them.

I would have breathed a sigh of relief, but I felt a tug at my foot.

Chapter Eight

He had me by the foot!

I gasped, squirming at the hold on my foot, the song of the sea filling my ears again as my head plunged beneath the waves.

Something fast shot past me and I curled my body, trying to shake the hand on my foot. The grim-faced sailor holding me held on tight, his teeth gritted and bubbles pouring from his mouth.

A little burst of flame hit him right in the face as Nasataa blasted him with an underwater flame. My baby! He could flame under water! Was that magical?

I didn't have time to be shocked or even pleased.

Aiming for his face, I kicked out with my other foot and planted a solid kick to his nose. He didn't let go, so I pushed hard against his eyes, curling my toes to grind into his eyes as I shoved as hard as I could with my free foot. His hold on my foot faltered, shifting to my breeches until he only had a handful of fabric in his grip. Quickly, I grabbed the ties to my breeches and pulled them loose, kicking free of my breeches and diving down, down, down. I was faster without the material clinging to my legs, but I felt vulnerable in just my underthings, blouse and leather corset.

Even with my greater speed, Nasataa was still faster. He dove toward the sandy bottom of the sea and I felt almost as if he was following the sound of the ocean that I heard, too. The direction he was headed was becoming rocky. We were following the shoreline of the island toward the north of Abergande – a place I'd never seen above the water.

The rock here looked bubbly – huge craters and smaller holes filled the rocks as they piled up along the shore. How fascinating!

I stole a glance back. The boat was right overhead. One of the sailors was kicking up to it in a flurry of bubbles, but as I watched, another dove down with a heavy weight in his arms.

A burst of adrenaline filled me, kicking my heart to a faster pace and making my lungs work double time as I gulped down big breaths of water – water! That wasn't right! – and hurried after Nasataa. I hoped he was going the right direction. I hoped that we could both trust the urgings of the song of the sea.

Despite the wordlessness of the call, I was certain it was leading us, steering us just by the feel of it, toward where the sand dropped off here to a rocky mass.

Bright sea plants waved in the calm of the ocean lullaby and swirls of colorful fish puffed up from them in startled clouds. We sliced through the first burst of yellow fish, losing sight of our pursuers as the water behind us filled with yellow, flashing bodies.

I nearly breathed a sigh of relief when I turned back and lost sight of my pursuers.

Where was Nasataa? Was he okay?

I couldn't see him anywhere.

Panicked, I spun in the water, looking in every direction. We had descended to a channel between rising clumps of coral and bright plants, to a narrow channel between them. I shivered as a silky plant washed against my bare leg. Another touch followed the first as I slid between the waving waterweeds, the sound of the sea singing hauntingly to my mind.

I'd lost him.

He was only a baby and I'd lost him.

I felt worse than I had on the docks when the sailors had seized my father. Worse than I had when Heron said he was leaving. A little creature had needed me and depended on me and I'd lost him. What if he starved out here without me? What if one of the sailors had grabbed him? What if a big fish ate him?

I spun again, peering between the weeds, but he was nowhere to be found.

My heart plummeted.

And then a little blue head darted out from a rock and I nearly laughed in relief.

He'd found a cave! I swam toward him, relief filling every pore of me. He was okay! He was here and he was safe!

I surged into the cave with him, looking over my shoulder for only a moment before I darted inside. A dark shape was moving through the crowd of yellow fish and the leaves of the waving plants. One of my pursuers wasn't far behind.

I kicked into the hole in the rock, following Nasataa into the deep cave beyond. It was scary to go into the dark without being able to see more than shadows. Scarier still with enemies outside. The opening was narrow, and I had to squeeze my hips and push hard to kick through. Even so, the coral scratched up my legs and hips, scoring them where it broke through the skin. I winced at the feeling of salt-water on my wounds and sucked in a deep breath.

In the low water-filtered light, I could barely make out the interior of the little cave. It wasn't really a cave, but more like a tunnel. I followed it, still too far behind Nasataa to catch him.

It led into a wider cave, still made of coral and mostly empty except for a few crabs. It felt dank, even though an underwater cave couldn't be dank.

If I had to return to the surface to breathe, I wouldn't have gotten this far. I was probably safe as long as I stayed here. But I was hungry and thirsty and tired and there was only one way out of the cave – through that tight tunnel.

Worry seized my heart. I'd made it inside, but what if I couldn't go back out? I couldn't stay here forever.

I chewed my lip as Nasataa crawled into my arms and curled into a ball. I stroked his head and back gently. His scales felt sleeker underwater and his wings, fins, and tail felt filmy in the water. He was so beautiful and so vulnerable. He needed someone to take care of him. Someone better suited to the task than a hunted teenage girl.

"Don't worry little buddy," I tried to say underwater, but it came out garbled. "I'll take care of you."

He didn't seem worried. He'd already drifted off to sleep in my arms.

I clung to him, worried enough for both of us as the bright water filtering through the holes in the porous rock faded darker and darker until I was sure it must be night outside.

What was I going to do?

Chapter Nine

Eventually, I nodded off, still clutching Nasataa. His warmth and his little fluttering heartbeat reminded me that I wasn't alone. I had this little guy to keep safe.

I woke with a start in the dark. Long, eerie beams of blue light rippled into the cave, but they were faint, as if lit by the moon. I blinked and it felt strange in the ocean water. I was chilled to the core – but not as cold as I would have expected. Was that a part of this special ability I had? – and so thirsty. I snorted a laugh, surprised by the spurt of water from my nose. How funny was it to be this thirsty while completely surrounded by water?

Gently, I eased Nasataa off my lap. By now, my pursuers must be done chasing me. By now, it must be safe to leave this cave and go find my family.

I'd check first and then come back for Nasataa if the coast was clear. I slipped down the rocky tunnel to the smaller cave and peeked my head out. A flare of light surprised me, and I ducked back around the rock.

Light? Where was that coming from?

I poked my head back out of the cave entrance and gasped.

Yellow light danced from a waterproof lantern hanging down from the side of a boat into the water far above me. It was small enough from that far away that it was hard to make out details but in the glow of the lantern, a diver leapt into the water, streaking down through the sea's embrace toward my cave.

I jumped in surprise. They knew where I was! They hadn't been able to get to me yet, but they knew!

The diver froze. He'd seen my surprised jump! He surged forward and I ducked back into the cave, scrambling into the tunnel and back into the wider cave beyond. Fear surged through my veins as my heart hammered in my chest.

It's going to be okay, Seleska. Just find another way out.

I scrambled along the edges of the cave, looking, but while the rocks were porous and there were many holes, none seemed large enough to fit me.

Gasping in frustration, I returned to the center of the cave where I'd left Nasataa. I'd just sit with him for a moment and compose myself and then I'd think of another plan. That would be best, right?

But where was he?

The little Blue Dragon wasn't where I'd left him. My heart leapt into my throat as I swam in circles. What if he'd wandered off? What if he'd gone out of the tunnel and the cave like I had, only the diver had snatched him and brought him up to the boat?

I couldn't let anything happen to the poor little guy. He was only a baby!

I tried to call his name, but it distorted in the water. Frustrated, I spun again, darting down the tunnel and back out to the first cave. Had he snuck past me when I was looking at the boat?

Where was he? Was he lost? Hurt?

I poked my head out of the cave and into the sea beyond. I just needed to see. I just needed to know if he was okay. Fingers tangled in my hair and with a gasp, I looked into the eyes of the man who had grabbed me on the boardwalk. His hair swirled in the dark water and his cheeks and eyes bulged with surprise. I planted my feet against the rock and pulled backward, tugging at his grip. He was too strong. His eyes narrowed as he fought me, but then a look of panic filled his eyes and he released me, kicking in a sudden flurry toward the surface. He must be out of breath.

I breathed a sigh of relief, but I didn't have time to revel in my escape. Another two divers were already streaking toward me and there was no sign outside the entrance of a little Blue Dragon.

Frustrated, I dove back into the cave. I couldn't go out. Not without being caught. But where had Nasataa gone?

I searched the larger cave for him.

Was one of those loose rocks in a different place? Brow furrowed, I swam toward the spot. Yes. It had tumbled down a little, revealing a dark gap in the rock about the right size for a baby Blue Dragon.

That must be where Nasataa had gone! Worried, I pulled at the loose rock, tumbling it further aside and widening the gap. The stones here were loose and easy to move. Could I move enough of them to make a gap big enough for me to swim to?

After a few minutes of work, I had cleared the entrance to another tunnel, but this tunnel was black as ink. Did I dare risk going in there with no light and no idea what came next?

I was going to have to. There was a baby dragon depending on me and I was the only one who knew he was there. I couldn't abandon him. Ramariri would never have abandoned me.

Besides, the song of the sea was louder here, as if it wanted me to follow.

With an indrawn breath to steady myself, I plunged into the dark cavern.

Chapter Ten

When I woke up yesterday morning, I hadn't expected to find myself feeling my way blindly through a black, rocky cavern in the middle of the night under so much water that no other human could find me.

But hey, life is like that. Unpredictable. And I did promise myself that I was going to have some adventures. I tried to remind myself of that as a gnawing worry lodged in my spine and bit into my sense of confidence.

Adventure.

I was an adventurer. Adventurers didn't stop just because things were a bit scary, right? That was what made it an adventure!

I was feeling along the rock tunnel – feeling to find my way and feeling to see if Nasataa was huddled against the wall somewhere. Maybe he was cold like me. Maybe that was why he'd gone into this tunnel. It did feel warmer in here. I shivered slightly as a current of warm water hit me. Weren't you supposed to shiver when it was cold? But I'd been cold for so long that the warmth reminded me of it, drawing me forward toward its source.

A very faint glow ahead outlined the edges of the rocks. What could be making that light? It wasn't the yellow glow of the lantern that the men had used to search for me. And it wasn't the blue-white glow of the moon through the water. It was more of an aqua color, like the sea on a sunny day. How strange.

As I swam, the glow grew brighter, until I could see as well as if it were day. I sped up, able to see far enough not to crack my head on the rock and invigorated by the warmth of the water here.

There was an opening up ahead, a pool of light. I kicked toward it and emerged into a wide cave with a flat bottom and a bright light in what almost looked like a well at the center. Strange markings were carved into the stone around it and into the walls and ceiling arching over the room. The tunnel I was climbing in from was the only way in.

What was a place like this doing here?

A blue blur launched itself at me, and I caught it, knocked back against the cave wall while the exuberant little dragon crawled all over me and finally settled in a ring around my neck.

"I missed you, too," I tried to say under the water.

He sent me a mental image of waking up alone and coming here to find me. Why hadn't I thought of that? I did my best to send him a mental image of my joy at finding him safe. He tightened his grip on my neck. That had to be affection, right? Which meant that my mental picture had worked! No more trying to talk to him under water. We had our own way to communicate. Success!

I stroked his little neck, relieved that he was okay, and circled the glowing well at the center of the room. Lucky for us that Nasataa was such a curious little thing, or we never would have found this interesting well of glowing light.

I tried to peer inside it, but beyond the light, I couldn't see anything else. The glow was so intense that it was hurting my eyes and if the markings carved around the room meant anything, then I couldn't read them.

But I knew that I was meant to find this well. Or someone was. I knew it because it sang to me – that wordless song of the sea I didn't understand but always heard. It sang to me louder and stronger and deeper than anything else I'd ever heard. I was drawn to it. I felt, somehow, that I needed to climb into that well and follow the light, that it meant to lead me somewhere.

But did I dare risk Nasataa? What if the light led somewhere dangerous? I glanced over my shoulder at the dark tunnel we'd followed to get here. It was just as dangerous, wasn't it? No matter where this well of light led us, if it didn't drop us right in front of an enemy, that was good enough, right?

Well, I liked to look on the bright side and this magical well had turned up right when I needed it. I was going to call that a 'very good thing' and accept this gift.

I smiled, glad I'd made up my mind and sent a mental image to Nasataa of dropping into that well. He sent me one back of staying on my shoulders and falling asleep.

Poor little guy had to be tired after that big adventure. I stroked the top of his head and took a step forward.

Here we go, now or never!

My bare toes hung over the edge of the well. I wasn't sure how to do this, but I took a deep breath and hopped into the well.

Light flared across my vision, blinding me, and then a powerful sensation like an undertow seized me and sucked me into the well and out to sea. A tingling feeling flashed across my skin and it was strangely familiar. With it came the smell of cinnamon and the memory of sweetly mumbled words. Had I been here before? I had no memory of a place like this, and yet it felt as familiar as my own name.

Maybe, there was more to being able to breathe under water than just a really strange skill. Maybe, I'd been in this place before. Maybe it had to do with my past life and with the family I had before I'd been adopted by my new family.

I swallowed, a little nervous at the thought.

Chapter Eleven

The powerful current released me, and I fell forward, swimming a little to get my feet under me in the water. My vision cleared as I looked around me. I was standing beside the well – no, not *the* well but rather *a* well. Because this well *here* looked just like the other well back *there*, but it wasn't in a cave. It rested on the seafloor, a skiff of sand piling up on one side of it and the ancient wreck of a ship on the other side.

The wreck was so far gone that all I could make out was a few ship ribs sticking up from a mass of barnacles and the homes of underwater creatures, but I recognized it from the stories the old men told sometimes around the fire. Stories of a time when the Havenwind Isles weren't forbidden to ships. Stories from a time when our fishermen went out in boats rather than netting fish from land. Stories from a time before the Blue Dragons rose up and tore down any man-made ship that bobbed on the water. Stories of storms and shipwrecks and diving for treasures.

Strange, how all the stories were becoming real. Because there were stories, too, of magical women who could live underwater, though in the stories they had swishy tails and seashells for clothes – which sounded even more uncomfortable than my spiky-heeled boots.

I looked around the magical well, but there was nothing here to keep me in this place. No writing that I could understand – though the well was ringed with more of those strange markings – no explanation at all for what had happened.

And Nasataa had fallen asleep on my shoulders.

Well, I had warmed up and I was safe again, and judging by the faint light above, the sun was coming up. I could swim up to the surface but I was too tired, so instead, I just swam along the bottom, taking my time as I meandered around coral and waving sea plants. I thought the land was sloping upward – hoped it was true – and that I was headed toward our island home.

After a night without much sleep, I almost didn't care. I was so tired that it was hard to think about anything at all.

Eventually, the land took a steep slope upward and I let myself bob to the surface and look around. I was a long way from Abergande. The Abergande beaches were dominated with views of the town and cleared trees. Old piers and docks coated in mold and barnacles were easy to pick out there, but as I scanned the island ahead of me, the treeline and the way the beach sloped was immediately familiar.

I was home again.

Worries that I'd been holding down bubbled up to the surface of my mind. Was my father okay? What had happened after I left and swam out to sea? What would he and my mother think when I strolled into the village. Would they think something was wrong with me because I could breathe under water? Would everyone see that and remember that I was from somewhere else? Would they think that I didn't have a place here anymore? I had no other home but this village with these people.

My mouth felt suddenly dry as I thought about their reactions. And my lungs burned as I coughed up water, adjusting to breathing air again. How strange that they could do both. Was I part fish? Or was it simply magic? Either way, it wasn't something I had ever expected.

I'd been raised a princess in the tiny kingdom of Timbrel and then I'd watched my family slaughtered before my eyes and fled with my dying bodyguard and a borrowed dragon. They'd saved my life.

But the few memories I had of my childhood before the tragedy were tinged with love, affection, happy laughter, and big trees. There weren't any memories of surf or sand. All my memories of the sea came after – from being raised on this island by my adoptive parents. None of that explained an affinity for the water – certainly not a magical one that let me breathe water and live.

It was a puzzle. And not one that I was going to solve by worrying.

I swam until I could touch the sand with my feet and then began to walk up out of the surf. I was at the beach where I'd found little Nasataa. Almost at the very spot where I'd looked out longingly on my birthday and wondered what adventures I might have. Was that really only the day before yesterday?

Someone moved on the beach. Just a shadow in the trees.

And then the shadow was running toward me and I froze. Was this one of the sailors? Had they been waiting here for me, too? I should have thought of that. I should have realized they might come here for me.

I crouched down defensively, trying to decide what I should do.

The shadow ran into a bright patch of sunlight, raising his arms and waving to me in the rising light of dawn.

Oh.

It wasn't a sailor and it wasn't an enemy at all. It was Heron!

I straightened from my crouch. My cheeks felt hot as I realized I was climbing out of the water in just my shirt, corset, and underthings. I needed dry clothes right away.

I shook myself off as the last touch of the water left me and I was standing on the warm, flat sand of the beach.

Heron was pulling his shirt off and laughing as he reached me.

I blinked, surprised by his response, but my surprise didn't last long. As soon as he reached me, he wrapped the shirt around my waist for me like a makeshift skirt.

"Thanks," I gasped. "What are you doing here?"

"What am *I* doing here?" he looked like he didn't know if he should be surprised or if he should laugh again. "What are *you* doing here? We've been worried sick about you! I barely managed to drag your father back here!"

"But your apprenticeship!" I argued. "You're supposed to be with the blacksmith!"

Heron's face took on a hard expression.

"When the sailors turned their cannons on Abergande and threatened to flatten the town, the place shut down. Everyone fled to the surrounding villages. We came back here to protect our village. Our family. Our friends."

"But it's just one ship ..." I said, but I knew he was right. What could we do against cannons? Even I had heard of those.

"The power of cannons is intense," Heron said. "They could flatten our village from the sea, if they knew where it was. But the party looking for you seemed distracted. They kept diving into the sea."

He bit his lip like he was uncomfortable.

"Don't tell me you were worried about me?" I said coyly, giving him my best teasing look.

"Seleska," he said, his face lined with worry.

"As if I can't outswim a bunch of heavy-armed sailors!" I laughed, but inside I was more than a little nervous. I almost hadn't escaped them.

Heron grabbed my upper arms as if he planned to lift me up by them. Maybe he did. His grip was incredibly gentle, but the intensity in his eyes gave away his violent emotions.

"Seleska, you don't understand. They want you. They want to take you back with them to the people who hired them."

"Hired them?" my voice shook a little. Partly from surprise at his actions and partly from surprise at his words.

"I heard one of them let that slip. They're a hired ship. Hired just to get *you*."

"That whole ship?" I couldn't imagine what that must have cost. "All to get me?"

He nodded grimly.

"But why?" I asked. "I'm not that important."

He laughed and then looked surprised at his own laughter.

"Seleska, you dove into the water and didn't come up again. They held you under water and you didn't drown. How long were you under for?"

I didn't answer. What would he think if he knew I wasn't normal? On my shoulder, Nasataa yawned loudly but Heron's eyes didn't even flick away from my face. Uh oh. If he wasn't bothered by the Blue Dragon, then this was really serious.

"Seleska?"

"All night," I said in a tiny voice.

He blew out a long breath. "Wow."

I watched him, worried about what he'd say but he smiled a wry grin and pulled me in close so he could lean his forehead against mine.

"I guess you'll be the one having adventures without *me*."

"Not if you come with me," I said, trying to be coy again, but my voice faltered. "You don't think ... you don't think there's something wrong with me, do you?"

He pulled back so I could see his smile as he said, "I think there's something right about you, Seleska, and I'll never think otherwise."

I grinned with him, treasuring this moment of friendship, however fleeting. I still had Heron.

My belly rumbled loudly, spoiling the moment.

"Let's get you something to eat and some dry clothes."

Chapter Twelve

"There are a lot of things we don't know about your past, Seleska," my adoptive mother was saying. "And that is okay."

I slipped into dry clothes behind the dressing screen as she spoke. Nasataa was curled up in my leather bag, hidden from prying eyes. Heron hadn't said anything when I hid him before we entered the village.

"You always have a place and a home with us. And who you are or where your family came from have nothing to do with that. But the sea is dangerous, daughter. It swallowed so many fishermen that we stopped using boats altogether. We stopped allowing ships to sail here. It's just not safe. Not with Blue Dragons lurking under the surface."

I hadn't seen any Blue Dragons last night. Except for Nasataa. I'd already grabbed a hunk of bread off the table when my mother wasn't looking and slipped it into the leather bag for him. Would he eat bread? That didn't seem very dragony. I'd have to get him a fish as soon as I could.

"But I can breathe underwater," I protested. "Maybe that's for a reason."

"There are a lot of things people *can* do," my mother objected. "But that doesn't mean that they *should* do them. It's not safe out there right now, Seleska. You need to stay here with us."

I carefully laid my boots to the side. I liked them, but if I was going to walk under the water again – and I was definitely planning something like that – then sandals made more sense right now. I shuffled into my usual pair of sandals as I spoke.

"Is the village in danger because of me?"

My mother didn't answer, but the door creaked as it opened.

"Mama? Is the village in danger because of me?"

The sigh I heard as I came out from behind the screen was my father's. I ran to him, forgetting my question in the relief of seeing him okay.

"I was so worried about you," I said as I hugged him. "How did you get away?"

"It wasn't me that they came for and they thought they knew where their quarry was." His smile was gentle, but there was something about the way he was looking at me – like how he looked at his nets just before he did something to them to improve how they worked. "You surprised me."

"I surprised myself!" I said, stepping back a bit and looking nervously at them both.

"Don't worry," my father said. His face was grim and determined but I didn't think he realized that his hands shook a little while he spoke. "The men of our village are preparing to defend it. We will not let them take you from us."

"Heron said they have a ship with cannons. He said they could flatten our village with it," I said nervously. "I love you and mama. I love our home here. I don't want to ruin everything."

"Seleska," my father said sternly. "Don't surrender to these mercenaries. You might think you would be saving us, but you would only be breaking our hearts."

A tear ran down my mother's face as she nodded her agreement. Our cottage was in disarray, the beds unmade and the dishes sitting beside the bowl my mother usually washed them in. Halana was such a tidy woman that our home spoke volumes – she was worried.

I couldn't believe that Renny had guessed what I was thinking the second I started thinking it. Of course my gut response was that I needed to turn myself in. How could I live with myself if anything happened to my family because of me?

"Yes, father," I said, but my mind was racing. I couldn't let my tiny village fight a ship full of cannons and soldiers with weapons just to protect me. And I couldn't give myself up to them or it would break my parents' hearts. There had to be some other way.

I thought about it for the rest of the day while we prepared the village, gathering anything that could be used as a weapon, constructing a wall of sharpened stakes – there was only one side to the wall by the end of the day.

I'd barely done any work at all. It seemed every member of the village wanted to tell me personally that nothing had changed – that I was one of them, a valued part of the village – and that they were happy to fight for me. I was touched and so grateful. But between their well-wishes, I barely had time to tend to Nasataa, never mind get anything else done and before I knew it, it was dark.

Fortunately, there was no attack as the village ate the evening meal and began to turn in to their own houses. Everyone in the village hugged me or gave me a strong smile as they passed and with each encouraging nod and determined look, I grew more and more certain that I had to keep these people safe. They were willing to risk everything for me – an outsider who had been adopted into their village ten years ago. They were willing to risk their homes and families and lives. That wasn't right. And I had to do something about it.

Fortunately, Nasataa had slept most of the day without causing any kind of trouble, though he'd gobbled down the fish I'd slipped into the bag for him. As I settled into my cot, the leather bag clutched close, my mind raced with my plan.

I just had to wait for my parents to fall asleep first. I didn't want to get them involved – not when it meant doing something this risky. But I couldn't just let them risk everything for me – again. This time, it was my turn to keep *them* safe and make sure that *they* had a home.

It was too bad that I had to bring Nasataa on such a dangerous errand, but I could hardly leave him behind. He was only a baby and he needed me.

Chapter Thirteen

I snuck out of the house and into the velvet night. Little glowbugs darted through the waving palm trees and the birds and insects of the jungle island were wide awake, singing their chorus so loudly that it masked my furtive movements as I slipped away to the edge of the water.

My plan was a simple one. I would go to the mercenaries' ship and I would sink it. It couldn't be that hard to do. After all, there were sunken ships all around the Havenwind Isles.

I felt a little bad about it. Destroying property was wrong. But, so was kidnapping – or attempting to kidnap – girls. And it wasn't like I was destroying the ship completely, I was just going to move it to underneath the water instead of on top of the water. That way, the cannons couldn't hurt my village or my people. Simple enough, right?

Or at least, that's what I told myself. I had a feeling that enacting the plan wouldn't be simple at all and an even worse feeling that sinking a boat wasn't as morally neutral as I was pretending. It was probably wrong.

At least I wasn't planning to kill anyone. They would just lose their ship and have to learn how to live on the islands with the rest of us. That seemed simple enough.

I kept telling myself that as I snuck out of the village toward the little cove on the other side of Pebble Beach that I knew contained the old, dilapidated shed that used to house Elder Yandee's canoes back when people still used boats on the island. Heron and I had gone there once as kids and slipped inside the tumbledown building, stepping carefully over the places where the roof had collapsed and one of the walls had caved in. More importantly, we'd found the old paddles in a heap in one corner and two rotting canoes on the floor of the shed. And one not-so rotten canoe stacked on top of them.

It was that canoe that I was aiming for. Sure, I could swim out to the ship, but that would take a lot of strength and I was still tired from all my swimming yesterday and my lack of sleep. A canoe would make everything simpler.

Or so I thought.

A twig snapped behind me and I spun in place on the beach path. Who was following me?

"Seleska?" Heron whispered from behind me.

"Heron! What are you doing here?" I was trying to be quiet. We were still too close to the village and anyone might hear us.

"Following you. You shouldn't be sneaking out! You should be at home in bed getting ready for tomorrow when we defend ourselves." He caught up to me on the path, his footsteps quiet on the sand and the moonlight gleaming off his worried expression. "Now is not the time for harebrained adventures!"

"Is it harebrained to save the village before it even comes to a fight?" I challenged in a whisper. But I needed to stop talking. I didn't want to be overheard.

I spun and raced down the path, hoping he wouldn't alert anyone, hoping he'd just let it go. I didn't dare let word of this get back to my parents or they'd want to stop me. They'd see protecting me as the first priority, but to me, protecting them was just as important.

"Seleska!" Heron had caught up to me. He was faster than he looked despite the bulk of those blacksmith's muscles. "Whatever you're doing, I'm coming, too."

I trotted down the beach path, ignoring him. We were almost out of earshot of the village. Just a little further.

When I reached the rocky point where the wind blew along the beach and carried sound away from the village on most nights, I spun again.

"You can't come, Heron! It's too dangerous!"

"If that's true, then you shouldn't be going." He had a condescending look on his face that made me frown. I could do this! No one else needed to get involved.

"If you want to help, then watch Nasataa for me," I said, trying to hand him the leather satchel.

"Is that what you've named that thing?" he asked. "Not a chance!"

"Please? It's not safe for him to come with me!"

"Then leave him here."

"If the village finds him, they'll kill him."

"Umm, yeah. He's a Blue Dragon."

"He's just a baby," I protested, turning back to stride down the path. We were almost at the old shed.

"He can still do a lot of damage. The Elders say they are poisonous."

"He hasn't poisoned me," I said, not looking back as I finally reached the shed door and wrenched it open. It leaned precariously to the side, resting on a single hinge.

"The boathouse? This is not a good idea, Seleska," Heron said with a frown. His arms were crossed over his thick chest.

"Then stay here," I huffed, gathering a paddle out of the stack and throwing it out of the shed before diving back in to try to free the top canoe from the fallen roof pieces.

Strong arms reached past me to help me tug the boat free.

"If you're going, then I'm going, too. Someone needs to keep an eye on you."

I rolled my eyes, but inside I was thrilled. I could use the help. I had no idea what was involved in breaking into a ship and sinking it. Except that I'd need something to chop a hole in the bottom of the boat, which was why I was looking for the rusty axe that used to be in the shed.

"Don't tell me that you're looking for that axe!" Heron looked alarmed.

"How else would I chop a hole in the bottom of a boat?" I asked.

Heron looked at the canoe.

"Not that one! The one with the mercenaries," I said.

He tried to wipe the grin away as soon as it appeared on his face, but his eyes were still dancing when he spoke, even though his face was straight.

"Do you know how thick the hull of a ship is? There are better ways to sink it. They have pumps in the bottom to push water out. We can reverse the process and pump the water back in."

That sounded like it would take a while.

"Trust me," he said, as if he could read my thoughts. "It will take less time and draw less attention than your plan will."

"How do you know what ships are like inside?" I asked.

This time, his knowing grin got under my skin. "I'm a blacksmith's apprentice. We are supposed to know about all kinds of engineering. There are old plans for ships in the smithies. Just because we don't repair ships anymore, doesn't mean we didn't before."

"I wonder what this place was like before the ships stopped coming," I said as we hauled the canoe to the water.

"Busier," Heron said dryly.

"I bet that was exciting," I said, as my mind danced with visions of a bustling Abergande and thriving villages.

"We've been lucky to be protected from the world for so long," Heron said with a sigh. "I guess that's over."

"Personally, I prefer the adventure." I ran back and grabbed the paddles before returning to him on the beach.

He had the canoe mostly in the water, but his arms were crossed over his chest.

"Promise me that you'll be careful, Seleska. This is serious business."

"Cross my heart," I said with a wide smile before leaping into the canoe and climbing to the front of it with my satchel full of Nasataa and the paddle I'd chosen for myself.

Heron could be as grumpy as he liked, but he wouldn't dull my fun. I'd been itching for adventures only days ago and now I was having them all the time! Oh. And I was also trying to save my village. That was important, too.

Chapter Fourteen

"Shhh," Heron whispered as we drifted in toward the ship.

Despite being the dead of night, the ship was alight with lanterns and shapes moved on the deck. I'd hoped everyone would be asleep and now that it was clear that they weren't, I was getting worried. We didn't have weapons of any kind or even a very fast boat. The canoe bobbed in the ocean waves and with a lot of encouragement, it had floated up the coast and out to the ship. But it wasn't a fast boat.

Out in the distance, the small ship's boat with the lanterns and divers was still anchored near the reef where I'd disappeared into the caves. They must still be looking for me. Divers dropped from the boat to take turns in the water. Good thing I'd found that portal or I'd still be trapped in there. What the portal was and how it worked was a worry for another day – or maybe a mystery I would never solve.

In the distance, Abergande lay dark and abandoned – a shocking sight.

"Are you okay in there, little buddy?" I whispered to Nasataa.

He sent back an image of him scurrying up the ropes on the side of the ship and leaping onto the deck, flaming wildly.

"I don't think that's a good idea."

He sent an image of himself running up the leg of a screaming sailor and gnawing on his ear. It was adorable – but also dangerous.

"Just stay in the bag until I tell you its safe to come out, okay?" I whispered.

"Shh!" Heron reminded.

I should have left Nasataa somewhere safe. Somewhere that didn't put him at risk of being caught by mercenaries. But where would that have been?

Even my parents wouldn't have welcomed a Blue Dragon to the village – not even a baby one.

We were getting close to the ship. Fortunately, they didn't seem to be watching the waters on this side of the ship. And why would they? There were no other boats or ships around here except for theirs.

And wasn't it interesting that theirs was still here? After all, the Havenwind Isles had given up boats because of the wrath of the Blue Dragons. Wouldn't it make sense that those same dragons would pull this ship into the waves? But they hadn't. Why not? Had the dragons stopped attacking ships? Or was there some other reason for it?

"Seleska!" Heron whispered, pointing urgently toward the ship ahead.

Oh. Yes. I scooted up to the tip of the narrow canoe and caught the side of the ship before we hit it with the canoe.

We'd made it this far. Hope soared through me. Maybe we could stop these mercenaries and save our village! We just had to get into the ship without being caught and pump water into it. Easy, right?

A stab of nerves shot through me, reminding me that it was not as easy as that, but I ignored them. We had work to do and getting all wound up about it wouldn't help the job get done any faster. Besides, adventures were meant to be nerve-wracking!

I pulled us along the side of the ship until we reached a point where a rope hung down from the side. It looked like it was meant to be used to tie up that boat the divers were using. Well, I could use it to climb up into the ship.

I glanced back at Heron. He shook his head, pointing at himself. He wanted to go first, did he? Typical. But that didn't make any sense. He was bulkier than I was, and it would be harder for him to hide. I smiled at him, pretending that I didn't understand what he meant and then grabbed the rope firmly in both hands, planted my feet against the side of the ship and began to climb.

Nasataa squeaked in the satchel hanging from my shoulder and I sent him a visual image of waiting quietly and patiently in the bag. If he made sounds like that on deck, I'd be sure to be discovered!

My arms were already aching by the time I was halfway up the rope. Good thing I hadn't let Heron go first! He'd already be up on deck with arms like his and then I'd have to scramble to catch up!

My heart was in my throat when I finally reached the deck and eased myself carefully over the rail. Fortunately, despite the bright lights from the lanterns, there were only two men actually on the deck. One was standing at the stern of the ship near something shaped like a wheel and the other at the bow. I slunk to where a stack of crates was lashed down, hiding behind their bulk. What would be in those crates? Food they'd bought in Abergande, maybe? It must take a lot of food to feed a crew like this.

I felt a touch on my shoulder and froze. They'd found me!

"Next time, wait!" Heron hissed in my ear.

The breath gusted out of me like a cloud of steam. I'd thought I'd been caught! Maybe this was more dangerous than I'd thought. Maybe I should have been more careful.

But Heron was already pointing to a hatch where a man was climbing up onto the deck. He carried a tray and strode to where the man at the stern was standing watch. Heron shot me a significant look. This was our chance.

I bit my lip, but I couldn't back out now. Not when we were so close and not when I'd gotten Heron into this with me.

Gripping my satchel and holding tightly to my courage, I slipped across the deck, my light sandals not making a sound. I reached the hatch and ducked inside, descending the ladder quickly to make way for Heron.

I slipped into the shadows, waiting, waiting.

There he was! I stepped out to show my relief.

But the figure descending the ladder was not Heron.

Chapter Fifteen

I leapt back into the shadows, tucking myself behind a barrel shoved in behind the ladder. We were in a long passage, poorly lit. Doors lined the long passage, heavy-framed and ominous. I hoped the figure would slip into one of the doors, but instead, he paused at the bottom of the ladder, a frown on his face. He looked up the ladder and then back down, as if he had forgotten something but couldn't remember what.

Sweat beaded across my brow. My mouth felt dry. He was going to see me back here. If I even moved an inch, he'd notice me. I stayed as still as possible, but that didn't stop the rustling at my side. Nasataa peeked his little head out of my bag.

Please, don't hear him!

I shot an image to him of him lying down in the bag and waiting patiently.

He ignored it, climbing slowly from the bag and crawling down my leg. His little claws dug through the fabric and into my leg as he scurried down.

No! This wasn't good! I needed him to stay safe and being safe meant staying where I could keep him from trouble!

I stayed frozen as the sailor looked up the ladder again and shook his head.

Nasataa, creeping along the edge of the wall, scurried over one of the sailor's feet.

"Skies and stars! The rats in this place!" the sailor cursed, stomping just inches from where Nasataa scurried along the passage.

My heart was in my throat. That had been so close!

Come back! I thought toward him. Please!

I tried to think an image of him returning to me, but it was garbled. My strong emotions made my thoughts tug at him, not just to scurry back along the passage to me, but to come from wherever he went, to pull toward me from far out at sea, from through portals and over islands.

I must really be starting to love that little guy, because I felt like if he were any of those places I would go and find him and keep him safe. He couldn't be trusted on his own yet. He'd only get himself killed.

The sailor shuffled down the passage, not even noticing that Nasataa was huddled in one of the doorways. As soon as I lost sight of the sailor, I crept out, following where my little dragon had gone.

"Seleska?" a hoarse whisper sounded from behind me.

I turned to see Heron, color drained from his face, clearing the last rung of the ladder.

"I thought you were going to be caught," he whispered.

"I lost Nasataa," I whispered back, worry filling my voice. What if he found something dangerous? There were probably fires on board, or even food laced with poison to kill mice and rats. If he got into it ... I couldn't think like that. I needed to find him first.

"The dragon? Forget him! We have more important things to do here."

My mouth firmed and my brows lowered. How would he feel if he was an orphaned baby dragon who was lost on an enemy ship? Would he want to be forgotten? No? Then why did he think it was okay to forget Nasataa?

With a huff, I hurried down the corridor, not turning to look at Heron when he whispered my name again. If he didn't care about baby dragons, how heartless was he?

The passage plunged deep into the ship, but now I was getting worried. I had lost track of Nasataa, and no matter how often I called to him, reaching as far as I could mentally with the plea that he come to me, I couldn't get a reply. Where had he gone?

The ship was quiet, snores coming from some of the doors and the creak of timbers and ropes moving and rubbing against each other in the waves of the ocean swell cloaked the noises we were making.

At the other end of the passage, there was a ladder leading downward again. We needed to go down there to complete our task. But where was

Nasataa? Had he thought the same thing and hurried down the ladder? I could only hope so.

I was about to go down it, too, when Heron grabbed my arm, spinning me around.

"Seleska," he whispered into my ear, his mouth so close that I could feel his lips brushing my ear as he whispered. "Don't be like that. I came with you, didn't I? I care."

He was right. I was being unreasonable. And we needed to work together. But I couldn't help myself.

"Nasataa matters, too," I whispered back.

He looked like he was trying to hold in his temper, but he nodded tightly. Poor guy. He was trying really hard, even if his thick head couldn't seem to grasp that a baby was a baby no matter what species it was, and it needed protecting.

"Sorry," I whispered. "Friends?"

He smiled. "Friends."

He ducked down into the hatch and with a sigh of relief, I scrambled after him.

Time to sink this ship!

Chapter Sixteen

There was a dull thunk below me, but from my place on the ladder, I couldn't see what had happened.

"Heron?" I whispered, worried, but there was no reply.

I scrambled down the rest of the way and spun, looking for him.

I gasped when I saw his body laid out on the wooden beams of the ship's hold. There was blood on his temple and his huge form was slumped over like a dead whale on the beach.

A tiny cry ripped from my lips before I could prevent it. I raced to his side. He was still alive. His breath was shallow, but he *was* breathing.

"If he lives, he'll wake up with quite the headache," a voice said from above.

With my teeth gritted, I looked up.

All I'd noticed when I turned at the bottom of the ladder, was Heron – his situation so grim that it blocked out everything else, but now that I knew he was alive, other details began to filter in.

The hold was open here, with a trickle of water down the center and barrels stacked along the sides of the hold with coiled ropes and tools hanging on the sides. I couldn't really call them walls, since the floor and walls were all just hold. A bobbing lantern hung from the ceiling, swaying with every roll of the ship and a big pump sat in the center of the floor. It was currently unmanned.

It would have been the perfect opportunity to enact Heron's plan and fill the ship with water while the crew slept and the pump was easy to access.

Would have been.

Instead, the man in the flowing white shirt – the very one who had dunked my head under water – stood over Heron's slumped form. He held a cutlass in one hand. Fortunately, he'd settled for hitting Heron with the hilt, rather than slashing him with the wicked blade. My enemy's light-colored hair – so like mine – glinted in the lantern light, reminding me that there was a reason they had come to our shores and that reason was me.

"What do you want?" I asked, my voice tight.

"You're the one who came to my ship, Princess. I think I should be asking that question," he said with a look that could almost be called a grin if it wasn't so cruel.

"I want you all to go away and leave my village alone!" I said boldly.

"Done," he said with a laugh. "I don't need any villagers."

"Then you'll just go ?" I asked, even though I knew that if he left, he would want to take me with him. He wanted me. But I needed to buy time so I could think of a way out of here.

I called to Nasataa, desperately begging him to return to me. I didn't want to flee without him. Although, I couldn't really flee anyway, could I? Not with Heron knocked on the head. I wouldn't even be able to carry him. He was three times my size.

I swallowed, my mouth dry as my situation finally registered.

I'd come here for adventure.

I'd found disaster.

I couldn't see a way out of this mess now.

"Ah. It's beginning to become clear to you," the man said with a smile. "I think I should introduce myself Princess Seleska. I am Branson Kendark. Does that ring a bell?"

Kendark? The name did sound familiar. My brow furrowed as I tried to remember where I'd heard it before.

"Your mother's people were Kendarks. From the lands of the Rock Eaters to the east. I am your mother's half-brother's son. Your cousin. Which is how I recognized you immediately. Not that it's very hard. After all, there aren't many girls with light colored hair so far to the south. And there are even fewer who can breathe water."

He seemed to want to talk. I let him keep talking while my mind reached out to Nasataa, trying to find him. Where was that little fellow?

"It's an abnormal gift – even among our people. So abnormal, that we need it now. We need you."

"I thought you were mercenaries," I said.

What if I managed to catch him off guard and then I flooded the ship and just kept Heron's head above water as we followed the passages to the surface? He'd be much lighter if he was floating. Maybe we still had a chance here if I was careful. I stood up, thinking hard about what to do to get my cousin – if that was really who he was – off guard.

"You can be more than one thing at a time, Seleska. I thought you'd realize that. After all, you are a princess and island trash at the same time."

Trash? He was an awful person to be calling all my friends and family 'trash.'

"Which is why you should come with me of your own will. Why fight it? You're valuable to the Rock Eaters – and to me. And you can ask the price you want for your services."

"Services?"

"Haven't you heard? Magic is leaving our world. The dragons are all that is left of Dominion magic. Baojang has lost theirs almost entirely. Even far-away Ko'Torenth is rumored to be stripped of all magic but a few strange objects. That leaves only us – the Rock Eaters – to salvage the magic of this world."

"I thought Rock Eaters were painted with bones and wore ceremonial clothing," I said. That was what the island tales told.

"I'm not your typical Rock Eater. I have to present myself in a way that doesn't threaten people at our ports of call, or I can't trade," he said dismissively. "But I'm, as committed to the cause as anyone. We must find a way to bring back the world's magic or face the consequences. And just because we dress in a way you find laughable, doesn't mean we aren't incredibly powerful people."

"What does that have to do with me?" I asked.

I was edging forward, trying to get close. If I was close enough to him, maybe I could surprise him and take that cutlass.

"Well, sweet cousin, the old stories say that magic first came to the world from volcanoes under the sea."

"That's nice," I said, smiling and stepping a little closer. His sword tip dropped a little, taken off guard by my friendly response.

"And the only person who can reach so far into the sea would be someone who can breathe under water."

"And then what?" I said sweetly.

That sword point was lowering even more.

"And then," he said, matching my smile with his own friendly smile, "we call your bluff."

He reached out and grabbed me by the top, spinning me around and putting the cutlass to my throat.

"Nice try, little cousin," he said as the razor-sharp edge nicked my skin.

Chapter Seventeen

I'd been wrong to call Nasataa to me. Now I begged him to stay away, sending pictures in my mind to him of diving overboard and fleeing.

Almost the moment that I sent them, I saw a glimmer of his shining blue scales as he darted behind a barrel. Oh no! We were all trapped now! He was stuck in here with us.

"Don't move and this will all be over quickly," Branson Kendark said. "I have a cabin ready for you. You won't even have to travel in the brig."

Ice lanced through my belly but I couldn't think of a way to squirm out of his grasp without that razor-sharp cutlass slicing through my throat. I blinked back tears of frustration as my mind raced. What to do? What to do?

I couldn't save myself. I couldn't save Heron. But there was still hope for Nasataa. With all my mental might, I tried to project to him that this ship was evil and dangerous. That he must flee it at all costs. I tried to show him that he would be captured and forced to stay. That he must leave no matter what.

A groan of timber on timber filled the air and then suddenly Nasataa was leaping through the air, his small wings fluttering as he landed on Branson's shoulder and flamed his ear.

"Ugh! Get off of me!" The mercenary twisted against the surprise attack, a scream ripping from his throat as the blue flames stuck to his ear. His arm holding me never faltered, his sword blade stayed poised at my throat even as his other hand beat the fire out.

"Run, Nasataa!" I called.

The sides of the ship moaned again and there was a crash from above.

"What the – " the mercenary began but a loud *snap* from above cut him off, followed by a scream. His sword arm sagged slightly as his gaze turned upward.

I didn't hesitate. I ducked under the sword blade, spinning to slip free. Nasataa sailed through the air and landed on my shoulder, wrapping protectively around my neck.

"It's okay, little buddy. It's okay," I said. He wasn't lost. He wasn't hurt. Yet.

It was up to me to keep the little dragon safe. But I also had brought Heron here and I had to help him, too.

I'd only run one step toward him when the ship bucked, the sides bulging.

Everything seemed to move in slow motion. Behind me, Kendark cursed.

The timbers beside me creaked, and then one snapped like a dry stick. Followed by another and another. Water plunged into the hull through the open holes, surging forward. Barrels knocked loose from where they were tied bobbed along the surface. The water was knee deep by my second stride, waist deep by my third.

Heron!

He was going to drown!

I reached him as the water suddenly lowered, pouring away. I had the sensation of soaring upward, even though my feet were still braced against the hull.

I reached Heron as the water level lowered to ankle deep, pulling him up from the water. He gasped, his eyelids flickering open a little as he choked on water, coughing and sputtering to bring it up.

I could hear Branson Kendark's loud calls for an explanation. Screams rippled from far above us. I wrapped my arms around Heron, trying to pull him to his feet as he fought for breath. He was dazed and choking on water. We couldn't stay here. The ship was going to go down – or something – I was a little confused about why the water was running *out*.

And then the floor beneath us fell out and we were falling through the air.

Chapter Eighteen

I was seeing things that my mind couldn't make sense of. Above me, fluffy white clouds tinged with pink announced that dawn had arrived. Between me and the clouds was what was left of the ship we'd been on – a splintered wreck of shredded wood. One mast and sail dangled from the wreckage by a long rope, swinging back and forth. Bodies of sailors, barrels, and tackle tumbled down, falling like crumbs from the ship.

Around the ship, a long sinuous body – or maybe a tail? – was wrapped. Gleaming blue scales and semi-translucent, wispy fins lined it. It was squeezing the ship like a constrictor snake squeezed its island prey.

And suddenly, the warnings in my village about Blue Dragons made a lot of sense. Suddenly, it didn't seem so crazy to fear them or to lock up all the paddles and demand to know if anyone had heard or seen one.

Suddenly, the songs I'd been hearing all this time made sense, too. Because I was hearing the song right now, and it was coming from this Blue Dragon.

I saw all of that in the blink of an eye.

My next thought was that we were falling. I was still holding Heron and Nasataa was wrapped around my neck and we were falling through the air like a piece of wreckage toward the boiling sea below. How far could you drop before hitting the water and still live? And what about Heron who was still struggling to pull in a breath?

I tried to twist in the air to look under me, but the sea was coming up too quickly. I'd failed Nasataa and I'd failed Heron and now they were both going to die because of me.

Please, don't let them die!

An image filled my mind – the same image that I'd sent Nasataa of how the ship was evil and dangerous. But this image was amplified and bigger, larger, rougher. I blinked from the intensity of it as it tore through my mind, leaving me aching from the pain of it. That wasn't my dragon.

My heart was in my throat. My mind was swirling with confusion and fear. I felt spray on my face. We must be close to the surface.

Please, just don't let them die!

I didn't even know who I was pleading with as we broke through the surface, smashing painfully against the waves. Heron slipped through my hands as we plunged into the water. And then my descent slowed, and I was kicking up to the surface, spinning in the water as I searched for Heron.

My heart raced so quickly that I couldn't keep up. Even though I could breathe under water, I was still holding my breath.

Where was he?

Wreckage drifted in the water all around us and I couldn't see him between chunks of wood and undulating ropes, bobbing barrels and sinking pulleys.

Heron? Panic burst up into my mind. If I didn't find him quickly, he was going to drown for sure. With a head injury and his lungs already filled with water once, he didn't stand much of a chance on his own.

Where was he?

There!

I saw him sinking below me and I dove down, struggling to reach him. He was sinking too fast. I wouldn't get to him fast enough to pull him up through the waves!

Please, please! Don't let him drown!

A huge horned head plunged through the water between us. It glittered in the ocean light, blue and beautiful, tendrils and fins swirled translucently in the water as the mouth opened, rows of teeth gleaming in the dawn light, and it scooped Heron up, pulling him to the surface.

Fear surged through me. This dragon was so much larger than Ramariri had been – so huge and powerful and it had my friend right in its jaws. I was about to scream when suddenly, I was snatched up in another set of huge jaws and pulled back up into the air.

I'd expected the jaws to crush me – or at least hurt a bit, but they were gentle and delicate and the song of the sea – the song I heard every time I went down to it or thought about it at all – filled my mind along with words that were foreign and yet understandable.

Keep the little one safe.

Nasataa squirmed against my neck as the huge head arched around and set us gently on the old canoe bobbing out in the ocean. The other head laid a coughing, choking Heron down right in front of me.

I scrambled forward, pulling him into my lap and wrapping my arms around him protectively as he sucked in a long breath. Nasataa, for his part, was playing the part of scarf. He was wrapped so tightly around my neck that it was becoming uncomfortable.

Keep him safe.

This time, the sound in my mind echoed as if two voices were saying it at once and images tumbled in my mind. An image of Nasataa first seeing me and rushing toward me. An image of him in the cave with the portal and me following him. An image of him running away on the ship and then one of him leaping to wrap around my neck. It was as if the dragons were trying to tell me all about Nasataa and me in one momentary burst. It was painful and beautiful, and it explained things to me that I couldn't have said in words.

We were bound together, the little dragon and I. I was meant to be his protector and helper.

"I will," I said as the two huge heads stayed close, watching me with hawk-like eyes. "I promise."

They rose then, towering above me, before plunging back into the sea. A burst of water jetted up where each head had been and then, in the distance, the length of body, or tail – or whatever that was gripping the ship – plunged back into the water, smashing the ship against the surface of the ocean and splintering the last shards of it into a million pieces.

"I don't think you need to worry about the ship anymore," Heron said between coughs. His head was still bleeding and I was holding him upright or he would have fallen over, but he was speaking. That had to mean he was okay, right?

I reached up, stroking Nasataa's head gently as I pulled Heron in tighter.

They were going to be okay. They were alive and breathing and okay.

I took a deep, grateful breath.

"I don't think you need to be so prejudiced against Blue Dragons," I replied. "After all, they just saved our lives."

Episode Two: Dragon Staff

Chapter One

We drifted into shore, worn and thirsty, our canoe bobbing wildly in the waves. Wind blew onshore so strongly that it confused the mind, filling the ears with whispers and suggestions of secrets. It had been all I could do to get the canoe back to the beach with Heron slumped against my chest and Nasataa wrapped around my neck.

I'd kept a lookout for sailors who might be swimming after us, but all I saw of them were small dark spots bobbing on the waves or clinging to wreckage as they made for the nearest shore. If I was honest with myself, I felt guilty that I wasn't back there making sure they all made it ashore safely. Even if they were my enemies, it was clear that I had the advantage when it came to saving people who might be trapped in a sinking ship – after all, I was the one who could breathe underwater.

And I was the reason their ship had sunk, which made me doubly guilty. I'd gone there to sink it and it had been me calling to Nasataa that had alerted the giant Blue Dragons to the presence of the ship and the threat it was to the little baby dragon.

But if I'd stayed to help them, who would help Heron and Nasataa?

Nasataa clung to me like a frightened baby – which was what he was, dragon or no – and sent me mental pictures of lying safely on the beach or eating juicy fruit. He was tired and hungry and scared. He needed a safe place to rest and eat and he was my responsibility. I reached up to stroke his head as often as I dared without capsizing the tippy boat.

Heron was drifting in and out of consciousness. That blow to his head had been hard. If I'd left him in the canoe, he might have drowned. The old rickety canoe had a slow leak, and anyone lying on the bottom of it would have to be able to breathe water like me. Even now, he lay heavily against me, his sun-darkened skin ashen in the morning light.

I'd paddled this whole way with incredible slowness, supporting Heron's head up on my lap out of the water, keeping his big muscled body balanced on the canoe, bailing water with a little wooden cup attached to the canoe by a string, and paddling when I could. And by the way, who knows their canoe has a leak and is careful to tie a bailing cup to it, but then doesn't fix the hole? Who?

Our canoe hit the sand, sliding up the beach to come to a stop and slowly topple over.

I was too tired to care. And Heron was too heavy on land. We fell into a heap on the smooth sand and with difficulty, I crawled out from under him and propped him up against the canoe.

"Wait here while I get help," I said, breathlessly. The village should be getting up now. I should be able to find enough people to help me carry Heron – or maybe we could borrow the donkey and his cart. Heron was a big man.

His eyelids fluttered open and he smiled slightly at me as he murmured, "Stay out of trouble."

"You're one to talk!" I replied, wobbling to my feet and hurrying toward the village path.

Nasataa had begun to snore. I could have sworn he was already bigger than he had been four days ago when I found him newly-hatched. How fast did dragons grow? I was going to find out.

For now, I tucked my hair around him to keep him from prying eyes. No one would feel safe if they knew I had a baby dragon with me, and I'd lost his pouch somewhere along the way last night. I'd need a new one or a better way to carry him.

I'd lost my sandals, too, and my bare feet trod the dirt path to the village carefully, as I watched for goat's head thorns and other spiky debris. I was so concentrated on not hurting my feet that my father's relieved voice came out of nowhere.

"Seleska! We were so worried!"

"Dad!" I exclaimed, losing my fear of hurting my feet and running to hug him.

He froze as my arms wrapped around him. "Seleska? What is around your neck?"

I pulled back to see him still frozen in a half-hug as if he were afraid to move.

"A baby Blue Dragon," I said sheepishly. I made my eyes go as wide as they could trying to look innocent.

The dark cloud that rolled over his expression told me it hadn't worked.

"*That* is going to be a problem," he said.

Chapter Two

"Seleska," my mother said again, in full lecture mode, "There is a reason that Blue Dragons are forbidden. Even their scales are tossed back into the ocean if they wash ashore. We must have no part in them or their affairs."

She had me backed up to a tree as she lectured while in the distance, the men of my village loaded Heron up onto the donkey cart to take him home. Elder Lutrind was fussing over him with a cool drink and herbs. I wished I was getting that kind of kind treatment instead of this berating.

"Mama," I tried to say.

"Blue Dragons are trouble, Seleska. My father died when his fishing boat was capsized by a Blue Dragon. Your father's brother died when he swam out too far into the ocean and was swallowed up by one of them. You can't keep that dragon. You have to give it to the Elders."

The cart was moving now, bumping its way toward us. I watched, worried as it drew close and stopped. Heron smiled weakly from in the cart.

"Hey, Seleska," he said.

"I'm so sorry, Heron," I said, slipping past my mother and ignoring her sigh and shaking head. "I should never have got you into this mess."

"We saved the village, didn't we?" he said with a wry grin as Elder Lutrind pushed him back to a prone position. "We stopped the ship and the cannons."

"We did," I said, laying a gentle hand on his shoulder.

Elder Lutrind clucked her tongue. "No touching!"

"Why not?" I asked, pulling my hand back sharply. Was Heron in worse condition than I'd feared?

"Not while you're touching that cursed thing!" the Elder said, pointing to the sleeping dragon around my neck. "Drive on Talan. Old Horace needs the cart when we're through." She looked at my mother as the cart lurched back into motion. "Convince her, Halana!"

My mother rounded on me as the cart hurried away, the rest of the villagers following it.

"See, Seleska? The whole village is worried about you! You can't keep that creature!"

"Mama," I said as calmly as I could. "He's my responsibility and he's just a baby. Didn't you take me in when I needed you? And foreigners aren't welcome on the islands, either! How could I leave him to the elements when you showed me that welcoming those in need is such a good thing?"

My mother crossed her arms over her chest, a stern look on her face. "You were a human child, Seleska."

"He's only a baby," I protested. "And he's mine."

"Halana," my father interrupted, saving me from more of a lecture. He was trailing behind the last of the villagers who had helped Heron. "I'll take her with me, alright? We're going to go up the beaches and collect the sailors floating into shore."

"They were about to fire their cannons on our village!" Halana protested, anger in her tone.

My father nodded grimly. "So, it seems to us that it would be dangerous to let them run free on our islands. The men of the village are going to collect them and then we will decide what to do with them."

"Oh," my mother looked pacified by that. "And Seleska?"

"Let me talk sense into her, while you help the women prepare. We'll have more mouths for dinner tonight – hungry mouths. And even if they are our prisoners, they will have to eat."

She nodded and I breathed a sigh of relief when she hugged him goodbye and shook her head at me.

"I would hug you, too, but I won't go near that thing. Get rid of it, daughter."

She strode away with purpose and I was left standing awkwardly next to my father just a few short paces from a knot of village men carrying fish spears and machetes.

"It looks like you lost your sandals," my father said, handing me my tall spiky-heeled boots with a blank expression.

I frowned as I took them and put them on. They were so impractical. And I could tell he was laughing behind his stony expression. They all were.

Well, at least I got to go have an adventure instead of waiting behind and making food with the village women. I was starting to suspect, though, that everyone thought these boots were a joke. Maybe they were. I'd have to ask Heron about that when he felt better.

I strode after my father thinking about how much trouble Heron was going to be in when he was better again.

"Your mother is right," he said after long minutes of tromping down the path.

"Would you have left me on that beach when I arrived, six years old, frightened, alone except for my dying friend?" I asked boldly. "A dragon brought me. And you took me in anyway."

"Mmm," he agreed but I couldn't tell if my point had been taken or if he just wanted me to be quiet.

We walked in silence after that, following the others until shouts from up ahead alerted us that the first of the sailors had been found.

The sailor had not survived the night. Nor had two of his friends. They were washed up along the beach, their tangled limbs and awkward poses the first signs that the waves had taken their lives. Dapnee strode inland and began to dig. I hadn't even realized that he was carrying a shovel. Two other men from our village joined him as the rest of us lifted the sailors and carried them into shore. I helped my father and two other men lift one of the dead sailors. The sight of him soured my stomach.

A pang seized my heart. These men had meant to kidnap me or fire on our village. And both those things were really wrong, but it was my fault that they were dead. Guilt made me bite my lip and look away as we carried them to their graves.

"Mark the spot," my father said, "and we'll make proper stones for them when we can."

"We can have their friends do it," Jamrie suggested. "It will keep them busy while we decide what to do with them."

Murmurs of agreement surrounded us and more than one of the village men looked at the sleeping baby dragon around my neck.

"It would be easier to defend you, Seleska, if you would get rid of that thing," Jamrie said, suddenly. "It's hard to defend a girl – even one of us – when she's carrying around poison."

"He's not poisonous," I protested, but the frowns around the group told me that no one meant that literally.

By noon, we had rounded up five survivors and four more bodies. Dapnee, Jamrie, and the other village men continued up the coast while my father and I took the first five prisoners back to our village. With haunted eyes and slumped postures, they didn't look like they wanted to make any kind of trouble, and they hadn't said a word as we'd bound their hands with jute rope and tied them to a long line of rope as thick as my forearm.

But every one of them watched the dragon around my neck with worried eyes and I was beginning to feel like I was the one who was dangerous and poisonous.

We walked back to the village in silence, my father at the front of the line and me bringing up the rear. We were almost back home when Renny tried one more time.

"Just give it up, Seleska. It will be easier for everyone. It isn't your responsibility."

"Would you have given me up?" I asked him, hurt in my eyes.

"Never," was all he said.

"Then why do you think I would leave poor Nasataa with no one to take care of him?"

And that was the crux of the matter. If I didn't take care of Nasataa, no one would. And he didn't deserve to be abandoned and alone. What kind of a person would choose to do that to him? It didn't matter that he was a dragon and not a human. He mattered to me, if for no other reason than that he had to matter to someone.

Chapter Three

The feeling of the village that night was somber. Altogether, nine men and women had survived the shipwreck, not counting Heron and me. And there might have been more if the other villages or the townspeople of Abergande had found any.

Heron was feeling much better, his head bandaged up. He was under strict orders not to overexert himself, but he sat around the village fire with the rest of us, his old grin on his face and the firelight dancing in his eyes.

"I've heard you have everyone at loose ends about what to do with you," he said when I sauntered up to him and sat down to share his bread and fish. I slipped a piece to Nasataa and his eyebrows rose. "It's going to get worse if you feed that dragon in front of everyone."

"Then I won't feed him in front of everyone," I said, bristling. Why was I so much more angry at Heron for saying that than I was at everyone else? That didn't even make sense.

I stalked off to the beach where I could be alone, my ridiculous heels making my hips sway too much. I could hear the village debating what to do with the prisoners as I left. And I heard more than one villager whispering that maybe I'd brought this down on us. After all, anyone who carried around a baby Blue Dragon was clearly bad luck. It stung. I was only trying to do the right thing. And I was the one who had saved everyone! Sort of. I had a lot of help. And no one would have been in danger in the first place if they hadn't been searching for me here. Okay, fine, it was my fault.

As I passed the line of prisoners, I felt Branson's eyes following me. He had survived the wreck, just like I had – though with an ear so badly burned that even the village Elders weren't sure how best to bandage it. None of the prisoners were talking. They ate in silence. They hadn't been willing to talk to the Elders, either. But I could tell by watching them that they hadn't given up. Their backs were straight, and their gaze followed me sharply. They were just biding their time, waiting to escape and take me home to the Rock Eaters who were paying them.

I gritted my teeth together. I had enemies on one side and angry friends on the other. I'd heard an expression once about being caught between a rock and a hard place. This must be what that expression meant. With no allies left – not even my parents and not even Heron – I didn't know what to do. I wasn't going to give up on Nasataa. He needed me. So, then what was left for me?

The village was out of sight by the time I stopped, settling onto a big driftwood log and pulling Nasataa into my lap to feed him the rest of the bread.

"Are you okay, little guy?" I asked gently, sending calming images to his mind. "You had a big day yesterday. That's enough to wear anyone out!"

He made a sound like a purr, rubbing his filmy back-fin against my palm. I smiled and patted him gently, offering him more food.

He shot me images of colorful fish and I chuckled. "Maybe next meal."

He tugged at my hand with his little teeth and I played with him, tugging back and forth until he got tired and curled up in my lap again his small head on his tiny haunches. He was asleep before he'd even finished settling in.

"I'll take care of you, Nasataa," I said gently. "Don't worry. You don't have to be afraid. I'm not going to leave you."

Tears sprung to my eyes at the memory of my first parents – who had died as they tried to get me to safety – of my bodyguard, who had died doing the same – of Ramariri who had made it as far as this island, fighting death for hours so he could bring me somewhere safe. All those people had died for me. It didn't make sense just to live for myself. And I wasn't going to. No matter what people said about it being easier. My parents were being silly, too. Because they had taken me in – a helpless foreigner – and I knew they'd be doing the same thing for Nasataa if they weren't so worried about me.

I hadn't realized I was crying until someone sat down beside me. Hurriedly, I brushed my tears away.

"I have something for you," Heron said, offering me a bead-sewn bag with double shoulder straps and a flap closure at the top. It was big enough to carry two Nasataa's – or one Nasataa for another couple of weeks if he kept growing like he was. "I saw that you lost your other bag."

"Thank you," I said with a sniff. Where had he even found such a pretty bag? I was pretty sure that was a curling wave beaded onto the back.

"Don't be mad, Seleska," he said.

"I'm not mad at you," I said. "But I have promised this little guy that I'm going to take care of him, and nothing is going to stop that." I looked at him as fiercely as I could. "Not the village, or my parents, or even you."

Nasataa snuggled in closer as I felt the beadwork on the bag Heron had given me. It was really well made. Not something from the village. Had he gotten it in Abergande? When would he have done that?

"I'm not going to try to convince you to send him away," Heron said, his dark eyes glittering under the light of the rising moon. "If the Elders and the village and your parents can't, then I sure can't. But can I convince you not to do crazy things like boarding mercenary ships and trying to sink them? Or whatever that thing was that you did that actually sunk the ship? I can't really remember that part."

"It wasn't me," I admitted. "It was a Blue Dragon."

Heron chuckled, the bandage around his head slipping a little so that he looked almost jaunty. "And you act like everyone is crazy to call them dangerous!"

"I didn't say they weren't dangerous," I protested. "I said that Nasataa is only a baby and that he needs my protection."

"You know," Heron said with a gentle smile. "I think you might be right that he isn't the most dangerous thing around here. You are. You're way worse than he is for drawing trouble." He laughed and I glared at him, but eventually, he sobered up and spoke again. "Just promise me that you'll stay out of trouble, Seleska."

"I'll try," I said.

"I have to finish this apprenticeship, so I can't be around all the time to keep you safe."

"I was the one who saved *you* last night!"

He chuckled. "Just promise."

I leaned in close so that we were inches apart before giving him a wicked grin. "I will do nothing of the sort, Heron. You'll just have to trust me."

"Tradewinds protect us! You couldn't have asked for something easier? Like bringing you a chest full of rubies?" I laughed as he stood up. "I'd better get back to the village, before someone starts to worry about me. Friends?"

"Always," I agreed.

But as he sauntered back to the village, I bit my lip and turned to the sea. I couldn't stay here and endanger everyone, and I couldn't abandon Nasataa. And that meant that my options were limited. Where else could I go? How could I stop more ships from coming here and more people from hunting down my village, and family, and friends?

There had to be a way to head off trouble before it got here.

Chapter Four

I t wasn't so much a decision. 'Decision' implies that you thought something through and looked at all the angles before action. Decision implies carefully weighing the risk rather than following the song of the sea.

When I slipped Nasataa into the bag Heron gave me and closed the flap, that was more of an action. When I slipped it on my back and stole a wistful glance back at my village and the silhouette of my parent's cabin, that was more of a longing. When I followed the song of the sea and took my first step toward the water, that was more of an instinct. I wouldn't have called any of that a decision.

Instead, it was with a sad, but singing heart and a determined set to my jaw that I strode out into the waves and kept on walking long after they'd flowed over my head and covered my swirling hair.

If it had been a decision, I would have shed those ridiculous boots for a sensible pair of sandals and I would have packed extra clothes and blankets, a waterskin and some food. If it had been a decision, I would have said goodbye to everyone before I went. But because it was an action inspired entirely by emotion, I just went.

And I kept on going, searching the sea bottom in the direction I remembered emerging from, until I was led to the old wreck by the glow of the portal.

It would be silly to go through that, right? It would just take me back to the cave north of Abergande. I circled the glowing portal, feeling Nasataa's breathing as he inhaled and exhaled the water all around us. He was comforting to have there, even if I was the one charged with taking care of *him*.

The strange markings around the portal were impossible for me to understand. I could see them easily – squiggles and lines and dots and triangles – but I couldn't read them. One of them – a circle with a squiggly line beside it – was glowing. Experimentally, I touched another sign on the rim – two triangles with a dot beside them. At the touch of my finger, they depressed slightly and began to glow as the circle and squiggly line winked out.

Maybe the runes determined where this portal took you. Maybe each rune took you a different place. I could try that out. At least I knew where one rune went – the circle with the squiggle must lead to the rocky cave I'd sheltered in before. So, if I followed this portal to another place, I wouldn't be stuck. I could choose the circle and squiggle and go home – or close to home – quite easily.

Well, I'd be crazy not to try, right? After all, I needed a way to get far away from here. Maybe not for good, and maybe not right now, but eventually. If I knew how this worked, it would be a good option for me. I'd just try one rune. But which one?

I let my gaze flick along the runes trying to see if one of them appealed to me.

I kind of liked the one with the circle inside the triangle and the wavy line under it. I'd try that one. And hope there weren't sharks on the other side. Or Blue Dragons.

But that was the genius of this. If I didn't like where I went, I could just come right back home again. Besides, the village would be happy to have me safely out of their way for a few hours. They had conversations to talk through and decisions to make and my presence only made all of that more awkward. Even my parents needed time to process all of this in peace.

I was doing the right thing by giving them that space.

I pressed the sign that appealed to me so much – the circle inside the triangle with the wavy line under it – and stepped into the glow.

The world vanished and everything went dark.

A moment later, I blinked my vision back. Wherever I was, it was day here. The water was clear, but colder than at home – and yet the cold didn't seem to bother me as much as I would have expected. Was there more magic to who I was than just the ability to breathe under water?

This water was less turquoise and more of a steely grey. Neat.

A rocky bottom surrounded the portal here with waving weeds, taller than I was. I shouldn't go too far. It would be easy to get lost in this. But I did want to know what kind of place I'd found.

Taking a deep breath, I swam up to the surface. The water here was not very deep at all and my head broke the surface far more quickly than I had expected.

I coughed on the air – always a surprise after water- and my eyes grew huge as I took in the sight before me. I was looking at a city – a city anchored to the land but sprawling out across the water. Boardwalks hung or swung between towers rooted in the water and boats swanned in and out from among the towers. Branches sprouted from every side of these towers, bearing round houses and inns and shops, spiral stairways, ladders, and swinging bridges connecting them.

A smile spread across my face at the marvelous sight. Well, this was a good idea! Good thing I hadn't talked myself out of coming here or I never would have seen this amazing place.

I was still grinning like an idiot when something hit me from behind and the world went black.

Chapter Five

I awoke in a woven cage of reeds. Or at least, they looked like reeds, but when I tugged at them, they didn't budge at all and they slashed my hands like they were made of metal. Nasataa squirmed against my back and I reached awkwardly over my shoulder to unclasp the flap and let him out.

He squealed with delight, running across my shoulders and then leaping into my lap. I shot him a quick warning about the steel basket, sending a mental image of how it had cut me, and he sent a mental image of himself flaming the basket.

I didn't expect that to work, but I was still disappointed when it did nothing. At least whoever had put us in this cage had left food and water. We both ate and drank immediately.

This basket – cage? – had a view, that was for sure. We were dangling over the water from the side of one of those towers. This one – a green tower with silver ornamentation – was at the very edge of the tower and water city. Underneath it, boats moved as often and quickly as people moved in the boardwalks of Abergande back home. There were sailboats and rowboats, fishing boats and fancy boats with canopies carrying people. I watched them for the first long while before letting my gaze move to the other towers and the people moving on the walkways and ladders, through the shops and open-sided restaurants, into homes and into the thick towers themselves. In the distance, big ships lay at anchor, smaller boats running to and from them like baby ducks to their mothers.

If I had not been a prisoner, I would have enjoyed this sight. If I had not been a prisoner, I would have been delightfully curious about this city –

what was it called? Who lived here? How did they get along when so many of them lived in one place?

But I was a prisoner, and the tightening knot in my belly was growing tighter by the hour, slowly choking out my appetite, my joy, my certainty, and even my curiosity. I no longer cared about who had taken me or why. I only cared about getting home. I clung to Nasataa, whispering comforting words to him as he played with my hair or slept in my lap.

Eventually, there was a creak and I looked down the long, narrow arm of my basket to see a strange figure approaching. He – or maybe she – was clad in flowing red clothing, tied tightly around the wrists and ankles. It billowed out like a sail around him – obscuring the shape of his body almost entirely – while round glass pieces obscured his eyes and a tight-fitting leather mask covered his mouth and nose. The rest of his head was hidden by a heavy red hood that was part of the billowing outfit.

Who in the world could this be?

He approached the cage with caution, looking back and forth from the tower to the cage as if he were nervous about approaching me. Which was ridiculous, since *I* was the one in the cage. I stayed sitting cross-legged with Nasataa playing in my lap. I couldn't have stood up anyway. The cage was too small for that.

"Who are you?" I asked boldly as soon as he was close. "You'd better have a good reason for putting me in this cage!"

He froze, watching me for a long moment before pulling down the leather mask and revealing a chin and nose that looked decidedly feminine.

"I'm a Bubbler of the Rock Eater City of Metamora." Definitely a woman, but the way she spoke sounded distracted, like her mind was on something else.

"What do you want with me?"

There was no response.

"Well?" I demanded. "Why have you put me in a cage?"

"You trespassed."

"In the sea?" I tried to keep the scoffing out of my voice.

"The sea is ours and all that lies within."

"That's a pretty big claim." If I'd been standing, I would have put my hands on my hips.

"You and your creature are to be inspected by the Saaasallla and your fate will be determined at that time."

"Fate?" I pressed. "What do you mean fate?"

"Your manner of death."

"Shouldn't there be a trial?" I wasn't sure if I was more angry or afraid at these words. "A chance to present my case to the Elders and be found innocent or guilty?"

"You are already guilty. Your manner of death is all that is left to be determined. The Saaasallla favors drowning."

Well, he'd be waiting a long time if he tried that on me.

"Is there no mercy in this place?" I protested.

"This explanation is our mercy. You are owed nothing. Not even that."

She spun and left me gaping. I should never have stepped into that portal and entered this mad world. I needed to get out of this cage and back to my home as fast as I could go. No amount of disappointment from my community could be as bad as this!

Chapter Six

The sea sang to me. Out of reach – far beneath my hanging basket – and yet it sang to me of rippling currents, of lapping waters, of schooling fish, of rain on the surface, and winds whipping up waves. It sang to me the siren song of freedom, of flying through wind and surf with my hair streaming behind me and my cheeks flushed with exertion. It sang to me the glorious song of dawn catching each ripple of water and painting it gold and pink, of sunset doing the same in the autumn tones of orange and red. It sang of the deeps where great creatures moved unseen, where blindness was no barrier and new worlds sprang forth with creatures strange and magnificent.

And that song filled me up and kept my heart strong as I watched the foreign city around me prepare for my execution.

"It's been decided," my strange visitor said when she came again, removing her mask for long enough to speak to me. "Death by fire."

"Fire? You seem to have a lot more water around here than you do fire." My heart had leapt into overdrive. I hadn't really expected this. Even with all the talk about killing me, it hadn't occurred to me that they were actually going to find a way to do it. I swallowed uncomfortably.

"Even so. Thus, it is declared by the Saaasalla."

"But this Saaasallla doesn't know me!" I said. Would Nasataa survive this? He could breathe underwater, but what about fire? Did dragons have any immunity to fire? I sure hoped so. I felt like I might be ill.

"It matters not."

"He might change his mind if he knew me. I'm valuable."

The blank face didn't change. "Not valuable enough."

How much should I tell her? I should tell her something that would keep me from being burned alive. After all, if her people had sent mercenaries looking for me, then I must be worth keeping alive, right?

"I can breathe underwater," I said, starting with the most remarkable thing that I knew for sure.

"So can I."

I hadn't expected that. An icy chill shot through me. Maybe I really wasn't all that special.

"I'm a princess," I said through a dry mouth, offering my last tidbit up.

"So am I."

Oh. Well. I'd run out of protests.

After a moment, she turned and walked away and I tried not to let panic and despair seize me as I sat helplessly in a cage awaiting a horrific death.

There had to be some way out of this.

Below us, on another platform, they were beginning to pile wood for a huge fire. A fire that would put my village bonfires to shame.

Nasataa yawned sleepily, stretching out on my lap. I could have sworn he'd grown in the night. He was the size of a large cat now, his tail as long as my arm. He chewed sleepily at my sleeve, a string of drool running from his mouth, and sent me a mental image of leaving the cage and going back into the sea. He was sick of being trapped here.

So was I. And fear filled me, running along my bones until it became a part of me. How could I protect this little life when I couldn't even protect myself?

"Wait!" I called to the Bubbler. She was almost too far away to hear, but she must have heard me anyway. She strode back down the walkway and I waited until she was close before I continued. "I know that you're executing me, but what about him?" I held Nasataa up. "Couldn't he go free?"

"No."

"But he's not the one who broke your law."

"The Enemy is killed on sight. He was only spared this long because he was with you."

She turned on her heel and strode away again.

The enemy? Why did everyone hate Blue Dragons so much? Had they sunk ships here, too? But there were so many in the harbor that it was hard to believe. If Blue Dragons wanted to sink them, they easily could. It must be for some other reason.

Poor Nasataa. He lived in a world that hated him for what he was no matter that he was only a baby and so far, entirely innocent of any crime.

I tried not to give in to the sinking feeling in the pit of my belly, but I was all out of options. I'd tried everything that I could to save us – given up all my secrets and even tried to just get him free without me. There were no other options left to me.

Unless...

What had I done on that mercenary ship? I'd been calling to Nasataa – I had stretched my mind as far as I could as I tried to call him. Maybe I could try that. Maybe there would be a Blue Dragon out there somewhere who would hear our call and come to rescue us again.

I reached out as far as I could with my mind, calling, calling, begging for help. I tried to project an image of Nasataa and me in this cage and of the fire they were preparing on a platform below us. I tried to project the danger of the situation as I called, called, called to anyone who would listen.

Please! Please hear and help us!

Was that a tiny tremor I felt in the song?

The last ray of light fell behind the horizon and below me, they lit the fire. It shot hungrily into the air, crackling and popping with fury.

My insides froze at the sight even as sweat popped out along my brow. We were out of time. It was too late.

Chapter Seven

I hadn't realized that the cage could be lowered until it slowly began to sink through a trapdoor in the platform and descend downward toward the fire.

A crowd had turned out to watch my death. Great. I was not just going to die horribly, I was also going to be entertainment for the people of this awful city. I'd always wanted to see a city. I had so much fun visiting Abergande that I was sure I'd love the excitement of an even bigger place – all the varied people and the many shops and inns. But this city was not anything like what I'd hoped for. These people were villains! And they thought it was fun to watch someone die!

My anger grew with every moment that my cage was lowered slowly downward. I held Nasataa protectively to my chest, my jaw clenched and a fierce look on my face. I wouldn't cry. I wouldn't. Oh, skies and stars, I already was!

A tear leaked down my face, but I scowled and brushed it roughly away. I wouldn't give them the satisfaction of watching me cry.

Nasataa seemed mostly unaffected. Fortunately, he didn't realize the danger we were in. I hoped he wouldn't realize it, that he wouldn't suffer. The poor little guy. He deserved so much better than this! I should have been able to protect him from these monsters.

I felt a quiver in the song of the sea, and I cried out to it to save me. Please! Please! Whatever you are, please help us! Help us!

I sent out a visual image of Nasataa, sweet, innocent baby Blue Dragon Nasataa. Surely whatever creature stirred in the depths of the sea would see him and want to help – right?

The fire was getting closer and now the murmur of the crowd was settling into a quiet chant of words I didn't understand. I'd never understood hating a group of people. After all, people were individuals and each one was different, but I couldn't help but hate these people right now. They didn't seem like individuals. They seemed like one huge moving entity of hate and destruction – and I wanted to turn that destruction right back on them!

I gritted my teeth and then an image filled my mind. It was wobbly and hard to see, but it looked like my cage, far, far up in the air hanging over the roaring fire.

Yes! I tried to send the message to the mind far away.

Who was it? Who had seen our plight?

It's us! I tried to call.

Please, help!

Another image filled my mind, but it wobbled weakly and fell apart before I could understand it. I just hoped it meant help was on the way. I was already too hot, sweat pouring off of me. My skin hurt from the heat of the fire below. Gusts of smoke filled the basket, leaving both me and Nasataa coughing and choking on it. We might breathe water, but we sure didn't breathe smoke!

We hadn't even reached the real fire yet and I already felt like this was too much to bear.

Another wobbly, incomprehensible communication filled my mind.

Please! Please hurry! I begged the mind. We didn't have much time. My lungs felt scorched.

And then, suddenly, the basket was wobbling and shaking like a fish on the end of a line. The crowd around us were all looking to a spot above my head. If they weren't so swathed in cloth, I might have seen looks of surprise on their faces to match the surprise on mine as our basket was snatched from the air and the chain holding it wrenched apart with the sound of tearing metal.

I squirmed in the cage trying to get a good look at what had a hold of us, but everything was happening too quickly. We were falling toward the water, narrowly missing a boat loaded with cloth-wrapped bales, and then dragged under the surf. I coughed on the water, grateful when it washed my lungs clean of smoke. Black trails filled the water when I exhaled.

I clung to Nasataa as we sped through the water so quickly that all I saw were bubbles around us. Water tugged at me, swirling my hair so that I couldn't see anything. It seemed to go on forever until finally, we stopped, the cage settling on a sandy seafloor.

But we were still trapped inside. We'd die of starvation if we couldn't get out.

There was a squealing of metal and the side of my basket opened, wrenched apart by two massive ... tentacles?

They retreated and I hurried out of the basket, stepping out on the sandy ocean floor on wobbly legs. My breathing was returning to normal in the wake of our salvation.

I tried to send images of joy and gratitude as I looked up, up, up into the single eye of our savior. I gasped, shock filling me.

I tried not to stumble backward at the sight of him. We'd been saved, it would seem, by a squid the size of my village. He rose proud and magnificent before me, his beak opening and closing and his long, tangled arms swirling in the ocean current.

"Th – thank you," I tried to say underwater. I send gratitude as hard as I could toward him and he sent back another one of his garbled communications.

All at once, his eyes snapped shut and he drew his arms in, and then he shot away, the burst of water from his flight so powerful that it knocked me backward, sending me tumbling through the water like a leaf in the wind. When I finally caught myself and found my feet again, the squid was gone.

I clutched Nasataa close to my chest. I had no idea where we were. No idea how to get back to the portal and I was terrified to look up on the surface to get my bearings. Last time, that had been a terrible decision.

I took a deep breath.

I should be thankful that the squid had saved us. I was thankful.

Why had he come when I called? Was he just that kind and helpful? I had hoped for and expected a Blue Dragon, but I'd never even thought to hope that other sea creatures could hear me, too.

But that didn't stop apprehension from filling me.

I had no idea what to do next.

Chapter Eight

I found my way to the coastline where the water was shallower. I was so tired that I almost stumbled into a round metal object as large as my parents' cabin before I noticed it. As soon as I did, I shrank back into the shadows.

I was just in time.

A woman – maybe? – with goggles and a facemask just like my captor had, swam out of the metal structure and out to sea. She didn't look behind her or she would have seen me. I huddled in the shadows, shaking at the thought of being captured again.

The Bubbler had not lied. These people did breathe under water.

So why had the mercenaries needed *me* if they had them? I hid for long minutes, waiting to see if anyone else came out or if the woman returned. When no one did, I slipped back out to sea and found a deep and rocky trench. I stayed in the trench, following it for hours until my legs began to give out from under me. I was cold and shivering – not from the cold of the sea but from the shock of the past day. Fear kept me beneath the waves and away from the shore.

Nasataa was restless in his bag on my back, signaling often that he was hungry and thirsty with images in my mind. I couldn't let him starve. And I was thirsty, too. Eventually, I'd have to go up to the shore and find us fresh water and something to eat. But what if I was captured again? It was clear that any discovery by these Rock Eaters would mean our deaths.

I was still worrying about it, my belly knotting up inside me, when Nasataa slipped out from the bag on my back and shot out in front of me.

I sent him an image of him returning to me. Come back!

He didn't listen, swimming inland and snatching up colorful fish as he went, gulping them down in a single bite. He was hungry. No wonder he wasn't listening. Strange that a creature so suited to life underwater would be thirsty, though. What did the big Blue Dragons do about that? Maybe there were fountains of fresh water under the sea if you knew where to look.

I chased after him with tired limbs, kicking through the water. I would go faster if I lost these silly boots, but I didn't want to be without shoes, so I kept them on my feet.

Come back, Nasataa!

The water was growing shallower. This was not good! What if he broke the surface and they caught him? And then part of him disappeared as he leapt into the air.

Skies and Stars! He was going to get us killed!

I chased after him and when my own head broke the surface, I spun around, scanning in every direction, ready to duck under again at the first sign of trouble.

There was no one there. I gasped in relief. No people, no structures on the horizon. Nothing but rocky beach and cold clouds, grey sea, and waving trees. I drew in long, relieved breaths. But where was Nasataa?

I found him in a small cave, lapping fresh water from a natural bowl in the rock. I took a handful of it myself before slumping on the smooth rock of the cave floor.

I was so tired. I'd just rest for a moment. I wouldn't fall asleep. That would be far too dangerous. Just one moment of rest.

A warm body cuddled up against me. And I let Nasataa's gentle snores wash over me. He was a good dragon. I tried to send him an image of what a good dragon he was as I listened to his soft breathing, in and out, in and out.

My eyes fluttered shut and I fell asleep in a cave I'd never seen before, on a beach I didn't know, in a hostile land.

Maybe that wasn't such a good idea.

I ignored that thought and let myself drift off to sleep.

Chapter Nine

"What have we here?"

I woke with a start. My mind spun, trying to remember where I was or why a dark silhouette stood over me, framed by sunlight.

A cave. I was in a cave. I'd fallen asleep. Nasataa woke beside me, flaming the wall of the cave as he yawned.

"And a baby dragon, too. And you thought you'd just sleep in a cave along the Rock Coast?" the woman standing over me clucked her tongue.

I sat up, scrambling to my feet.

"Who are you?" I asked, my voice thick with sleep.

She snorted as she drew back and began to arrange driftwood into a tent for a fire. She pulled a flint from her pocket, sparking a handful of grass and after a moment, a merry driftwood fire lit. Blue and green flames licked along the driftwood as the salt of the sea tainted the orange flame.

"Pretty isn't it?" the woman said. "But still dangerous. Like you and like the baby dragon."

I flinched back at her words. Was she an enemy, too? The dancing flames illuminated her face. She was a woman in her forties or early fifties. Still beautiful but worn by wind and sun so that her face was wrinkled and thin and her black hair had thick bands of silver running through it. She was narrow and lithe, but she moved carefully like she had an old injury to nurse, and I saw that she was fitted in leather and metal armor. She carried a long staff with a curved blade at the end of it with the air of someone who knew exactly how to use it.

"Are you here to capture us?" I asked, putting my back against the cave wall. There wouldn't be much that I could do if I had to fight. She was the one with the staff.

Nasataa leapt into my arms, his little flame lighting up the cave.

"I'm here to make you some tea and something hot to eat," my visitor said with a smirk. "Why don't we start there?"

There was probably a catch to that, right? But I couldn't think of what it might be. I still wasn't ready to relax, but when she filled a kettle and placed it on the fire and then started to cook soup, I stepped a bit closer, letting the fire warm me.

"Do you know of the Troglodytes?" the strange woman asked.

"No," I said, enjoying the warmth of the fire.

"They are the Elders of the Dragons. They hold the wisdom of drag-onkind and they shepherd the dragon peoples through the difficulties of their generations. They have been with us since the dawn of magic."

Why was she telling me this? I cocked my head to the side as she poured tea, handing me the first cup. It was fragrant and warm and my whole body relaxed as I sipped it.

"Long ago, one of the Troglodytes had a vision of a time to come when magic would leave the land."

I felt a tingling feeling as she spoke those words. Did she know that time was now? She poured herself tea and continued.

"They saw a champion arise. That champion would require guidance and protection. Care and training. That champion would need a fierce protector to guard them so that they could bring magic back to this world. In the return of magic, there is hope for many people and nations. Right now, the magic has left us and the people war over the scraps left in the world. If it could be restored, we could bring peace and prosperity back to the nations."

"We?" I asked. What did she think I had to do with this? Unless ... she didn't think I was this champion, did she?

"I am here to find the champion," the woman said sincerely before taking a sip of her tea.

"Are you saying that you are the fierce protector?" I asked warily. She certainly looked fierce.

She laughed. "No. I'm here to train the protector and make her fierce. You're not the champion, Seleska. You're the protector. Nasataa is that champion."

My face went pale. "How do you know our names?"

The tea, soothing a moment ago, was making me feel ill with this news.

"I am Vyvera Kyrynos and I serve the Troglodytes. I was sent by them to find you and your little charge. It is not for us to choose the champion or the protector, but we can at least help you. I am here to help teach you what you need to know to help him save the world."

My mouth fell open at her words.

Save the world?

Was she crazy?

"Will you accept my help?" she asked.

"Ummm, yes." I agreed. After all, I was stuck in a foreign land, lost on the shores, with no supplies and no hope and here was a strong warrior with hot food offering to help me. I'd have to be crazy to say no.

She smiled widely. "Good. It is agreed."

She held out a hand and I took it awkwardly. Her hand clasp was firm and strong.

"Now what?" I asked as she released my hand and began to pour soup. There were four bowls.

"Now, I will take you to the Troglodytes. They will have more that they wish to say to you. And I'll be teaching you what to do with this." She handed me the bladed staff. "It's a Dragon Staff – an ancient crafting of the Troglodytes and it is yours now."

"Oh," I said as I took it. "I really can't accept something so valuable."

"It's meant for you." Her words were curt.

"Umm, thank you? But what will you fight with?"

"I have my own," she said.

I looked surreptitiously around the cave, but she had nothing else with her. No bags. No staff.

Vyvera pushed one of the bowls of soup toward Nasataa and he leapt from my arms to the ground and began to eat. She handed another one to me and took up the third before turning to call out the cave mouth.

"Heron! Soup is ready!"

I nearly dropped my soup when my best friend strode into the cave, his usual grin spread wide across his face.

Heron? Here?

I set the soup down carefully and ran to throw myself at him, hugging him so tightly that I thought my arms might not be able to let go.

"Ngh," he grunted before patting my back gently. "Are you okay, Seleska? Vyvera said she needed a moment alone with you. But I didn't know you were upset. Seleska?"

Ooops. I hadn't meant to cry, but the safety I felt at his presence just drew the tears right out of me. I wiped my eyes hastily.

"I'm just so glad to see you," I said.

He rubbed the back of his neck awkwardly.

"I'm kind of hungry. If it's okay with you, can we eat that soup?"

The soup was the best thing I'd ever tasted. I couldn't have told you what was in it or what it tasted like, but it was the best.

Chapter Ten

"We can't linger," Vyvera said as soon as we had finished eating our soup. "The Rock Eaters hunt you. It seems you had quite the brush with them. I'll get Damokas."

She stood up, striding out of the cave while I was still processing her words. There were more people out there?

"How many of you came to find me?" I asked Heron.

His gaze hadn't left me since we started to eat. It was almost as if he couldn't believe I was there.

"Just Vyvera and her dragon Damokas." His smile seemed to say more than I could understand.

"She rides a dragon?"

"A big one. You should have seen the Elders when it set down on the beach! Your parents had just reported that you hadn't come home. We were about to start searching for you."

"Oh," I said stupidly, feeling my cheeks get hot. "I didn't mean to make people worry. I thought it would be simpler for everyone if I just left."

"And has it been simpler?" his smile didn't change, but it seemed like he was laughing at me from behind his eyes.

"No, just more dangerous." I paused. I wasn't ready to tell that story yet. "What happened then? How did you get here so quickly?"

"There are portals over the ocean. They're a secret, but because Vyvera works for some sort of special dragon elders, they told her where they were. It only took a day to fly over the entire ocean! Can you believe that? She said her dragon staff could tell that you'd used some sort of underwater portals.

But the air portals don't come out in the same places, so it took us a while to find you."

"And what are you doing here?" I bit my lip. We'd disagreed the last time I saw him.

He tucked a stray strand of hair behind my ear. The gesture felt oddly protective.

"Are you kidding me? I didn't trust you to go running off to another country on your own. You'd probably do something crazy and get caught for it in the first hour. I didn't want a bunch of strangers to punish you for all the risks you take – that's my job."

He winked.

Why did my cheeks feel so hot? He was just being a good friend. There was no reason to be embarrassed about that. But I still was. It only made it worse that he was right. I had ended up in trouble almost as soon as I had arrived in this place.

We collected the dishes, cleaning them in the pool of water, and doused the fire. I coaxed Nasataa back into the bag on my back while Heron packed the wooden dishes and the kettle into a leather bag.

"You could have stayed home where it was safe," I said nervously as I settled Nasataa and helped him get comfortable.

"Sure," Heron agreed. "So, could you."

"But Nasataa is my responsibility. I couldn't just let him go on his own. He might get hurt and have no one to help him."

"Maybe you're my responsibility. What happens if you get hurt and have no one to help you?" His smile was almost tender.

"What about your apprenticeship?" I asked. I felt awkward at how sweet he was being.

"By the time the Elders sort out what to do about the captives, the sunken ship, the return of the Blue Dragons, and the shock of seeing Damokas fly into their village, you and I will be back again."

He laughed as if he'd made a joke, but I had a bad feeling that things wouldn't resolve themselves so quickly.

"Well," I said, leading the way out of the cave, "I'm glad you came with Vyvera. It's nice to have a friend a –"

Chapter Eleven

We flew down the rocky coast, avoiding any sign of people or cities. It was difficult to do. The Rock Eaters were far more populous than I could have dreamed of and their cities sprung up all along the coast, with small villages and large fishing installations in between the cities.

"Shouldn't we fly out to sea away from them all?" I asked when we skirted the first town, flying low through the trees in a nearby forest to avoid notice.

"The Troglodytes have arranged a meeting with you south of here. This is the fastest route to get there," Vyvera said. "And despite the danger, the meeting is too important to risk missing. We have to get you and Nasataa there as quickly as possible."

Despite the need to avoid towns, Vyvera talked often when we were in safer locations.

"Baby dragons grow quickly," she said about an hour after we took off from the cave. "He'll double in size every week for the first few months and he'll sleep most of the day."

Nasataa was sleeping in the pack on my back, completely unimpressed or unafraid by our flight through the air.

"He'll eat almost anything he can, so make sure you keep him fed or he'll eat that bag he's in," Vyvera warned. "He doesn't need a lot, just constant care and love. He'll get into trouble if you aren't watching carefully, and dragons need a close bond with the ones who raise them – in this case, you – in order to grow to healthy adult dragons."

It was a big responsibility, but of course I was willing to do all of that for Nasataa. He deserved a protector who was willing to care for him the way he deserved.

"He'll start talking soon. Dragons learn that quickly. So, be ready. It can be a shock when they speak into your mind."

She paused as we all went silent, avoiding a large, sprawling farm.

"How do you know all of this?" I asked her when we'd passed the farm. "Do they teach this somewhere?"

Vyvera laughed. "There are training schools for dragon riders, like Dragon School in the Dominion. And there are other lands where dragons are ridden – a different type of dragon than the dragons descended from Haz'Drazen. I was trained in Dragon School, but I didn't stay there. I was visiting Haz'drazen's lands on a request from the Dominar when the Truth Wars started. I would have wanted to return home to help defend my city, but Damokas was wounded and we had to stay while he healed. I was found by the Troglodytes while I waited there and they set me on a different course."

"What course?" I asked.

She laughed. "Finding Nasataa. His birth was prophesied and so was yours. I only had to find you in time."

"I guess I'm lucky that you found me now," I said.

"I was almost too late. The staff can help guide me, but it is not very clear sometimes. I've been looking for months. If you hadn't used those portals, I might not have found you at all. But their use was easily detected – and they have not been used for quite some time."

Good thing that I'd used those portals! If I hadn't, I'd be lost here in the land of the Rock Eaters without any guidance at all.

"Why are these people called Rock Eaters?" I asked.

"They eat rocks."

I should have guessed that.

"Seems like a poor diet," Heron offered from behind us.

"Small ones. They swallow them whole. They think that some rocks have magical properties that can be passed to the person who eats them," Vyvera said.

"And can they?" I asked.

"I have not witnessed it," Vyvera replied. "I have never spent any time in this land. Foreigners are not welcome."

"Then don't you think we should be leaving?" Heron asked.

We were ducked low between the hilltops, passing a tall tower on the edge of the ocean. A bright light shone from it, like the sun reflecting off a polished metal sheet. What were those for?

"The Troglodytes are – ancient. And with magic seeping from the world, they are dying. We need to speak to one of them, but he is close to the surface of these lands, and he will not live to travel anywhere else – he is near death. Travel will kill him. We must go to him – no matter the risk."

I felt a little nervous at the word 'risk' especially with a baby dragon dependant on me. But I needed to be brave for him and keep him safe.

"The bond between a guardian and her dragon is a sacred one," Vyvera said as if she could tell what I'd been thinking. "You must be willing to be fully responsible for the safety and care of your little dragon."

"Of course," I said. And I meant it. So far, I'd been willing to do whatever it took to keep him safe.

"No sacrifice can be too great."

I'd been willing to leave my home and my family to keep him safe. That had to count for something, right?

She was still talking, "It will be your job to raise him up to be the hero he needs to be, to comfort him, guide him, protect him, and to rescue him from danger. You can't possibly be ready for that task, but I will try to help you find your way."

"I understand," I said, and I thought that maybe I did understand, because hadn't I seen my parents do those things for me? And hadn't Ramariri done them for me? It was my turn to be responsible for someone else. My turn to sacrifice for someone else.

"And I think the first sacrifice you will need to make," Vyvera said, "is to get rid of those ridiculous boots."

"What?"

Was that Heron laughing? I shot him a baleful glare, but it only made him laugh more.

"We'll see what we can find at the next stop, but we can't have you tripping all over the place while you're guarding our Chosen One, can we?"

I was willing to give up my home and even my life for this little dragon. So why did the idea of giving up my boots sting so much?

Chapter Twelve

We flew for hours and it was well into the afternoon before we made our first stop. Vyvera set us down in a small valley between two huge hills. There were little farms and hamlets all around, making this a difficult place to find anywhere to hide so large a dragon. He'd been flying with his feet almost brushing the ground for hours. His gnarled face looked irritated when we finally landed and he immediately flamed, setting two bushes on fire before Vyvera patted his shoulder and calmed him down.

"There's a creek. Go vent your frustrations there," she offered him, and he slunk toward it, head low until he could plunge his entire head under the water and flame. Steam and bubbles rolled off the surface, flashing up into the air and my eyes went wide.

Would Nasataa be so large someday? Would he be larger? I really had no idea what I was getting into with him, did I? But I bet Ramariri didn't know what it would cost him to take me on as a charge. So, I couldn't let my worries about his eventual size stop me.

I dismounted carefully, opening the bag to let Nasataa out to run around and trying to juggle the staff I'd been given as I freed it from the saddle. He scampered out of the bag immediately, chasing after a butterfly. Fortunately, the butterfly was flying circles around the little valley, so I didn't have to chase after him as he bobbed up and down through the long grass.

I joined Heron at the edge of the creek to refill our canteens and waterskins.

"Fill these, too," Vyvera said, handing me two more skins as she strode off into the trees.

"Are you adjusting to all of this?" Heron asked me gently.

"Sure," I said, fiddling with the long staff. It was awkward to haul that thing around with me. Too bad it wasn't a sword. Then it would have a scabbard. "I mean, I don't want anything bad to happen to Nasataa."

"But that doesn't mean it's easy to find out that your job is to raise him and protect him. That's a big commitment," he said. "Nasataa will probably outlive you by centuries."

I hadn't even thought of that. Watching him leap through the grass after a frog – the butterfly had fled to the trees – his little snout flaming from time to time, was adorable. He was a sweet little dragon full of joy and excitement. He drank from the creek and then leapt toward me to snuggle against me, his eyes closed in satisfaction. How could I say no to that?

I couldn't.

"How did you know you wanted to be a blacksmith?" I asked.

Heron shrugged. "It's the only thing I've ever been good at. It wasn't hard to commit."

"I guess some things are worth committing to," I said with a wry smile. "And if I said no, I'd regret it all my life."

Heron was nodding with a knowing smile on his face as Nasataa leapt from my arms again, snarling suddenly and flaming wildly.

Vyvera strode from the trees with another person at her side. A person wearing crimson flowing clothing tied at ankles and wrists, a pair of goggles and a face mask.

My heart started racing before I had time to think. We were under attack! Vyvera had betrayed us!

I brandished my dragon staff in front of me, darting forward to where Nasataa crouched. I stood over him as he flamed at the stranger, my staff ready to defend us both.

"Good instincts, but not much skill. We'll need to work on that," Vyvera said with a smile.

What was she talking about?

Beside her, the Bubbler lowered his mask and pulled the goggles back to rest on the top of his head.

"A stranger group of people I have never seen before, but you have given the sign and sung the song, so I am at your disposal."

"Thank you," Vyvera said sincerely.

"The Lightbringers stand to serve, to bring light to the nations and foster the hope of the peoples," our visitor said formally.

"You can stop looking like you're about to fight for your life, Seleska," Vyvera said to me. "This is Octon – a Lightbringer – part of a secret society that spans this globe working to bring light to dark places. He will not harm us."

"What help do you require?" Octon asked.

"Local clothing for the three of us and food. I can pay in gold."

Octon shook his head. "I will not take your payment. No, I am not being generous. I cannot afford to take it. If I were to spend a foreign coin here, they would kill both me and my friends. Keep your gold coins."

I watched him curiously. He spoke our language but with an accent slow and smooth like butter. It fascinated me. So did his looks – different from Vyvera's leathered look, or Heron's dark island look, or even my pale look. Octon's hair where it peeked from his hood was bright red and his skin was bronze. I wondered if that was common here. It was impossible to tell when they all covered up so much.

"We must hurry," Octon said. "A Saaasallla Patrol is in the nearby village. They will eradicate any foreigners on sight. And they will certainly slay this creature with you."

He pointed at Damokas and I felt a stab of icy fear shoot through me. That meant they would also kill Nasataa and none of this was his fault. He was just a baby who I had brought to this strange and severe land. It seemed strange that Octon wasn't pointing him out, too.

I looked around for the little fellow. Where had he gotten to?

"How long will it take you to bring them here?" Vyvera asked. "And can I pay you some other way?"

Octon was replying, but I wasn't listening. I was looking for Nasataa.

He wasn't near Damokas. He wasn't along the creek. My eyes swept along the grass and flowers of the valley, following any flicker of movement from a fly or butterfly. Where was he?

"I've lost Nasataa," I said after a moment. My head felt light and my heart began to beat so quickly that I could hardly hear Heron asking me if I was sure.

My little dragon! I'd lost him.

Chapter Thirteen

"Nasataa!" I called. "Nasataa!"

I reached out with my mind, desperately trying to find any trace of him, begging him with pictures to return to me, but I felt nothing in return. He was out there somewhere, and he couldn't have gone far. But which direction would he have headed?

I ran toward the nearest hill, the staff in my hand catching on the grass around me. I could hear snarls and people calling to me while trying to keep their voices low, but I didn't have time to stop and listen to them. I needed to find my little dragon before something happened to him. I could imagine him out here, cold and alone, afraid and starving without a friend in the world and surrounded by enemies who would kill him on sight. It would all be my fault because I wasn't watching him carefully enough. He'd die out there thinking he was unloved – maybe even calling for me – and never getting a reply.

I was already crying in fear as I climbed the hill, my heart pounding so hard that I couldn't hear anything else. I spun every few seconds, scanning the terrain around me, my gaze flicking over trees and grass and rocks, searching for that little fellow.

He had to be here somewhere. If I could just find him.

My head whipped back and forth as I searched. I could see the whole valley from here. I could see Heron running through the deep grass toward me. I could see Damokas rearing up and Vyvera rushing toward him. I could see Octon frozen in a crouch, watching me. But there was no sign of my little friend. He was not in the valley.

I spun back to where the trees thinned a little ahead. Maybe if I got higher, I could see past the valley and catch a glimpse of where he'd gone.

"Nasataa!" I called, "Nasataa!"

I reached the top of the hill and I could see over the hill to the road beyond and the rolling farmlands. Where was he?

There he was!

He was hurrying through the grasses chasing after a bright blue butterfly. I was about to cheer with relief when I saw what else he was running toward. A group of men and women on horses – holding long lances and wrapped in the same loose clothing as Octon – but without the goggles and masks and with tabards bearing rock-shaped sigils – were stopped, pointing up at me. One of them appeared to be shouting.

I froze in place. If I ran to Nasataa, I would draw their attention. If I did nothing, he would run right to them. I didn't know what to do. Should I charge them and seize their attention?

There was a loud roar behind me and Damokas surged into the air, wings flapping powerfully and head reaching high into the air as his scream tore through the afternoon sun. Vyvera was on his back, her glittering eyes fixed on the patrol.

I didn't wait. I seized the opportunity to run down the hill toward Nasataa as the patrol sent a stream of arrows toward Damokas. I hadn't even noticed their bows! I glanced toward them as I ran, and I saw them aiming at the Black dragon, pointing strange devices that looked like bows held horizontally. They snapped rapidly, firing at the dragon as he climbed higher and higher.

If I hadn't drawn their attention, they wouldn't be attacking my friends. I should have controlled my panic.

I called to Nasataa with my mind, but he didn't seem to hear. He was still running headlong toward our enemies and the gap was too big to get to him first. That didn't stop me from running. Not even when I turned my ankle in my heeled boots, pain flooding my mind at the *pop* sound of it twisting under me. I fell to the ground, smacking hard against the hard earth, and then scrambled back to my feet again, grabbing my staff from where it had fallen in the grass. One foot didn't want to take my weight.

I waved my arms, trying to get Nasataa's attention.

I was too late. One of the men sprang from his horse and ran to the little dragon, grabbing him in both arms and dragging him to the horses. I was still running, despite the pain and the strange way my foot kept turning under me at every step as if it couldn't quite support my weight.

They couldn't take him! Not my Nasataa!

An ache so strong I didn't think I could hurt that badly seized me as the horse he was on reared. The eyes of all the patrol were turned to me and I could tell that they wanted me, too, but then I was pulled backward, strong arms gripping me and fighting me into the grass.

I saw the leader of the patrol watching me. His expression hardened and then he pointed forward and they charged down the road away from me.

They were taking my Nasataa and I didn't know where they were going. A sob tore through my lungs and I fought the arms holding me. Why hadn't the patrol turned back to get us, too?

Heat seared me as strong arms lifted me up and jostled me as my captor ran. I knew it was Heron without having to look, but why was he carrying me?

It took some effort to keep the staff held out from us so that the blade on the end didn't hurt him as he ran.

A wave of heat hit me in the face and I turned to see flames rushing through the grass all around us. The trees on the hillside were already in flames. The whole valley was like a crown of flame and ash.

"I can run," I called out to Heron. I was only slowing him down.

"Not on that ankle," he said.

And I should have been grateful that he was saving my life and carrying me to safety, but my eyes were still fixed on the retreating backs of the soldiers carrying my baby away.

Where were they taking him? I wished with all my heart that I had paid better attention and that I'd been able to keep him safe.

In the distance, Vyvera's Black dragon was nothing but a dot in the sky.

Chapter Fourteen

"This way," Octon said bursting out of the flaming grass like a bird from her nest. I gasped as he led us at a run across the road, ducking into a wooded copse and then past that to a flowing river – clearly the source of the creek we'd been drinking from.

At the edge of the river, he pulled a wall of woven branches and vines aside and tugged out a small boat he had hidden there.

"Put her in there," he ordered Heron, and Heron practically threw me into the boat before tugging a big canvas over my head. He shoved the butt of my staff roughly under the canvas.

"Stay put," he hissed and then I heard the banging of oars being thrown in the boat and a scrambling sound.

"Tug them on over your clothes. They'll be a close fit. You're a big man," Octon said.

There was a rustle of cloth and then the boat was jostled back and forth and pushed forward – launched, I assumed – into the river. The splash of oars hitting the water was followed by another whisper from Octon.

"Follow my lead. We row in time and against the river."

Heron grunted in response and they shot through the water.

I tugged at the canvas, trying to see but before I could get out a hand pushed me down.

"Stay under the canvas," Heron hissed.

I didn't know how long I waited there, tension filling me. Every moment felt like an hour. The longer I hid here, the further away my enemies took Nasataa. What if they were killing him already? What if he was hurt or hungry and no one was there to take care of him?

And where had Vyvera gone? She'd disappeared in a flash without one second's thought about the rest of us. I'd trusted her. I'd been a fool.

It felt like hours before I heard Octon whispering to Heron.

"This channel, this one here."

And even longer before the boat bottom scraped on something and the canvas was pulled off my head.

"Sorry for the delay, little lady," Octon drawled in his honey-thick accent. "But it was the only way to get you out of there before the Bubblers came to put out the fire. A clever distraction your friend made. It gave us time to escape while their Patrol went chasing after her and the dragon."

"But the little dragon. Nasataa," I said. I could barely keep from crying as I said his name. I'd failed him.

"They won't dispose of him until they've talked to their authorities. No one does anything in our lands without a written judgment from an authority. So, you have time to rescue him if you wish. But for now, let's deal with you." He looked up at Heron. "Can you carry her again?"

I looked back at him and nearly jumped. Heron was swathed in the red clothing and goggles of the people here and he looked like a giant Rock Eater.

He chuckled at my shocked expression.

"There are a lot of people on the river. Good thing Octon had extra clothing!"

He lifted me with ease, carrying me as we followed Octon out of the boat. It had been pulled up on a grassy bank along the river. Beside it, a small cabin sat, squat and ensconced by massive, sprawling trees.

Octon opened the door and we followed him into a cluttered home. Tools and implements and stacks of books filled every available space and were hung from the walls and from lines strung across the top of the room. Gnarled knot art hung on the walls and fishing buoys were strung out across the floor. Someone was mending a net. Someone else was half-way through stitching something leather. Someone else had started a beadwork project and then walked away. Heron set me down on a bench on top of a pile of books, putting my feet up on his knee as he squatted down and began to remove my boots.

"I can do that," I protested but he didn't stop.

"We can wrap the ankle," Octon said, bringing a long bandage to where I was. "But I don't have shoes for her except for the soft woodland boots the people to the south favor. They don't have to fit precisely, so she could wear a pair of those."

As soon as Heron had my boots off he began to feel my foot, rocking it back and forth and flexing it up and down until I gasped. Then, he began to spool the bandage Octon gave us around my ankle, tying it tightly and expertly.

"It's not a bad sprain," he said, his touch gentle on my hurt foot. "If you keep it wrapped and are careful, it will heal fast. Just keep this strand of bandage tight to support it while it heals."

"Thank you," I said, feeling my cheeks heat at the kindness he was showing.

"Let me find you those boots," Octon said as Heron fussed over the bandage.

Octon returned with soft boots that only went as high as my ankles. They were made of soft fur and he was right – despite being a bit big on me, the soft shape of them made that unimportant. He also offered me goggles, a mask, and the red flowing outfit.

"Thank you," I said sincerely. If we had to sneak in somewhere to rescue Nasataa, it would be easier with local clothing. "What is the purpose of the goggles and mask?"

He looked uncomfortable at the question but eventually, he answered.

"Our land has grown barren of magic. The Saaasallla's Finders often use their special abilities to blow holes in the earth and sea looking for new sources of magic. We wear the goggles and masks to protect ourselves from the things that fly up in the dust. There are strange things buried in the ground – things men were not meant to disturb."

That was unsettling. I pointed at the goggles on the top of his head. "How do you know to make sure they are on?"

"You'll know," he said shortly.

"By what manner do these Finders 'blow holes'?" Heron asked with narrowed eyes. It made sense that would be the part that got his attention.

"It's a secret," Octon said. "But it involves combining powders and liquids."

Heron was still frowning when a boom sounded outside the cabin and Octon pulled his goggles over his eyes so quickly that it looked like instinct. Eyes wide, we copied him, but after a moment he pulled them back up and strode to the door, opening it wide. An exhausted looking Vyvera stepped through.

"We need to go," she said. "Now."

Chapter Fifteen

"Why?" Octon asked.

"Your cabin is surrounded."

I scrambled to my feet and Heron slung an arm under me while with my other hand I leaned on the staff and with his help, I hobbled out of the cabin. Behind us, Octon riffled through his things, going from stack to stack as he tossed things into a huge pack.

"Hurry!" Vyvera said to him. "We'll all have to cram onto Damokas' back. Four is a big load."

Heron helped me outside and up onto Damokas while Vyvera tried to chivvy Octon into hurrying. Around the cabin, I heard the snap of sticks and the creak of branches – telltale signs of sneaking around us. I clutched the Dragon Staff, too worried to speak out loud. My other hand found one of Heron's as he settled in place, gripping it tightly. He squeezed it reassuringly.

Things had gotten scary fast.

At the first flash of red in the trees, I gave a strangled cry and at the same moment, Vyvera and Octon ran from the cabin, a long scarf and some device I didn't recognize trailing from Octon's bag as their clothing flapped behind them.

Damokas shifted nervously from foot to foot and with good reason. The first arrow zipped toward us and embedded in a tree beside Damokas' head with a *thunk*. It was still quivering when Vyvera launched herself onto Damokas' back.

Octon shoved his overly-full bag to me and I gripped it, trying to shift it into a position where it could balance on Damokas' back while Heron grabbed the smaller man and pulled him up behind the saddle. He was still tying him in when Damokas kicked up into the air.

There was a yell from the treeline and a series of curses as red figures emerged. A hail of arrows was let loose – more enthusiastic than accurate. They streaked around us, some of them bouncing off the dragon's belly.

Octon bit off a scream as we sailed upward and Vyvera bit off a curse.

"They're everywhere. I thought you said it was only a patrol!"

"A Patrol is the military name for a group of a thousand soldiers," Octon protested.

"Did an arrow hit you?" I asked him. I was worried about that scream.

"No," Octon said, breathlessly.

Vyvera's curses rang through the sky as Damokas climbed, bursting into the cloud layer with an aura of relief. We were hidden from view up here and though the occasional arrow broke through the clouds, none of them had the strength to even pierce the air by the time they reached us.

"I guess we're safe as long as we're on the dragon," Heron said and Vyvera snorted.

"Sure. As long as the cloud cover holds."

"The arrows can't reach us," he objected.

"The towers will wipe out any enemies who fly," Octon said. "We're hidden in the clouds, but the clouds won't last forever."

"Towers?" Heron asked.

"Didn't you see them gleaming along the shores and the city walls? They say that a tower can amplify a stream of fire to hit a seagull a mile away."

"Well, Damokas is bigger than a seagull," Heron said. "And that report sounds exaggerated."

"How comforting," Octon said wryly.

"Nasataa was captured by the men on horses," I broke into the discussion. To me, that was the most important part. Arrows, towers, arguments – none of that mattered compared to the little dragon.

"I saw where they went with him," Vyvera said. "There is one of those towers beside a town."

"Aaavtar – that's the town," Octon agreed. "But if he is in the tower, no one will be able to rescue him there. Certainly not something that flies. They'll see you in a moment and blast you from the sky."

"What about if we hid Damokas somewhere and snuck in?" I asked. It was clear we were flying in circles as we thought of what to do next and if they were right and the clouds were our only protection, then we needed to decide what to do quickly before the clouds blew away and left us vulnerable.

"And who would do the sneaking?" Vyvera asked.

"I would!" I said boldly.

What was I thinking? Was I really volunteering to sneak into an enemy tower? I didn't even know how to fight if someone attacked me and they were firing real arrows out there! But Nasataa was in there somewhere and I wasn't going to leave him in danger no matter how frightening it might be to go after him.

"You have a sprained ankle," Vyvera said.

"I don't," Heron said. "I'll go with her."

I squeezed his hand gratefully. I wouldn't have to do it alone.

"You don't know how to go unnoticed in a strange land," she protested.

Octon sighed. "I'll go with them."

"Then why don't you go alone and leave them with me?" Vyvera asked.

"I'm not touching a dragon!" Octon said. "I'll help them get him out so you can all leave, but I don't want trouble with the patrol and I definitely don't want to have to touch a dragon."

"You're riding a dragon!"

"That's different." He adjusted his goggles over his eyes. It gave him a strange, faraway look.

"And what do you expect that I will do in this master plan of yours?" Vyvera asked me dryly.

"Could you come and get us when we escape?" I asked. "I mean, once we're out of the range of the tower, couldn't we meet you somewhere?"

Vyvera sighed so loudly that we could hear her over the sound of the wind.

"I can't think of a better plan. You'd better pick a good rendezvous spot, Lightbringer," she said to Octon.

I smiled. We were going to go rescue Nasataa.

Chapter Sixteen

It felt strange to try to sneak in the flowing red clothing.

"Why red?" I whispered to Octon when Vyvera dropped us off in the woods. She'd sent Damokas in a nosedive through the clouds to land in the woods and then she'd launched back into the air immediately, flying low to draw attention away from us. Watching her leave like that left a knot in my belly. Would she be okay? What she was doing was really risky. What all of us were doing was risky. But I couldn't just leave Nasataa. "Red stands out so much!"

"We don't all wear red," Octon said, forging a path through the trees.

I leaned heavily on my staff, following him. My ankle hurt and I was sweating from walking on it, even if most of my weight was on the bladed staff, but I didn't dare stop. If they had to stop for me, they might all decide to turn around and give up on this quest.

"Red denotes warriors. Other classes wear other colors."

"So that means you're a warrior?" I pressed.

Heron followed us silently. Something was on his mind and he watched the woods constantly.

"Yes."

"Where are your weapons?"

I'd been too busy before to really notice how different this world was from home. The forest was thick and tangled and smelled of plants I didn't even know existed before. Heavy fronds rose up from the soft forest floor. But the ground seemed to be made entirely of dead plants – nothing like the sand back home and I couldn't smell the sea. It felt wrong not to be smelling the sea.

"I fight with hands and feet," Octon said.

"And you're helping us. Against your own people." Heron said and now I realized why he was so quiet. He didn't trust Octon. His voice as thick with wariness.

"*For* my people," Octon corrected, shooting a firm look over his shoulder at Heron. "My people have suffered long under the harsh rule of the Saaasallla. Our suffering increases with her desperation. If magic is not found again in the wells of the earth, more and more people will be sacrificed in the quest for power."

"You seem to have a lot of people here," Heron remarked.

Octon stopped dead and I almost walked into him before he turned, glaring at Heron.

"Let us be clear, islander. There are many people here, yes, but they are no less precious to us than if we lived where there were few. A person's value does not depend on the community around them or what they bring to the world. A person's value lies in being a person. So, sacrificing people for power – even when there are many people, even when in a land with so many people it can be easy to overlook the value of individuals – it's still wrong. It's still a horrific waste."

"Sorry," Heron said, surprise all over his face. "I didn't mean that your people weren't important."

Octon huffed, but he turned and kept walking.

"Are your people dying while they are looking for magic?" I asked gently, trying to show that we did care about the problem. "Are they digging wells or exploring caves or spending too much time under the sea?"

He stopped again and I backed up a step, worried that I'd said the wrong thing, too. It was hard to know what to say that wouldn't be wrong. I knew nothing about this land or its customs and even the most innocent observations or questions were perilous.

"Magic comes from life. If it is no longer pooled under the earth and sea, it can be sucked from the land."

"How terrible," I said, trying to be careful. "Does it kill your trees and flowers?"

There were so many trees and flowers around that it was hard to imagine this place without them. They waved gently in the breeze around us.

He snorted. "You can only pull so much life out of non-sentient things. It's inefficient. The Saaasallla prefers efficiency."

"Oh."

We emerged from the trees, but Octon motioned to stay low as we watched the tower from the treeline. There was a watchman patrolling a ring around the camp at the base of the tower and there were probably more guards at the tower, too. I felt sweat beginning to bead on my forehead. This was going to be harder than I'd even imagined. Where, in this huge camp, would they have kept Nasataa? The tents and pavilions flew flags over them – different combinations of colors. Did that mean something?

"Which is why," Octon whispered as his gaze flicked over the camp, "the Bubblers prefer sentient creatures. Humans ... and dragons."

Heron's whisper was hoarse. "Are you saying that they suck the life out of people to fuel their magical efforts?"

I felt like I needed to sit down. My head was suddenly light.

It was all I could do to keep whispering when I said, "Are you saying that they'll suck the life out of Nasataa?"

"All trespassers are considered good sources of life and magical power. What do you think they would do with you if they caught you?"

"Burn me alive."

His expression looked impressed. "They might. That's one way to suck the magic out of someone."

I exchanged a terrified glance with Heron.

"But don't think you're special. I'm not just doing this to help you," Octon said grimly. "I turned to the Lightbringers after the rulers sucked my family dry and tossed them in a mass grave like buried refuse."

And these were the people we were going to try to sneak past?

Maybe this wasn't such a great idea after all.

And then I heard a little voice in my head.

Sela?

Nasataa! He just spoke his first word!

And it was probably meant to be *my* name!

Chapter Seventeen

"He's in there," I said with a gasp. "I heard him!"

"Good," Octon said, his eyes narrowing. "Try not to talk. You sound foreign. Follow my lead."

"How will we get into the tower?" Heron asked.

"The tower isn't our goal. It's offensive. They won't have the dragon in there. They'll have him in the Bubbler tent – the one with the blue and white flag over it," Octon said. "Now, follow my lead and no more talking!"

He was already moving before I could say anything. I looked at Heron but he only shrugged, waiting for me to move before he followed. I pulled the goggles down over my eyes – they felt strange like that, but I thought that anything that distorted my face was a good idea when I was sneaking into an enemy compound – and followed Octon. I tried not to wince at my ankle. Maybe I should have worn the mask, too, instead of leaving it hanging around my neck, but it felt too strange and panic welled up in me whenever I put it on.

The next time I glanced back, Heron had his mask and goggles on. He was still too bulky for the outfit, though. I hadn't seen a Rock Eater yet who was as tall as he was or as thick with muscle.

We reached the guard station first. Two guards stood on either side of the well-worn road, long weapons in their hands that looked an awful lot like my spear, but instead of a single blade on the end, theirs had a pair of prongs with barbs on the ends.

"Business?" the first guard demanded.

"With the Faaallland," Octon replied curtly.

Behind the guards, a pair of Rock Eaters walked by pushing a wheelbarrow, their flowing red clothing pulled down to the waist and tied there as they worked. It was all I could do not to gape. Their bodies were marked with white – whether that was paint or something else that tinged the skin, it seemed to flex with their every move. It ended at their necks, but from collar to waist their bones were picked out, drawn on top of their skin, and patterns of flowers and birds made swirls around the bones as if they had decorated their insides and then put it all on display.

I was glad I was wearing goggles so that no one would see my eyes bugging out.

"Details?" the guard asked.

"Private," Octon said.

"Password?"

"Daxillius."

The guard stepped back for us to pass. Now, why would Octon have the password? Were we just incredibly lucky to have found him, or was there more going on here than met the eye? Nervously, I followed, hoping that this wasn't some kind of trap.

There was a commotion at the other side of the camp. Voices rose up and a loud crash boomed across the encampment.

I didn't dare ask Octon any questions. He ducked behind a tent the moment the chaos started and I followed him. Heron collided into my back, but I was just glad he was there.

We followed Octon through the camp as the sun sank past the horizon. The camp was bigger than it had seemed from the air. Without Octon, I would have easily been lost. The flags were hard to see and I still hadn't caught sight of one that was white and blue.

A group of men holding those strange twin-tipped spears trotted past and then Octon ducked his head into one of the tents before motioning us to follow. He lit a lamp inside and grabbed a double-pronged spear from a rack of them at one side of the tent.

"Supply tents have a pure white banner," he said briskly as he filled a belt pouch with other supplies.

"What are those?" Heron asked him.

"Bubble masks," Octon said as he stuffed filmy things in his bag. They glowed slightly like they were powered by magic. "Let you breathe for up to twenty-four hours under water and they regulate your heat and pressure under the waves. Bubblers use them."

"What do you need them for?" Heron asked.

"They're hard to find."

"So, you decided to just pause and steal a few?" He looked shocked.

Octon leaned in close, growling. "I've been living on edges for years, boy, and thanks to you, they ransacked my cabin and I can't get my stuff, so yeah, I'll take what I need when I can. If you have half a brain, you'll grab some, too. They're priceless."

He grabbed a handful and jammed them at Heron.

Heron shook his head, his wide eyes meeting mine, but I noticed that he did stuff them in his pocket.

"We shouldn't stay here long," I said. "Anything can happen in a few minutes and they've already had Nasataa for too long."

I called to him, reaching out, and found his little mind instantly. He was worried about me. He was hungry.

I grabbed a few sticks of something that looked like dried meat from a barrel beside us and put them in my own bag. I'd hidden it under the red clothes. If we were going to steal – and I didn't like doing it, but then again, they'd stolen Nasataa from me – then we might as well steal something useful.

I sent a feeling of reassurance to Nasataa and felt a burst of pleasure at his response.

Sela!

Hold on, little buddy. I'm coming.

"Come on, Octon," I said, tugging at his sleeve. I noticed that Heron had pulled a big hammer off the rack and was swinging it as if he was testing the weight. It looked a lot like the blacksmith hammers he used at home. He wasn't thinking of bringing that, was he? "We have to hurry!"

They both needed to focus. There was a baby dragon waiting for us.

"We're just gearing up, Seleska," Heron said. "There might be trouble."

"There won't be if we hurry!" I whispered. I could tell that Nasataa was still unhurt. But how long would that last if we delayed? The last light had faded outside the tent and I was equally worried about being caught. Surely, they must keep an eye on their supply tents.

I was about to say more but then the screams started.

We froze, looking at the wall of the tent as if we could see through it.

"Did that voice sound familiar to you?" Heron asked worriedly.

Chapter Eighteen

I didn't have time to reply before Heron was charging out of the tent and through the darkness. I hobbled after him, slowed by my sprained ankle and quickly falling behind. I heard a curse in the darkness as Octon overtook me, speeding past toward where Heron rushed into the night.

A tent blocked them from view as they quickly outpaced me. This ankle was a real problem. What would I do if I lost them? My heart beat faster and I pushed my goggles onto my forehead so I could see more easily. The night was alight, despite the darkness. The tower in the center of the camp was on fire and people ran from every direction toward it, barking orders or yelling to one another.

I hurried as fast as I could, trying to look like I was doing the same thing that they all were, but now I was worried. There was no way I was going to catch up with Heron and Octon and without them, I was lost.

And how could I free Nasataa if I didn't even know where I was?

As if called by his name, Nasataa reached out to me.

Sela!

Was he close to where I was? For some reason, he'd sounded louder. Closer.

He sent me an image of the inside of a tent, which wasn't a lot of help, but the walls were orange. Could I tell what color the walls of the tents were in the dark?

Some of them had lights inside and those glowed orange or dull red through the tent fabric. One of the ones to my left seemed to be glowing extra orange. Or maybe it was my imagination.

I tried to look for the flag at the top of the tent, but I couldn't see it in the darkness. Should I take the gamble and go check it out? After all, everyone seemed distracted by the fire and the screams and I couldn't possibly catch up to Heron and Octon.

I licked my lips, wavering.

Indecision would help nothing.

Clenching my jaw with determination, I hurried toward the more orange tent as fast as I could on my painful ankle.

There was no one outside it. I scurried to the doorway, looking furtively around me, but every person I saw was running toward the tower, buckets or weapons in hand.

Okay, might as well look. I took a deep breath, bracing myself and ducked into the tent.

A squeal of excitement pierced the air.

Nasataa!

I flew to where he was sitting in a golden lace cage. My eyes felt wet as I reached toward him, sticking my fingers through the bars of the cage.

"You're okay! Oh, Nasataa, I was so worried!"

Sela!

I reached into my bag, pulling out a strip of the dried meat for him. I couldn't stop the tears from pouring down my face. I'd been so worried about him. I felt like a heavy weight had been lifted off my chest. He was okay! He was trapped – but okay.

So, how did I get him out of this cage?

He licked my fingers gently, looking up at me with huge, sweet eyes, and then began to chomp happily at the meat. He really was hungry.

There was no key left on the nearby tables or chairs. Though this place had the look of occupancy. Cups of tea still rested on a low table, steam stirring the air above them. Whoever had been here must have run to the fire with everyone else.

That meant they'd be back as soon as it was out.

I needed to hurry.

"Okay, watch out, Nasataa," I said. "I'm going to try to break you out."

I jammed the butt of my spear through the bars of his cage and tried to pry them apart, but I only managed to spin the cage around. I needed more leverage.

Carefully, I lifted the cage down to the floor, wedging it between my feet, and tried again. One of the bars bent slightly, but not enough to set Nasataa free. I pulled the spear out and sat on the ground, gripping one bar with my fingers and wedging the heel of my unsprained ankle in the marginally wider gap I'd made. I pulled with my hands and pushed with my foot as hard as I could.

They budged!

With a gasp and a huge breath, I tried again.

This time, to my delight, the bars squealed as they pulled apart.

Would it be enough?

A joyful Nasataa squeezed through the bars, climbing up to sit on my shoulder and chew my ear. I hugged him close, tears blinding me for a moment.

"It's okay," I said. "I'll never let anyone take you again!"

"That might be a hard promise to keep," a voice said from the tent door.

I spun, Nasataa still clutched in my arms.

In the door of the tent, the Bubbler from Metamor stood, her mask hanging loose, and her goggles pushed up. She was barely older than I was, I realized. But the look on her face was deadly.

"Unless you want him to die with you."

Chapter Nineteen

I opened the flap of my bag and Nasataa leapt inside while I scrambled to grab my staff. I could feel the little dragon peeking over my shoulder as I stood up, wobbling against the staff.

"You can't even stand, and you think you're going to fight me? You foreigners are a joke," the Bubbler said.

"Who are you anyway?" I asked. "How did you get so far south so quickly?"

One of her eyebrows rose. "I could ask you the same question. Only I thought you came here the same way I did – by rail."

I didn't even know what she was talking about. I swallowed, holding the staff in front of me defensively. She only laughed.

"That won't do anything, girl. I'm trained in the life force arts. I'll suck your life from your bones and then use it to make you dance without your skin."

"Ugh! You wouldn't really do that, would you?" I asked. "That's sick."

Her eyes widened like she was surprised by my reaction.

"Is that fun for you?" I pressed. "You like to do gross creepy things, and that makes you smile in the dark when you're sitting all alone because you killed all the people who could have been your friends?"

Her eyes widened further, and her hand reached out, claw-like. Had no one ever told her the truth about who she was? It was coming as a total shock. I could see that.

"It's not too late," I said, trying to be gentle. Maybe no one had ever loved her enough to tell her that her behavior was terrible. "You could become a nice person. Make friends. Be a positive force in the world."

Sweat broke out across her brow and her hood fell, revealing hair frizzling at the ends as her face screwed up in an expression of concentration.

"It's not working," she gasped.

"It could work. If you gave compassion and kindness more of a try, it could work for you," I encouraged.

Her eyes were so wide now that I was afraid they might pop out of her face, and her cheeks were stained with purple. Had she even taken a breath while we were talking? She raised the other hand, claw-like.

"The magic. It's not working."

Oh.

She was trying to kill us. And I'd been encouraging her to be kind.

Ooops.

There was a heavy *thunk* and then she fell to the ground and Heron ran into the tent, a body slung over one shoulder and blood pouring down his cheek from a gash on his face.

"You have the dragon?" he asked, breathlessly.

"Yes! Heron, are you –"

"Run!" he shouted and then he turned on his heel and ran from the tent. Was that Vyvera hanging over his shoulders? Her head lolled and bounced as he ran, her clothing was torn and bloody.

Where was Octon? Where was Damokas?

I hobbled after Heron as he darted from tent to tent, trying to keep out of sight as people continued to run toward the fire.

"Octon?" I gasped, pain in my voice when we reached the next tent.

"Providing a distraction."

We darted to the next tent. I could barely keep up with him, even though he was carrying a full human and all I had was Nasataa and the staff.

I could feel Nasataa curling up in the bag on my back. Were those snores I heard? At least someone felt safe. And that was good. He deserved to feel safe and protected. He never should have been at risk in the first place. But how could I keep him safe in a world like this?

We were closer to the perimeter than I'd expected. The river ran past this part of the encampment and I could tell Heron was angling toward it.

"Shouldn't we go to the rendezvous?" I asked Heron at the next tent.

"We can't, Seleska." His voice sounded worried ... panicked?

There was a shout from behind us.

We ran from where the last tent stood out across the open field toward the river.

"Can't Damokas come and get us?" I tried again, forcing the worlds out between strained breaths.

My ankle rolled under me again and I fell, but I scrambled back to my feet, recovering my staff, and blinking back tears of pain as I ran.

More shouts filled the air behind us and then we were running again.

We reached the riverbank and I scanned it, looking for a boat. There was no boat.

Heron's eyes were wide as he turned to me.

"Damokas?" I gasped.

"Dead," he said, his breathing gusting heavily.

Behind us, the footfalls were getting closer. We had to get out of here. We had to leave right now.

I swallowed, reached into Heron's pocket and pulled out two of the magic masks he'd stolen in the tent. I slapped one over Vyvera's mouth, hoping she was still alive enough to need it, and the other over Heron's.

"I sure hope these work," I said, before grabbing his hand and pulling him after me into the river.

His warm hand felt comforting as the cold water pulled us into the fast-flowing current, erasing any trace that we'd ever been there at all. I clung to it, hoping that knowing he was depending on me would give me some sort of burst of inspiration, because I had no idea what to do next.

Sela! Water!

At least Nasataa sounded pleased.

Episode Three: Desperate Flight

Chapter One

I clung to Heron's hand, pulling him underwater. He was carrying Vyvera, stumbling along the river bottom. The current pushed against me and more than once Heron shot me a puzzled look as I pulled him upstream. But our enemies would expect us to go downstream. And if we did what they expected, then they'd catch us quickly.

We were outnumbered. One of our number was unconscious, and the dragon we'd all relied on to get us out of this mess was dead. And where was Octon? He was our local guide and we'd lost him in the commotion.

I wanted so badly to talk this through with Heron but talking underwater didn't work and Heron's mouth was under the magic patch that made it possible for him to breathe under the water. Hopefully, those patches gave him all my abilities – the warmth stabilization, ability to handle the water pressure, ability to walk underwater and control easily whether to walk or swim, and the ability to breathe underwater.

Frustrated, I pressed on, walking along the river bottom and holding my staff at the ready. Fortunately, my ankle was bothering me less in the water. Adding a sprained ankle to everything else we were up against only complicated things further. And I was fed up with complicated.

A *whoosh* filled my ears and then, in a cloud of bubbles, something plunged through the water just in front of us. I braced myself, staff held firmly in both hands. Heron's hands were occupied with Vyvera. It was up to me to defend us. My heart was already pounding but I clenched my jaw and readied myself. No one ever said this would be easy.

The bubbles cleared and the dark figure in the shadowed river plunged toward us. I stabbed forward with my staff and he froze, eyes widening.

Oh no! It was Octon!

I tried to give a sign of apology as he scowled at me around his magical breathing patch, urgently signaling for us to follow him.

The rush of the river filled my ears as we fought from shadow to shadow.

Another burst of bubbles ahead and I rushed forward. Octon was our only ally here, which made that an enemy. I stabbed with the staff, connecting almost by accident with the enemy's leg. A burst of darkness clouded the water around his leg as his flowing garments pulled at the currents. There was a surprised look on his face and then he plunged upward back to the surface.

For that matter, what was keeping Heron and Octon here on the river floor? I could guess that I was held down by the water in my lungs, replacing the air. But did their magical patches over their mouths do the same thing? If not, wouldn't they rise to the surface?

I looked back to where they were, and my eyes grew wide. I hadn't even heard a sound, and yet they were surrounded by Bubblers!

And now I knew why they were called Bubblers.

Bubbles surrounded them, pouring out of the ends of rods they held, but they weren't normal bubbles. They were tinged a dark color. I was hard to make out the exact shade underwater in the dark. They held small lamps in their hands to light the way. How long could those burn underwater? Or were they magical?

I rushed toward the others, slashing one of the Bubblers in the back with my bladed staff. I flinched as a puff of darkness filled the water around him.

What was I doing? If I flinched every time I hurt someone, then I wouldn't be able to defend my friends. But I couldn't help but feel the pain of a knife slash across the back when I inflicted it. It wasn't an easy thing to hurt another person – and it shouldn't be.

Gritting my teeth, my inner self crying at the necessity, I stabbed the bladed staff forward, hitting a second bubbler. I didn't know where I hit him, only that he stumbled and then kicked upward toward the surface. The bubbler I'd hit the first time seemed to be in shock. He clutched his back, arching backward with pain.

It felt strange to fight underwater – the water slowing our movements and the sound of the rushing water blocking out all other sounds. Dark bubbles streamed away with clouds of dark blood.

But now three more Bubblers were closing in, ignoring Heron and Octon to join together against me. I was clearly the biggest threat. I was the only one with a weapon.

I held my staff out, firm and ready. Behind them, I saw Heron catch a stumbling Octon. Octon must have been injured in the battle. Or maybe those colored bubbles were even more toxic than I first thought.

One of the Bubblers launched a stream of bubbles at me. I ducked under them, feeling awkward as I tried to dodge the slow-moving stream. The way they rippled through the current made them unpredictable and difficult to avoid.

A second stream rippled toward me. I ducked out of the way, slashing wildly with my staff and popping some of the bubbles.

Uh oh. Bad idea.

The bubbles burst, filling the water with a glittering haze of red and then pain shot through my lungs like inhaling pepper. I sneezed violently, temporarily disabled by the burning wave.

I recovered as fast as I could, slashing my bladed staff out and connecting again. But now I was in trouble. Heron swayed in the water as he tried to support two unconscious people and drag them forward, a look of anxiety on his face as he glanced constantly back toward me. But what else could he do? He couldn't take my place. I couldn't carry two people – not even in the water.

My lungs were screaming as I lunged again, this time I hit so hard that my blade lodged in my victim. My stomach bucked as I yanked the staff back and forth, trying to dislodge the blade. The feeling of it catching on something hard, and then catching in the other direction before finally pulling free, made me want to throw up. I swallowed down nausea as the broken bubbler I had just mangled hung heavy in the water, blood gushing from a gaping chest wound.

There were three more, and these ones weren't going to make the same mistake. Had more bubblers joined in the fight? I couldn't keep track of them in the chaos. All I could do was fight the ones I could see.

Their expressions hardened as they turned their bubble staffs on me, taking care not to come into range of my staff.

With nods to each other, they let out a burst of bubbles toward Heron.

With a feeling near panic, I leapt forward, slashing bubbles as quick as I could, trying to defend him, but as the bubbles burst close to me, their effects washed over me. I felt hot and feverish, visions and illusions dancing across my vision. Was that Ramariri swimming through the water? Was that my birth mother calling to me?

No! Get a hold of yourself, Seleska! They were hallucinations, nothing more. I gripped my staff, trying to blink my vision clear as the last three enemies closed in. I tasted blood, sick at the thought that I was breathing that in with the water. I was going to be ill.

And then I was going to die, because there was just no way that I could defend myself from three enemies while fighting the effects of their poison. Did I say three? There appeared to be five now. No, eight. Wait. Was I hallucinating? Which ones were the real ones?

Help! I called in my mind. Help!

Chapter Two

A blur rushed by me and I flinched, flicking the staff up in defense. I hit nothing but water. There was another blur and then a third one and then I was hit hard from the side and I stumbled, barely catching my balance with the staff. I was thrown from my feet a second time and I fell against Heron.

His eyes were wide, and he pointed with his chin toward something behind me. I glanced back and my own eyes widened at the sight of the sleek bodies swirling in the water surrounded by clouds of inky darkness.

Those weren't sharks ... were they? Not in a river.

But they were some sort of huge fish. And they ... no, I couldn't think about that. The scent of blood filled my nose and I hurried to put a shoulder under Octon and help Heron as he dragged Octon with one arm while he carried Vyvera with the other.

We were too slow. We couldn't possibly go fast enough with two people to carry underwater and walking against the current. Frustration made me clench my jaw as I pushed forward.

At least we weren't being shredded by river fish.

Yet.

I pushed harder, fear giving me strength that I didn't know I had. It was long minutes until the scent of blood was gone from the water. Even longer before I could turn and look behind my shoulder and see nothing but darkness.

My heart hammered in my chest and every wave of seaweed or brush of the current set my nerves aflame with fear. At any moment they could turn from their feast and come after us. We were easy targets, simple prey.

Eventually, my feet began to drag as the fear wore into exhaustion. I couldn't go on much longer. I could feel it on my bones, dragging me down, making my steps drag and my ankle groan with pain.

I thought I was going to have to stop, going to have to quit on everyone, when suddenly Octon shook his head, and though it fell back to his chest, his feet stopped dragging and started to stumble between us.

It felt like a lifetime before he was carrying his own weight. I wanted to look at Heron and see his reaction, but I was too tired for even that. It was all I could do to stay upright and keep going.

When finally, Octon was carrying himself again, stumbling but on his own two feet, I let go of him and sent a grateful glance toward Heron. His eyes were set dead ahead and his face was drawn. Octon might be carrying himself again, but Heron was still carrying Vyvera and he looked like he couldn't take even one more minute of it.

Fortunately for me, Nasataa was asleep in his bag. But even his lighter weight was beginning to drag at me as my strength faded in the cold of the water.

I nearly walked into the anchor in the water in front of me. At the last second, I grabbed the rope instead, stumbling to a stop. Up the rope, the small craft was a dark outline rimmed by moonlight. The water here must be shallow.

I paused for a moment, catching my breath.

I nearly screamed a warning when Octon leapt up, kicking toward the surface. What was he doing? What was he thinking?

Heron followed him, kicking against Vyvera's weight – but he was too tired from carrying her and he sank again. Should I help him? I felt the draw to come to his aid, but I didn't think we should go to the surface.

I shook my head at him, trying to communicate that it would be a terrible mistake to go back up to where the Bubblers and Rock Eaters were. Surely, they were looking for us. Surely, they would be hot on our path. And it would be easier to find us if we were above the surface of the water. At least down here, we had the advantage of being hard to reach.

Heron thrust his jaw toward the surface, a determined look on his face. I followed his gaze to where Octon's head dipped into the water from the surface. He was nothing more than a silhouette, but he was beckoning toward us energetically.

This was a terrible idea.

Heron shook his head, frustration in his eyes. He knew what I was thinking, and he wanted to go with Octon. That was clear from his expression.

Trying not to sigh with worry, I grabbed Vyvera's legs, helping Heron move her from the slumped position over his shoulders. He rolled his shoulders in relief the second she was down from them, and together we kicked up and made our way to the surface.

Octon had better know what he was doing.

Or this pointy staff of mine would be the least of his worries.

Chapter Three

We broke the surface and I choked, coughing out water. I was never going to get used to that. It took me a moment to realize what the panicked look on Heron's face was. I reached out and ripped the magical patch from his mouth. The light faded from it as he coughed and choked just like I had, finally spitting out the water so he could breathe air. Vyvera was next. Fortunately, even unconscious she was able to cough up the water she had been breathing. I'd been worried about that.

The boat, it turned out, was empty and small. It was anchored in the river near a dilapidated landing and covered in a tarp. Octon, exhaustion marking his every movement, helped us pull and push Vyvera into the boat and then the rest of us tumbled in, covering ourselves with the tarp. We were cold and wet, but no one had enough energy to complain about being crammed into a tiny space and shoved against everyone else. At least it was warm this way.

Nasataa's snores eased me into sleep.

I woke to him licking my face and burping tiny flames into the air. The tarp had sagged at one end and morning light was filtering into the moldy boat. I struggled to sit up. I hadn't slept nearly long enough. Had it even been more than a few hours? I didn't think so.

But the morning light brought better spirits. Sure, we were being hunted and chased and sure my ankle throbbed from walking on it while it was sprained, but today would be better. We'd find some way to go forward. Everything could start new again.

Nasataa flamed again and I fished out some of what had been dried meat from my pocket. It wasn't very dry now and it hung soggy and stinking from my hand. He didn't seem to mind, eating it with enough relish for a fine feast. I shrugged. At least river water wasn't brackish. He could drink that.

His wet feet walked across Octon and Vyvera before he found the prow of the boat, shrugged out from under the tarp and leaned down to drink. He sure was an indomitable little thing. Here we were in a foreign place – and one full of adversaries! – he'd been caught and caged twice, all he had to eat was soggy old meat, and he seemed as happy as a fish in water. I liked that spirit!

I smiled tenderly before I heard a cough behind me and turned to see a sleepy-eyed Heron rubbing his eyes. He'd slept beside me – almost over top of me as if he could guard me with his body. Maybe he could.

"We're alive," I said, surprised by how raw my voice sounded.

"For now," he agreed, but the strain of the situation made his voice tight.

"Today will be better," I assured him with a bright smile. It would be. I would make it better.

Vyvera sat up so suddenly that I nearly jumped. She coughed, a fit wracking her body so that she shook and heaved before spitting out a glob of black tar. She was in worse shape than I remembered. Wicked wounds ran down her arms and legs. One of her arms hung lifeless at her side.

Hadn't Heron had a head wound last night, too?

I stole a glance at him to see concern written across his face. His head wound had scabbed over. It must not have been very bad, but his concern was growing to a tight anxiety. And no wonder. Vyvera was our way out of this place. The one who knew where we were and how to get where we were going, and she looked ... bad. Very bad.

"He's dead," she gasped. "I'd hoped ... I'd feared ... well, he must be dead."

"Damokas?" Heron asked gently, continuing at her nod. "I saw him when we grabbed you. They mounted his head on their tower like a trophy."

She gasped, her body shaking, and then she coughed again, a terrible barking cough that seemed to come from her very core. The black tar she was spitting up couldn't be good. I exchanged a worried look with Heron before moving to her side.

"Let's get that arm in some kind of a sling," I offered, tearing off the mask that dangled around my neck – part of my disguise, and lengthening the strap with the buckles. It would have to do for a sling. We didn't have much else.

She let me sling her arm, barely flinching at my touch, though her arm seemed completely immobile.

"I think we need a real healer," I said grimly. "I think it's broken."

I'd seen a broken arm before in the village. The healers would make sure the bone was right and then tie things up so they couldn't move until it knit. I didn't know how to do that right and doing it wrong might be worse than doing nothing at all.

"No point," Vyvera said, pain etched across her face. "We must press on. The Troglodytes wait for you and getting you and Nasataa to them has to be our first priority."

Nasataa ran past along the gunwale of the boat as if he had heard his name, leaping and snapping at flying insects. He was so innocent. Too innocent for all of this.

"We will do that," I assured her. "But first, let us get you to a healer."

She barked a laugh that held no humor.

"When I said there was no point, I meant it. I won't live past two weeks. Dragons and their riders are bound to each other. If one dies, the other dies, too. That cough of mine – the black goo I am spitting up – it's the result of that. We have just two weeks – maybe much less than that – to get you to the Troglodytes. And I will get you there if I have to die trying."

Chapter Four

Ishivered at her words, memories of Ramariri flashed through my mind, a bevy of images from our short few days together. He had meant so much to me. I hadn't even realized he was dying until he was almost gone. I hadn't had time to really tell him how much he meant to me. It was that feeling that lingered, burning through me and making me clench my fists and jaw even after the memories were gone. That terrible feeling of loss and helplessness combined with anxiety. I hated that feeling. But it felt as familiar as breathing.

Just breathe Seleska. You're okay. You will be fine. Just breathe.

I'd had to say that so much to myself in the early days without him. I could say that again. And it would be true. My eyes snapped open and I saw Nasataa hopping along the side of the boat doing little summersaults. I had to be strong for him. I couldn't panic or back out because I was afraid. I had to be strong.

I didn't realize that I was still shaking from the feeling whipsawing through me, until Heron wrapped an arm around me. He pulled me in, drawing me against his strong, immovable body. There was something about how solid he was that made me feel safe – like all the world around us could fall apart, but Heron would still be there. I let out a long breath.

"How can we help you?" Heron asked Vyvera.

Her smile was wry. "By hurrying so that I don't waste my last days in failure."

Well, that was direct!

I was surprised by a cough from behind Vyvera. I hadn't even realized that Octon was awake until he sat up, rubbing red eyes.

"If you need to go upriver and you need to hurry, and if Heron still has those patches we stole, then I can help you."

"Oh?" Vyvera asked.

"I know a safehouse not far from here. We can walk. But we should hurry. We are easy targets here. They will be searching the river surface."

"Only the surface?" I asked.

He shrugged. "It's easiest. And the patches don't last forever. Everyone has to come up for air eventually."

"How long do they last?" I asked.

"Twenty-four hours or as long as you are submerged." He pointed to where the three patches lay in the bottom of the boat, shriveled and dry as dead leaves. "But if you surface, the patch is done, and you'll need a new one."

"And how many do you have?" I asked Heron, biting my lip. We would have enough, right? We had to have enough.

"Seven," he said, after counting them.

That was three trips underwater for him and Vyvera and one left.

I swallowed, feeling the pressure of our low supplies. Would they be enough?

Of course, they would be. No point on worrying about what couldn't be helped. We'd find a way somehow. I always found a way to do what I needed to do.

"Come on, Nasataa!"

He ran to me as I followed the others onto shore, leaping into my outstretched arms and licking my face.

"Yeah, I love you, too."

Selesa! Ride!

I opened the bag for him, and he climbed in, keeping his head out so he could watch as we slipped onto a narrow path between high leafy fronds. The trail was packed dirt, but small plants sprang up along it as if it was not often used. My feet squelched unpleasantly in the soft leather boots Octon had given me and my sprained ankle ached painfully. I missed my sandals. I would need to replace them as soon as I could. If I was going to spend this much time in the water, none of the boots were going to be a good fit.

The path wound along the river until it finally emerged at a tall, narrow house with a huge wheel on the side of it. A long shaft ran from the narrow house to a larger house beyond.

"It's a watermill," Octon said, as if that made any sense.

"A way to use water to grind grain," Vyvera explained.

I watched the wheel move, fascinated by the paddles that caught the water of the river as it tumbled past and spun the wheel. How strange. This land was full of wonders. If only they didn't want to kill me so badly, I would really enjoy seeing all these new things.

There were a few different boats moored by the wheel – some of them large enough to carry cargo in sacks and bales.

"Wait here for me. I will make sure it's safe for you," Octon said, slipping down the dirt path where the foliage cleared into a wide grassy space, edged with bright flowers.

Vyvera launched into a coughing fit but she stopped herself, struggling for a moment and then breathing out a long breath.

"While we have a moment, let me tell you about the staff," she said looking at it wistfully. I hadn't even realized that we'd lost her staff until that moment. What other important things had we lost with her dragon? I shouldn't be thinking like that. The dragon was a person and enough of a loss without counting the other things we'd never see again. But I couldn't help but wonder what battles we might face and lose because we'd lost Vyvera's staff.

"Your staff," she said, taking it gently from my hands, "can be fought with. You can use it to slash and hack and stab. But it also serves more purposes than that. With this staff, you can access magic."

Chapter Five

"Magic?" I asked.

"No time for questions. If we're traveling underwater, we won't be able to talk, and my time is limited. So, listen. Watch the physical moves first." She whirled, demonstrating each one as she spoke. "Block. Jab. Feint. Parry. Slash. Backhand. Pivot. Show me."

I took the staff carefully and tried to copy her moves. They were more halted than hers had been, more of trying to remember what they were than actually executing them well, but I did remember.

"Okay. Good start. Every time we stop for a break or rest, run through those. Do it every day and you might even begin to get good enough to spar with someone. And now, the magic. It's not your own magic. Rather, the staff can suck up any magic thrown against you. Maybe you've seen that happen already?"

I nodded. I had seen that, hadn't I? I'd seen that bubbler with her hands curled trying to do *something* while I was lecturing her about how to become a better person. Had that been my staff picking up magic?

"I thought so," Vyvera said. "Because I can feel the power in this staff. Using it, that will take more time. These are tuned to their owners. How you access that magic and how you make it work for you varies from person to person. Just keep using it to deflect magic attacks and absorb them and in time, as you practice the physical moves, you will learn to harness the magic, too. Oh, and if you ever start to get good at those moves, you should find a good sparring partner."

I nodded seriously, trying not to look too excited. A magic staff? I had no idea this was so valuable! It had been great when it was a weapon and a support to me. Now, it was even better!

I whirled the staff the way she'd shown me, testing out the moves. Could I feel the power in it like she had? Or was that all in my mind.

"And don't take off your friend's head by accident," Vyvera said wryly.

My eyes went big when I looked behind me to see Heron ducking with an unimpressed look on his face.

"I'm going to go see what's keeping Octon," Vyvera said, slipping down the path.

I was about to follow her when Heron laid a hand on my shoulder. "Seleska?"

"Yes?" I paused as he swallowed. What was so hard for him to say?

"Maybe we shouldn't be going upriver. Maybe we should be going downriver."

"But they'll expect us there," I said, confused.

He licked his lips nervously, his dark brows drawing downward. "We expected to be going with Vyvera and to have her dragon to help us if things went poorly. But Seleska, the Havenwind Isles are a long way from here. If you can really go through portals under the sea, well that might be the only way to get back. And if Vyvera is dying, she might die before we find a safe place here. Maybe it's a better idea to go home right now and to bring Nasataa with us. Where better to keep him safe than where we have friends and family?"

I shook my head. "We'd be endangering them."

"No one will know where we are. Right now, lots of people know." He looked around at the bushes as if he could see enemies creeping in from every side.

"Vyvera is giving her life for this," I said, torn.

If I didn't agree to go, it wasn't like he could go without me. He'd be trapped here surrounded by enemies. But if I stopped and turned back with him, then the Troglodyte would die before we could arrive to meet him and everything Vyvera had worked for would be useless. Her dragon would have died for nothing. She looked calm on the outside, but I knew what it was like to lose a dragon friend. And Ramariri and I had only been friends for days, not years like Vyvera and her dragon.

Besides, if evil forces were really after Nasataa – and me, too – then there was nowhere we could go to flee and be safe. Our only hope was to fight back.

"I'm sorry, Heron," I said. "But I can't just run away. If I run, I'll always be running. If I stay and fight, I could win."

He nodded, but there was tension in his jaw and face that hadn't been there before. He was as worried as I was.

I wanted to comfort him, but at that moment, Octon and Vyvera returned.

"We're in luck," Octon said with a beaming smile. "A fellow Lightbringer is headed upriver in that supply barge and he's agreed to let you ride on the hull."

"On the hull?" I asked. He couldn't really mean what he said, could he?

"Sure. Underwater and free from prying eyes! It's a perfect setup!"

Perfect? That's not what I would have called it. Heron and Vyvera wouldn't be able to put their heads above water without ruining their patches, and a journey like that couldn't be short.

"How many days upriver is this meeting of yours?" I asked Vyvera.

"At least five," she said.

"And Yvon can get you as far as Tinlin City, three days upriver," Octon said proudly.

"That will do," Vyvera said seriously. The expression on her face was of pure concentration, as if she were counting out her last coins. In a way, she was. After all, those three days would be some of the last few days of her life.

I felt a knot forming in my throat at the thought of her sacrifice. I really couldn't back out. Not now. I reached for Heron's hand, surprised when I didn't find it. He stood a few steps away, looking down the river toward the sea. He didn't like the choice I'd made.

I swallowed hard, trying to get rid of the lump forming in my throat. I had to do what was right, even if my friend didn't like it.

"Thank you, Octon," I said, trying to keep worry out of my voice. Three days was not far enough, and we didn't have enough patches to go farther than that underwater. My hands were sweating as he led us to the boat, a reluctant Heron following a few paces behind.

Why did I feel so guilty for saying yes?

Chapter Six

This had been a mistake. I was trying not to think of that. Instead, I was trying to think about how it was also an adventure and all my life I had wanted adventures. When I went back home and told my parents about it, none of the discomfort or difficulty would matter, only the amazing adventure and the people I'd gone on it with. Right?

I thought about that as we put patches over Heron and Vyvera's mouths and noses and slipped into the water with a last wave to Octon. I thought about what a grand adventure it was as I tried to convince Nasataa to stay in his carrier and as I jammed the supplies Octon had given me into the carrier – a canteen of clean water, a pair of sandals, a package of dried meat wrapped in oilcloth and a few coins.

"All my friend can spare," he'd said quietly as he'd handed them to me.

I thought about what a grand adventure it was as the barge captain wrapped ropes around the hull of his ship and we scooted down the side of the hull, under the dark waves, and clung to the ropes like barnacles.

Heron was trying to be positive, too, with a squeeze of my hand as I secured my staff to the rope and got a good grip on it.

We were off on a grand adventure into unknown places!

But I still felt too ill to be upset about the lack of food. My nervous belly did not seem to understand how adventures worked.

Neither did my heart, still aching over the injuries Vyvera was enduring – we'd bandaged her wounds as we could, but they were bad. Anyone who planned to live more than a few more days would be concerned about them.

Even my muscles couldn't understand how adventures worked. They were aching and protesting after the first hour. It was all I could do to keep holding the rope during the second hour. I adjusted constantly, squirming to find a good place. I didn't dare fall off. At the back of the barge, a huge paddle turned, carrying the boat upstream against the river. I didn't understand how that worked, but Heron had been incredibly interested, peering at the wheel and a tall stack at the center of the boat as if he could make out how it operated. Maybe he could. He saw the world differently than I did.

I was beginning to think that my arms were going to give out and I'd be sucked downstream and battered by the paddles when the boat began to slow. It stopped and then an anchor fell through the water, plunging to the floor of the river.

Heron gave me a confused look. But I didn't know any more than he did what was going on. He pointed up. Oh yeah, I was the only one who could afford to go check.

With aching, stiff arms, I pulled myself along the rope and up to the surface, careful to hug the boat tightly when my head surfaced. It was all I could do not to cough. Instead, I choked quietly on the water coming up as I sucked in air.

Voices rang out from the boat above.

"...patrol coming. Stand ready!"

There was the sound of a boat bumping against our barge. Good thing I hadn't surfaced on the other side! And then there were more voices.

"This is the Saaasallla's River Guard, accompanied by Bubbler Atura Feliciano. We are looking for three fugitives. Do you have any passengers on your boat?"

I didn't need to hear more than that. I scrambled down into the water again. Bubblers could breathe underwater, too. They could send someone down to check for us. We needed to hide right now before they did.

I hurried, hand over hand down the rope. I couldn't call to them to warn them but my heart was pounding in my chest as I rushed to my friends. How could I warn them without words?

I wasn't sure. The second I saw Heron, I made my eyes as wide as I could, trying to signal fear. We were both wearing the Bubbler goggles – strange contraptions of glass panes, metal cases, and leather straps – that we'd had with us when we infiltrated their camp and Vyvera had been given a pair by Octon. They helped in the water making everything clearer and easier to see.

I pointed toward the stern, beginning to swim in that direction. We could hide in the water wheel. They wouldn't look there, right? Because you'd have to be crazy to go in there. After all, if it started moving again, that wheel could kill you.

Fortunately, Heron was following me, helping Vyvera along. She looked ill. She probably needed to spit more of that black guck, but she couldn't with the patch over her mouth. She pulled it off for a moment, spitting black goo into the water and then managed to pull it back over her nose and mouth before devolving into a fit of coughing again. My stomach knotted at the sight. I wished so badly that I could fix this for her.

We worked our way to the paddle wheel, climbing between the paddles to hide inside them. The others seemed to understand somehow, though Heron looked extremely worried about it. They settled in between the paddles, bracing themselves and trying to be as small as they could be.

In his bag, Nasataa was waking up.

Stay inside!

I sent him a visual image of staying quiet inside the bag. He could come out when all of this was over.

I felt a creeping sensation come over me, as if the water was trying to tell me something. I couldn't help myself. I leaned down, peeking out from the bottom side of the paddle at the boat hull.

There was a flash of red as someone ducked under the hull and I pulled my head back in. They really were searching for us underwater! There were bubblers crawling along the bottom of the ship! I clenched my jaw and stole a second glance.

There was one swimming along the rope, goggles pulled over her eyes and mask over her face. I cringed back behind the paddle.

Please don't look here! Please don't look here!

I thought the words as hard as I could.

Chapter Seven

I could hear them on deck, my ears straining to listen to any bump or sound. I put my finger up over my lips to warn Heron and Vyvera, but I didn't need to. They were both motionless, frozen in place and out of sight. They were better at this than I was!

Nasataa squirmed in the bag on my back and I help my breath.

Still! Be still!

I sent him calm images of lying still and being relaxed. He sent me the image of cramped muscles and wanting to swim.

No! Be still!

He wasn't listening. Instead, he squirmed against my back and a few bubbles drifted out of the pack, gliding up to the surface. Teeth gritted and one hand on my staff, I reached around my back with the other arm and hugged him tight against it. He was going to give us away!

Long seconds passed and then I heard the crank of the anchor chain.

Heron ducked his head down past the paddle, looking at the hull like I had and then popped back around, urgently motioning to us to follow. I swam under the paddle but Vyvera was slow, her limbs moving awkwardly and her body bucking with supressed coughs. Heron seized her clothing, tugging her hard to pull her past the paddles.

Close to the bow, I saw the anchor lifting on its chain. It was almost completely up.

Heron and I kicked forward in the water, swimming as fast as we could. We were barely far enough when the big paddle began to turn again, sucking the water toward it.

I swam hard, kicking and clawing with my free hand as fast as I could while my other kept a grip on the Dragon Staff. I couldn't afford to lose such a priceless relic.

Heron fought hard, too, pulling Vyvera along with him.

By the time we reached the ropes we were exhausted, wrapping our legs and arms around them and hanging from them as the current tugged all around us. The look we shared was one of mutual gratitude. We were grateful to be alive and free. Or at least, I was.

Vyvera didn't share our look. She was clinging to the rope desperately, head curled into her chest. Gently, Heron wrapped an arm around her so she wouldn't have to hold on by herself. He was always like that – gentle with other people. Reliable in a crisis. I should appreciate that more.

I was beginning to smile when I felt a tug at the back of my pack. I spun. Afraid we'd been caught after all, but it was only Nasataa slipping out and darting through the water beside me. He'd better stick close! Could he manage to swim against such a strong current? He seemed just fine, but I kept a close eye on him as the hours passed until finally, the boat anchored again.

I swam up to the surface, checking on what was happening and Captain Yvon called down to me.

"We're at anchor for the night. The hands and I will sleep on deck, but the shore is close. We leave again at first light."

I nodded, grateful for his help but so tired I could hardly rest at all.

We made camp on the shore, lighting a fire on a sandy beach and sharing the canteen and dried meat. Nasataa was out immediately, curling up so close to the fire that the flames almost licked his gleaming scales. Heron slumped nearby, not even bidding us goodnight before he was asleep. I was about to join him when Vyvera shook with wracking coughs and then pointed to me.

"No sleep. Practice."

"What?" I asked, incredulous.

"The Staff. You need to practice. It will guide you."

She curled up by the fire, coughing her terrible barking cough and I was left sitting there with a choice. She could hardly force me to practice when she was so ill. And I was so tired that I wanted to ignore her instruction. But then again. How could I defend Nasataa if I didn't have any ability to use this staff?

With a tired sigh, I stood up, paced down the beach and then began the forms Vyvera had shown me, slowly and carefully at first but picking up speed as they grew more familiar. I was probably imagining things, but the staff seemed to glow slightly as I worked with it. And it did feel as if it was guiding me in my awkward forms, helping me to adjust them as I practiced. I must be really tired to think that.

I worked until I was so tired that I was beginning to forget what I was doing. Eventually, I returned to the fire and collapsed beside Nasataa, drifting off to sleep.

Our next two days were the same as the first – a combination of clinging to ropes until our muscles hurt and desperately avoiding the notice of the patrols that roamed the river. Sometimes their hulls went by so close that I could see what color they were in the dark water. Other times, we had to scramble to hide from bubblers boarding or riding along their own patrol boat hulls. It was nerve-wracking and exhausting, but I kept reminding myself that it was still an adventure and adventures were not comfortable things. Captain Yvon passed food to us at night – just enough to keep us going – and I worked the staff on each break, but so far, no magic had come to me.

On the second night, Vyvera drew us a map in the sand of where we were going, demanding that we memorize it and repeat it back to her. Our destination lay under a waterfall. I would like to see a waterfall. There weren't any on the Havenwind Isles and I felt like seeing one would be a true adventure.

"Just in case," Vyvera said the third time she made us repeat her directions. Her coughs had grown worse and black fluid sometimes leaked from her eyes. I was beginning to worry that she didn't have two weeks. She might not even have two more days.

I wanted to say or do something to comfort her, but the only thing I could think of was to comply to her wishes, so I memorized the map, and I worked the staff, and I hoped with all my heart that she would live to see the Troglodyte she was going to die to serve.

Chapter Eight

The third morning Captain Yvon had a quick word with us before we ducked under the waves.

"We've been hearing news all up the river that revolution is spreading from the coast."

"Revolution?" Vyvera asked before beginning another coughing fit.

"They say that a dragon attacked one of the Sentinel Towers. Since then, the people have been astir. Some have wanted to see the Saaasallla overthrown for a long time." He looked around warily. "But I shouldn't be discussing such things. I only mention it to remind you to be careful. I agreed to hide you until Tinlin City, but I've never seen so many patrols and Bubbler Atura Feliciano herself is hunting for you. It's going to be hard for you to hide – especially since you look like foreigners. And now with tensions so high, any attention drawn to you could lead to violence. Be careful. Watch yourselves. Try not to stand out in any way."

We nodded, and Heron looked worried.

"Do you think there will be a war?" he asked.

I shivered. I hated the thought of war. People killing other people was such a terrible thing. No one deserved to die just because someone else wanted what they had. But that hadn't stopped me from lashing out with the staff when Nasataa was threatened, did it? That was blood I'd seen in the water and bones my blade had caught on. I wasn't innocent in this.

The Captain shrugged at the question. "Who can say? When we reach Tinlin City I will anchor in the docks there for a few hours while we unload. That will be the best time for you to make your way to shore and on to the next leg of your journey. I hope you arrive at your destination safely."

We nodded.

"Thank you for helping us," I said, smiling my sweetest smile. I had nothing else to offer him. "I hope you don't get into trouble for it."

"I won't if you don't get caught," he said. "So, don't get caught. We will be at Tinlin City by midday."

It had felt longer than just a morning, but the sun was high in the sky when we started to see other hulls and the paddles stopped and we drifted in beside the base of a pier. The anchor dropped, and Heron and I made eye contact and nodded.

It was time.

We needed to get away from the barge and into the city and we needed to do it without anyone watching.

I looked to Vyvera to see if she realized where we were, but she seemed barely conscious. Heron shook her gently, putting an arm around her to help guide her to the muddy river bottom along the pier. I felt for Nasataa's mind with my own, but he was worn out from a night chasing and snacking on glowbugs while the rest of us slept and he was – fortunately – fast asleep. My belly rumbled at the thought of food – even glowbugs – but I ignored it. Adventurers were always hungry in the stories. Eventually, I'd find food again.

We slid along the mud bottom, and my senses were on high alert, watching for any Bubblers. We couldn't surface here. People would notice soaking wet people coming out of a river they hadn't gone into. So where could we go? We needed somewhere quiet. I led us along the shoreline, keeping far enough back from the bank that we wouldn't be seen.

The world above could be seen from under the waves, but it was too blurry to make anything out beyond vague shapes and colors. I was going to have to risk putting my face above the water soon, but I didn't dare do it too soon.

Eventually, we found another dock. This one was more worn with rotting wood and old debris around it. Good. There were only a few boats tied up here. A better place to try to scope out our chances.

I crept to the far side of the dock and carefully crept to the surface, bobbing up between two of the boats. I managed not to cough, choking quietly as the water came up out of my lungs. I was in luck! No one was in the boats tied here and they were small and shabby. I risked rising a little higher to look past their hulls.

We were on the far side of the river port, on the furthest dock upriver and the most decrepit of them all. Debris from the river was stuck in a churning eddy at the shore and tall trees draped over the water, trailing their unkempt branches into the pollen-coated surface. Further along the river, the real docks were teeming with boats and people. I could make out the barge we'd traveled under and on its deck, a Bubbler patrol was boarding. They wouldn't find anything, but I sure hoped they wouldn't make trouble for Captain Yvon.

We needed to get to shore quickly before they thought to look under the water, too.

I dove back under, signaling Heron and Vyvera to follow me, and I led them up the muddy bank to surface near the heap of debris and the trailing tree branches. They lent us perfect cover as we slid quietly out of the water, trying to wring out our clothing as we made it to shore. Heron and Vyvera tore off their patches, leaving them in the heap of debris.

"We will do better in our own clothing than the Bubbler robes we're wearing on top," Vyvera said, and Heron quickly shed the waterlogged red cloth as she spoke, flinging the mask and goggles aside. "Bubblers get noticed more than foreigners do and you two won't pass as bubblers."

I was more reluctant, but I saw her logic, and quickly stripped my own disguise off, stuffing it and the others in my pack.

There was a shout from down the beach, and I peeked through the branches to see what it was.

The Bubbler patrol had Captain Yvon between them, hands tied in front of him as they marched him swiftly away from the docks. A spike of cold shot down my spine.

"I guess we'd better hurry," I said, sharing a worried glance at Heron and Vyvera.

Chapter Nine

There was nothing we could do for Captain Yvon.

"They have no evidence that he helped us," Vyvera said through muffled coughs. "They won't keep him for long."

I wasn't so sure. Our enemies hadn't seemed terribly reasonable so far.

"We need dry clothes. We stand out in these wet ones," Heron grumbled as we scrambled up an alley, dodging an old man who was scowling at us from a bench where he sat feeding birds.

"Follow me," Vyvera said, leading us further up the alley. "You'll find if you travel much that most cities operate the same way. There are only so many ways for a lot of people to live in one place."

"What does that mean?" Heron asked.

"It means they hang their washing in the alleys and if we are lucky, we can steal some clothing to wear."

I didn't like the idea of stealing. What if I took someone's favorite shirt or pants?

Heron hung back a step to walk beside me. "I think that having your world saved is probably worth losing an outfit from your laundry line."

"Won't they be watching them if theft is such a possibility?"

He shrugged. "What do I know? No one steals in the islands. Not much, anyway. And we don't have alleys."

It didn't take long to find and steal clothing that fit us. I felt strange in my outfit. I was wearing sandals again, which I was grateful for, but the clothing here was all of a soft fiber I wasn't used to and they used more cloth than we did in the islands. My clothing felt bulky. So did the pack on my back.

We wrapped our old clothing into a tight package and added it to my pack under a sleepy – and irritated Nasataa. Hopefully, he would go back to sleep. If he popped a head out of the bag in this city, someone would notice, and we'd be in huge trouble.

I strapped the canteen over my shoulder. It didn't fit in the bag anymore. We'd need to make difficult decisions about what to keep soon – the bag was stuffed to the top.

Almost everyone in Tinlin wore hoods – which was handy when trying to disguise a foreign complexion. We kept ours pulled low to disguise our features in shadow. But we were still garnering looks as we strolled out onto the streets.

"I think it's the seaweed," Heron whispered after a few minutes.

I looked down, but there were no weeds clinging to me. What was he talking about? But then I saw it. All along the street, the people walked with chains of seaweed around their necks. Some wore purple and some green and those with green seemed to avoid those wearing purple and vice versa. What in the world was going on?

We paused beside a cart selling the necklaces and Vyvera ran her fingers over a purple chain of seaweed.

"Best seaweed in stock, mistress. Shipped from the sea yesterday," the vendor said, which was clearly a lie since it had taken us three days to make the same route. "You'll need to wear your own. You and your friends. No one is willing to trust anyone who hasn't declared just yet."

"Declared?" I asked as a shout broke out from down the street. Heron's head whipped in that direction, like a dog scenting prey.

"The seaweed declares your side in the discussion, mistress," the vendor said, but the look he gave me was longsuffering, like he was used to young women being a bit slow to follow politics. I bit my tongue. If I tried to show him that he was wrong about me, I would only be exposing us.

"It seems that those in purple are not fond of the Saaasallla's patrols," Heron muttered.

"The rebels, you mean," the vendor said. "Yes, purple is a dangerous color to wear."

"Coins," Vyvera said, looking at me.

Reluctantly, I fished out a pair of coins from my pack, trying not to disturb Nasataa as I reached blindly around his sleeping body, and handed them to her.

"We'll take three green," Vyvera said.

The vendor grinned. "An excellent choice!"

I struggled to mask my shock as Vyvera and Heron hustled me away from the cart, jamming the seaweed over my head.

"But," I began, and Heron shushed me.

"Disguises aren't meant to express your true thoughts. They are meant to make you blend in!" Vyvera reminded me. "And we need a way to find a ship headed upriver, so we need to go to an inn and listen to what the riverboat captains are saying. And that will mean looking loyal."

I kept my mouth shut but I didn't like this plan. Lying didn't seem like a good idea and I hated the looks of disapproval and headshakes I was getting from every person wearing a purple necklace. I agreed with them! We should be natural allies, not enemies!

But Vyvera was right. By the time we found a good inn near the river where the river captains were drinking, it was obvious that no one in a purple necklace was even being allowed in. If we'd chosen purple, we wouldn't be either.

No sooner had we crossed the threshold of an inn called *The Betting Betty* than I saw what I was looking for. Chalked up on the wall were the names of boats with a list of when each was departing and for where. By the rough map scrawled beside us, we could hitch a ride on *The Sea Serpent, The Dash and Roll,* or *The Potbellied Pig.*

Perfect.

A smile was already spreading across my face when someone in the inn cursed and every eye followed his shaking hand to where it pointed at me.

"What is that?" he asked.

Nasataa chose that moment to lick my ear.

Chapter Ten

I opened my mouth to speak, but Heron already had me by the waist. He lifted me up and practically threw me out of the inn door.

"Run!" he cried, and we were running.

We dashed down the streets, our feet flying as we skidded across cobbles and down winding stone staircases, past shops, and around carts selling fruits and street foods. Calls and shouts filled the air behind us, but we were gaining distance from them. If we could just keep it up!

Nasataa flashed me a feeling of chagrin. He realized that somehow licking my ear had caused this. But it was actually my fault. In all the sneaking and stealthiness, I'd forgotten to keep an eye on him and make sure he was still asleep.

We zigged and zagged from street to alley to street again, up one staircase and down another until we were close to the docks again. I ran past a half-rotten boathouse with a roof half caved-in when Heron whispered to me.

"Seleska!"

I spun to see him and Vyvera ducking into the tumbledown shed and I hurried after them. Heron jammed the door closed again and pressed his eye to a hole in the wall while we collapsed in a heap among the dead leaves and debris in the small shed. Old oars and abandoned pottery were stacked in corners of the shed and everything smelled of mildew and rotting wood.

Nasataa squirmed out of the bag and leapt into my arms, laying his hot little head on my shoulder.

"It's okay," I whispered. "It's not your fault."

He licked my jaw excitedly.

"Shhhh!" Heron whispered to me.

In the distance, I heard the sound of feet passing and voices calling. Some were near and some further, but when they finally passed us, no one stopped to look in the dilapidated boathouse.

Eventually, Heron joined us at the back of the shed, trying to catch his breath with the rest of us. Vyvera muffled a cough.

"I don't think I'll last much longer," she whispered in the darkness. Outside, the light was fading to dark. "I pushed too hard when we were running."

"We won't have to run again if we're more careful," Heron assured her.

"I don't mean that. I'm finding it hard to breathe."

We were silent for long moments.

"I'm sorry, Vyvera," I said.

"I need you to know two things," she whispered as the moments drew out. Even her speaking seemed labored and difficult. "First, you are essential to the healing of the world, Seleska. Keep that knowledge close, don't forget it, and don't give up. I need you to get to the Troglodytes. The world needs you to. Nasataa needs you to. Without the Troglodyte's blessing, the Rock Eaters will find you and kill you. Promise me that you'll go."

"I promise," I whispered.

"Second, you must keep practicing with that Dragon Staff. The fate of the world hangs in your mastery of that."

Well, that seemed extreme.

"Promise me," she insisted.

"I promise."

Heron shifted uncomfortably beside me. He had wanted to turn back before, and I suspected that he still did. These promises couldn't be easy for him to hear.

"There was a prophecy that led me to you," Vyvera said, and then her voice changed as she began to quote it. "*One born on distant island far from home. One brought to keep him safe if he roam. One given as a strength to face that day. One who with her life for them will pay.*" She paused to cough violently before continuing. "Do you see what it means? What it has to mean? It's the prophecy of the Restoration – of the return of magic. And it prophesies the birth of Nasataa far from home, of Seleska who will guard him, of Heron who will lend them strength, and of me who will die to help you."

I wasn't sure what to say. It didn't seem that clear to me. Besides, prophecies were weird religious things, weren't they? What did they have to do with real life? But you couldn't tell someone that when they were dying.

Instead, I reached through the dark and took her hand. "Don't give up, Vyvera,"

"I am not giving up," she said, struggling for breath between each word. "I just don't want you to give up either. Any of you."

Heron coughed awkwardly. "I won't leave Seleska and Nasataa."

Her voice seemed to contain a smile as she said, "That's all I needed to hear."

We grew quiet then and soon Nasataa began to snore again. I listened for a long time to Vyvera's breathing as I held her hand. I wished I knew what to say to help in some way, or at least ease her worry about all this.

I still hadn't thought of anything when she drew her last breath.

There was silence in the shed for a long moment.

"Vyvera?" I whispered.

"I think she's gone," Heron said.

Her hand was cooling when I finally let it go. I felt – heavy. It turned out that adventures weren't always fun. And they weren't always good stories. Sometimes they just hurt and people died for seemingly no reason when you just wished they could live.

I didn't even realize my breath was trembling until Heron found me in the dark and wrapped me in his big arms. He held me like that for a long time and I thought he may have even kissed the top of my head before he finally cleared his throat and spoke.

"I still have one more patch. If we knew of a ship headed upriver, it might be enough to get us to Vyvera's goal. I remember her sand map."

And that was all he needed to say to tell me he was still with me. At least Nasataa and I weren't alone. I squeezed him in a grateful hug, so incredibly grateful, but afraid he'd change his mind if I mentioned his change of heart.

"I know of just the right one," I said.

Chapter Eleven

Hiding under a strange boat was far more difficult than hiding under a friendly one had been. I adjusted my grip on the rope carefully. Heron's eyes were closed as he fought to stay strong and keep holding on. He couldn't surface and adjust his grip, and the hours were wearing on him. I reached out again to pat his shoulder with the back of the hand holding my staff, and he looked up tiredly and gave me a dull nod to tell me he was still holding on inside.

With one hand on the rope and one holding my staff, I couldn't help him. I could pop up to the surface and get my bearings, but he was stuck under the water since this was the last magical patch we had.

We hung this rope in an inconspicuous spot from the prow of the boat when it was still dark outside. We'd stolen it from the shed and dragged it with us, knowing we'd need any advantage that we could get. Even though it had been a full day since then, I couldn't stop thinking about the moment that Heron picked it up.

We'd both been standing there, shaking, looking at Vyvera. It didn't feel right just to leave her in the shed. She was a precious person. She wasn't disposable. But there were no Elders here to say the Words of Respect, no women of the tribe to wash her body with Xyana flower water, no men of the tribe to build the Great Fire to return her to the embrace of the earth.

"We can't stay, Seleska," Heron had said. "If we stay, they will catch us."

But all day, all I could think about was Vyvera. Had they found her body? Would they honor her, or did they even do that for foreigners? The guilt plagued me.

On top of that, Nasataa was hungry. He had been sending me mental images of eating for hours. And if I didn't find a way to feed him, he was going to go crazy. I was pretty sure that he'd already eaten the last of the meat in the bag and maybe some of the leather clothing, too.

He was scrambling circles in the bag on my back. How long until he decided to leave it and what would I do with him then?

Heron's hand slipped on the rope. I gritted my teeth, hoping he could catch himself, but his other hand slipped and then he was spinning through the water away from the boat. I kicked off from the hull, kicking hard to chase after him.

From over my head, a blue streak shot out in front of me, gaining on Heron. Nasataa. I knew he was going to slip out of that bag soon!

I swam as fast as I could with one arm and two feet, fighting to get to where they were. The dark currents of the river between us obscured everything. That was good, right? If anyone was looking out from the deck of the boat, they wouldn't see us in the water. But they would definitely see us if we poked our heads above the waves.

I found Heron in a huddle in the shallow water next to the shore. He was careful to keep his face underwater, but his arms were wrapped around his head.

If only I could talk to him. Nasataa was running circles around him as if he could communicate that way, but I knew that this wasn't good. I'd never seen Heron like this before. Had he been injured and I didn't know it?

I popped my head above the surface, choking on the water silently. I was getting better at that. The boat was already long gone. I watched the stern slip around a bend in the river. There was no one else here. I could try to find a different boat, but I didn't think Heron had that in him right now. I needed to worry about him.

I ducked back under the water and found Nasataa gulping down minnows as he swam circles around Heron. Well, at least there was one problem solved.

Gently, I took Heron by the shoulders and pulled him up out of the water, ripping the path from his mouth.

"Can you walk?" I asked.

He nodded and I took his hand and drew him into the forest, choosing a place where the bushes were thick. At least we'd have some cover. Nasataa followed me, snapping at bugs and picking them out of the air. He was having more success than we would have. My own belly rumbled hungrily. I hadn't eaten in more than a day and that hadn't been very much.

"Heron," I said as soon as we reached the bushes. "Are you okay?"

He nodded, but he was rubbing his eyes, his face lined with worry.

"What's going on?" I asked him.

"Seleska, I just feel lost." He paused. "I came out here with Vyvera to find you – to make sure you were okay and could come home safely, but the farther we go, the farther we are from home. And Vyvera's dragon died and with him our chance of quick escape, and now she is gone, too. Without her, we don't know where we are or what we're doing. Neither of us has been off the islands – not since we grew up. We don't know what to do or how to handle this place. I know she quoted that prophecy and I know you promised her we would keep going, but this feels like a fool's errand."

"We're only a day away from the place she drew on the map. Remember, it was just two more days past Tinlin City."

"That was when we were under a boat," he said, looking grimly at the forest ahead.

I swallowed, following his gaze. I had a knot in my throat thicker than the rope we'd been holding. What was I going to do if Heron lost hope? I didn't know what I was doing either, but I didn't see what other choice we had than to keep going. It would be even worse to turn back now.

"Don't give up on me, Heron."

"I'm not giving up, Seleska. I just … I just don't know what to do."

"Follow me," I said. "I'll keep you safe. I'll keep everyone safe."

And how was I going to do that? He seemed to share my uncertainty as he laughed grimly.

"I came out here to keep you safe, Seleska."

"Well, Heron," I said coyly. "How can you do that if you leave? You know I need a lot of help to stay out of trouble."

He laughed, smiling for a moment before his smile faded again.

I stood up on my tiptoes, wrapped him in a hug – though my arms barely reached around his bulky muscles – and kissed his cheek.

"Stop worrying so much," I said. "How can you enjoy an adventure if you spend the whole time upset to be on it?"

He smiled again, this time a little more genuinely.

"Let's build a fire and get dry before we continue," I said, but if I was being honest, I was worried. I needed Heron to be strong and stable. I wasn't sure I could do the task Vyvera had left me and keep his spirits up at the same time.

Chapter Twelve

It felt good to be on land again. Nasataa ran from bush to bush and flower to flower, stripping anything edible from the surrounding countryside. He was happy and vibrant and totally unconcerned about our situation. I loved that about him.

Heron, on the other hand, had me worried. He was lost in thought and even though we could talk again, he'd hardly said two words to me. At first, I felt worried, trying to think about how to cheer him up but soon that worry faded into irritation. We were all in this together. I didn't force him to come along on the adventure, so it wasn't up to me to make everything fine for him. I'd just have to ignore his moodiness and carry on.

The brush along the river was thick enough to mask us from the water but sparse enough that we traveled through it easily and I was beginning to think we should have spent the whole trip on land instead of clinging to boats in the water.

A dull *thunk* like a paddle hitting a hull caught my attention and I dodged quickly behind a clump of bushes, motioning for Heron to join me. Nasataa swarmed in, running up my leg and back to perch on my shoulder with his chin on top of my head. He was starting to get too heavy for that maneuver.

We peered anxiously at the water as a boat emerged from a bend in the river, skimming quietly along the water. A stack rose up from the center of the boat, black smoke billowing from it as the paddle worked against the current. Was that some kind of magic? It didn't look like it. If anything, it reminded me of Heron's forge.

I turned a questioning eye to him but he shook his head.

At the tip of the prow, a pair of Bubblers leaned against the rail, searching the water with their gazes.

"I don't know why you are so set on this course, Atura. Your father will not be impressed by the capture of a single foreigner. You should set your sights higher." A female voice drifted across the water as clear as if I had been on deck with her.

I froze at the reply. This voice, I recognized. It was the Bubbler who had threatened both Nasataa and me, first when I was imprisoned in a cage and then when I was rescuing him in the tent.

"This foreigner is different, Sanala. I will do anything to catch her and the abomination. This foreigner is an enemy prophesied from times past. Defeat her, and our land will soar. Fail, and she will ruin us."

The other woman barked a laugh. "You're being overly dramatic. What could ruin the Rock Regime? We have stood proud for generations. The other nations think we are barbarians. And since we destroy any trespassers, they don't know our secrets."

"Secrets!" Atura spat. "If you think that rough mechanics and burning hunks of rock is a great power, then you have no idea what magic can do. We can't afford to lose it. What would you do without bubble patches?"

"Find some other way to breathe underwater. If we can power boats with rocks, who knows what other things we can do. I swear, Atura, the rock you swallowed made you so salty I can hardly stand you sometimes."

Most of that was nonsense to me, though Heron's eyes grew big when they spoke about mechanics. The one thing I did catch was the one that made me most worried. Atura really was hunting me. And now she had passed me on the river and anywhere I went, I would have to worry that she was already there.

And her friend was right. She was too salty! She should have taken my advice about becoming a better person.

"Do you realize what this means?" Heron whispered when they were finally past.

"That Atura is an ill-tempered frog who should have listened to me when I told her to be nicer to people?"

His eyebrows rose. "I meant the rocks. Somehow, they power those things with rock. Do you have any idea what that knowledge could do for our village? We could make so many things. I wonder what kind of rock it is."

Well, at least someone was pleased. My delight didn't last. Ahead of us, the boat pulled into land.

"We'll do a land sweep here before carrying on. Check everywhere."

Chapter Thirteen

"Hurry," I whispered, scrambling behind Heron as we raced to find cover. He hid under a tangle of roots in a small overhang. He was partly hidden from view by the fallen tree and a man-sized rock that had left the hole in the bank when they fell, but would that be enough?

Nasataa wrapped himself around my neck, sensing our worry. I tried to signal to him to get into the bag, but he ignored me, only tightening his grip. Well, it wouldn't matter if I could breathe underwater if I couldn't breathe at all! I tugged at him, trying to release his grip.

Heron grabbed me, ignoring my battle with Nasataa, and pulled me behind him, pushing me as deep as he could into the dip formed by the roots. He stood in front of me in a crouch, clearly ready to take on any attackers. He was like a wall of man and muscle.

Long moments passed as we heard the rustle of feet in the bushes and the occasional call back and forth from the search party. I was already sweating, tension filling me. Why had they picked this exact spot to look for us? I wished Octon was here to shed light on it. Or Vyvera. She would have known. Instead, it was just me and Heron trying to figure this out for ourselves.

There was a snap as someone trod on a branch nearby. I froze, icy fear stabbing down through me as I waited. Out of nowhere, Nasataa let out a chittering sound. Was that his fear leaking out?

"This way," the searcher said, pushing through the trees toward us, his red clothing – tight at wrists and ankles – billowing around him as he hurried.

I shrank back into the bank, trying to be small and unnoticed. Heron shrank back to, pressing me into the dirt. He was too big to be doing that! My lungs squeezed at the pressure of his weight and I gasped as Nasataa gripped tighter still.

It's going to be okay, Seleska, I told myself. You will be okay. And so will Heron and Nasataa. But it was hard to have a cheerful outlook with our enemies closing in on us.

The Bubbler was searching, eyes up in the trees scanning the branches, then down to the ground looking for hiding spots. He kicked at dry leaves and sticks as he came into view from around the roots of the fallen tree and the huge rock.

"You find anything yet?" another Bubbler asked as the first one stepped close to where we were huddled.

All he had to do was look in this direction and he'd see us. He looked over his shoulder as he replied.

"Not yet. It's a wild dragon chase. Atura needs to get over herself."

He spun back around, and his eyes widened as he spotted us. He opened his mouth to call out, but Heron was faster. He leapt from our cover like a dragon flying through the air and pinning the man against the tangle of up-turned roots from the fallen tree. He snatched a rock up with one hand while the other gripped the man's neck, pushing him backward and strangling his cry of alarm. Fast as lightning, the hand with the rock came up and smashed him over the head.

No! My hands flew up, covering my mouth. I'd never expected to see such violence from Heron. Not mild, gentle Heron who always took care of people!

The Bubbler fell lifeless to the ground, his eyes rolling back and a terrible caved-in dent in his head. I turned to the side and threw up noisily.

"Not feeling well, Malan?" the second bubbler asked, turning around the big rock. His eyes widened as he took in Heron, still clutching the rock. He brought up a long spear, jabbing it toward Heron.

Heron ducked silently to the side, but another jab shot toward him just as quickly. You couldn't fight a rock with a spear.

Soundlessly, horror filling me, I leveled my staff and lunged from the cover of the overhand, darting toward the Bubbler. The blade of the staff slid into his back so easily that it almost didn't feel real. Heron leapt forward, clamping his hand over the man's mouth before he could scream. His other hand wrapped around his neck, holding the Bubbler in place while he thrashed on the end of my bladed staff.

When he was finally still, we were both out of breath, looking in wide-eyed horror at what we'd done.

"The others going to notice that they don't come back," I said eventually. I thought I might throw up again. What had we done?

When I longed for adventure, I'd never realized that I would have to become a terrible person if I went on one. Heron hadn't even wanted to come – and yet he'd been so good at killing. All of his instincts had been perfect. I turned my wide-eyed gaze to him, my hands shaking so badly that I nearly dropped the staff.

"Do you still have the Bubbler clothing that we were wearing before?" Heron asked, breathlessly. After a moment of my wordless gaping, he clarified. "In the bag?"

"Y – yes," I said, pulling the bag off with shaking hands and digging into it to draw out the red flowing clothes and the goggles and masks.

"Put them on over your clothes. We'll pose as these two."

I complied, shaking so badly that I could barely dress.

"You'll have to put the bag on under the clothes. Can you do that?" Heron pressed.

I nodded, still unable to speak as I did as he directed. They'd never buy it. We didn't look anything like them.

"We won't go on the ship. They'll know it's us in a heartbeat," Heron explained as he dressed. "We'll run into the woods and let them just see glimpses of us. They don't have time to chase deserters. Right?"

I was shaking so hard that I could barely hold the staff. Heron took it, wiping the blade on the clothing of the fallen Bubbler. I flinched at the act. That wasn't right. Hadn't he suffered enough indignity?

"Seleska?"

I was still staring at the blood on the clothing where Heron had wiped the blade.

"Seleska!"

I looked up then to meet Heron's fiery eyes.

"If we're going to live, we need to do what we have to do. Do you understand?"

I nodded, but my heart felt so empty that I was afraid it might never fill up again. My eyes were huge as they drifted back to the dead men.

"And Seleska?"

I looked back at Heron. He moved so that his bulky body blocked the sight of the dead. His eyes were still blazing with fire.

"Heron?" My voice sounded weak even to myself. Nasataa slid down the neck of the billowing clothing and I felt him wriggling into the bag.

"I think that before we risk our lives again, I should give you something."

"What?" I asked weakly.

"This."

He leaned down and kissed my lips so gently that I was afraid it might not be real. Afraid I might be just making it up to distract myself. But it was his warm smile that filled up my empty heart again when he had finished.

"Now, follow me. We need to be seen, but not recognized. Got it?"

"Got it," I said, glad he was leading since I was sure I was far too light-headed to lead anything.

Chapter Fourteen

Having the worst and best moments of my life in quick succession really had my mind spinning.

Heron quickly dragged the bodies of the two men we'd killed into the overhang and pulled at the roots above them, shaking enough earth to lightly cover the bodies. It wouldn't keep predators out, but a quick glance in the overhang wouldn't show anything had happened here.

He nodded to me as soon as he was done, and we pulled the goggles down and the masks up before striding through the underbrush.

"Hexon? Malan?" I heard someone nearby call. "Where did the two of you go? We're done our grid and ready to move on! Hexon? If you make me late for dinner, I will take yours, too! Malan?!"

Heron aimed us toward the calling voices, careful to stay far enough into the trees that you could only see glimpses of us between them.

"There you are!" Someone called. Heron increased his pace, kicking it up to a light jog and I matched him stride for stride.

"Where are you two going? Bubbles from the deeps!"

"What are they doing?"

"We aren't going to wait while they run around in the woods!"

"Do you think they saw something?"

"No! It's only them and that's not even their search sector."

I followed Heron, not looking to the right or the left as we hurried into the woods, still following a generally parallel path next to the river. This was a crazy idea, but it was the best one I could think of.

When we passed the last of the Bubblers, I recognized her as Atura. She paused, watching us with narrowed eyes.

"Bubblers! Under Article XVSI, I demand that you stop and return to your posts or orders will be issued for your arrest," she called, but she looked confused as we continued on without stopping. We were too far away and going too quickly for her to catch us on her own, even though she ran a few steps toward us. My only worry was that she might recognize my staff. I didn't dare look back to see if she did or if she was following.

I was winded and aching when we finally lost them, huddled together in a dip in the ground breathing heavily. We hadn't heard anyone else in hours, but we'd kept running long after any sound of pursuit. And I was still worried that one of them might pop out from hiding and seize us.

"Do you think they're following us?" I gasped.

"Running?" Heron asked. "No. In the boat."

I nodded. "We must be getting close."

"There was a waterfall," Heron said. "We had to find the base of the waterfall. If we stick with the river, we'll find it eventually."

I nodded, exhausted. We shared a brief hand squeeze of support and started again, this time at a brisk walk. What I really wanted to do was talk about that kiss. Had he meant that, or was he just distracting me? Had he followed me for more than just to keep me out of trouble?

But now was not the time for that. Now was the time to keep my eyes open and prevent disaster.

The sun was beginning to sink through the trees when we heard the roar of the waterfall in the distance. We'd made it. It was there, on the river somewhere and we'd found it!

There was no discussion about food – we didn't have any and it didn't make sense to complain about that. No discussion about whether to go looking for the waterfall in the dark. That could mean death if we lost our footing nearby. No discussion of a fire – after all, we were still being hunted.

Instead, the three of us curled up together in a heap at the roots of a tree and listened for the enemy. If only we could last until morning without being found. We were so close. If we could only hold out a little bit longer.

My last thoughts – before I drifted into a troubled sleep – were about how to keep everyone safe.

Chapter Fifteen

I woke to the sound of a twig snapping, sitting up with a start. I'd fallen asleep with my head on Heron's broad chest and he was still breathing deeply beside me. Nasataa scrambled up into my arms and I hugged him tightly, petting his head as I looked around. It must have been a stray animal or something like that.

Now that it was light, our situation was dawning on me. We'd followed the sounds of the waterfall, alright. There it was, just upriver of where we were, pouring down into a wide basin below that narrowed into the river. Through the dawn light, rainbows danced across the base of the waterfall, and spray filled the air, slicking the rocks all around.

It would have been tranquil and idyllic under any other circumstances.

But up on the cliffs at the top of the waterfall, and down at its base, stone structures stood hard and unyielding. They bulged with bubbles of glass at the sides and sticking out into the water of the river. On the tops of the structures and all around them, Bubblers swarmed – working, guarding, unloading boats from the docks there or loading them with goods. In the distance, long cables brought goods up and down on a wide platform from the structures at the top of the cliffs to the ones at the bottom.

Of course. Why would they let a waterfall interrupt river trade when there were other options? But this complicated things. According to Vyvera's map, we needed to get to the base of the waterfall. But to do that, we'd have to pass all those Bubblers guarding these very falls, not to mention the other workers and boat Captains dotting the docks and surrounding the river.

My mouth went dry and I tried to fend off feelings of bleak despair as I cooed to Nasataa.

"Who is a good boy, then?" I cooed to him. He flamed my fingers excitedly. "Who is great at sleeping when I need to flee danger? You are! Who keeps everyone warmer at night? Yeah, that's you, too! Who flames Seleska but doesn't hurt her? Yeah, that's you, too!"

And then my own words hit me. Nasataa's flames were so magical and strong that he could flame things underwater. Maybe that was the key here. What if we swam under the water and created a distraction, setting one of those docks or boats on fire? Would that be enough to get Heron an opening to make it to the base of the waterfall without a mask? We could swim underwater to where he was and join him then. It seemed like a bad idea, but what other idea was there?

I glanced back at my sleeping friend. He seemed so innocent when he slept, lashes framing his closed eyes and all those powerful muscles relaxed against the tree. But he was big and powerful. I needed to remember that. He hadn't hesitated to help me when those bubblers attacked – and he'd been almost scary in his attack.

Another twig snapped.

Well, that was strange, wasn't it?

I put a hand on Heron, grabbing my staff with the other and was about to shake Heron awake when Atura stepped out from around the tree we'd slept under.

"And there you are," she said.

I scrambled to my feet. She held a simple rod and it looked so innocent, but I remembered those rods from when we fought those Bubblers underwater. The bubbles they had produced had been toxic.

"And here you are," I said. "You know it's very impolite to sneak up on people."

She stepped forward, stepping right over Heron's sleeping form as she closed in on me. I took another step backward toward the water.

"Is it as impolite as spying?" she asked, one eyebrow arched. Her goggles were on her head and her mask was hanging around her neck. I hadn't seen her face so close before. She was my age and pretty, with the same copper hair and brown skin that Octon had. And she was about my height, too.

"Who is spying?" I asked. "I'm sure you don't mean me. I'm just running for my life. Next time that you want to keep someone around, you shouldn't try to burn them alive. Or attack them in a tent. That's not how to gain new friends, you know."

Her dry expression told me she didn't care for my tips.

"You're a fool. You ran straight to a Bubbler Outpost. This is the heart of my power. I will offer you and the abomination up as the final payment for my rock."

"Payment?" I asked, bending down quickly and scooping up a river rock from the shore. "You mean these things mean so much to you that you have to pay for them a bit at a time? I hate to break it to you, but I just took this one for free."

"Ignorant fool. That's nothing more than a river stone. The rock I swallowed gives me a power you can't dream of."

"Really?" I asked, feigning my best impressed look. "Care to tell me about it?"

"I don't see a patch in your hand," Atura said. "Which means that when you back up you won't be able to stay submerged for very long. I doubt you have any left or you wouldn't have been running on foot. And that means you'll be easy prey."

"I don't see a patch in your hand, either," I pointed out.

She grinned and it wasn't a pretty grin of a happy girl. It was laced with malevolence.

"I don't need patches – or at least I won't for much longer. That's the power my rock is giving me. And with the last payment, that power will fully mature and I will be able to seize my destiny."

"You know that you sound evil, right?" I said. "It's phrases like 'seize my destiny' that really hammer that home."

She sneered. "Oh no, foreigner. I'm not the evil one in this story. There are prophecies about me and how I will return magic to the world."

I froze. There were prophecies about *her?*

She laughed. "I bet you didn't know about that."

Chapter Sixteen

It didn't matter even if those prophecies were real. Prophecies didn't matter. What mattered was what people did or didn't do about them. So, what if there was some kind of prophecy about Atura? So far, she'd shown that she was an awful person. If that was what following a prophecy did to you, then maybe it was an evil prophecy. I gritted my teeth and held my staff out as Nasataa moved to crouch on my shoulders, his head above my own. Hopefully, he didn't burn all my pretty hair off if he decided to flame!

I braced my staff as Atura held out her rod. There was a snapping sound behind her. There must be more Bubblers back there waiting to pick up where she had left off.

"Now," she said, "what setting should I use? Do we just want to incapacitate you, or shall we make it hurt, too?"

"We? Are there two of you in that big head of yours?" I asked, but I was getting worried. You weren't really the hero of the story unless you had a great rival. But Atura might be more rival than I could handle. And we were in her world fighting on her ground.

"I think we'll make it hurt."

Her grin made my belly flip flop, but whatever she was going to do was stopped when a heavy stick slammed down on her head. She fell forward, her eyes closing as she hit the sand.

Heron stood over her with a tree branch in his hand. "I don't think I killed her, and there might be more of them."

I nodded, hurrying forward to check Atura's pockets and pouches. Yes! She had more patches. I grabbed them from the pouch on her belt and handed them to Heron.

"You're going to need these if we're going to swim under that waterfall," I said, seriously. Then my smile turned teasing. "My mama always said that when you were grown, you'd 'have to beat admirers off with a stick'."

He snorted. "I don't think she qualifies as an admirer. She stepped right over me like I wasn't even a threat."

He checked her breathing and then pulled her up a bit further on shore. I looked at her speculatively. He'd brought up a good point. *Why* had she ignored bulky Heron to go after Nasataa and me? Was she just that single-minded? It was a puzzle. Maybe that rod of hers made her so powerful that she hadn't seen him as a threat.

"We don't want her to drown," Heron said as he pulled her behind the tree. "And we don't want to be discovered too soon."

I looked around. I didn't think anyone had seen us. While the area was well-populated and busy, we were still too far away to draw much notice.

"Take that rod of hers," I said. "I don't know what it does beyond those clouds of red that made Octon so ill, but she must think it will pack a real punch."

He nodded, gripping the rod with one hand and holding a patch in the other.

I licked my lips. I wasn't so sure about this part. It was easy to be an adventurer when adventure came to you but hard to step out and choose danger.

"Ready to go?" he asked as I adjusted the straps on the bag and made sure Nasataa was secure on my shoulders.

"Not yet," I said, giving him a saucy grin before placing a hand on his chest and standing on tiptoes to give him a light kiss – an exact mirror of the one he'd given me.

He opened his mouth to say something and I grabbed the patch from his hand and slapped it over his mouth with a wink.

"Now I'm ready. I think I like being the only one who can talk."

His lowered brows told me he didn't agree, so I gave him my sweetest smile to soften the teasing and then leapt from the bank into the river, letting the water sweep over me, swirling my hair out behind me as I faced into the current. The kiss hadn't just been for him. It had been for me. I needed to know that I was still okay. That there were still people who cared about me.

Okay. It was time to focus and to get to the bottom of that waterfall. Time to stop worrying over Atura and letting my heart flutter over Heron. Who was with me?

Nasataa!

I had one solid ally.

Heron joined us in a blur of bubbles. He'd pulled his goggles and mask on, but when he got close enough, he winked at me. He wasn't taking the teasing to heart. Or maybe he even liked it. With one last smile, I led the way through the current toward the waterfall. My ankle was feeling a lot better. I hadn't noticed it healing, but it took my weight without protest now.

After an hour of fighting the current, I was especially glad for a healed ankle. It still felt like we'd barely made any ground despite struggling against the water. We had to resort to walking on the bottom braced against the current instead of swimming at all. Somehow, I hadn't realized that the waterfall and then the narrowing of the river would make the current so strong. At this rate, it would take us all day to get where we were going.

I wasn't wrong. By noon – or what I thought must be noon – we were in the center of the channel, but we were only just reaching the wide basin and the river was getting deeper and deeper. On either side of us, boats were docked or coming and going from the docks. The old plan I had of sneaking in to light one of them on fire was looking more and more ridiculous. Good thing Heron had that patch!

But now our slow progress was worrying me. The longer we were in this pool beneath the falls, the more chance we had of being discovered, or of Atura recovering and alerting people to our presence. I exchanged more than one worried glance with Heron, but there was no other choice. We were already exhausted from fighting the current and our only choice was to keep going forward. Even Nasataa had grown tired and retreated to the bag where he sent me sleepy images of shells and fish.

I tried to keep the images I sent him comforting, but I was getting a bit worried.

When the first party of Bubblers leapt into the water just behind us, my worry turned to fear.

Chapter Seventeen

How were they catching up to us? We were pushing against the current as fast as humanly possible, and yet the Bubblers moved faster than we could, even though they were swimming. I exchanged a frustrated look with Heron.

They were gaining so fast that we wouldn't be able to outrun them. Very soon, we would have to take a stand.

There was something strange in the water ahead, blurring it in a cloud of bubbles. What could be causing that? It had slowly been growing louder and louder as we approached.

Wait. Was that where the waterfall plunged into the basin?

We were getting close. If we could only reach that cloud of bubbles before the Bubblers reached us, we could hide in the cloud of bubbles.

My heart raced as I pushed harder, jamming my staff against the river bottom and pushing off as hard as I could.

Heron grabbed my arm, whirling to spin his body and then squaring off, rod raised.

We were out of time.

I spun, too, Dragon Staff raised.

There were five of them. Three held rods and two more held something that looked like a handle attached to a smooth stone with a glowing rune cut into it. The rocks with the runes pulled them through the water. They were like super-rocks.

Was that the secret to their speed?

I could use one of those!

Heron fiddled with the handle of his rod, like he was trying to activate it. He'd better be careful with that thing. If he hit us with those bubbles, this attack could backfire on us!

The Bubblers ahead pointed their own rods at us, shooting huge bubbles toward us in an array of colors – purple, green, red.

I braced for them. We couldn't outrun the bubbles racing toward us and we couldn't maneuver around such a big cloud. My only option was to pop every one of them before they hit us.

Staff outstretched, I clenched my jaw and slashed my staff through the water as the first bubbles arrived, popping them as quickly as I could, as far away as I could. With the bubbles bursting downstream, their effects couldn't reach us – but only if I kept popping them in time.

The water dragged at the staff and working it under the waves took all my strength. If I could sweat underwater, I would be slicked in sweat at the sheer effort of trying to move the staff at any speed underwater. Maybe slashing wasn't the best idea.

I changed my approach, jabbing at bubbles as they came toward us, but my heart was pounding. There was no way I could destroy them fast enough this way, and Heron still hadn't figured out his rod.

Fortunately, they'd fired from too far away and into the current instead of with it. The last bubbles coming toward me stalled and then floated the wrong way, leaving the Bubblers on their tail to dodge their own weapons. I slashed toward them with my staff, but with those super-rocks they used were just too fast!

Each super-rock was steered by one Bubbler while one or two passengers hung onto the handles and shot bubbles from their rods. They were formidable. They outnumbered us. They were faster than we were. They were better armed.

Frustration filled me as they swept in so close that they could almost touch me, and fired a second cloud of bubbles. I fought to pop them all, but one bubble landed, searing the skin on my arm. I screamed underwater, my eyes searching for Heron.

He had given up on trying to use the rod as a bubble weapon. I caught sight of him at the same moment that the group of two Bubblers reached him, firing off their rod. He waited as bubbles floated toward him. He wasn't even trying to slash them. What was he doing?

My attackers had passed, but they were probably circling around to attack me again. And yet, I couldn't peel my eyes off of Heron, wondering what he was thinking frozen like that.

And then he moved so quickly – quick despite the weight of the waters! – and clipped the pilot of the super-rock on the back of the head, grabbing the handle of his super-rock. He held on with one hand, dropping his bubble rod and reaching out to snatch the mask and the patch from the mouth of the shocked Bubbler beside him.

The Bubbler dropped the handle like it was hot, kicking upward toward the surface.

Yeah! Right on!

But now my enemies were back again, and I wasn't a muscle-bound blacksmith's apprentice who could hit people over the head and steal their super-rocks.

As the bubbles rushed toward me, I slashed and hacked wildly. Two more small bubbles hit my legs, searing them with painful agony. They burned – even underwater they burned! I screamed and then forced myself to stop screaming, biting my lip instead.

Something grabbed me from behind. An arm as thick as a tree.

Heron!

I adjusted my staff to keep it away from him as we streaked through the water. He nodded to the handle, indicating that I should hold on and the minute I turned and grabbed it with my free hand, he reached out with his spare hand.

What was he reaching for?

In the whirling bubbles, and flowing underwater cloth filling my vision, I barely managed to see my enemies beside us holding their own super-rock.

Heron had seen. His arm wrenched the rod from the nearest Bubbler, turning it on him and whacking him so hard in the face that he lost his grip and spun away from the super-rock.

Heron leaned as far out from our super-rock as he could while still gripping it, aiming another blow at the face of a second Bubbler. I wanted to watch, but I realized suddenly that if he was fighting, I should be steering us.

I kicked my legs, using them like rudders to keep us aimed toward the wall of bubbles and churning water where the waterfall entered the basin.

We were almost there!

I felt Heron tugging madly at the handle, but I couldn't look at him or I wouldn't be able to steer. Hopefully, he was holding on!

Hopefully ...

We plunged into the wall of bubbles and my vision and hearing were filled with nothing but the chaos of water crashing into water.

Chapter Eighteen

I'd never been under a waterfall before. I wished I could have enjoyed it instead of fearing for my life.

Nasataa spun loops in the bag, agitated by the roaring falls and Heron's tugs at the handle bothered me. I couldn't see more than his arm holding the handle and a blurry outline of the rest of him. Even that was hard to see well. What was he doing that was causing so much turbulence?

And what would we find here? We'd been sent to go under the waterfall, but where did we go from here and what could be found that would be different from what the Bubblers could find?

If only Vyvera were here to tell us.

And then we emerged from the flurry of water.

I hadn't even realized I was holding my breath until the water was suddenly calmer and I could breathe easily again. Heron bucked and I looked back to see him fighting against the last two Bubblers. One of them had his rod wrapped around Heron's neck and he was pulling, pulling, pulling against it.

Horrified, I spun, trying to get closer and ease the pressure from Heron's neck, but my movement only seemed to make it worse as his face darkened a shade.

Help! Help us!

I cried in my mind. If only we were in the ocean where friendly Blue Dragons could hear our cry or even a passing squid.

Please! We will die!

As I thought that, a second pair shot out of the wall of water, waving their bubble rods. And then a third. And then a fourth. And then a fifth.

Oh no.

Please!

I was nearly in tears now.

Something bumped my super-rock and I looked to see we'd hit the rocky wall of the cliff behind the waterfall.

And there was nothing here. Nothing at all.

I gritted my teeth. Well, Seleska didn't just give up. Seleska didn't just stop fighting when there didn't seem to be hope.

I let the super-rock stay against the wall, and I twisted to face outward, my feet behind me getting leverage from the super-rock. I'd have to aim this attack carefully.

I aimed with my Staff and then jabbed it as hard as I could. It slipped under Heron's flailing arm into the body of the man strangling him.

I knew I'd hit him hard when Heron fell forward, nearly knocking into me as all his fighting energy propelled him forward. His arms reached for me and he clung to my waist, his legs hanging limply, like he'd lost the strength to do more than cling for dear life to my waist.

I jerked the staff, trying to free it, but instead, it shook my enemy on the other end like a fish on the end of a spear.

He fell free after long seconds passed, but a ring of Bubblers was around me now and closing in while my back was to the wall. They raised hands and rods.

This was it.

They were going to finish us off. I gritted my teeth, flinching.

Here it came.

But they were waiting for something. One of them looked behind him as if what he was waiting for was about to emerge from the bubbles.

I tried one last plea.

If anyone can hear me, please, please, this is my last chance. This is Heron's last chance. This is Nasataa's last chance. Please, don't let us stand alone. Stand with us!

I didn't know who I was hoping would help us, but I nearly cursed when I saw who our enemies were waiting for.

She shot from the wall of bubbles like an arrow from a bow.

I knew it was Atura even with her mask and goggles on. It was impossible to mistake the confident arrogance of her stance for anyone else. Impossible to miss the laughter as she saw me surrounded and helpless.

Please.

Well, if it was time to die, I wasn't going to cower. I held my chin high, ready for what was going to happen.

And then the sound of rock scraping against rock filled the water and light lit the faces of my enemies from below.

I looked down into bright light.

And then something seized my foot and dragged me down, so fast that I couldn't catch a breath in the rushing water. I clung to my staff and the propelling super-rock as the waters rushed around me and the light grew ever nearer.

Chapter Nineteen

I was pulled into an underground cave through a crack in the rock. Rocks bumped me as I was dragged through a cavern. I hoped Heron was holding on!

The thing holding my leg was long and thin like the tail of a dragon, with translucent skin and glowing bones and veins. My eyes were practically bulging out of my head when we were finally dragged above the surface of the water into a cavern filled with air. Waves of green light – something living or a plant? I couldn't tell – rippled along the dark walls.

And in the center of the room was a glowing portal like the ones I had come through under the water to get to the land of the Rock Eaters. Only this portal was huge. It lit the room with rippling aqua light so that while we were breathing air, the light made it look like we were still underwater.

Heron ripped the patch from his mouth, choking and gasping for air as the tail of the giant creature in front of us released its grip on me.

We swam to the rocky ledge and climbed up. As soon as the super-rock propeller hit the air it stopped pulling. I kept a hold of it. I didn't want to lose something so useful.

But my eyes never left the creature in front of us. Not even to check the wounds on my legs – burning worse now that we were in the air – or Heron. I could hear him gasping beside me. That would have to be enough assurance of his safety.

Towering above us, a huge creature – like a chameleon but translucent and glowing – towered above us, a single eye looking down at us. Something crunched under our feet as we walked toward him. Something like glass.

It took a moment for me to realize that it was scales. Translucent scales. Vyvera had said that the Troglodyte could not move because he was dying. Was that what I was seeing? Scales shedding as this magnificent creature died?

YES.

I gasped as pain filled my brain along with a voice so overpowering and heavy that it shot through every nerve of my body at once, like they had been hit with a thousand blacksmith hammers.

OUR TIME IS FADING. WE MUST SEE THE CHOSEN ONE SUC-CEED BEFORE WE FADE FROM THIS EARTH.

Vyvera said we needed to restore magic to the earth – not that I had any idea how to do that.

YOU MUST BE DELVED.

That horrific nerve-smashing feeling shot through me again and I froze in the pain of it. Behind me, I heard the rocks cracking. The Troglodyte wasn't opening them up again, was he?

YOU ARE FOUND ACCEPTABLE.

There was the sound of a stone crashing. Heron crowded in close, taking the super-rock propeller from me so he could hold my hand.

OUR ENEMIES GATHER. NOW THAT I HAVE REVEALED MY LOCATION THEY WILL BREAK INTO THIS CAVE.

And then what?

AND THEY WILL KILL ME. BUT FIRST I WILL SERVE MY LAST PURPOSE. I HAVE FOUND THE CHOSEN ONE AND THE GUARDIAN AND VERIFIED YOU ARE THE ONES WE HAVE WAIT-ED FOR. YOU ARE CAUGHT, CHILD, IN A WAR YOU KNOW NOTHING OF. A WAR BETWEEN THE TROGLODYTES AND OUR ANCIENT ALLIES, THE DRAVEN.

MANY CENTURIES AGO, WE EACH BIRTHED DESCEN-DANTS – FOR THE TROGLODYTES IT WAS THE DRAGONS, OUR BELOVED CREATURES. FOR THE DRAVEN IT WAS THE MANTI-CORES.

BUT WE WARRED ON THE OTHER SIDE OF THIS WORLD. THE DRAGONS FLED AND WERE NEARLY DESTROYED AND WE – THEIR ELDERS – HID IN THE DEPTHS OF THE EARTH. OUR

DAUGHTER, HAZ'DRAZEN HAS FORGED A NEW AGE FOR THE DRAGONS.

BUT EVEN AS SHE ESTABLISHED THEM, OUR ENEMIES HAVE BEEN WORKING. THEY ESTABLISHED THEIR MANTI-CORE RANKS. THEY FOUND THEIR OWN HUMAN ALLIES. PASSED ON THEIR OWN PROPHECIES. GAVE THEIR OWN RELICS.

THEIR PROPHECIES SPEAK OF THEIR HEROES: HANCOR – THE DISSIDENT, ISKARIS – THE USURPER, STARIE – THE CHO-SEN ONE, HALBAZAR – THE CONQUERER, APEQ – THE ARTIFI-CER, ATURA- THE GUARDIAN, FELROC – HER CHARGE. MANY MORE. EACH WORSE THAN THE LAST.

SELESKA, THEY ARE OUR SHADOWS, OUR OPPOSITES, THE TERRIBLE DARKNESS THAT MIMICS OUR LIGHT. WE HAVE TRIED AND TRIED TO STOP THEM BUT EVERY VICTORY HAS ONLY DELAYED THEM. YOU ARE OUR LAST CHANCE TO TURN THE TIDES TO US. TAKE BACK THE MAGIC THEY STOLE FROM US.

But wasn't magic fading from the earth?

There was another loud boom from behind me. Heron gripped my hand pulling me toward the bright portal.

THEY WANT YOU TO THINK SO. IT IS NOT SO. THEY HAVE BEEN STEALING IT ALL, STORING IT UP TO SECURE THEIR VIC-TORY.

IF THEIR BABY MANTICORE – FELROC – IS PLACED IN THE HAROC INSTEAD OF NASATAA, ALL WILL BE LOST FOR THEY WILL HAVE WON. YOU MUST STOP THEM. GET NASATAA THERE. GET HIM TO THE HAROC.

The what?

FIND THE HAROC. IT IS THE SEAT OF LIFE.

There was a final crash and then the floor shook, and light poured into the darkness, blinding me. Heron tugged me backward and I followed the leading of his hand, trying to blink away the bright light.

A sound like a garbled scream – long and gut-wrenching – filled the air and then my vision cleared and what I saw made no sense at all.

Strange creatures, ridden by Bubblers in flowing red, swarmed into the cave, light streaming in all around them. With long harpoons, they speared the Troglodyte, throwing one after another after another, like knives driven into a sleeping goat.

What was his name? How could I honor him if I didn't know?

I AM KO. I WAS KO. NOW, FLEE DAUGHTER!

I gasped as a harpoon lanced toward me, clattering on the rock as it missed me by inches.

"Come on," Heron said, pulling me the last step toward the stone ring portal.

"We need to pick the right symbol," I said, my throat tightening as translucent ooze ran down the sides of the groaning Troglodyte. His ancient scales shattered under our feet as we stepped up onto the rim of the portal.

Heron turned to me to say something but his eyes went big and then pain lanced through me – pain so powerful that it knocked me forward and the last thing I remembered before blackness took me were a pair of powerful arms wrapping around me and a voice slowly fading away as it spoke in Heron's husky voice.

"Don't Seleska. Stop moving or it will kill you. Just hold on. I'll get you to help. Just hold on, please!"

Episode Four: Bubbles of Hope

Chapter One

I woke from a troubled sleep, surfacing briefly to see a dark face and a pair of worried eyes. Heron.

"Try to stay still, Seleska. Try not to move. I'm getting you help."

"Heron," I murmured.

"Please, sweet honey, keep breathing. Don't stop. I'll find you help. I promise."

He shouldn't be so worried. Everything would be okay. I felt fine. A bit numb, maybe. And it was hard to breathe. But I didn't like seeing him so upset.

A little face poked out from around his head – little Nasataa standing on Heron's shoulder. I wanted to laugh at the absurdity of a Blue Dragon so close to Heron who had always been prejudiced against them, but something choked me up and then everything faded to black again.

I thought I could hear voices echoing outside the darkness of my own head.

"What is this place, little guy? It seems ... oh!"

There were scuffles and then nothing and then I wasn't sure how much time had passed until my eyes were flickering open again.

We were stepping out of a cave into the light and the vista before me would have taken my breath away if I wasn't gasping for it with every jarring step of Heron's feet. He carried me in his arms like a child, clutched close to his chest as he walked. His head was thrust forward as if he was doing the most important task on the planet and wreathed around his head like a crown sat Nasataa, his head also thrust forward to look at the amazing scene spread before us in the golden half-light.

Black peaks of volcanoes rose up from the landscape like dark dragon teeth – the tops of some of them broken from the violent splashes of lava that spurted up unexpectedly. The slopes falling away from the jagged peaks were sleek with black sand and stunted trees.

We were stepping out of a cave mouth toward a very strange feature, a double-peaked dormant volcano with a wide shelf between the peaks. A massive arch made of stone – a dragon biting its own tail - was centered on the middle of the shelf. Its proportions were so gargantuan that a dozen dragons could have flown through in a cluster without breaking formation. I tried to follow the twist of the tail, which dipped down into the ground before rearing up again into the dragon's mouth, but one edge of the pattern became another seamlessly and my eye lost its reference point as it twisted in on itself. A winding road led to the arch from the low land below, like a ribbon twisting through a ring.

My eyelids fluttered and blackness took me, voices fading in and out again.

"Can't you see he's a baby dragon? Doesn't he get access to your precious Dragon Door?" A pause. "Dawn's Gate? Whatever. Will you help her or not?"

Murmuring. Voices. Then Heron again.

"Are you just a scaly sack of bones or are you going to help?"

Frantic voices and then a calming one. I blinked and my eyes opened to see a pair of new eyes looking into mine. The rest of the face was hidden by cloths wrapped around face and head, but those eyes – those lizard-like eyes blinked at me in golden disapproval.

"There is no passage for humans without a special edict. You must be – weighed."

"There isn't time for any of that," Heron said as my vision began to narrow again. His voice sounded panicked, on the edge of tears. "Can't you see she's dying? Can't you see that there just isn't time?"

"We have many questions."

There was something hard on my back. Had I been set down?

Yelling.

Fear.

Something warm curled on my chest while loud threats and the clash of steel met my ears.

A whisper in my ear and a hand gently cupping my cheek.

"Please don't die, Seleska. Please hold on. I will return to you."

And then blackness. Nothing but blackness and darkness.

I sank into the darkness, letting it encircle and embrace me. I wanted nothing more than to sink deep, deep into that velvet softness. But why had Heron sounded so distressed? I should be fighting this to help him. I should be trying my best to get back to him, not giving in to all my instincts to rest.

I fought against the constraints of sleep, but the heaviness in my chest was too difficult.

Nothingness stole me away.

Chapter Two

I woke to quiet murmurs and this time, I didn't let myself sink back into the depths of darkness. I forced my eyes opened and clawed at the cloth covering me. I had to get up. I had to find Heron and Nasataa.

Something snapped – an irritated sound. A hot tongue licked my face and all I could see were blue scales and gleaming eyes as Nasataa lunged and jumped at my face, licking my cheeks and nose. His breath smelled like a campfire.

"Ungh," I said.

Selesa! Selesa!

"Nasataa," I moaned. "You're okay."

And of course, he was. That little fellow could survive just about anything with his adventurous spirit and his big heart. I smiled weakly at the thought as I fought against an unwilling body to sit up. Something heavy clamped my legs to the ground.

"Easy, there!" a strange voice cautioned me. "You've been through a lot. You can't get up yet."

My eyes blinked at unfamiliar light. Everything around me except Nasataa was shades of white. Gleaming white, soft white, dappled light.

A face emerged swathed in white cloth and a deep white hood. All I could see was a pair of reptilian eyes. I froze.

"Don't be afraid. That's the usual reaction I'm afraid. You'd think it would be more comforting to see one of your own – someone who speaks your language and yet it's always this. Shock. Fear. Turmoil. It seems so unfair."

"Why is it unfair?" I murmured. The white around me wasn't soft exactly, but it was warm and the feeling I was getting from that radiating warmth was a good one – as if I was feeling my body being knit back together.

"Because the Ilerioc are humans – sort of. We started as humans – Haz's portion of the debt to Haz'drazen."

"Who are Haz and Haz'drazen?" I asked tiredly. This seemed all so unreal. The warmth, the whiteness, the chatter of bedtime stories. Perhaps I was dreaming.

Nasataa crawled in close and tucked himself under my chin, promptly falling asleep. I wouldn't be sitting up now that he was asleep there. That was okay.

The Ilerioc – if that's what this person was – looked shocked. Or at least as shocked as you can look when all you are showing the world is your eyes.

"Haz was the great king of humans. Long, long ago he made a treaty with Haz'drazen, the Queen of all Dragons. Both of them led dwindling groups of people fleeing the wars of the Ifrits and their allies. Both needed each other to rebuild and find safety. To seal their treaty, the dragons agreed to send a specific number of dragons based on their population every year to serve as transportation and defense for the humans. This practice is still carried on today in the form of a lottery. The humans sealed their side of the bargain a different way – by gifting the dragons a set number of humans to keep forever as servants. Their children were bound by the same agreement – to serve. In theory, it was a better idea. No need to send more humans every year, just a one-time pledge. In practice, there are more of the Ilerioc living with the dragons than there are dragons living with Haz's people – the Dominion. The dragons were wiser, it would seem, in how they chose to keep their bargain. More than that. Dragons keep their dragon traits because only a few are sent to the humans every year and they are born and raised among their own kind. Whereas we Ilerioc, are raised and born among dragons. Our humanity is – lessened. We have become our own race. Our own people. Our own tribe."

"That sounds so unfair," I said. My mouth had been opening slowly more and more as this Ilerioc spoke, in surprise and then in horror. "You are never free? You are born to serve and die serving?"

He shrugged. "Sort of. And yet, the dragons have never forced us to stay. We are not forced to serve. Theoretically, we could go at any time – back to lands where we are misunderstood and feared. To people who have gone on without us. To cultures we find barbaric and disgusting. It has never made sense for us to go. So, we have chosen to stay."

"But you are servants?"

"We serve. And we are gifted things for our service."

"What kinds of things?" I asked, still confused.

"The fruits of our labor – food, clothing, artifacts, metals, woods, all the things required of life."

"So, you're paid?" I asked. "That doesn't sound like a servant."

The Ilerioc shrugged. "I don't know. I have not left the lands of Haz'drazen. What would I know about these things? What do you know about them?"

Apparently not much. I'd assumed that no one would willingly serve someone else when they could be free. I still wasn't sure I believed him.

"And what do you do to serve?" I asked, hesitantly.

"I translate language for those who come from outside – like you. The dragons do not like to speak into the minds of men – except for the Purples, but they are a strange lot. And so, they require someone else to speak. I am that someone."

"Oh," I said, trying to smile. I didn't want him to think that I was unfriendly and judging him – though I was. "And do you get many visitors from outside?"

"Few make it through the Dawn Gate, but even there, interpreters are needed to send those unwanted away."

"I guess I should feel lucky to be here," I said brightly.

He nodded seriously. "You should."

"Oh." I paused a long moment. "My name is Seleska."

"I know."

"Oh." I felt a little foolish. I didn't know his name.

"Nasataa told me," he said.

"And your name is ...?" I asked.

"Tereoc."

"Can you tell me where Heron is, Tereoc?" I asked brightly. I didn't want to make him upset when I had so much information that I needed.

"Was that the man who brought you here? He is in custody, awaiting judgment."

I gasped. "What can I do to get him free?"

Poor Heron!

Tereoc chuckled. "That has nothing to do with you. You are meant to stay here and to heal. See how three white dragons ensconce you? Their strength heals you. You would do well to remember that and be grateful."

"Oh," I said, "I am very grateful."

Curiously, I looked around, realizing he was right. What I had taken for walls and floor and even furniture were actually the scaly legs and winding tails of three large White Dragons. Their breathing bore me up and down in a gently rocking sling and the strength of their healing power was what was radiating into me and healing my injuries.

"And now you must rest. You were stabbed through the chest. Healing from that takes time – even with all this extra help. Sleep, and we will speak more in the morning."

I was worried about Heron. I should be getting up and trying to find him. But even as I said those things to myself, exhaustion overtook me, and I drifted off to a dreamless sleep.

Chapter Three

This time when I woke, there was no one there but Nasataa and the white dragons, and all of them were asleep. Moonlight spilled over the sleeping whites, filtering through their semi-translucent manes and rippling over their reflective scales. They were truly beautiful.

I slipped my legs out from under a tail, surprised to see that I'd been stripped to my underthings, but if the puckering scar in my side was anything to judge by, my clothing was probably ruined.

Nasataa slept beside me, curled in a ball with his small head resting on his back haunches. Was it just me, or was he larger? I stroked his head, feather-light so as not to wake him, and assessed my situation.

I felt buoyant – light, energetic, ready to go. Nothing ached or hurt or grumbled in my body – even my ankle had stopped throbbing, and it had been hurting for days. The burns on my legs were gone. Only that one huge scar remained.

Oh well.

Scars made you look tough and capable. I liked that.

I could be tough, right? And every day I got just a little more capable.

So, Nasataa was well. I was well. I turned my attention to my surroundings. I was under a dome woven of something thick and white like a hard lace patterned in flower-like sprays. Inside, the three dragons lay all tangled around one another. Through the lace, the moonlight made patterns of flower shadows across our bodies.

I stood carefully, slipping around the tangled dragons as best I could, on-ly climbing on them when necessary. They didn't seem to notice, and soon I was at the edge of their nest, looking out through the white lace.

My breath caught in my throat. The moonlight spilled over a world of vertical heights and waterfalls, gleaming on the tumbling falls, outlining the heights in silver gilding. It was velvet shadows and silver gleams, shushing winds and the scent of jasmine. It was the things dreams were made of. I could barely believe I was there at all.

Was this the world Nasataa was born for? Not the rough and tumble fun of island life or the stark violence of the land of the Rock Regime, but this glorious, angelic place? Was this the world Ramariri was meant for – the world he had denied himself when he saved me?

My eyes stung as I let them travel from one raised platform wreathed in lace to the pool nearby where flashing fish leapt into the sky. They skittered over hanging flowers made of carved stone where tiny lights told me that people slept inside the hanging flowers. They caressed the forms of the mountains, strong and shielding, surrounding a white, water-filled city far too pristine for an island girl like me.

I felt strangely sad at the sight, like glimpsing something beautiful you could never have or smelling some delicious food you could never taste.

Reluctantly, I drew back and felt along the stone-lace wall. There must be a door somewhere.

I found a table first. A small round mirror stood above it. On the table, a pitcher of water and a bowl and a stack of clothing awaited me. I washed hurriedly, slipping on the leather pants, flowing shirt, corset, and spiky-heeled boots. They looked a lot like my old ones – almost as if someone had recovered my things and tried to replace them.

Biting my lip, I made my way around the back of one of the dragons and finally found the door. It opened to a narrow platform and then nothing.

My breath caught at the drop into darkness.

"Dragons don't need stairs."

I startled at the sound of the voice and from the side of the platform – hidden when you looked straight out the door, a man holding a Dragon Staff an awful lot like mine, stepped forward. He was dressed in tidy white leather, cut into breeches, a vest and various straps buckled with silver. Under the vest, even his shirt was a pale color – hard to discern in the moonlight. Just like the first Ilerioc to greet me, his head was wreathed in white cloth, so that nothing but his eyes showed – and they shone in the night like a cat's.

"I'm sorry," I said, realizing I'd been staring for too long. "I don't know what I expected, but it wasn't a guard. I'm Seleska."

"You're both under guard until we sort you out," he said. It was strange how easy he was to understand – no accent. And shouldn't he have an accent? When I'd come to the island, everyone had an accent – a lilting cheerful accent. And the Rock Eaters had that slow, drawling accent. So why didn't it seem like the Ilerioc had one?

"Nasataa hasn't done anything," I protested. "He's innocent."

"I meant both pairs of girls and dragons." He said it like it was the most obvious thing in the world.

"Both ... what?"

His reptilian eyes narrowed on me at the same time that Nasataa bounded out of the room and out to the narrow platform, leaping into my arms. I cuddled him close, letting my cheek rest on his head and listen to his purring sound as the Ilerioc answered.

"You arrived, carried by a dark islander and with a baby Blue Dragon. Our guards were stunned. They were even more stunned when less than an hour later another girl – about your age – arrived with her own baby Red Dragon. Both she and your islander claimed the dragon is a Chosen One meant to restore magic to the world. Both she and your islander claimed that you are the dragon's guardians. We didn't know who to believe, so for now, Prince Taoslil allowed both of you to enter the Lands of Haz'drazen. You will be sorted out soon by the dragons."

"Can't you ask the Troglodytes?" I asked. He looked surprised.

"Would you believe that the other girl asked the same thing?"

I felt the blood rushing from my face. Who was this other girl?

He sniffed. "The Troglodytes have not chosen to comment on this."

"Don't you have mind-reading dragons?" I pushed.

"If you mean the Purples – well, they don't just go around reading minds without a good reason. That's not how they operate."

"This seems like a good reason," I said reprovingly. I would have crossed my arms if I wasn't holding Nasataa.

"Even so, they cannot tell."

"Well," I said.

"Exactly. We're in a conundrum. Who do we trust? Which story do we believe?"

"Were you the Ilerioc speaking to me when I woke up?" I asked. He didn't sound like a servant. He made it sound like he would be in on the decision while the other one had made it sound like he was basically just a plaything of the dragons.

He scoffed. "Tereoc? No. Don't let his strange ideas get in your head. He's too caught up in history."

"He said you were slaves."

His posture stiffened. "We have not been slaves for many generations."

"And if you aren't a slave, why didn't you tell me your name?" I asked, pouting. "That hardly seems polite. I told you mine."

He seemed startled. "I'm Jeriath, Top White of the Ilerioc Guard."

I smiled, teasingly. "And how did you get up here, Jeriath? I don't see any wings on your back."

He snorted. "I climbed the stairs. But don't even think about it. There will be orders to get you in the morning. You should go back to sleep and wait for your escort."

"With my friend in custody and Nasataa and I hanging in the balance you think I will go back to sleep?" I could feel my expression turning stubborn. And with good reason. I was going nowhere until someone showed me Heron and proved he was okay.

"I *think* that if you take one step toward the stairs, I'll have to stop you with physical force," he replied.

With a mischievous look, I stepped toward the edge of the platform until he gasped at my closeness, but he couldn't admit that he cared if I fell, and I hadn't looked down, so the height didn't bother me. In one graceful move, I sank down to sit with my legs hanging over the edge.

"I think I'll sit here," I said breezily.

"Suit yourself."

"And while I'm sitting here, maybe you can tell me where you thieves put my Dragon Staff."

There was no response to that or to any other questions until dawn lit the sky.

Chapter Four

It started with drums.

At first, I didn't even realize that they were drums. I thought it was just my beating heart, speeding up as the first rays of dawn lit the sky. Who was this other girl, and what would happen to me if the dragons chose her? Would Nasataa and I just be left to carry on in life – not a bad thing at all! – or would we suffer some kind of punishment for coming here? Jeriath – of course – said nothing. He simply stood and guarded all night long, ignoring my teasing and various attempts to get a rise out of him until, tired, I retreated into silence.

Nasataa was unconcerned about any tension between us or about our captivity in a lace prison. He dove and leapt, grabbing at my hair, chittering and doing tiny flips. I played with him half-heartedly, tussling him around and tickling him under the chin. It was dangerous on the edge of the platform – and I wasn't sure if Nasataa could even fly – but he was surefooted and quick, never getting too close to the edge.

When the drums finally started, he was curled up around my shoulders like the world's heaviest scarf, snoring almost as loudly as they were. He was starting to get too big for that position, the tip of his tail dangling down as far as my waist. I was going to have to get stronger shoulders if he wanted to keep riding on them. I was trying to hold off worry. Worry wouldn't help and I didn't like it when I was worrying. It made my belly hurt. A bright, cheerful spirit was a better tool than endless fussing.

I forced a bright smile on my face and held my head up high. I'd keep the smile on my face until I felt it for real.

I had expected dragons to arrive, but what I hadn't expected was so many. A swarm of the huge creatures started as dots in the distance near the great waterfall, but as they grew nearer, I could count twenty of them. What worried me was that a similar sized group took flight moments later, headed in a different direction. So. They were sending groups for both of us. Me and the other girl.

I tried not to tighten with tension, focusing instead on keeping my face relaxed and my smile in place. The drum was on the back of one of the dragons – or maybe it was just one of the drums. Maybe there was a drum for the other girl, too. An Ilerioc stood on the dragon's back, pounding the drum as they flew toward us. He must be very surefooted and very certain that the dragon wouldn't drop him.

The lead dragon – a huge Gold Dragon, led the way. Behind him was the drummer riding a Green dragon with two other Greens on either side. Behind them, a pair of Black Dragons carried a wide, white lace litter hanging between them. I didn't even look at the other dragons following. My eyes were glued to that litter, my breath hitching as I realized I was going to be riding in it.

I had not ridden high in the air since Vyvera strapped us in and Damokas winged his way into the sky. But we had been precious to them. And I had been precious to Ramariri when he carried my child self to safety. This would be different. Did these dragons care about whether we fell? Did anyone care?

And I was also worried that there was no sign of Heron. What had they done with him?

One dragon swept up from the back of the pack, a White Dragon bearing an Ilerioc with her hands full. She leapt gracefully from the back of the dragon onto the platform like she did that all the time. In her hands was a Dragon Staff and a strange headdress – wait. That was my Dragon Staff!

"That's mine," I said, severely.

"Indeed," she agreed, her reptilian eyes narrowing from behind the veil. Other than the head wrap, her white clothing was looser and lighter than the guard's was and I caught a glimpse of her skin – was it slightly green? How odd.

She handed me the staff and I took it with my eyes widening. They were giving me a weapon? But then again, was I going to try to fight twenty dragons with just this staff? Unlikely.

With care, she took the headdress and placed it on my head. It was shaped like an elaborate star made of stiff white lace, the points sticking out around my head and a tassel dangling down on each side of my face. It felt strange and bulky.

"You'll ride to the place of judgment," she said soberly, gesturing toward where the litter carried by Black dragons was hovering closer and closer to the platform.

It could only get so close. Even though it dangled on white ropes between the dragons, they couldn't get much closer to the structure and still be flying. I'd have to take a solid leap from the platform to the lace litter.

Oh. I didn't like this at all.

But what was the alternative? To be dragged like a child?

I liked that a lot less.

Gritting my teeth, I tossed the Dragon Staff onto the litter, stuck my tongue out in concentration, held onto Nasataa and took a running leap to the litter, landing awkwardly in the net. The heels of my boots caught on the lace and it was long moments until I caught my balance and settled in a cross-legged sit on the white lace. I was still shaking when I gathered up the Dragon Staff in one hand and reached up with the other hand to hold Nasataa tight against my shoulder and chest.

He'd slept through the whole thing, of course. Nothing bothered him.

I hoped he had a good reason to so relaxed. I hoped all my nerves would turn out to be over nothing.

"Seleska!" the Ilerioc guard called to me as I rose into the sky. "I think I will bet on you. You have a better sense of humor than Atura does."

Chapter Five

A tura?

Atura was the other girl?

And suddenly my biggest concern wasn't falling from this net. My biggest concern was protecting Nasataa from the one person who wanted him dead more than anything else. I gripped my Dragon Staff until my knuckles ached and my cheery smile turned into my mama whale face.

I'd seen a whale once from far away, out in the ocean and my father had told me a story about how whales only had one calf, and they protected that calf with their own lives, smacking their powerful tails to fight off any predators. If I had to smack someone with my tail today, I was going to smack as hard as I could. I'd practiced. I'd fought. I was ready.

Sort of.

It was hard – in all my determined stubbornness – to enjoy what should have been one of the most spectacular sights of my life. The dragon city lay all around me. None of it was built on the ground. Every structure was lofted into the sky, on pillars or bridges or long arms, suspended from wires or balanced nimbly on the edge of a cliff.

It was long minutes of silent brooding before I realized that the structures had a nest-like quality to them. Each structure was woven in white lace-like patterns. I still hadn't figured out what they were woven off, but someone had taken care with the work. The patterns were not random. They were flowers or leaves or the silhouettes of dragons.

Water was everywhere – so strange for a mountain range marked by volcanoes. The water flowed blue and flashing white in falls from the heights, through woven nests, and even from one level to another. It followed the small walkways weaving between some of the structures in rivers and ended in brilliant blue pools. Rainbows formed in the bright clouds at the bottoms of the falls and glinted off the pools. They seemed to linger in the air everywhere.

If I had imagined paradise, it would look like this.

And everywhere, there were dragons.

Dragons lined the mountains peaks, sat in the nests, darted through the falls. They spun and dove and leapt and soared. They rippled in every color and shape and size.

Except for Blue.

There were no Blue Dragons anywhere except the precious sleeping dragon on my shoulders. My brow furrowed. I could feel the loss – like a missing friend. And the song of the sea was gone. I shivered as I suddenly realized I had been missing it all along. All this water and no song.

Where were the Blue Dragons? Why weren't they here in this dragon city?

I gripped the Staff as we flew toward the highest peak in the range. It rose high above the others and at the top, where a waterfall fell from the peak, a rounded area had been carved, overlooking the city. It seemed important. The rock wall above the rounded area was shaped in a lacey star – like the hat they'd given me to wear. There must be some significance to that.

As we drew closer, I could make out shapes of dragons waiting in the rounded bowl. At their center, on a raised platform, a rainbow dragon sat, looking down over the rest like a mother. Like a queen.

Haz'drazen. I was going to see her. Maybe even meet her. My mouth felt dry and my tongue was swollen. What would I say? How could I plead Nasataa's case to this glorious monarch?

I wished that Halana and Renny were with me. They were so wise about these things. They would know exactly what to do and what to say if they were here. My mother would be leaning over my shoulder saying, 'Remember, Seleska, you must,' and there were would be a thousand things for me to remember. I missed her. If only I hadn't left the way I did before. They were probably worried sick about me.

If only I still had Heron with me, too. He was more level-headed than I was. He wouldn't put his foot in his mouth or say something people could misinterpret. Losing his company left a hollow feeling. I knew he was my best friend and that I liked having him around, but I didn't realize how much I depended on him to keep me steady.

I swallowed, forcing back tears. This was not the time for that. This was the time for steadiness and strength. With difficulty, I found my feet, standing in the lace net and keeping my feet under me. I would face them with dignity and strength.

No matter what.

Chapter Six

I was too small for this world.

I stroked Nasataa's scales gently as our litter came to land at a platform reaching out from the rounded bowl at the top of the mountain. It was clear I was meant to step onto the outstretched rock to exit the litter, but I felt so small compared to everything else.

Around me, my escort was all watching, their dragon eyes glittering, their wings flapping almost idly. They were all huge. And foreign. Ramariri had felt huge, but he had never been anything but loving and kind. Damokas had been large, too, but he had clearly been close to Vyvera and I hadn't felt concerned about him. Even the Blue Dragons had always been on my side, but here it felt different. I was surrounded by huge predators, all looking at me, and I felt small, vulnerable, and utterly alone.

Well – if I was the biggest one here, or the best one here, it wouldn't be much of an adventure, would it?

"All we're guaranteed in life is an adventure, Nasataa," I said, thrusting my chin out determinedly. I wasn't going to let them see me looking nervous. I gave him my most encouraging smile.

I leapt from the net to the platform and strode down it to where an Ilerioc was waiting at the end of the platform. Beyond her, dragons were arranged in ranks before their queen and a few humans in strange clothing dotted the landscape – as small and negligible as I was.

The Ilerioc turned before I reached her, leading the way through ranks of tall dragons, sitting on their haunches. Within moments, I lost sight of the queen's platform or anything else. I was dwarfed in a forest of dragons. They towered over me in every color of dragon – Gold, Red, Black, Purple, Green, and White. From the crusty hard scales of the armored Reds to the ethereal smoothness of the Whites, each dragon gleamed in the sun, snapping occasionally or snorting thick clouds of steam. Every instinct in my body told me to run or hide, but I kept my head high, walking with wobbling knees as I followed the Ilerioc.

When Vyvera first told me the prophecy, and when Nasataa and I were first saved by Blue Dragons, I thought it made some sense that he was special and that they needed us. But right now, standing between these powerful beasts – creatures that did not deign to even speak to me – I couldn't understand it at all. Why would they need us? What could they possibly need someone else to do?

And if Nasataa was so special, shouldn't these massive creatures be his guardians and not a small, fragile human who didn't even have any experience or power of her own?

I swallowed at the thought. I ached thinking about letting anyone else take my place with Nasataa. He was my little guy. He made me smile in the worst of circumstances. He filled my heart with joy. I'd give up any comfort to make him more comfortable. And yet ... wouldn't it be better for him to be raised by his own?

Nasataa stays with Seleska.

He yawned dramatically on my shoulder and shifted so he could rest his jaw on the top of my head. I almost laughed at his thoughts. Maybe he was attached to me, too.

Seleska! Seleska!

Well, I'd do what I could.

It seemed to take ages to cross the rock bowl between the rows of the assembled dragons. I'd seen more tails – some barbed, some sharp, some clubbed – than I could count and more glittering eyes and sharp looks than I'd ever remember – except for maybe in my nightmares.

And then the way opened up, and the Ilerioc led me to a lacey platform, raised just a foot above the rock floor. It looked like a wide, shallow nest and it was positioned so that anyone standing in it could be easily viewed by the queen on her own perch above. The Ilerioc led me to a spot a little to the right from the center of the nest and pointed dramatically to it before stepping a pace ahead of me and sinking to one knee.

Should I be bowing, too? Probably.

And yet.

I was a little offended by how I'd been treated. They'd taken Heron. They said my fate and the fate of my small dragon rested on their decision. My eyes narrowed as I thought.

I was Nasataa's protector and guardian. Guardians didn't kneel to potential enemies. Guardians stood strong and firm. I spaced my legs shoulder-width apart and settled into a firm stance, Staff held out and braced firmly against the ground and my other hand made a fist on my hip. I was the guardian of this dragonlet and I was powerful and strong.

Sort of.

Okay. Whatever came next, I was ready.

I looked up at the queen on her throne. Rainbows flashed along her bright scales, making it hard to look at her directly. But I thought that perhaps I saw the glitter of her eye looking at me. Was that a wink? Of course not. It was simply a trick of the light.

Beneath her, standing right below her throne, a magnificent White Dragon paced back and forth, shaking his mane from time to time as if he found waiting difficult.

Long minutes passed in silence and then the click, click, click of boots on stone caught my attention and I turned to see a girl of my height and size dressed almost exactly like I was – except that where my clothing was blue and white, hers was red and black. She shook out her long black hair – hadn't that been red before? How did she change it like that? – and her copper skin shone in the light. I wished I could show that kind of confidence. I wished I was that gloriously beautiful.

I swallowed down the disconcerting feeling that I was looking in a strange mirror. From her heeled boots to the Red Dragon baby on her shoulders, Atura was styled like my mirror image and the wicked smirk she shot me sent icy fear down my spine.

Chapter Seven

"I present myself and my charge to you, oh ancestor dragons!" Atura said boldly before her Ilerioc could even finish bowing and the bow Atura gave was elaborate. She held her Red Dragonlet before her like an offering. "I am the Guardian prophesied of old, and this is the Chosen One. As the prophecy says: *One born on distant island far from home. One brought to keep him safe, if he roam. One given as a strength to face that day. One who with her life for them will pay.* This dragonlet is the one born far from home in the Rock Regime under the Saaasallla's rule. I am that one to keep him safe." She shot me a nasty look. "This Blue Dragonlet is here to give his strength to Felroc so that Felroc may ascend and the woman carrying him will give her life to see this accomplished."

Oh no, I would not.

Fury bubbled up inside me. She had a whole speech prepared based on the prophecy and why she and her dragonlet should be chosen! And why Nasataa and I should die!

I'd been worried about doing the right thing for Nasataa and worried about Heron and she'd been planning this big old speech! Where had she even found a dragonlet? You couldn't just find one anywhere. And why was she fighting for this? I didn't even want Nasataa to be their Chosen One. It put him at too much risk – but what other option was there if magic was being stolen by an enemy.

Wait. Maybe that was it. Maybe somehow those magic thieves had manufactured that little Red Dragon to manipulate the Dragons to do their bidding.

My eyes narrowed and my grip on the Dragon Staff grew firmer as I watched Atura. Little snake.

The Ilerioc in front of Atura spun and intoned, "Queen Haz'drazen welcomes you and receives your offering of honor. And yet, a question remains. Two have washed up on the shores of our mountains – two who have no right to carry a dragonlet or involve themselves in our affairs. And yet, one of you is the one prophesied."

"Where is Heron," I demanded quietly. I didn't know any fancy words. I probably would have tried charm and smiles, but no one was greeting me or talking to me and I felt an edge of concern creeping over me and making me salty as the sea. No Blue Dragons to plead for us was bad enough, but they still held my ally and now they seemed inclined to be charmed by my adversary. I didn't want to fight for a role I'd never asked for. I just wanted Heron free and we could be on our way. And if the Manticores and Ifrits and Dragons all decided to have a huge war between themselves, what was that to us?

My Ileroc spun. "Show respect to the Queen."

"Respectfully," I said, trying to keep the bite from my voice, "where is my companion? He is innocent of any wrongdoing."

The Ilerioc's eyes narrowed. "Your companion fought our guards, demanding with violence that we take you in and save your life. He is a criminal – a needlessly violent man. His judgment is separate from this affair."

I gritted my teeth. Oh no. This was worse than I could have imagined. I looked around me and the situation I was in hammered itself into my brain. There would be no escaping this contest. I couldn't fight my way out – I might not even be able to get down from this mountainside on my own. And my best friend was locked in a cell.

I tried what I did best. I smiled charmingly and made my prettiest face.

"Surely, you don't really think he's a criminal."

Atura snorted loudly.

The Ileroc seemed unimpressed. "What I think matters not. What the queen thinks is the only thing that matters. Now, show some respect."

I bowed, sinking to one knee like the rest, but I gritted my teeth as I did it. How did you show respect to someone who did not deserve it? I hadn't asked for any of this and they were treating me and Heron like criminals. Meanwhile, they were treating Atura oh so nicely just because she had a pretty speech and the ability to lie through her teeth to get what she wanted. Fine lot of character judges they were!

Your objection is noted. The voice in my head was like a gentle whisper and I froze, looking up at the glittering eye of the Queen of Dragons. I could swear that was her. Beneath her throne, the White Dragon snarled something, punctuating it with a burst of flame.

The Ilerioc in front of Atura spoke to translate "We will ask our Elders, the honored Troglodytes to choose between these two."

Silence filled the air, and it dawned on me that every dragon was still – not just here in the bowl, but everywhere. The dragons flying below had found perches. Those already perched were still as statues. Not an ear flicked or tail snapped. They were utterly still.

Only gusts of steam still spurted from nostrils and mouths, filling the bowl with wisps of hot mist.

Long moments passed before the White Dragon snarled loudly and around me, dragons turned their heads up and flamed into the sky.

Uh oh. This didn't look good.

I looked to my Ilerioc translator. She was standing again, her knees shaking as she turned to me.

"The Troglodyte Elders," she said with a shaking voice, "for the first time in our known history, are silent."

Chapter Eight

"Maybe they are sleeping," I suggested. After all, they'd gone to a lot of trouble to get me here. You'd think that they would say something now. "Vyvera brought me to one of them but he died. I don't remember his name, but maybe one of the other Troglodytes will mention it when they wake up."

"Lies!" Atura hissed, shooting a viperous look at me.

Whatever I expected, it hadn't been the reaction around me. They weren't even listening to my words about Troglodytes or Vyvera.

Mournful songs felled the air as the dragons poured out their sorrow, flaming – almost constantly into the air in between their moans of despair.

I looked around me, edgy now at the change in atmosphere, recognizing the fact that one upset dragon could stumble at any time and accidentally step on me or sneeze and flame me to cinders. This was not a great time to be a human. Not at all.

What were they so upset about? Maybe I should have broken the news about the dead Troglodyte a little more gently.

There was a loud hiss from the throne and the flames slowly flickered out and the mournful song grew quiet. Smoke hung in the air above us – a reminder of the high emotions surrounding us in the dragon community. I felt like my emotions were twanging like a fishing rod with a bite. There was something incredibly unnerving about this many dragons upset.

I held Nasataa close as he yawned again. Oddly, the little dragon in Atura's arms was still completely still.

Silence. The whisper in my mind spoke again.

After long moments where the dragons twitched and shifted as if they were listening to something, the Ilerioc spun to translate.

"A decision has been reached temporarily. You will relinquish your dragonlet."

"Of course," Atura said, offering hers to her Ilerioc. "Whatever the Queen wishes is hers. My Felroc is pleased to serve."

My Ilerioc reached for Nasataa and I leapt to my feet, stepping backward and holding my staff out in a protective stance. They weren't taking Nasataa. I could see their emotions were high. I could see this meant a lot to them. But I didn't trust them with Nasataa. They might call him a criminal and lock him up like they did to Heron.

There was a hush around us and then Ileriocs rushed in from every side. I thought I might recognize Jeriath in one of the ones who rushed to surround me. They all carried Dragon Staffs just like mine, and they formed up in protective rings around both Atura and me.

I watched them, puzzled. I couldn't take on this many fighters if they wanted to take Nasataa from me, but they didn't seem to want that at all.

Atura's Ilerioc handed Felroc back to her and mine said calmly, "It has been determined that you will keep the care of the dragonlets ... for now."

Why ask for him if they were just going to let me keep him after all? I looked around me, confused and still on edge.

"It was a test," Jeriath whispered under his breath.

But had I passed it or failed it?

It was impossible to say which, as the interpreter spoke again.

"Prince Taoslil has determined you will need protection as this matter is decided. The Ilerioc Guard of the White has chosen to guard you. The Ilerioc Guard of the Red has chosen to guard your competitor. You will remain in their care as this next test proceeds. The Queen would like to take your measure and the measure of your dragonlet."

Well, that was better than taking him away. And at least Jeriath seemed to be trying to help a bit.

"The guardian of a dragonlet should not be cowardly," my interpreter said.

Fair enough.

"This next test will test your courage to see if you are made of strong enough stuff to care for a baby dragon."

Uh oh. That didn't sound good.

"You will remove those boots and give me your staff."

Reluctantly, I passed her the staff, quickly removing my boots. I didn't mind being barefoot. If I was being honest, I'd had it with these heeled boots. They could kick them off the edge of the falls forever for all I cared.

"This next task will be dangerous. You should not ask the dragonlet to do it with you. What if he were harmed?"

Were they just trying to trick me to take Nasataa after all? He clung to my neck so tightly that I choked a little.

"I will hold the dragonlet for you," Jeriath offered, his eyes sober. "I swear to you that no harm will come to him and I will return him to you when your task is complete."

Could I trust him? I bit my lip, thinking.

Across from me, Atura was easily handing over her dragonlet. I was pretty sure he was a fake somehow. How else could she give him up so easily?

I pulled Nasataa off my neck, cuddling him to my chest for a moment. "Look, I'll be back quickly, okay? But you need to stay with Jeriath. He'll take care of you while I'm gone."

Nasataa chittered, cocking his head to one side.

"I'll be fine and so will you, but I need you to promise to be good for Jeriath."

Nasataa flamed my hand. Fortunately, that didn't hurt me.

"No flaming him. No running away. No eating his head scarf thing."

Nasataa seemed to snigger. Or was that my imagination? But he leapt easily into Jeriath's arms, scrambling up to sit on his shoulder. Jeriath's eyes were wide. He was probably worried that Nasataa really would eat his headscarf. That made me want to laugh. I wouldn't put it past the baby dragon.

"Be good, okay?" I said, leaning over to kiss Nasataa before I followed the Ilerioc translator out of the nest and toward the cliffs overlooking the city.

I didn't like that part. Why did we need to be so close to the edge?

Atura's interpreter already had her stepping up an open-sided bridge that spanned the top of the falls. They stopped at the very center as we followed.

The mist of the top of the waterfall made the bridge slick and I was grateful not to be in those slippery heeled boots.

When I was side by side with Atura there was silence again.

I was beginning to realize that was when the dragons speak with their minds in the ways that we couldn't hear.

"At the determination of the Queen, you will leap off the edge of these falls to prove your courage to the Drazenloft of Haz'drazen. Fail, and your journey ends here."

Chapter Nine

Wow! If I'd wanted an adventure, then I really had my wish! Leaping off waterfalls so high that I couldn't see the bottom of them definitely counted as an adventure.

You'd think these dragons would be more concerned with the missing Troglodytes than with testing us, but their priorities were different than mine would be. Or maybe they were taking care of that at the same time using their silent mind speech.

My heart was pounding so hard that I could hardly think, my breath catching in my throat. I could breathe underwater. I could stay warm deep in the sea. What I could not do was survive enormous falls – or fly.

"You will leap on my count," our Ileriocs called in unison. Behind us, a growl rolled from the throats of many dragons, rumbling through the air like thunder.

My insides felt like water, my legs like jelly. I was going to throw up. I could just tell.

"Three."

Was I really going to jump? I wasn't suicidal! This was crazy!

"Two."

But if I didn't then I'd be branded a coward and they'd take Nasataa and who knows if I'd be able to negotiate Heron's freedom and ...

"One."

... and Atura would win. And besides, there must be some catch. They wouldn't really plan to have both of us die, right?

"JUMP!"

Atura leapt first. Skies and Stars, but that girl was better than me at everything! I couldn't let her beat me at this, too!

With a grimace, I leapt, too. I arched up, turned, spreading my arms and dove head-first.

I was going to die.

My heart raced in my throat – which was where it seemed to have lodged itself.

I was going to die.

My eyes streamed with tears.

I was going to die.

I thought that maybe I was screaming. Or maybe that was Atura.

I was going to die!

A white body with a filmy, translucent mane rose up through the mist of the falls from underneath me, hovering on powerful wings. It was coming up too quickly! I was going to hit it!

Ungh!

The white dragon bobbed in the air under me as my hands grasped at that mane, tangling through the tendrils of it to hold on for dear life. I couldn't hear a thing except my speeding heart. I tasted blood in my mouth and my head spun until I felt nothing but ill.

Who came up with this brilliant idea? Just jump off a ledge. That will sort everything out.

But it had definitely been an adventure.

We soared up through the mist of the waterfall, the White Dragon dashing into the sky and me clinging for dear life. I expected him to level off at the rounded mountaintop where Haz'drazen held court, but instead, he climbed high in the air, speeding toward the other end of the city, plunging through clouds and burst of bright sunlight.

I should have been scared.

Instead, exhilaration filled me. I was alive. And I was riding a dragon. With no safety gear, no one to guide him, nothing but the dragon and me and the bright air whipping around us. We sped toward the sun and then, just like I had, the dragon arched upward and spun into a downward dive.

I might have been screaming. But if I was, it was in sheer delight.

There was no way I was holding on. I was holding his shoulders, of course, but that wouldn't have stopped me from falling. We were just falling together in the same direction. The dragon plunged to the far end of the city and just when I thought I might be dashed to the ground, he dipped under me, catching my weight.

I was laughing so hard and I couldn't stop.

This!

This was the kind of adventure I'd been longing for. I was riding a dragon through the clouds, our exhilaration feeding off each other so that my joy was mingling with his and back again.

I could hear his throaty chuckle mixing with my whoops of delight as we plunged through the city, close to the ground. His tail tip flicked a pond and his wing slapped at a dragon leaning too far forward as he tried to catch a glimpse of us.

I giggled when he barrel-rolled, flicking his tail teasingly at a group of young dragons in a nest.

This was glorious, perfect, fantastical. I was running out of words for it.

Who was this magnificent, fun-loving beast? Here I'd been thinking the Whites were all stuffy protocol-followers.

Oh, we do like our protocol.

I shrieked in delight at his voice in my mind. I thought they didn't like doing that.

We don't. But I like you. You're different. And I taste the shadow of another mind. A Gold?

Ramariri! My beloved dragon savior.

I knew that one. He was a salty old dog. He saved you, did he?

He was wonderful. The best of dragons.

I felt a mental chuckle ripple through me, and I tried to hold onto the sensation. It was like laughing through your soul. My smile was ear-to-ear with excitement and if I could have smiled more, I would have.

And the voice of the Blue – I taste that, too. He is powerful.

And precious.

And that, too.

And who was this White Dragon who broke all custom to speak to me? And to save my life – I should thank him for that.

No thanks necessary. We were both playing our parts in the ritual and for some reason, the Ilerioc's decided to take you on despite no support from the White Dragons. That intrigued me, so I offered to catch you. Now I know why. Your good spirits are infectious.

Who is saying so?

I felt his mental laugh again.

I am Taoslil, son of Haz'drazen, Prince of Dragons. And your friend. Whatever happens in these trials, you will have a place in my nest.

Well, that was comforting. But what about Nasataa.

Nasataa has always been welcome here. He is one of us.

I felt bubbles of hope welling up in me, tickling my brain with promises of safety, comfort, fun and most of all – of exhilarating flights through the clouds and rainbows of this ethereal place.

When we landed back on the platform to the fountaining cheers of the dragons around us, I couldn't wipe my grin off my face.

Not until I saw Atura already standing there, arms crossed and boots back on. She'd beat me back. Would that mean something?

Chapter Ten

I could hardly believe how quickly we were hustled away after Taoslil dropped me onto the rock floor. I had barely caught a leaping Nasataa and fished my hair out of his playfully tugging mouth and retrieved my Dragon Staff before my Ilerioc translator was rushing over.

"Another test will be arranged," my translator said. "But first, the dragons know the fragility of dragonlets and humans. We will feed you and make sure you are rested before the next challenge."

I glanced at Taoslil. He was approaching the throne of Haz'drazen, already distant and looking the other way. There would be no help from him on knowing what to do next.

Fear not. I have chosen to speak for you. Let the Ileriocs take you for rest.

I obeyed, nodding to my translator and following her as she led me back to the edge of the cliff. This time, she steered me to a narrow staircase cut into the rock. My heart did flip flops as we approached the stairs, but I had no real reason to fear. Hadn't I just leapt from this cliff and lived? Though, in fairness, that had all been Taoslil. My heart soared at the thought of our flight. I was never going to forget that.

Neither will I. I had no idea humans were so entertaining when you found the right one. It explains a lot about my brother.

His brother? But he didn't say anything more and it took all my concentration to follow my translator down the narrow, steep steps. I was glad I hadn't put those boots back on. On a whim, I'd left them on the ground where I'd tossed them. In a time so long ago that it was hard to remember, I'd wanted those boots. Now, I just wanted to get all of us out alive.

The guard I'd been assigned crowded around us, but we didn't have to go far. A short flight down the steps led to a landing and a door cut into the cliffs. The translator led me inside.

"This is Ilerioc property, so please show respect. We offer you the hospitality of our home for a brief respite."

The room she opened had a long row of windows carved in the rock wall, looking out over the city. On low tables, food and drink were heaped and chairs pulled up, but it didn't look like it was usually a dining room. It looked like it was usually used for something else. As if reading my mind, she explained.

"This is usually a waiting room for those waiting to seek the ear of Haz'drazen. Today, please stay only in this room and the small lavatory through that door."

I nodded in agreement, hurrying to the lavatory. I had been wondering if they had those here – they must, but I hadn't been offered one and things were getting dire. When I emerged again, Nasataa chittered in my ear and looked across the room to see my Ilerioc guard arranged around the room with Jeriath at the door. He nodded to me.

At the table, two strange people sat, watching me as if they were waiting for me to join them. They were not Ileriocs. Their heads and faces were uncovered and bare and one of the men – an ancient worn looking leathery man – wore his hair long with small braids interspersed through his gray locks. Feathers and beads were woven into the braids and his chiseled face was rough with day-old growth. Both men wore close-fitting black leathers with colorful scarves tied around wrists, elbows, and waist. One – a golden-haired man – had golden scarves and the old man's scarves were purple.

"Hello," I said uncertainly, placing Nasataa on one end of the table. He promptly dove at a platter of meat, gulping it down in huge mouthfuls. He should be careful. I tried to shoot him an image of himself laying on the ground moaning to show that he'd get a belly ache, but he ignored me.

"My name is Gerond Carthauler," the man with the golden hair said with a smile. "Are you Seleska and is this Nasataa?"

"Yes," I said, uncertainly, helping myself to water and food. Whatever they had to say, they would have to say while I ate. It had been days since I'd had anything to eat and my belly was rumbling audibly.

The golden-haired man smiled. "I am a Dragon Rider of the Gold – an ambassador from the Dominion. I watched your testing today."

I tried to smile around a mouthful of food, nodding to let him know he could keep speaking. I was more interested in the food.

"The Dominar sent me here to witness your arrival. She saw in a dream that a young dragon would arrive with an inexperienced protector and that this dragon would be the key to saving the world."

I looked up at him sharply and he smiled. I swallowed down my food hastily so I could speak.

"Then why are you speaking to me now? You saw that the dragons have not determined who the real Chosen One and Guardian are."

"Ah, but we are here to lend the help of the Dominion to the true Chosen One."

"And how do you know that is Nasataa?" I pressed.

"The Dominar's dragon told her to watch to see who was caught by his brother – the Eldest Prince of Dragons. And that was you. It was our sign."

"Oh," I said, feeling foolish that I had nothing better to say. "Umm, thank you. It's so kind of you to offer help, but I don't know what you can –"

"We're offering you a mentor. Someone to teach you about dragons and help you in the middle of all of this," Gerond said.

"Oh, I'm sure you have better things to do than to help me," I said, my face heating. Gerond seemed like a very important person and it made me feel incredibly uncomfortable to think of myself being a burden to him.

He chuckled, "Oh, I definitely do." He clapped the old man on the shoulder. "But this is Hubric Duneshifter, and he doesn't have anything more important to do at all, do you, Hubric?"

Chapter Eleven

Hubric snorted, his leathery features crinkling into what might have been a grin or even a snarl.

"Speak for yourself, Gerond. I've never needed anyone to do my speaking for me."

"I'm not sure anyone really wants to be my mentor," I said, helping myself to more fruit as Nasataa grabbed an entire roast chicken, circling around it with snaps and snarls and then grabbing a leg and shaking it like he thought it still needed to be killed. "My last mentor died when her dragon was killed and the one before that died saving my life." I tried to keep my tone light, but there was a lump in my throat. "Can we just be friends without a mentorship?"

"No," Hubric said gruffly. "And I don't die easy, so you won't be getting out of this so easily."

"Do you also breathe underwater? Because you might have trouble keeping up if you don't." I said, making my eyes large but trying not to show that I was laughing inside. The old fellow was all gruff and growls and I could just tell he was a huge softy inside. I could probably tease that out of him given enough time.

"I do not. But keeping up will not be a problem."

"What a pity," I said with my most innocent look. "We spend a lot of time underwater. I suppose you'll need a lot of time to sleep though, won't you?"

"Sleep?"

"Don't old people sleep a lot? Old Janny in the village spends most of her time sleeping or drinking soup."

The snarl he made was a combination of disbelief and irritation. I hid my grin behind a huge slice of melon.

"I am not so old as that!" he said when he was finished sputtering.

"It's just I'd hate to see you wasting all your precious time mentoring squirrels and trees while I'm underwater. That hardly seems fair. Maybe you deserve a better person to mentor?" I batted my eyelashes innocently. I didn't need a minder. And I didn't like the idea of putting yet another person in harm's way.

He snorted. "Nice try, little girl. I'll have you know that we have a way around the underwater part – devices that make it possible to breathe underwater."

"Like the Rock Eater's patches?" I asked innocently.

His eyes narrowed for a moment and then he laughed. "I'm going to like you. I thought my last two charges were challenging, but you're going to keep me on my toes, aren't you?"

"I don't know what you mean," I said, smiling broadly. I was beginning to like the old fellow. "But, if you really want to help me, you can start by getting Heron free."

"Heron?"

"My friend. He saved my life, but the dragons are holding him as a prisoner."

"Well," Hubric started to say, but he was cut off by a rumble in the ground beneath us. We all paused, listening.

The rumble intensified, growing deeper and heavier by the moment. Was that an earthquake? There were legends of those in our village – horrible events where the foundations of the world shook and moved. No one knew what caused them. The Elders said that their grandparents had felt one once. It shook down every home on the island.

"What in the –" Gerond began, but I was already moving.

There was a basket with a cover nearby. It wasn't my bag, but it would do. Frantically, I filled it with as much food and bottles of water as I could stuff into the basket while Nasataa shook the chicken for the last time and then leapt onto my shoulders.

This time when we ran, I wasn't going to be without food. I hated being hungry and thirsty all the time.

Hubric was on his feet first. He gripped the handle of a short sword at his waist and I grabbed my own Dragon Staff, ready to go. Even with our quick reactions, we were hardly even ready before the Ilerioc Guard of the White closed in around us.

"We need to head lower into the mountain while we can," Jeriath said as our guard formed up. "Those are our orders."

"You'll keep the girl and baby dragon safe?" Gerond asked urgently.

"We will. And the Ilerioc Guard of the Red will keep the *other* girl and dragonlet safe. We don't know which of them is the Chosen One and his guardian. We must be cautious."

Well, I felt a lot better knowing that they were protecting Atura. Ha!

Gerond nodded briskly and hurried toward the door and I found my eyes watching him leave. He was a stable presence and I hated to see him leaving just when things were getting dangerous.

"Don't worry about Gerond," Hubric said gruffly. "He always lands on his feet."

"What about you?" I asked, challengingly.

Hubric barked a laugh. "I always land on *someone else's* feet."

Around him, the Ilerioc Guard chuckled under their veils.

"Come on," Jeriath said, leading us to a mural at the back of the room. He touched a button and it clicked aside, revealing a doorway and stairs leading down. "We have to hurry. I don't know what is going on, but my instructions are clear. I am to move you to the lower levels and await further instructions."

As he took the first step into the doorway, the ground shook again, throwing him against the wall. It was all I could do to keep my own feet. What was happening out there? It wasn't an earthquake, was it?

I hadn't realized I'd asked that aloud until Hubric answered.

"I don't think it's an earthquake or even a volcano erupting. I think it's something else – a debt long unpaid. A reckoning coming due."

And at his words, I couldn't help the shiver that slid up my spine.

Chapter Twelve

Two steps after we walked through the door, Hubric took the basket from me gently, whispering as we walked.

"I know the temptation to keep what you can get, Seleska, but this is going to slow you down. You already have your hands full guarding that dragonlet, don't you think?"

Reluctantly, I let it go. I did have Nasataa to take care of. He was right about that. I reached up to stroke his head with a finger as Hubric set the basket down on the ground and we followed Jeriath and two other Ilerioc Guards down the stairs.

But I kept glancing back at it as we walked. Hubric made sense, but I didn't like leaving it behind. It felt like I never had enough anymore. Right now, I didn't even have shoes. I'd left those boots up top on the cliffside.

Snap, snap, crunch.

Nasataa's little voice sounded distracted and he moved nervously over my shoulders, shifting his weight constantly as I hurried down the steps.

Crunch. Snap.

"It's okay, little guy," I said gently, but I was more worried by his thoughts than I wanted to let on. Was he okay? That was a strange thing to say and he wasn't adding any images to clarify what he meant.

Hubric watched me wordlessly as we hurried down the steps, like he was making a list in his head of everything we were doing. I felt my face grow hot at the thought. Did he think I wasn't good enough guard for Nasataa? Honestly, who wouldn't?

I was untaught and untrained.

And I was young. Hubric could probably fight in his sleep and he had a lot of life experience.

But I wasn't about to let that get me down. I was the right person to take care of Nasataa because I loved him the most and because I'd never leave him or let any harm come to him as long as I had strength in my arms and breath in my lungs. That brought a confident smile to my lips. If I needed to learn to be a great warrior woman to take care of my little flamer, then that was what I'd be.

I liked that as a nickname. Flamer. What do you think Nasataa?

Flamer. Crunch. Snap.

Yeah! He liked it!

The stairway shook again, and I stumbled down the last step into a crowded landing that I hadn't seen because of Jeriath blocking the path in front of me. My feet slipped as I struggled for balance on the slick rock floor of the landing and stumbled headlong into red leather and loud cursing. I grabbed at the other person, trying to stabilize myself and felt something tear free into my hand. At least the Dragon Staff was still far from that other person and unlikely to take an eye out.

When my balance returned, I was face to face with Atura. She scowled at me and then leaned forward so fast that I thought she was going to bite me or spit in my face but instead, she leaned in close to my ear and hissed.

"Say anything and I kill you."

Yeah, very friendly.

She drew back and then gave me a smile that she must have thought was sweet but was laced with venom. I wanted to bite her, but instead I clenched my hands hard to keep my temper.

"I'm so glad we found you," she said in a tone that I didn't trust at all. "Whatever is happening is so dangerous. It's a good thing that we're together!"

Yeah. Good. Keep your friends close and your enemies closer, right? Only, I'd never had any enemies until I met her. Well, other than my cousin and his pirates.

"And the prophecy made it clear that we needed you – remember?" she said oh so innocently. "*One born on distant island far from home. One brought to keep him safe, if he roam. One given as a strength to face that day. One who with her life for them will pay.* We still need your part of that, Seleska."

Nasataa hissed and Hubric stepped between us with a dry look on his face.

"If you ladies are done making each other's acquaintance, maybe we can keep fleeing to safety, hmmm?"

Our guards were already heading down the next staircase going in a different direction into the darkness below. Lit torches lined the walls of the staircase.

My cheeks felt hot. I should be worried about keeping Nasataa safe and instead I was letting Atura be a burr in my sandal.

"Can we get to Heron?" I asked, looking for Jeriath's eyes before he disappeared down the stairs. "He shouldn't be imprisoned at a time like this."

"That's not my affair," the Ilerioc said from behind his leather veil.

"Please," I asked, giving him my most winning look. "If everything falls apart, he could be trapped or hurt."

He sighed. "But our path will take us close to where he is being ... detained. I will make a judgment then."

So, he had that kind of power, did he? I slipped in a little closer to where he stood, smiling encouragingly. If I was close, then he wouldn't be able to forget I was there and that there was something I wanted.

He shook his head and slipped down the stairway and I followed close behind.

If I didn't think about Heron right now, no one else would and if this volcano really did blow or there was an earthquake, he might need to flee with us. I was having a hard time believing this shaking was anything other than a massive disaster coming, despite Hubric's creepy words about debts and reckonings. Which reminded me – I still had something in my palm that had torn loose from Atura.

As I walked, I looked down into my palm and saw a small leather pouch that had torn away from her clothing. Was it a pocket? It was sewn shut. Carefully, I picked away at the seams.

"What's in your hand, Seleska?" Atura asked, slipping close from the stair behind me.

A small stone no larger than the last joint of my littlest finger slipped from the pouch into my hand as the earth shook beneath us again. A bright rune glowed on it.

"Show me your hand!" she demanded.

I didn't want to. I wanted to know more about this rock. I slipped it into my cheek. I could show her an empty hand and spit it out again in a moment. It felt strange – almost warm – against my tongue.

"Show me!"

She grabbed me, spinning me against the wall of the staircase while I was trying to show her my empty hand.

I was so surprised, I sucked in a breath suddenly, sucking in the stone and then coughing. It lodged in my throat and then I felt it slowly moving down.

Oops. I had swallowed it.

And I had no idea what it did.

Chapter Thirteen

"Shut up!" Jeriath hissed and Atura's mouth snapped shut with an audible click. "Do you hear that?"

There was a rumbling again, but fainter. And this time, the sound of rock scraping on rock.

I shivered, remembering the last time I'd heard that sound as the Troglodyte desperately passed his message to me. I met Atura's eyes and behind her feigned concern, I saw I look of satisfaction. Her palm was pressed against the rock wall as if she was feeling for something or gaining some kind of strength from the rock.

I frowned at that. She wasn't ... she wasn't *causing* this, was she?

"That sounded close," Jeriath muttered. "From now on, we need silence."

The Head of the Red Ileriocs nodded briskly, pushing forward to trot down the stairs first.

We followed, pressed against one another as we hurried down the stairs. Frustration filled me at every turn. I couldn't see past Atura's head in front of me. She was still wearing heeled boots like the ones I had abandoned, and she was taller than I was. All I could see was her back and patches of light between the people ahead of us, constantly moving as they hurried down the stairs.

If I looked behind me, all I saw was Hubric scowling and occasionally rubbing his chin in thought. His eyes met mine anytime I looked back, and his eyebrows rose questioningly. I felt my face heating. The way I'd hidden that rock in my mouth was embarrassing. What was I? Six?

Worse, I'd swallowed it and I still felt it making its way slowly from my throat to my belly. It left a strange, hot sensation in its wake. Was it one of those magical rocks the Rock Eaters ate? And if it was, had it been activated? Atura said hers had not been activated until she finished her task. What if it was meant for an enemy? After all, if it was something good, wouldn't she have already swallowed it?

We reached another landing and this one branched in four directions. Jeriath and the Head of the Red Ilerioc Guard nodded to each other and then made hand signals and two of each of their guards darted down the steps. One of them returned seconds later with a shake of his head.

Jeriath's eyes tightened behind his veil. I made a frustrated sound in my throat. I hated those veils.

Hubric leaned in close, whispering in my ear – again it was like he could read my mind!

"When the people of Haz gave a tithe to serve the dragons those people swore they would never again show their faces as free men. When the Ilerioc people were granted their freedom, they chose to honor their old vow by always keeping their heads and faces covered. I respect people who honor their vows."

I nodded. But it was still frustrating not to see their faces. And it had to get hot under all that cloth. I hoped I hadn't made promises that would bind me and my descendants like that.

Two more groups returned both shaking their heads.

"The stairways are blocked?" Hubric asked.

"Falling rock," Jeriath replied shortly.

A moment later, the fourth scout waved from the stairway and we followed Jeriath as he hurried down that set of stairs.

"There's only one way out through there and it is slow," the guard protested. "We should turn back."

"I was given strict orders," Jeriath protested.

"We will have to choose which has precedence if we go that way, and neither of these has yet given their vows. That's what they are here for in the first place!"

"Anyone can take a vow," Jeriath said.

"But it should be done before Haz'drazen and the Council."

We were all listening, not sure of what they were talking about.

"I will give any vow necessary," Atura said boldly as we hurried down the steps. They were growing steeper. "I am your true Guardian. As the prophecies state, I was rescued by a dragon as a child."

Wait? *That* was in the prophecies?

"Really?" Hubric asked dryly. He didn't believe her? Actually, neither did I. Atura would say anything to get what she wanted. And she'd wanted to burn me alive when we first met. I still thought she might. She hadn't been very subtle about wanting to see me dead.

"I was rescued by a huge Blue Dragon from a sinking ship. He bore me on his back to land. That's in your prophecies, isn't it?" she asked, quoting in a slightly different tone. "*On the backs of Blues, they bear her to shore, child in distress, child sacrificed for, child rescued from death. On their backs they bear up golden hope. Memory will not be forgotten. And in her belly will bloom the strength of gratitude.*"

Ilerioc and the First Red Ilerioc Guard gave identical grunts as if they had been punched in the belly.

"I thought those prophecies were sealed to only a few," Hubric said neutrally.

"They are," Jeriath said and it almost sounded like a curse. "How did you hear of them, diplomat?"

"When the Dominar sent me on this mission to represent her, Raolcan Prince of Dragons spoke the words to me."

Jeriath grunted again, but this time it sounded like respect. "Then you know that if her words are true, she is the true guardian of the Chosen One and she must speak her vows over him." He shot a harsh glance at me. "And I have chosen incorrectly."

I felt my face heating, but it felt silly to chime in right now. Would anyone believe me if I told them that the Gold Dragon who rescued me was carried on the backs of Blue Dragons as he flew his last hours to the Haven Isles to bring me to safety? His memory would never be forgotten. Not by me. Not by them. And I believed the prophecy. I believed it because I did get strength from my gratitude to him. It was what gave me fuel for every day.

I put my hand to my heart, silently thanking my old friend again.

Ramariri, I thought. You are not with me anymore. But I will always be grateful. I promise that I will protect little Nasataa and guard him in his task. Just like you guarded me. For your memory. For your sacrifice.

Chapter Fourteen

And that *was the vow they were talking about.*

The strange voice shattered my thoughts and I gasped. Who was that?

Taoslil. Sorry. I shouldn't be spying. We don't usually do that, but I heard you making the promise – you were broadcasting your thoughts so loudly it was like you were an actual dragon. Giving the vow without being asked – well, to me that means you must be the one meant to protect the dragonlet.

Could he help us get Natastaa somewhere safe?

Not now. We are under attack. All able dragons must fight. But don't worry. Your Ilerioc Guard will keep you safe.

He should know that the prophecies were about me – that Ramariri, the Gold Dragon who saved me was carried on the backs of Blue Dragons as he died saving me.

I will remember and I will honor him.

His voice was gone suddenly, and I could almost feel him pulling free from my mind. I blinked my eyes as we reached the bottom of the stairs and rushed forward.

"Where are we?" I gasped as the light of flickering lanterns finally registered.

The room was huge. And it wasn't all lit with lanterns. Light filtered in from holes in the wall, sealed with glass. Water was on the other side of the glass and fish swam past the portholes.

I spun, trying to figure out where we were. I hadn't seen an ocean when I looked out from the nest.

"It's a river that leads to the ocean. The ocean is not far, but that's a river," Hubric said as we ran further into the room. His ability to read my mind just by watching me was getting spooky.

At the center of the room was a metal orb with rivets all along the sides. It was perched over a round pool that glowed mysteriously. Racks of equipment and garments were set up around the pool.

It drew the eye so strongly that I didn't even notice the other wall until a hoarse voice called my name.

"Seleska!"

Like a shot, Nasataa leapt from my shoulders and flew – flew! – a few wobbly flaps before hitting the ground and running full speed to the dark barred cells along the other side of the room.

I knew exactly why. My quavering gasp came only moments later.

"Heron! You're here!"

I chased after Nasataa, following his lead as my own eyes tried to adjust to the darkness of the other side of the room and find where Heron's voice was coming from.

I almost stubbed my toe on the bars when I finally reached him. He was on the other side of a wall of bars, gripping them in either hand, his face pressed up against them as if he could get through just by wanting it enough. If that was a prison cell, it was an awful one. It was dark and damp with only a narrow rock wall for a bench and a drain in the middle of the floor. There were no other prisoners, no guards and no sign that Heron had been given food or water.

"Seleska! You're alive! You're okay! I've been so worried. You look like you aren't even injured anymore." His words poured out like a torrent of relief. Were his eyes glassy? His smile was wide, and his too-bright eyes flashed in the low light.

I leaned in close to try to get a good look at him and his hand snaked through the bars to find the back of my head and tangle in my hair, holding me gently but firmly like he was afraid that if his grip slipped at all I would vanish like a ghost.

"I brought you to their door and I begged them to take you, but they wouldn't, Seleska. Not until I forced them to. I'm sorry. I'm so sorry."

"What did you do to force them?" I asked, my eyes wide at the thought of gentle kind Heron forcing a dragon to do as he wished.

"Stay back from the prisoner," Jeriath warned, coming up from behind me. "We don't have leave to free him. He is under judgment."

"I thought you said you would consider it," I said.

"I fought them," Heron said, not letting go of me. "I fought them and demanded that they take you and help you or I would kill them."

"He broke Carhan's arm and leg and nearly killed him," Jeriath said harshly.

"Please," I begged, turning to him. "You can't leave him here. You promised to reconsider."

"I have reconsidered. He's a criminal." There was a sound of finality in his voice. "He stays here. Get your gear on and get ready. After we send the Chosen One and his guardian down, we'll send you next. Even if you're a fraud, you're still under our protection."

"A *what*?" Now I was reeling from all the crazy conclusions he was jumping to. Heron a criminal? Impossible! Me, a fraud? He was joking, right?

"The other girl is the True Guardian. We will watch her say her vows and then send her to safety with the guard. We can only send eight people at a time and it is essential that she is properly guarded."

I clenched my jaw and put a hand on my hip, and turned my whole body to him – but I made sure to stay close enough to Heron that he could keep his hand in my hair.

"Then why don't you go ahead and take care of that, Jeriath? If it's so important to you, then I don't know why you're wasting your time here?"

He made an angry sound in his throat, but he said one more thing before he stalked away.

"If that's how you feel, then you're on your own, imposter. We have important charges to protect and we don't have time for your dramatics."

My face grew hot at the finality of his tone. I'd just lost my guard with my sharp words.

Chapter Fifteen

I heard them begin to prepare Atura for her vow as Hubric stepped closer.

"You should be more careful with that temper, Seleska. You're going to get your friend in even more trouble if you provoke Jeriath."

"It's unfair, Hubric," I said irritably. "They've imprisoned him and all he was trying to do was save my life and now they all believe Atura just because she's such a great liar."

Hubric snorted. "Way of the world, kid."

"That doesn't mean it's right!"

"Of course, it's not right. People believe what they want to believe – even what it's patently false. And they are swayed by confidence and a tidy story but in real life, true stories are never tidy and the people telling them are rarely confident."

"So, what do I do?" I asked. "We can't just leave Heron here!"

"Wait here a minute."

He hurried off and I turned back to Heron. He smiled warmly at me, tenderness in his eyes but also concern.

"Seleska," he said. "You shouldn't stay here trying to free me if it puts you in danger. Go with the others. I'll be okay."

"I wouldn't do that," I said. And it was just the truth. I would never leave Heron when he needed me, just like he would never leave me when I needed him. "Did you really fight guards and dragons to get me help?"

"I'd do it all over again, too." The look in his eyes was blazing.

I stood up on my tiptoes, pressing into the bars so that I could reach him and with great effort, I managed to stand high enough to just brush his lips with mine.

When I pulled back, he bit his bottom lip.

"Seleska?"

"Yes?" I asked innocently.

"You need to stop doing that."

"Why?" I made my eyes as large as I could.

"You're my best friend. But if you keep doing that, I might just fall in love with you."

"Oh," I said as if I had no idea that was possible. "Oops."

But that left it in my hands, didn't it? I could decide to keep things the way they were, and we could be friends forever – the kind of friends where he went away to Abergande and apprenticed there without telling me first. I frowned.

Or, I could keep kissing him and we could maybe be more.

I felt all tingly at the thought of it. That would be ... nice. The wicked smile I shot at him as I thought of exactly how nice it would be probably suggested the truth – that I planned to keep kissing him and see what happened next.

I would have followed up on it right away, but Hubric was back with his arms full.

"These are rare. Swimsuits and goggles. They are insulated and light-weight and cover you from neck to wrists to ankles, but they are a tight fit, so they're hard to change into. There's a screen over there that you can change behind, Seleska. By the look of this place, I think it's more of a staging area for river expeditions than it is a prison," Hubric said, handing me a strange suit made of a material I'd never felt before. "Heron and I need to wear the breathing patches, too. Why don't you leave us to it?"

"And I have the super-rock still," Heron said, reaching down and then holding it up in the air. "No one knew what it was, so they left it with me."

Hubric grunted, pointing to Nasataa. "Take your charge with you. He shouldn't be burning holes through the bars."

I glanced down the line of bars to where Nasataa was flaming the bars so hard that he had left little tears and holes all along the bottom of the cells.

"Oops," I said.

"Yeah. Ooops," Hubric said dryly.

With my face blazing, I caught Nasataa and tucked him under one arm as I hurried behind the screen. Hubric was right. The suit was hard to put on. It fit far too snugly, but I could tell it would be easy to move in once I was underwater and it wouldn't be catching at the waves all the time like my regular clothing did. Worse, the rock under our feet was shaking even harder than before and it made it hard to balance and dress with the floor rippling like water.

It was all I could do to keep a positive attitude and not to panic. It wouldn't help anyone if I was scared of the floor, would it?

From behind the screen, I heard Atura finishing her vow and her new guards hurrying to get her into the metal orb together.

"It's on a cable and it will take us out to the ocean. It's a quick way out of Haz'drazen's Drazenloft," one of the guards was saying. "We must keep you safe, Honored Guardian. For the sake of the world."

"Your loyalty pleases me," Atura said.

I made a face behind the screen. Atura was terrible. She'd probably called for the attack going on above us.

Wait.

Had she? I'd asked that question before, but I knew I was biased. The thing was, it was very possible that somehow she had betrayed us. After all, why else was she here? She hadn't attacked Nasataa or me – which was what I'd thought she was here for at first. And I knew that the Rock Eaters wanted to kill dragons and drain their lives to fill up magic reservoirs. Maybe she had been here all along to find a way in for her people. Was that crazy? Was I just thinking these things because I hated her so much?

There was a crash in the distance.

Crash. Smash.

Do you sense something, Nasataa?

Trouble comes. Crash!

I darted out from the screen, Nasataa in my arms and the Dragon Staff in one hand. The last guards were loading into the orb. They weren't even looking to where Hubric and Heron were changed into their swimsuits and trying to equip their breathing apparatuses. Maybe the need to keep the Chosen One safe was more important than stopping someone from slipping swimming gear to a man behind bars was. They were definitely not looking to where the doorway light was blocked and where suddenly dust and tiny bits of rock were raining down as a booming sound filled the air.

"We need to get her out!" Jeriath yelled as the last guards shoved into the orb and he pulled the door shut behind him.

I saw his eyes looking out through a single window on the door just before the orb shot down into the pool in its metal cable, zipping away. What manner of magic was that?

I didn't have time to think about that.

There was a loud click and I turned in time to see Hubric fiddling with the lock on the cell door and then Heron burst out from behind the bars – had Hubric picked the lock?

"Run to the pool!" Hubric shouted before slapping a breathing patch over his face.

I meant to run.

I really did, but as the huge head burst into the room from the stairway above, I wasn't able to move at all. I stood, frozen in place, completely immobile as I stared at the horrible creature breaking the rock to enter the room.

How was a thing like that even possible?

Chapter Sixteen

"Manticore," Hubric croaked and I knew he was right. I'd seen them before when they tore into the Troglodyte, but that didn't make them any less hideous. This one was massive – his almost human head was stuck into the room growling and snapping with broken, rotten teeth and his mane shook as he pushed against the rock.

A groaning sound ripped through the rock and then a crack. That must be magic. No matter how strong he was, he couldn't be breaking rocks with just his muscles!

Lightning fast, Nasataa dove from my arms and ran toward the pool. As if it had shaken me awake, I chased after him.

The Manticore slid into the room, his lion paws scuffling across the rock of the floor, crumpling cell doors along the one wall.

"Go!" Hubric yelled, shoving Heron into the pool. He fell rapidly holding the heavy super-stone and Nasataa leapt in right on his heels.

I was nearly there. Just a few more strides.

And then the Manticore was loose, barrelling toward us, driven by insane power. I threw up the Dragon Staff instinctively to protect us.

"You first," I called to Hubric and his answering growl could be heard even through the muffling of his breathing patch. He grabbed my arm, pulling me after him but I was the only one armed and I needed to protect them.

"You won't help anyone if you're dead, fool girl! Bravery is good. Sense is better!" he yelled, pulling the patch off so he could talk to me before replacing it and dragging me after him. Wouldn't that nullify the magic of the patch? Or were these patches different from Rock Eater ones?

We plunged into the embrace of the river, falling into the pool.

I breathed a sigh of relief.

Too soon.

The huge face of the Manticore plunged into the water behind us, searching, his dark eyes wide open in the fast-moving water of the river.

I swam as fast as I could, kicking with the current. My world was a haze of fast-moving images and panicked breaths, all drowned out by the frantic pounding of my heart.

In front of me, Heron and Nasataa swam through the water, the rock propelling them as they both clung to it, beckoning me to follow.

The river was long and straight and far ahead of them, I saw the round orb moving down the line. It was steady and sure, but not fast.

I spun to look at the thrashing Manticore. He fought against the rock rim of the pool. We'd have to swim fast to outdistance him before he broke through.

And there was no way we could swim that fast.

This was insanity. Why was I Nasataa's protector when I had nothing to protect him with? What was the point of this Dragon Staff if it couldn't help keep him safe?

The Manticore roared and then rock fell down from the pool entrance to the bottom of the river and bubbles roared toward us as his huge body tore through the water, his wings flapping in it like the fins of a great fish.

He was terribly fast. Faster than anything else I'd seen underwater other than a Blue Dragon.

And I had had enough.

I spun in the water, leveled my staff and screwed up my face.

"Okay, Staff," I said, but under the water, it was just bubbles. "You'd better be good for something! Come on! Do something!"

Vyvera said it would eventually have some kind of power. She said that if I practiced and got familiar with it, it would show me the power. And at least once before it had deflected magic back on the person doing the magic. But did Manticores have magic? Could this even work?

I hadn't had time to practice other than panicked fighting. And by the look of things, I never would. It was just one desperate battle after another for old Seleska, so if this Staff was ever going to be any good, now was the time for it.

I thought I could feel Hubric tugging at me from behind, but this time, I wouldn't be swayed. We couldn't outrun this creature, and it could clearly pulverize anything it got its grubby paws on.

And I was done. I was done running. I was done fleeing.

I was making a stand.

Focus.

That wasn't Taoslil or Nasataa! Who was that in my brain now? It was like a ship port with all these people coming and going!

No questions. Focus.

I saw an image in my mind of a Blue Dragon. Deep and mysterious. Its bright eyes turned to slits as it said again, *Focus.*

I focused on the Manticore as it swam toward me, bubbles streaming from its open mouth as if it was roaring as it tore through the water toward me. Mud and water weeds spun in clumps where they'd been torn up by its huge paws.

I focused on it with all my mental strength. It was everything dangerous trying to destroy us. It was everything I needed to protect Nasataa from. I focused as hard as I could.

Not that kind of focus. Don't focus on the evil thing you fight. Focus on why you fight.

I wanted to protect Nasataa like Ramariri had protected me.

Heat flared in my chest as I thought about the gratitude I felt for him – for his kindness and mercy. For his faithfulness.

It swelled, hotter, brighter.

Hubric was shouting from behind his patch through the water behind me. He must really be loud for me to hear his garbled voice.

The Manticore was nearly close enough to snatch me from the water with his paws. I saw the look of triumph begin in his eyes, the lips pulling back from jagged teeth.

I focused on gratitude instead.

Heat and light flared around me, so bright that it blinded me.

I blinked.

And when my vision cleared, there was no Manticore.

Chapter Seventeen

I turned to see Hubric's face, bug-eyed behind the googles. He looked like he was saying something under his breathing patch, but I couldn't hear him. This time, I followed when he tugged on my arm, swimming as fast as I could with one hand still gripping the staff.

Thank you, thank you, thank you, I thought to the Blue Dragons. If it hadn't been for them, we'd all be dead.

Keep the dragonlet safe.

Why hadn't they been at Haz'drazen's Council? Why hadn't their voices been heard? They knew who Nasataa was and who I was because of him.

We are not like other dragons. We prefer our privacy.

Well, that was a poor policy right now. Right now, all dragons needed to stick together.

We had almost caught up with Heron who was clutching Nasataa to his chest as if he could protect the little dragon forever, spinning the super-rock in wide loops as he waited for us. Nasataa squirmed away, launching himself at me and then scrambling to grip my shoulders and back in a sort of swimmer's piggy-back. That was fine by me. The closer he stayed, the happier I would be.

Heron's eyes showed his concern as he helped me grab one of the handles of the super-rock. He was worried about me. I gave him a bright smile. No need to let worry take over when we were all still alive. Besides, I'd learned a lesson just now.

Gratitude was a powerful thing. Powerful enough to destroy the most powerful of enemies.

Hubric joined us, grabbing the last handle and we let the super-rock tow us forward into the current.

I felt bold, the warmth in my chest growing as I kept thinking of all the things I was grateful for. For Renny and Halana who had loved me as a daughter for most of my life. For Nasataa who had turned my world upside down just by being born. For Heron who would never give up on me. For Vyvera who had died to help us all. For Hubric who was here now to help guide. For Taoslil who had believed in me. I felt warm all over.

And then, up ahead, three Manticores plunged into the water, ripping the big metal orb from its cable.

I would have screamed if I could scream underwater. Bubbles hazed everything in a flurry of activity as their wings and feet beat the water, pulling the orb upward and breaking through the surface.

I let go of the super-rock and swam up. I had to know what was happening. They hadn't believed in me, but that didn't mean that they deserved to be taken by Manticores!

I gasped as I saw them climbing up through the air with their wings fighting, battling for height. The door of the orb opened, and a figure tumbled out – a figure all dressed in white with his face swathed in cloth. He fell like a broken doll, landing awkwardly with a smack on the water downriver and spinning away.

I gasped as a head popped out of the orb just for long enough to confirm that the body was gone. Atura's gaze caught on me and I could have sworn she was laughing when she mock saluted me before ducking back into her orb.

Someone needed to catch them! Someone needed to stop them! Her Ilerioc guards were innocent in all of this and now they were her captives!

I spun in the water, looking for the Drazenloft and the dragons and that's when I saw what was happening above us.

I almost sank back into the water in horror.

Above me, the sky was dark with bodies, occasionally lit up by a stream of fire as dragons fought Manticores – hundreds upon hundreds of them. A massive body fell in the distance – so far away that I couldn't tell if it was friend or foe. Smoke billowed up from the landscape beyond.

And then a horrific cry sounded from above me and I looked straight up to see a dragon – eyes glazed with death – plummeting toward the river.

I ducked under just in time to see him plunge through the water upstream. Strong hands gripped me, pulling me out of the way as the huge body floated along with the current.

I looked back at Heron and we shared a look of horror.

That peaceful, paradise world of Haz'drazen's was a battlefield now. And there was nowhere to hide – not on land, or underground, in the water, or in the sky.

My heart was racing as a new body plunged under the water – a purple dragon, gnarled with age and with an angry sneer on his face. Ice shot through me at his underwater glare, but his gaze darted past me as if he was searching and then his head pulled out of the water again.

Someone was shaking my arm.

I spun to see Hubric signaling to us to surface.

But there were angry dragons and Manticores above! Better to stay down here where it was safe. I shook my head, refusing his direction.

He tugged again, pointing above insistently and then swam up toward the surface without waiting for us. I turned to Heron but he just shook his head, shrugged, and followed.

"What are you thinking?" I asked as soon as my head broke the surface, between my usual gasping sputters at switching from water to air again. "This is madness."

"The water is too slow," Hubric said, gasping as he swam toward shore. "We need to be faster."

"The enemy is all around!" I objected, pointing to where a black dragon fell in the distance, one of his wings broken in half. I clutched at Nasataa. He shouldn't be seeing this. He was just a baby.

"We'll go back underwater when we're clear of it. We just need to get to the ocean," Hubric said, a determined look on his face.

"No!" I said, more forcefully than I needed to. "That's heading right into danger! We can't walk to the ocean over the mountains anyway!"

We weren't planning on walking. My wings work just fine.

The cranky voice was from the gnarled purple dragon. He stepped out from around a rock on the riverbank, flaring fire at a cloud of flies stirred up along the riverbank.

I thought dragons didn't like talking to humans. So then why were all of them talking to me all the time?

I guess you're lucky.

"We're going to fly?" I asked, suddenly less sure of myself.

"It's faster. We'll stay close to the surface of the water. If you need to drop into it, Kyrowat here will let you jump. Good compromise? I thought so," Hubric said, talking over any objections. "Hurry. We don't have much time."

Chapter Eighteen

We were still tightening our straps when Kyrowat kicked up into the air, bobbing awkwardly as he tried to find a good rhythm close to the surface of the water.

"We're too heavy for him!" Heron called to Hubric.

"Tell me something I don't know, boy."

"He won't be able to carry us for long!"

"He won't have to."

"The patches are worn out. If he falls into the water, you and I will be in big trouble," Heron pressed.

"Would you stop whining?" Hubric's tone was irritable, but he reached behind him with a wrapped package and shoved it into Heron's hand. "There's a dozen more. Happy? Now quiet down and let's try not to die."

I'd only ever flown on such a wild and wobbling trajectory once before and the dragon I'd been riding that time had been dying. Kyrowat seemed almost as erratic as he followed the course of the river, dodging falling opponents and allies alike.

"There's another one, Kyro! Watch your tail!" Hubric called and we dodged roughly to the side.

I looked up, high above me, and caught a flash of light as the sun reflected off the side of the orb. The Manticores had carried it high above us and they were still climbing, trying to reach a huge group of them even higher up.

As I watched, another white-clad figure dropped.

"Jeriath!" I gasped – though I couldn't be sure it was him. But something about the way he fell made me think it was. "Hubric, can we catch him?"

Hubric's snarl was indecipherable, but the way Kyrowat turned in the air, flapping hard to gain height suggested that maybe we could.

"Seleska, tuck your staff in the saddle so you don't spear him like a sunfish!" Hubric called. "Heron. Hand her the dragonlet, and get ready. You're going to catch. Let's see if those big arms of yours are good for something, eh?"

"Can Kyrowat take the weight?" Heron asked as we all scrambled to obey.

"Stop doubting my dragon. He can breathe fire and he'll flame you to cinders if you keep annoying him."

Heron and I shared a worried look – irritated or not, Kyrowat seemed overloaded already. But what other choice was there?

We spun suddenly to the side and I curled over Nasataa, protecting him. We must be close!

There was a grunt from behind me and then Kyrowat dropped. I held my breath counting the seconds. After long moments of me clenching my eyes shut and holding onto Nasataa as hard as I could, he leveled off, his feet kicking up spray as they skimmed the water.

I spun to look back. Heron held Jeriath. It was definitely him! He slumped over Heron's lap bleeding profusely from the head.

"I don't know if he's dead." Heron was trying to feel for a pulse.

"Nothing you can do about it if he is. Everyone hold on tight!" Hubric called and then Kyrowat kicked forward with more speed than I would have guessed he could muster.

I glanced behind us to see a pair of Manticores splitting off from a group and flying toward us at full speed.

Seleska? That was Taoslil. He was still alive. I breathed a sigh of relief. *If you had passed the tests, we would have given you more information. Now that you are fleeing, you still need it. There were keys – three of them. You need them to unlock the Haroc under the ocean.*

Keys?

No time for questions. Just listen. None of us might survive this battle.

The Manticores were gaining despite all of Kyrowat's work. Could a dragon die from over-exertion?

I could see the ocean now, just a silver line in the distance.

The first key is in the Dominion. The second in a place now called Ko'Torenth. The third in the lands known as Baojang. Your rival will know this, and she will be seeking them, too. You must get them before she can. And you must hurry.

But those were just countries. A key could be anywhere in a country!

Ask my brother for help. He will know where to start looking. I have to —

His voice cut off.

Taoslil? Taoslil?

There was no answer.

A loud snarl from behind made me jump in the saddle.

I looked behind me to see a Manticore grab Kyrowat's tail.

We were too late! They had us!

I couldn't take my eyes off the ugly creature as his rotten teeth bit into Kyrowat's purple scales. The dragon roared in pain and Nasataa keened loudly. Had he been hurt? I looked over him frantically, but he seemed to be sharing Kyrowat's pain, not feeling pain of his own.

The Manticore shook Kyrowat and we bounced with him as he fought with his wings to get his balance in the air again.

Nasataa's keen was louder and I could feel him now in my mind, projecting an image of what he saw, loud and vibrant. I blinked hard, one hand coming up to my head to try to block the pain.

But I needed to get the staff and aim it at the Manticore. Why hadn't I thought of that?

I reached for it, but at that moment, the river below parted, and three huge creatures leapt up into the air.

Blue Dragons.

They were huge – dwarfing Kyrowat and even the Manticores. How had they even fit in the river? And they leapt like dolphins, arching up beautifully, light flashing off their scales as two of them snatched the Manticores up in wide-open mouths – ripping the one off of Kyrowat's tail with a wrenching shake – and then dove back into the murky river.

The third Manticore had risen under Kyrowat, his back accidentally buoying the older dragon up and then as the Blue Dragon surged forward, we surged forward with him, balanced on his shoulders as he sped toward the sea, legs and tail still in the river.

I had no idea a Blue Dragon could move so fast. We sped past land, past the river bank, past the looming hills and mountains and we were nearly as far as the sea when he finally sank below the water, leaving Kyrowat to flap tiredly to the shore.

Don't stop until you find the keys.

He vanished beneath the waves, leaving me blinking at a wide horizon with no idea what do to next.

Episode Five: Waves of Destiny

Chapter One

Behind us, screams and flares of flame still reached us as we left the Lands of Haz'drazen.

"Keep him from squirming!" Hubric called over his shoulder.

Wind tore at my wet clothing, drying the special underwater suit quickly. I clung to Nasataa as Kyrowat flew low over the edges of the ocean where the river tumbled into it, kicking up mud and fish where freshwater met salt.

Jeriath thrashed as Heron tried to keep him pinned in place.

"Traitors! Traitors!" he muttered.

"We're hardly the ones who let Manticores into the Lands of Haz'Drazen!" I objected. "If anyone is a traitor, he is for supporting Atura!"

"I think he's feverish," Heron said. "His head is hot."

"Why would he be feverish? I thought he was hit in the head."

"He was. Look, he's bleeding!" Heron was dabbing at Jeriath's head with part of his head covering. The man's scarf had dropped from his face, but I didn't know if that ghastly pale green skin was normal for an Ilerioc or a sign of fever taking hold.

"Quiet!" Hubric's command silenced us. I listened for what was worrying him but all I could hear were Kyrowat's wings flapping hard in the air and a tiny keening sound from Nasataa. I hugged him closer. He was getting too big for me to hold well, my arms barely wrapped all the way around him anymore.

When had he found the time to grow so much?

Kyrowat ducked behind a large standing rock, landing awkwardly on the sandy beach behind it and we all held our breath waiting for whatever Hubric had heard. Something hit me hard in the back.

Oof! What was that?

I looked behind me to see what had hit me.

Heron had Jeriath in some kind of lock, keeping him pinned under one arm while his hand was pressed tight over the man's mouth. Oh. He must have hit me as he thrashed. There was something wrong with Jeriath. Something that we'd need to dig into as soon as we dared stop.

His eyes looked wild and glazed at the same time, like he didn't know where he was.

We didn't dare to stop yet – not for long.

"Jeriath," I hissed. "You're okay. Calm down."

"Shh," Heron warned me, looking over his shoulder.

There was the sound of flapping wings and I relaxed for a moment until I heard an order barked sharply. Rock Eaters! I'd heard that language before!

They were just on the other side of that rock! At least a dozen, maybe more. And the sounds of wings and the crunch of something eating suggested it wasn't just humans. Were those – those weren't – Manticores, were they?

But they must be.

How had all these Rock Eaters and Manticores gotten here? The Troglodyte had opened up a portal to send us through to the dragons. But they couldn't have all come through that – could they? They had to have had some other way to get here.

Nasataa made a small noise and I petted him gently, trying to keep my shushing sounds as quiet as humanly possible. One dragon with five passengers on his back was no match for however many Manticores were out there.

Speak for yourself.

Oh. He was still talking to me.

Only when you insult me.

Well, it wasn't insulting to say that a dozen Manticores could take one old dragon, was it?

A dozen? There are thirty out there by my count.

See? Well, then he couldn't be insulted that I thought he was no match for them. I was just worried about his health.

Uh huh. If you think that's true then you don't know much about dragons. You're going to have to learn fast if you're going to fight for our side. We are tough! Tough and strong!

Whoa! I wasn't fighting for anyone. I was just trying to protect Nasataa!

What do you think being his protector means? It means you are the guardian to our Chosen One. Whether you realize it or not, you are fighting on our side!

Oh. Well. I kind of liked that. Seleska, Champion of Dragons!

Don't get too arrogant. You aren't actually *a dragon,* he grumbled.

Maybe not, but I was the closet thing to it while still being human, wasn't I? I felt pride swell in my breast. Seleska, Champion of Dragons.

After long minutes, the wings were flapping again, and the voices died away. We didn't move. Maybe they set a guard to look and see if anyone came running out from behind the rocks after they left. Or maybe Kyrowat was just very tired.

Of course, I'm tired. You try carrying five others and see how you do!

Well, it wouldn't make me so cranky that was for sure. Maybe we needed to see if any other dragons were willing to help out. We could use a few more to ride.

You think a dragon will just volunteer to carry some of you?

Well, he had, right? So, what was so crazy about seeing if anyone else would help out? They'd probably love the opportunity! We would all be great friends in no time.

There was no answer from Kyrowat. Either my question had him completely stunned, or he was sick of talking to me.

"We need a plan," Hubric whispered eventually. "There are Manticores everywhere."

"How could they all have come here?" I asked.

"Treachery. Someone had brought them into the Lands of Haz'Drazen."

"Who would do that?" I asked.

Heron cleared his throat and when we looked at him he just nodded to Jeriath. "This guy maybe? Why did you save him?"

"Because no one should die like that," I said at the same time that Hubric spoke. "And he was on my side before Atura came out with those lies about how she was saved by a dragon as a child."

"We're keeping him for information," Hubric said. "We need all we can get."

"We also need another dragon," I said. "Kyrowat can't carry all of us all the way to the Dominion."

Hubric nodded tiredly but before he could speak, voices rang out in the distance again, and once again, we were huddled against the rock waiting as they passed.

After long minutes, the voices faded again.

"We could go into the sea," I suggested. "That would be safer. And we're all dressed for it."

"And it would take far too long," Hubric said. "You're in a race, remember? A race where the first stop is in the Dominion."

"A race that will be over the moment we're caught," I whispered. "Unless you know a quicker way to get there."

"Mmmph," Hubric grunted. "Maybe. We could try the warrens – if we dare."

"Warrens?"

"Underground tunnels. They lead to unexpected places. But they're hard to navigate. Sometimes even impossible. And I don't know where the entrances to them might be in the Lands of Haz'drazen. If we get through the Dawn's Gate to the human lands again, we might be able to find one. But by then, we'd be close enough to Dominion City that it might not make a difference."

Kyrowat was already slipping out from behind the rock, flying low to the beach and hugging the rocky cliff along the side of the ocean. He'd have to be careful. His purple scales stood out along the blackened volcanic rocks and we didn't help him hide at all.

I retreated into my own mind, desperately looking for a way to defeat the Manticores and escape the Lands of the Dragons alive.

The next hours left my teeth on edge and my nerves sizzling. We hid in every rock, cave or outcrop we could find as we dodged groups of Manticores bearing riders in bunches of anywhere from five to a hundred. We saw no other dragons.

Nasataa was restless and I had chewed my bottom lip raw by the time the sun began to set.

"We need to stop soon," Heron announced. "I think this man is bleeding. And if you want that information we saved him for, we'll have to stop to tend his wounds."

A harsh voice cried out from the dusky light. A warning? A challenge?

We fell silent, but it called again.

"Hold on," Hubric whispered and then Kyrowat sprang forward, flying faster and harder than I thought a dragon of his age could possibly go.

You wound me, girl.

We flew in tense silence for what felt like hours as the darkness grew thicker and thicker.

As we flew, I thought.

I was in an impossible race against an adversary who outnumbered us in the one place you would think that lovers of dragons would have the most friends – the Lands of Haz'drazen. We were poorly supplied, didn't know where we were going, and were fleeing for our lives. And if we didn't succeed, little Nasataa would pay with his life. We had no option but to go on and keep trying. But everything in me was screaming that we'd already failed.

Heron leaned forward, whispering in my ear just as I thought that, "Be strong, Seleska. Bravery is doing the impossible because you hope in something bigger than yourself. Strength comes from love and gratitude, not the ability to rend and tear apart. Your bright eyes make my heart stronger every day."

I felt a warm little rush at his words and it kept me going as the hours passed and the wind whipped up, disguising the sound of our flight until it felt like we'd been flying half the night.

I thought I could see Manticores behind us every time I looked back, chasing us in the light of the moon, their broken teeth gleaming in the silver light.

But it was only my own terrors chasing me.

Chapter Two

The night was half-gone by the time Kyrowat collapsed in a rocky cave somewhere in a set of low mountains. In the darkness, with all the hiding and creeping through low rocky outcroppings, I'd lost my bearings almost entirely. I couldn't have judged east from west I was so tired, but I helped Heron pull Jeriath off Kyrowat's back and as Hubric tended his dragon and Nasataa curled up beside him to sleep, we wearily checked him over.

"He's been stabbed here, in the back," Heron said. "No wonder he's doing so poorly. He's lost a lot of blood."

"Do you think it's infected?" I whispered. "It's been hours since you caught him."

Heron shrugged, too tired to speak more. And what was there to say? If he was too hurt to live, there was nothing we could do about that, anyway. I bit my lip as we bandaged him.

Tiredness weighed on me like a heavy rock, slowing my movements and sinking my spirits. I fought against it as I worked with fumbling fingers, helping Heron to make Jeriath comfortable on the sand before collapsing in the sand myself. I hoped we wouldn't be discovered here. Hoped we would hear anyone coming before they found us. They wouldn't travel at night, would they? Hoped ...

The smell of the fire woke me from my troubled sleep and I pulled myself up to sitting with a start. Sunlight drifted in bright and golden into the sandy caves between the rocks. Someone's arm was draped over my waist.

Heron.

He must have fallen in the sand beside me. I couldn't see the sky from where I was. A good thing, considering our enemy could fly. I rubbed my eyes blearily.

Where was Nasataa? My heart was already racing before I was on my feet scouring the sand and cave with my gaze.

"Above," a deep voice rumbled.

I strode forward until I was out of the cliff's overhang and I could look to the cliffs above. I thought I saw the shape of a dragon silhouetted above with another, smaller dragon beside him. Before I could blink, the first dragon fell from the cliff and then the little dragon fell after him.

I gasped.

No!

Nasataa wasn't ready yet! He was too little to fly! I bit my lip looking for where I should stand to catch him – could I catch him? I'd have to try! There was no one else to do it.

"He's the size of a dog," the deep voice said. "I hope you don't plan to catch him. Come get some tea. It's much better."

"I'll do what I have to," I said through gritted teeth, sparing a quick glance for the voice. It was Hubric carefully drinking from a cup beside the fire. His drink steamed invitingly.

"Well, I'm glad you're not my mother fretting and worrying like that. You'd drive a sane person mad," he said. "And for the record, our prisoner's wounds are beginning to look better, though the fever still has him. I poured some water down his throat this morning."

My eyes were locked on Nasataa's little form. Was he scared? Was he panicked?

I opened my arms wide, ready, ready.

Just before he fell into them, he pulled up, his scaly belly swiping my reaching fingers. He shot into the sky with a look in his eye that made me think of a laughing dog.

Kyrowat, Hubric's full-grown dragon, flew a lazy circle around to him and the two of them glided side by side in an arc together.

I let out a long breath.

"They're dragons," Hubric said. "They fly. What did you think the wings were for, hmmm?"

"I thought he would need to be taught," I said tightly.

"Well, now is a good time to learn. We're being chased by enemies and between the five of us we're too heavy for Kyrowat. He barely made it through the flight last night and I worry for him. He's pushing himself too hard. If Nasataa can fly for himself, that's one fewer to carry."

I felt a tightness in my chest at not carrying him anymore. Would he be okay flying on his own? What if he got tired? I'd just have to watch for that. I was not going to have my little dragon worn out just because Hubric or Kyrowat thought it might be good training.

"They'll be seen up there in the sky!" I protested.

"Needs to be done."

"That's my decision," I said boldly but then withered under his sharp gaze "Don't you think? I mean, well, I *am* his guardian."

He laughed. "Well, now, I suppose it is. Why don't you tell him what he can and can't do?"

He winked at me as Kyrowat and Nasataa landed together right in front of us.

My eyes went big and with my biggest, brightest smile I rushed to Nasataa.

"You did it! You flew for the very first time! I saw you and it was amazing!"

He leapt up, fluttering a little in the air and knocking me backward. I stumbled back. Tripping against his enthusiastic weight and falling to the ground.

"Amazing, but maybe just a little too strong, aren't you?" He was nearly as high as my waist. It was almost as if he had grown more in the night. Or maybe flying had loosened his muscles and made them elongate.

Strong, Sela. Strong!

"Yes, very strong, Nasataa!"

"He'll need more practice before we set out," Hubric said with a grunt. He kept his face schooled to seriousness, but I thought he might just be a little touched by Nasataa's success, too.

"Wasn't he amazing, Hubric! Tell him how great he was!"

"Yes, it's truly amazing when a thing does what it's designed to do. Well done, dragon," he said dryly. He shoved a mug of tea in my hands as I stood. "Here. Drink."

"And what were you designed for, Hubric?" I asked innocently. "Making tea?"

He scowled as the dragons took off again. "Go wake your boy. I thought of something while you two were sleeping."

"Something good, I hope," I said giving him my brightest smile and indulging in a long sip of hot tea.

"Ha! Go charm him. It doesn't work on me."

But I was pretty sure that my smiles did work on him because he was failing at hiding his own smile under that grey mustache of his. Triumphantly, I returned to where Jeriath and Heron still slept. I checked Jeriath first. Still breathing, but not awake. Well, at least he hadn't died in the night.

Hopefully, whatever idea Hubric had was a good one, because, despite Nasataa's success and the joy I felt for him, we were still in a big mess here.

I crouched down beside Heron and shook him gently.

"Just a moment more," he muttered sleepily. "Just a moment more, sweet honey."

A stab of recognition shot through me. He'd said that when he was bringing me to the dragons for help, hadn't he? He'd called me "sweet honey" when I was fading in and out of consciousness. How had I forgotten that until now? I bit my lip. Maybe all his joking about making him fall in love with me – maybe it had just been the plain truth. Was it possible that Heron thought of me as more than just his best friend?

I opened my mouth, trying to form the exact right sentence when the hiss of steam and a sharp cry met my ears.

"We've got company!" Hubric called.

Chapter Three

I grabbed my staff from where I'd left it the night before, gulping down the rest of the tea and stuffing the tin mug into my belt pouch. I tugged at the tight swim clothing – not very useful away from the water – as I stumbled slightly in my haste to rush to Hubric's side. Nasataa dove from the sky, hitting the ground hard and skidding along it until he stopped at my feet in a cloud of dust.

"Are you okay, little guy?" I asked, but he was already rolling up on his feet and prancing forward to where Kyrowat had landed beside Hubric.

The older dragon flashed a bright-eyed wink at little Nasataa. Maybe he wasn't as crusty as he seemed.

I'm much crustier. My friends call me Metamorphic.

Was that a dragon joke? Was he joking *while* we were under attack?

Shadows darkened the ground, one after another and I shielded my eyes with a hand, looking up into the too-bright morning sky, my heart racing. How many were there?

My heart was stuttering so hard that I was having trouble breathing evenly. I clutched my dragon staff, ready to fight when the Manticores came. Those rotten teeth would never touch my Nasataa!

He spurted a small flame into the air like he was thinking the same thing.

"Good boy!" I said as I scanned the sky.

Dark bodies blotted out the sun, at least four or five silhouettes passed over us, curling around to lose altitude and get closer. They'd definitely seen us! They must have noticed Kyrowat and Nasataa's flights. I knew that would draw too much attention!

But wait. Those outlines didn't look like Manticores at all.

"They're dragons!" Heron's voice was full of awe despite the sleepy note to it. "Free dragons without riders."

"Now we can test your theory," Hubric said wryly. "How much are you willing to bet that a free dragon will be willing to carry your heavy frame around while fleeing the destruction of his home, hmmm? I'll wager my second best knife that you won't find any takers."

Heron looked uncertain as he shifted back and forth but he pointed to his belt buckle after a moment. "It's silver. Will you take it against the knife?"

Hubric laughed. "Keep the confidence. Dragons like confidence."

And then it was too loud to speak as winds beat against us in every direction. The dragons were landing in our small clearing in front of the cave – all of them at once – their cupped wings furling and huge feet hitting the sand sent a thrill through me. They were so large, so magnificent as the sun hit their scales and glinted off. Who would ever want to harm such magnificent creatures?

The Rock Eaters had no respect for life – not human life and not dragon life. And people who didn't respect life had lost something close to their hearts. My belly burned a little hot at that thought and I felt a wave of nausea. I'd swallowed one of their stones. One of the things that they made by sucking the life out of people. I'd made a terrible mistake doing that, hadn't I? Hopefully, it would turn out to be a dud and not do anything. After all, it hadn't done anything yet, right?

No point getting bogged down in worries about things that couldn't be changed. Confidence and enthusiasm were what we needed now. I held my staff in both hands and walked up boldly to the dragon closest to me – a thickly scaled red with ruby scales that made me just want to stare and stare at the subtle black striping wrapping around his back.

"I hope you won't be too offended," I said, "but we could really use your help."

Hubric snorted behind me and the Red dragon just stared at me, nostrils flaring.

"He must like you," Hubric said.

"Why do you say that?" I asked, smiling at the dragon, and reaching toward him in an invitation to come closer.

"Because you still have that hand. Didn't you pay any attention, Seleska? Dragons don't talk to people. Except for Purples, and they don't do it very often. Usually only to their riders."

But he was wrong about that because dragons talked to me all the time. Purples, yes, but also Blues and Taoslil who was a white. And these dragons were all looking at me.

No, wait. They were all looking behind me. I glanced behind me to see Nasataa preening under all the attention. They were curious about the little dragon, weren't they? I felt my face flaming in embarrassment, and I dropped my hand. Ooops. Not everything is about you, Seleska.

"We still need to get Nasataa to the Dominion, and he still needs our help," I said to Hubric, feeling like such a fool. Of course, the dragons didn't think I was something special. Why had I expected that? I was getting a swollen head, that was for sure! "And if we're going to get him out of here in the middle of this conflict, then we need the help of dragons."

One of the dragons pushed forward. He was thinner and a touch smaller than the others who were Red, Black, and Green. This one – a purple, looked almost lanky like he was young.

He is young, Kyrowat said to me. *Too young to be making such hasty decisions. Tell your blacksmith, 'no.'*

What could he mean by that? But before I could ask, the Purple bounded forward like an excited horse, knocking the Red to the side and skidding to a halt right beside me.

It was all I could do, as my eyes went wide, not to flinch. I swallowed. He was soooo big. Even a small dragon seemed huge and terrifying when it came barreling toward you. But it wasn't me he was interested in, or even Nasataa.

All his attention was on Heron, steam pouring from his nostrils as his yellow eyes narrowed and took all of Heron in like a wolf sizing up his prey. I spun to look back at Heron. Was he scared? Could he get out of the way? He'd been a prisoner of dragons only yesterday. Did this dragon know that?

Heron hadn't even flinched. He was leaning forward slightly, the sun glinting off his dark skin and hair and a look of delighted awe painting his face. I felt a tiny pang of jealousy – that looked like love in his eyes – and then the dragon spun in place and ran along the ground a little awkwardly. I dodged backward, barely avoiding his tail as it whipsawed back and forth along the ground. Nasataa hissed, spitting fire into the sky like he was watching a sporting event rather than the world's most confusing meeting, but when I looked back, I could see why.

Heron dashed along the black sand, running as fast as I'd ever seen him. The look in his eyes was pure exhilaration and then he was leaping through the air and grabbing the purple dragon by the tail at the same moment that the dragon kicked up from the ground into the sky.

Black sand flew up and swirled in the wind where his wings created turbulence. In the middle of all that sand and wind, was Heron, climbing up the dragon's tail hand over hand as if those slick scales had any kind of purchase at all.

My heart was in my throat. I thought I might have screamed his name, but now they were so high up that it was hard to see. I felt freezing cold as I watched them, my belly lurching with fear at the thought of Heron losing a handhold and falling, falling, falling all the way to the black rocks below.

What was he thinking?

What would I do if I lost him?

I gasped as he seemed to almost somersault forward along the dragon's spine and land right between his shoulders like a dragon rider with no saddle.

"Ah, the traditional way," Hubric said happily from beside me. He was still drinking his tea. His tea! As if nothing out of the ordinary was going on. "That's always nice. Purples are big suckers for people with wide-open hearts and I enjoy seeing the traditions upheld."

"Wide-open hearts?"

"Isn't your boy big-hearted? He sure seems stuck on you," Hubric said calmly. "Well, best pack up. We have miles to cover, danger on every horizon, an impossible quest, and two dragons so wet behind the ears that it will take all of Kyrowat's skill to keep them out of trouble."

Kyrowat rolled his eyes.

"Wha – "

"Don't look so stunned girl. How did you think dragons picked riders? They like to see some courage and a little bit of fire in the belly, you know?"

My own belly felt like it was on fire and as I helped him gather his things and check on Jeriath – still delirious as he moaned and muttered, though the bleeding seemed to have stopped – I couldn't help but feel like everything was spinning out of control.

Seleska, I tried to remind myself, it's not an adventure if you're in control. But when, after long minutes, there was still no sign of Heron and the Purple dragon, I had a hard time believing my own words.

Chapter Four

"Load up the Ilerioc behind you and strap him in behind the saddle," Hubric said.

I'd done what he said with a lot of difficulty, though it didn't look very comfortable for a wounded man. Jeriath could help me a little, but he was incoherent and mumbled constantly.

"There's nowhere else to put him and we can't afford to risk ourselves. We have miles to go today to reach the Dawn Gate and who knows what we'll find when we get there."

"There are no people between here and there?" I asked.

"Not that I've ever heard of. It's a place for dragons to roam free."

"What are these other dragons going to do?" I asked as I finished strapping Jeriath to the saddle. Hubric's other gear and my staff were already stowed in the proper bags and I would have been feeling worried about the lack of food or blankets if my belly wasn't burning like a hot ember was inside of it.

Should I tell someone about that, or would it just make them nervous? Maybe it was just all in my head, anyway. You could cause problems inside your body just by worrying too much, right? And I was pretty worried about swallowing that stone. That had been a bad idea.

I didn't like the idea of it staying inside, but I also didn't like any of the other alternatives.

"They're a group of juveniles traveling together. They didn't know about the conflict. They haven't decided what they're doing, but I think as long as Olfijum is partnering with Heron, they'll want to stick around."

I still hadn't seen them. I kept one eye on the sky as we took off and one eye on little Nasataa. He flew tucked under Kyrowat's left wing like a moon orbiting the larger dragon.

"Will he be able to fly for long?" I asked Hubric anxiously. "He's still so young!"

"Trust him. He'll be fine. You have to trust people – and dragons – to be able to do things without you. You show them disrespect if you pretend they can't function without your constant aid. It tells them you are capable and they are not. Do you want him to think he's capable?"

"Yes."

"Then trust his abilities."

It wasn't as easy to trust those things as Hubric seemed to think. I was a ball of nerves as I tried to keep an eye out for both the people I loved at once. It wasn't weird to say I loved Heron. That's what friends felt about each other.

I'd thought that the juvenile group had changed their minds about joining us but after an hour of flying they caught up, snorting and flaming in excitement as they pulled up beside Kyrowat, cupping the air with their huge wings.

At the back of the pack, Olfijum soared with Heron on his back. My best friend whooped like a kid riding a goat, one hand high in the air as he waved wildly to us. In any other circumstances, his sheer delight would have melted me. It still kind of did. But I was also worried.

Would an untrained dragon be able to take care of him so high up in the air? He didn't even have a saddle! Would things change between us now that he had this new friend? I glanced toward Nasataa, biting my lip. My dedication to him had changed Heron's life. How could his dragon not change mine?

On top of that, Hubric was making me worried. He glanced behind us often and every time he did, Kyrowat seemed to speed up. But whatever he was seeing, I wasn't seeing and after long hours my eyes began to hurt from looking at everything all at once.

"We'll set down at this creek for a drink," Hubric called back to me out of nowhere, and then we were diving toward the creek before I could respond, like a fleet of ships descending on an island.

The dragons, thirsty after hours of flying, plunged their heads into the creek, sending up columns of steam. Nasataa was right beside them, shoving his own head into the water before I could leap from Kyrowat's back and gather the little dragon into a hug. He seemed far more calm about being separated from me than I was from him. Here I thought he needed me, but really, he was ready for some independence.

He still needs you. He just needs you to let him fly.

Kyrowat seemed very wise.

Yes. It comes with age.

And very old, I teased.

Watch it!

I cuddled Nasataa to my chest as he drank, resting my cheek against him, just plain glad that he was okay. It felt wrong to be so far from the ocean as if we were walking away from life.

"Did you see?" Heron asked, excitement bubbling up from his deep voice. I'd never seen him so boyish – he was usually the responsible one, the worrying one. It was as if we'd exchanged roles overnight. "Did you see Olfijum? Isn't he amazing? He can speak to me! Right inside my mind!"

"Then I guess that maybe you won't be talking about going home all the time," I said. Why couldn't I just be happy for him? Why did it twist inside me painfully whenever he looked at the dragon with adoring eyes.

Ouch! He was doing it again.

He laughed and grabbed my hand, pulling me away from Nasataa who seemed just as happy to drink without being mauled by an overprotective guardian. No one needed me anymore, it seemed. I didn't mean to pout – but my lower lip did seem fuller than usual.

Heron pulled me up and into his arms laughing at my pout.

"Seleska, you silly little fool. Do you think that because I'm excited to meet Olfijum and fly in the air with him, that I'm any less attached to you? Hmm?"

"Maybe," I admitted, letting my eyes grow big and sad. "Maybe you'll forget me just like *that*."

I snapped my fingers on the word *that*.

He laughed. "I'm as likely to forget one of my eyes or leave my hand behind by accident. I've grown used to those pouty looks and mischievous smiles."

"Oh really," I said, giving him one of the mischievous smiles again. "Does that mean I can do this again?"

I stood up on tiptoes and offered him a light kiss. Just like last time, he froze, as if he was afraid to touch me.

"Seriously, Seleska. You ..." he cleared his throat. "You shouldn't play with me."

"But you're fun to play with," I said, smiling widely. At least he still seemed to notice me when I did *that*.

"Skies and Stars," Hubric growled from behind us. "Every young person I meet forgets I'm there the second they can look starry-eyed at someone else. It's as if I'm invisible. Can you see me? I didn't think so."

I laughed.

"You won't be laughing in a minute. The dragons have water and we must be off again. They're gaining on us."

"Who is gaining on us?" I asked, suddenly too worried to play games with Heron.

"The twenty Manticores and their riders who have been on our tails all morning. We had to stop for water, but if I had my way, we wouldn't have. We'll be lucky if we can stay ahead of them until dark and then we're going to have to maneuver quickly to lose them in the dark. Skies and Stars send a black night! There should be a new moon."

I exchanged a worried look with Heron but we were both scrambling back onto the dragons before Hubric was even done his speech. What would we do if they caught us? There just weren't enough of us to fight them. And Nasataa was just a baby. I watched him worriedly, trying not to upset him as we launched back into the air.

Skies and Stars send a black night and a chance to avoid the Manticores! My belly flared hot and ill at the thought.

Chapter Five

My eyes were so glued to Nasataa as we kicked up into the air that I barely noticed Heron shooting by on Olfijum.

"Boy's a natural," Hubric commented. "You could think about going easier on him."

As if I was hard on Heron! He was the one who was always leaving *me* feeling confused. I shook my head.

"He followed you all this way, didn't he?" Hubric pressed. "That's dedication. You won't find that just anywhere."

The sun was glaring and hot, making it hard to see far without squinting, but when I looked behind us, I saw what Hubric had seen. Silhouettes. Figures chasing us through the sky.

After that, I kept a close eye on my small dragon. If he started to flag – even for a moment – I wanted to be there to catch him and help him. The hours passed with the slowness of aging, one after another, after another. My seat hurt from sitting so long, my neck from craning down to keep an eye on Nasataa and my eyes from constant vigilance as I watched the sky behind and before. We were headed toward a black, teeth-like mountain range but as the hours passed, it hardly seemed to grow bigger.

"We're supposed to find a dragon named Raolcan in the Dominion," I said to Hubric, not able to keep worry out of my voice. "Any idea who he is?"

"Sure," Hubric said casually.

"Any idea where he might be?"

"With the Dominar," Hubric said. "He's her dragon. Or maybe she's his human. That can be tricky to sort out."

"What's a Dominar?"

Hubric chuckled. "The fearsome leader of the Dominion, ally of Haz'Drazen and guardian of the dragon's greatest human allies."

I swallowed. "Will it be hard to get to talk to him? Taoslil said I needed to talk to him in particular about where to find the keys we need to unlock the Haroc."

"I think I can get you a meeting," he said dryly. There was something he wasn't telling me. It was almost as if he was friends with this Raolcan.

He mentored the Dominar just like he's mentoring you. Although she was a bit less hotheaded.

As always, Kyrowat was a bit cranky. Hopefully, he was keeping an eye on Nasataa.

Believe it or not, he's important to us, too.

"And then I need to find keys in Ko'Torenth and Baojang. I don't suppose you know anyone in those countries, too?"

"Could be," Hubric said with a grunt.

"Maybe you could share that information?"

He was quiet for a moment. "Do you really want me to be your mentor?"

"I don't know. It seems like I need you. Do you mentor people who aren't dragon riders?" I was probably fine on my own, but Hubric had been helpful and it seemed ungracious to act like he hadn't been. I'd still be floundering in the river if not for him.

Ahem.

And Kyrowat.

"Not usually, but for you, I might make an exception. Usually, there are oaths."

I sniffed. "I don't really like being tied to things. I like to be free as a flag in the wind."

"Yes, I can see that. You haven't given any rash promises about guarding little dragons with your life or finding three keys before the Manticores do or anything like that."

I tapped him on the shoulder and when he looked behind him I gave him my very best smile. "Would you like to swear oaths, wise mentor?"

He snorted. "You're trouble, Seleska. Trouble on two legs. But I think you plan to be trouble to the Manticores and the Rock Eaters and that you'll be loyal and true to your friends and your dragon. That's why I'm willing to take you on and make you my responsibility. So. Repeat after me and try not to flinch. I, say your name."

"I, Seleska."

"You should put your fist over your heart for this part." He nodded when I did. "Swear fealty and full allegiance to Hubric Duneshifter, Dragon Rider of the Purple, until death takes one of us."

"But I'm sworn to Nasataa first," I objected. "You can't come before that."

"Fealty is different," he growled. "Fealty means you listen to me and I guide you. I won't ask you to do anything that isn't in the dragon's best interest."

I hesitated.

Just do it. He won't give up until you do, and seriously, you're getting the better end of the bargain.

For a supposedly choosy dragon, Kyrowat sure did speak to me a lot.

It's possible that I'm growing to like you.

Surprised, but a bit triumphant, I repeated Hubric's words. After all, I could use more allies, couldn't I?

"And I swear this by my honor and the Truth which is all I have to give." His knife flicked out of the sheath as I repeated his words and then he slit the end of his thumb and pressed the blood to my forehead.

Yuck. And I didn't even have a cloth to wash it off with.

"I, Hubric Duneshifter, accept your pledge, Seleska, and I swear to protect and guide you, shelter and provide for you, as my liegesworn until death takes one of us. I swear this by my honor and the Truth which is all I have to give." His smile widened. "It is done. Don't make me regret this!"

I laughed. "How could you regret it, old man? I'm going to make your last years the most exciting of your life."

He didn't laugh. "And now that we've done that, I think you should stop lying to me."

Chapter Six

My heart skipped a beat. "Lying?"

"Those Manticores are tracking us like they know exactly where we are. How can they do that, Seleska?"

I looked over my shoulder. There were so many of them back there. More than the dozen that Hubric had guessed before. And they were gaining on us. I bit my lip and thought fast.

It couldn't be the rock in my belly. Could it? Of course not. That was just a little mistake. It had nothing to do with this.

"I can tell from your expression that you're hiding something. And they're gaining on us."

"Well," I reasoned, "We're easy to see from the air."

"But if we went down in the rocks below, could we even hide if we wanted to?" Hubric asked. "What did you take from that Atura girl?"

"A rock," I said guiltily, my eyes still fixed on the Manticores. They were gaining on us. They were bigger than the dragons and on their backs, they carried multiple riders. I could almost make out covered faces and red hoods. Rock Eaters.

He let out a quiet curse. "A rock? Do you know what their rocks do? How they're made?"

"They suck the life out of people and use it to make magic. They put that power in the rocks," I said.

"Yes. Exactly. And you took one. Well, they also can track that magic anywhere, so it's an easy solution. Pull it out of whatever pocket it's in and throw it to the ground."

"Ummm." Was that – that couldn't be Atura on one of them, could it? She had something in her arms. Something just a little bit smaller than Nasataa.

"Well? What are you waiting for?"

"There's a tiny problem. Just a little one. Small, really."

"Spit it out."

"Yep, that's the problem." I felt my cheeks growing hot.

Hubric snarled. "Speak clearly, girl!"

"I swallowed the rock," I said, watching him with big worried eyes as he cursed so loudly that Kyrowat jumped beneath us.

When he was done, all he could do was shake his head. "You've doomed us, girl. You've doomed us all."

"Look, I'm sorry! I'm really sorry!" I said even though he wasn't listening to me. "I didn't mean to. I was just hiding it in my mouth so I could show her my empty hands and then I swallowed it by accident."

"Check Jeriath. Is he alive?"

I checked, frantic to do anything to make up for my mistake. Hubric was tearing through his saddlebags like a madman.

"He's alive but he still isn't doing very well."

"When he wakes up, you're going to interrogate him, okay? Start by asking how the Manticores got into the Lands of Haz'drazen. Make sure you let him know that you know he is Dusk Covenant."

"Dusk what?"

"Covenant. Don't ask questions, just listen. He's Dusk Covenant. I'm nearly sure. Their sign is tattooed on his ribs. There must still be some of them left. Ask him who and how many. Get as much information as you can, okay?"

"O – kay. But can't you do that?"

"Take this book. It's my book of Prophecies. Read them. You know how to read, right?"

"Yes." He was scaring me. "But you just promised that you'd be with me until you died. Why does it sound like you're planning to leave me?"

"See this scarf?" he asked, ignoring my question as he untied a scarf from around his head and put it around my neck. "The Dominar will recognize it. It's been mine for a long time and the pattern is unique. So will Tor Wine-spring, the ruler of Ko'Torenth. Tell them that I sent you, and they will help you in any way that you need. Trust no one else. Follow the prophecies."

I looked behind me. The Manticores were so close that I could see Atura's face. The triumphant look on it sent a chill through me.

"You're acting like you're going to die!" I didn't mean to make my voice sound hysterical, but it sounded like that anyway.

"Girl," Hubric said through clenched teeth. "If you told me the truth about that stone, I will be dying tonight."

Chapter Seven

The sun was dipping lower, staining the black rocks with an orange glow as the Manticores finally caught up with us. I'd been watching them for the last minutes, no longer trying to delve into what Hubric meant by saying he was going to die. I was too obsessed with the death that loomed for all of us right behind where we flew.

I looked down at Nasataa. He'd been doing so well, but the little dragon was flagging now, and Kyrowat had to slow down to keep him close. The gap between us and the juvenile dragons widened so quickly that when I called to Heron, he didn't hear my call.

"He can't fly like this for much longer," I told Hubric. "We need to find another way!"

"I'm open to suggestions," he said tightly, but when I glanced back, the Manticore behind us was so close that I could see the gleam in his rider's eyes. Any second now and they'd have us. We couldn't stay ahead of them like this.

"Come on, Nasataa!" I called. "You can do it! Keep going!"

"Caught you, imposter!" Atura called from her Manticore.

In her arms, the creature she held was a small Manticore. His eyes glowed red and his small teeth were as jagged and broken as the older Manticores' were. Could he fly, too? He was about Nasataa's size and weight.

Wait.

Where was the baby dragon she'd had back at the throne of Haz'Drazen?

"Never heard of cloaking magic, have you?" Atura called. "The dragons hadn't heard of it, either. They never even realized that little Felroc, the 'dragon' they chose as their Chosen One was a baby Manticore all along! And now *I* have the clues to the keys and I'll be taking him to the Haroc!"

"Turn! Skies and Stars, turn!" Hubric yelled to the dragons ahead of us, but whether they could understand him or hear him not, they didn't turn as the Manticores leapt forward with a burst.

Heron looked behind him, but he was too far ahead for me to catch his eye. I thought his mouth might be open, but whatever he was shouting was lost on the wind. We were too far behind. He and the other dragons wouldn't be able to turn in time.

I gasped in a deep breath, trying to catch sight of Nasataa, but I couldn't see him. Where was the little guy? This was why I didn't like him to be out of my arms!

Something shook Kyrowat's tail and then we were falling straight down before suddenly being whipped up again. I scrambled for my staff, tied to the saddle, my belly lurching as the scenery in front of me went from sky to rocks to sky again. I gritted my teeth, pulling at the lashings.

No, no, no!

One of the Manticores had Kyrowat by the tail, shaking him back and forth like a dog with a bone. Someone was screaming – was that me? I couldn't tell anymore.

I had the staff. I leveled it against the pull of the wind, trying to turn it toward the Manticores but now we were tumbling form the sky toward the rocks. My heart was in my throat. Nasataa! Where was Nasataa?

A high-pitched scream filled the air and my heart felt like it might burst. Nasataa! Nasataa!

Shut up! Kyrowat yelled through my mind. *I can't hear anyone else!*

I tried to calm my thoughts, but my breath was coming too fast as his wings suddenly shot to the sky and we stabilized, still falling, but slower now, just before crashing into the rock.

All my thoughts were upward as my neck craned toward the sky.

There was no sign of my baby dragon. I couldn't see him anywhere!

I tugged at the straps holding me to Kyrowat's saddle, but it was impossible to untie them while holding the staff. A burst like a powerful wind hit us, tumbling us over the rocks. Manticore magic! I'd felt this before. I aimed my staff forward, gritting my teeth and tried to think of the things I was grateful for. Nasataa, Heron, Hubric ... but my worry was too powerful. I couldn't feel that wave of hope like I had last time.

A second blast sent us spinning again. We tumbled end over end until we landed with a crunch. I was pinned under Kyrowat, my vision completely blocked by his back and spine.

I coughed, my lungs sucking at air that just wouldn't fill them. Coughed again. I couldn't see what was happening!

I could only see a sliver of sky and what I saw there made my heart freeze. The red and two black juvenile dragons battled a full-grown dragon with three Bubblers on his back. While they flamed, bursts of bubbles soared toward them.

"Hubric?" I couldn't see him at the angle I was twisted into and I couldn't move.

Above me, the bubbles hit the Black dragon square in the face and his flame went out immediately. He coughed, head whipsawing back and forth as if he were trying to shake a scent from his nose and then he coughed, his neck arching painfully before his entire body went limp and fell to the ground.

No.

Had he just ...

No.

NASATAA! I screamed in my mind as loudly as I could but there was no answer. No sign of him in the sky. No sign of Heron and his Purple dragon. No scolding from Kyrowat.

A second dragon fell from the sky, his landing shaking the ground under me.

"Hubric!" I called, panicked now as I tried to wiggle out from under Kyrowat. One of my hands was crushed under the staff, Kyrowat's weight pinning it against the rock. "Kyrowat! Please, someone, listen!"

"I'm listening, imposter. What do you want to say?"

Shivers shot down my spine at the sound of Atura's voice.

Chapter Eight

Her face appeared, leaning over me and she snatched away the mask over the lower half of it to reveal a venomous smile.

"How interesting. You didn't get very far, did you? And now that I don't have to pretend anymore, we can suck the life out of you and use it for something more ... interesting. The Saaasallla will be pleased. He was not amused when you went off on your own. Your impulsiveness nearly destroyed a plan that was decades in the making."

"I do try," I said through gritted teeth. "Nothing like threats about 'sucking the life out of you' to really make a girl want to foul up a plan."

Her expression went tight.

"Oh, it's not an idle threat." She wrapped her hand into my hair and began to tug. I screamed through clenched teeth as every nerve ending in my head caught on fire, but then the weight lifted off my legs and I was free of Kyrowat's weight. Atura dragged me across the rocks, snatching the Dragon Staff out of my hand as she went. My feet scrabbled across the ground as I tried to stand, tried to see what was happening. Was Kyrowat dead? Where were Hubric and Nasataa?

"Bubbler Atura," another voice said as I was still trying to catch my breath. "The dragons are destroyed. Captives will only slow us down."

Atura considered me carefully. "The Ilerioc?"

I looked to where Kyrowat was being dragged along the ground by a pair of Manticores. He looked badly beat up. His tail was missing chunks, his head rolled and flopped limply along the ground and one of his wings was at an awkward angle. I didn't think he was dead but ...

288

I felt thick – like I couldn't even feel all the emotions filling me. Not Kyrowat! Not the snappy dragon who pretended to be cranky when he was actually kind! What were they going to do to him?

"The Ilerioc lives, but he is gravely injured."

"He must have been part of this or they wouldn't have brought him with him. Revive him for questioning."

"But Bubbler Atura – "

"Don't question your orders. Go and prepare him. We have time now that we've caught my rival. The Saaasallla will be very disappointed if she is not contained and the old man and dragon will help us. Our reserves grow low."

There was no sign of anyone still in the air. No sign of anything other than Manticores and their riders on the ground. Were all the dragons dead? They couldn't be, could they?

No, no. no, Seleska!. Despair would help nothing. I had to hold out hope. As long as I didn't see Nasataa dead or lost or alone, he might be okay. As long as I didn't see Heron dead, he might be okay, too. I needed to cling to that. I needed to believe it.

"As you say, Honored One."

I tried again to stand but someone kicked me and I fell back to the ground. A boot stepped hard on my hand, bringing tears to my eyes. I blinked them away hurriedly. It wasn't time for tears. It was time to be brave and hope for the best. I hissed as they ground their heel into the small bones of my hand.

But I couldn't see Hubric anywhere. I couldn't even see Jeriath.

What was going on?

Fingers in my hair lifted me up as the foot released my hand.

"Do you remember how I told you that I am a master of the life arts?" Atura asked me. Her hand in my hair hurt but I gritted my teeth against the pain.

"Is this the list of your qualifications? Sorry, but I'm not hiring right now. You could see if the dragon city we left needs dungeon cleaners."

She spat at me and I flinched.

"I think I'd like to see your face when you realize what 'life arts' means. You might remember a man named Octon from our lands, hmmm?"

I did remember Octon. He'd worked so hard to help us. He'd done it despite all the risk to himself.

"I used my arts on him. An interesting subject. If you hadn't stolen that rock from me, maybe you could have seen how he turned out. I sucked his life out and I put it in that rock."

A flare of heat burned in my belly at her words and I felt ill.

"Ah. I can tell by how your face pales that you understand. I'm going to do the same thing to your friends. It's a convenient way to carry power around with you, don't you think?"

Chapter Nine

I felt the blood draining from my face and my head spun. I was going to be ill. I was going to be ill. I turned to the side and vomited. But unfortunately, no stone came out with the food and water in my belly.

Had I really eaten what was left of Octon? I would never have treated that stone with so much ... casualness ... if I'd realized that was what it was!

Maybe she was lying. She was evil and evil people lied, right?

And yet, I had a terrible feeling that she wasn't lying. That she really had taken the man who had helped us and turned him into a stone so she could use his life force to power her plans. And I'd swallowed that stone. And it didn't seem to be coming out any time soon. The heat in my belly increased.

Maybe it would kill me.

Maybe I deserved that.

Stars and skies, I was going to be ill!

Atura pushed me ahead of her over the black rocks and I winced at every step. One of my knees didn't feel right, pain lancing through it whenever there was weight on it. Blood and bruises marred my arms and hand and my face hurt on the side that had hit the rocks. But that wasn't what had me worried. They'd tied Hubric to a rock and they were marching me to where he was tied. Jeriath slumped against another rock. No one had bothered to tie him.

I checked Hubric over. Other than a black eye and a gash on his forehead, he looked okay. His eyes burned with fire and his mouth was fixed in a scowl. I hoped that I still had his book and his scarf. He'd be pretty upset if I'd lost those. I thought I felt the book pressing against my leg in my pocket, but it was hard to tell.

I sought his gaze and found it and he seemed to be trying to offer me strength and bravery in the look he shared with me.

Atura shoved me roughly against a man-sized rock and nodded to another bubbler who began to wind rope around me as he tied me in place. Bubblers were crawling all over the rocks, gathering sticks and building fires near their Manticores. I could barely stomach a glance at the horrific creatures, though their stink filled the hillside like a dirty farm.

"Tie her so that she can watch. I want her to see why her side is going to lose," Atura said with a smile. "You'll like that, won't you, Seleska? If that White Dragon hadn't made you such a pet, we never would have had to attack at all, but you just had to work your charms on him, didn't you?"

"They came over the mountains like a wave," Jeriath muttered.

"He's ready?" Atura asked.

"I think he's close to dead," one of the Bubblers said. "This is as ready as he'll be."

Atura sniffed.

"And the dragon?" the bubbler asked.

"Doesn't look like he has much life left, but we can try. No need to tie him down. The Manticores will snatch him from the air if he tries to fly."

"They flooded our land like a locust plague," Jeriath mumbled. Whatever dreams he was having while he fought for his life were not pleasant ones.

And just like that, we were reduced to broken refuse, barely even worth the trouble of tying up. Like driftwood washed up on the beach and ignored until someone wanted a beach fire.

Come on, Seleska! I tried to coach myself. Don't think like that. While there is life, there is hope! When Ramariri rescued me it had seemed hopeless, and then he'd saved me. There had been hope, after all. I didn't dare give up now, right? But it was hard to feel that way when every time I blinked, I thought I could imagine little Nasataa in distress somewhere in these rocks. What if even now he was crying, looking for help and I wasn't coming to help him? What if even now he was trying to get to me not realizing he would be in danger if he ever did? I bit my lip and tried not to think about it.

Hope, Seleska. Keep hoping!

I was still hoping as Atura strode away, head high, with a last comment. "I'll be back for you before nightfall."

I was still hoping as the Bubblers gathered around their fires and Hubric turned to me and spoke through thick lips. "This was prophesied. I heard it from the lips of Zin the Seer of the Kav'ai."

"What was prophesied?" I asked, still hoping this was all a mistake.

"That when the girl who swallowed the stone swore to me, that meant my life was coming to fulfillment. You'll die that day, Hubric, she said. But be strong. Your path does not end with death."

I swallowed. "Maybe she was wrong."

He shook his head sorrowfully and all my hope seemed to break like a waterskin filled too full. "She's never wrong."

"Everyone is wrong sometimes," I said. "And she just has to be wrong. She has to be. Because Atura and these disgusting Manticores can't win." I felt my eyes stinging as the tears came. Someone had leaned my staff against a nearby rock and the last rays of sunset glinted on the blade. "And you can't die, Hubric. And the dragons can't lose. And Nasataa can't be hurt. It just can't be, okay?"

And now hot tears were dripping down my nose as hard and fast as they could fall.

"There's no explaining why some things must be, child." I'd never heard his tone so warm and soft. "But some things must be so that other things can happen."

"Bad things? Wrong things? That just doesn't make sense! I don't want to live in a world where bad things have to happen!"

"Would you rather live in a world where none of it mattered at all?" His tone was gentle.

"What do you mean?"

"If nothing is risked, then nothing is gained. Great pain births great triumphs. I don't know why it has to be this way, but this is how it is and how it always has been since before magic first swelled in the heart of the earth and poured forth to bathe us in light. Life is a testing ground. It plows deep furrows through our hearts. But unless our ground is broken up and our furrows plowed, we cannot grow new life. Nothing can be birthed where something wasn't broken first."

"I just," I bit my lip. "I just don't want the bad things to be true."

"But they are," he said fiercely as the sun slipped over the horizon, bathing us in shadow so that the only light left was the light of the fires the Bubblers had set. "They are true. And wishing them away does you no good at all. Find that gratitude you had in your heart. Find that hope that made you powerful before, and find how you can drive good into the world like nails."

"There's got to be a way to save you," I said, my voice thick with the tears I wasn't willing to shed. "There's just got to be a way."

"Zin told me that if I didn't go on this quest, if I didn't find you, then the world would be swallowed in shadow. I did what I had to for the sake of the light and I have no regrets, girl." He said. And there were no tears in his voice. He seemed steady as he had hours ago when we flew together on the back of Kyrowat. "Do what you have to, Seleska. Don't let either of our lives go for a cheap price. Make what you do next worth the sacrifice and love that came before. Let the ground be tilled to grow something new."

I nodded, my chin wobbling as I pushed back tears. I'd known him such a short time, but I'd felt so safe with him. I'd felt like I finally knew where to go and what to do. I tugged at the ropes around my wrists, trying to loosen them. Maybe if I worked at them hard enough, I could work my way free.

"And Seleska?" Hubric's words sounded heavy.

"Yes?"

"If you can ... and I don't know if you can, but if you can." For the first time, his voice hitched a little. "Please take Kyrowat with you. He's been a faithful companion. He doesn't deserve to die like this."

Hot tears slid down my face. I fought against them, but the harder I fought, the more came at the thought of this man who loved his dragon so much that he was all he wanted to save.

"I will."

A voice rang out from the darkness.

"I've found a nice rock. Not as smooth as a river rock, but the right size. And he seems like he's made of hard edges, too, so maybe it will be a good fit for him."

Atura carried a torch and when she arrived, she planted it into a crack in the rock so that it lit Hubric, Jeriath and me with dancing orange light.

"They came but they did not stay. They died like locusts, falling from the air like dust." Jeriath was still deep in his fever dreams. What had they done to loosen his tongue like that?

"What do you think?" Atura asked. She held out a black, sparkling rock the size of her pinkie finger and my heart fell. Somehow, I'd still been hoping that these were all empty threats, but the rock and these words, they made it all feel real.

"Ready, old man?" she asked.

"Do your worst," Hubric said, eyes flashing in the torchlight.

"Oh, I plan to. You can count on that."

Chapter Ten

I would have expected that a magical rite that stole a person's life from them and turned it into power would take more than one person. I would have expected a lot of people – probably in terrifying costume and intoning in unison.

Instead, there was just Atura with a long rod in one hand and a stone in the other. She stood beside the torch, her head tilted slightly to the side, concentrating.

Seleska?

The voice in my head was weak.

Kyrowat?

I tried to keep my expression calm. If Atura saw me, I didn't want her to notice anything strange. There was a long silence – likely he was talking to Hubric.

"Hubric?" I said. "Hubric?"

He gasped, eyes wide.

And then he fell forward as if he was a puppet whose strings had been cut.

My breath was sucked away.

And that was all.

In one nearly silent moment, everything had changed.

Something bright and pure as spun gold spread from his body to the rod in Atura's hand and then into the stone in her other hand. The satisfied smile on her face was all I needed to know she'd succeeded.

My mentor was gone.

My mouth fell open as I gasped. I just ... didn't know what to feel.

Horror.

Horror that threaded through my ribcage reaching for my spine and bone-deep guilt. I'd told him not to be my mentor! I'd told him what had happened to Ramariri and Vyvera. Why hadn't he listened to me? He should have listened!

My thoughts raged, angry and horrified, sick and confused. Loud, but incoherent.

Hubric's head was slumped on his chest. His eyes were still open. I could feel the sob bubbling up in my chest. Someone needed to close his poor eyes. Someone needed to protect him from seeing what had happened to him, from seeing the victory on his tormentor's face, from seeing the hopelessness his death had birthed into the world.

All that nonsense about bad things being *for* something. I didn't believe that. Not for a second. This was nothing but a waste and a desecration. This was bone-deep *wrong* and if I made Atura pay for it forever it wouldn't be enough.

My belly burned hot from the stone within. Whatever magic was contained in it – dark or light or something else was longing to come out and I was longing to let it. Come out, little magic. Come and play! Let's show Atura a little life force magic, hmmm? How would she feel being sucked out of her body and fed into a rock, hmmm?

"Well, I can see why you have so many ropes," I said, trying hard to keep my flowing tears from clouding my tone of voice. "It's the only way you can keep people around. Even your friends over there are scared of you. Have you been making them into a rock collection, too?"

"You don't know what you're talking about," Atura said as she directed the rod to continue feeding the golden strands into the stone. My heart throbbed painfully as the stone began to glow brighter. It almost felt like that was the last breath of him. As if when the threads were done moving, he'd be really gone. "Do you have any idea what power it takes to do this kind of magic? You have to understand the essence of a person. What makes them tick. And then you can pull it out and put it in a ... container."

"And what? Walk around with a belly full of rocks for the rest of your life? You told me yourself that you need the Saaasallla to activate the rocks. You can't do that. All you can do is give yourself a belly ache."

It felt good to lash out at her. Felt good to poke at the person who was making me feel so much gut-deep pain. I hadn't even known Hubric for very long, but he'd been willing to offer me his protection for the rest of his life. And that had been enough to get him killed. He hadn't deserved that.

No one deserved that.

Stand ready. Kyrowat's mental voice was weak. *I call to them.*

Who was he calling? It had better be an army or we'd already lost. I was next. And then Kyrowat. I was not relishing living the rest of my life as a rock.

Atura laughed. Her laugh made me want to vomit. Nothing about this was funny.

"Those kinds of rocks are for greater power with manipulating life force magic. Those rocks are like ... tuners. They make it possible to manipulate the life in all living things to greater levels. And yes, for that, I need the blessing of the Saaasalla, may he live forever."

"Isn't he your dad? You did tell me you were a princess," I said. "If he lives forever doesn't that mean you'd never get a crack at being Saaasallla."

Her eyes flashed.

Yes! I'd finally hit a nerve! She ignored my words, but I could tell she was struggling with that.

"The rock I just made – the one I'm about to eat – is distilled from a person. And that's different. It makes it possible for me to absorb some of that person's skills and knowledge. And it doesn't require anything more than swallowing it to activate it. Don't you think that might be helpful?" Her smile was wicked. "I heard he has a lot of connections in the Dominion and Ko'Torenth. By the time I get there, I'll know what he knew, and I'll be a much more convincing "guardian" than you are. Especially once I put Felroc's little mask of light back in place and he plays pretty, pretty dragon baby for them."

The sound that came out of my mouth was pure guttural anger. I was going to kill her. I was going to rip her apart.

"Any help you thought you had," she said with a smile, "is mine now."

Chapter Eleven

Waves of despair washed over me one after another. She would have Hubric's knowledge and the ability to pretend that she had a baby dragon to protect. How could I possibly beat that? I would look like a fraud.

But if I didn't at least try, then all the magic left in the world would go to Atura and the Saaasallla and I'd seen what they would do with it. I'd seen how little they valued life beyond their own. They wouldn't stop at just killing everyone I ever knew. After all, they'd killed Octon's whole family. He'd said that they put them in mass graves.

If they killed their own people, they wouldn't even blink at killing mine.

A flash of a memory filled my mind – an image too painful to digest. I shoved it away, cold fear washing over me. I'd never seen all those bodies I was just remembering. I'd never seen them thrown into the earth.

Those were Octon's memories.

That I had.

Because I'd swallowed his rock.

Heat flared painfully in my belly, mixing with my emotions of regret and guilt. I shouldn't have swallowed that stone. What had I done?

There was no taking the past back. All I could do now was try to honor Octon. It wouldn't exactly make up for this, but it was all I had.

Atura was playing with my Dragon Staff now that her rock was made. She jabbed it into the air with a puzzled look on her face, twisting the haft, spinning the staff. Her expression only grew more cloudy as she worked until eventually, she set it back against the rock I was tied to – though woefully out of reach.

In the distance, the Bubblers had made camp and the quiet sounds of retiring for the night were drifting up to us. For them, the torture of strangers was just another night. Same old boring stuff happening all over again.

"The waves washed over them," Jeriath mumbled. "Waves of Destiny. And at their crest, a blue dragon rode."

I almost wished I knew what he meant. One thing was certain – Atura was unlikely to get any information of value from a man as out of things as Jeriath.

"I can tell by your expression that you finally realize the situation, Seleska." Atura was bathing in her victory, happiness making her face softer.

With a quick movement, she popped the freshly glowing stone into her mouth and swallowed, opening it after to show me her empty mouth.

"Your friend is mine and soon you will be, too. Not that you have much to offer me, but maybe that staff of yours will work once you're in my belly."

"I doubt it," I said through my numb feelings. "You're not the type of person who can use it."

It was wrong that she'd eaten Hubric's stone. Wrong that she had any part of him at all!

She laughed. "Ah, but you are. And that's all that matters here."

I clenched my jaw. But as my belly flared with heat, my hands began to work at the ropes of their own accord. What had I just done there? That was a trick I didn't know. The ropes began to loosen. Was it possible ... was it crazy to think it? ... that Octon's abilities really had transferred just a little to me?

"I have a special rock saved just for you," Atura said with a smile. I was beginning to hate her never-ending smiles. "I selected it after our first meeting. We've already proven that I can't just pull your soul out of your body with my magic, but that won't be a problem. Burning always works when simple magic doesn't. Something about the pain and heat, I think. And you're already tied perfectly for the process."

Burning? Fear slashed through my thoughts making it impossible to think as nausea swept over me. There were a lot of ways to die. Burning sounded like the worst of them.

Seleska?

Kyrowat. Sorry, old boy. I couldn't save your friend. My friend.

Coming for you.

He sounded so tired and so selfless. He was clearly hurting and barely conscious and yet he was trying to come to my aid. Well. At least I wouldn't die without friends. That was a kind of accomplishment, wasn't it?

If I was going to die, I wasn't going to do it cowering. I straightened my back still working on my bonds as I did it. I was going to make sure to take a moment to be grateful before I lost that chance.

And I was grateful.

You'd think that I'd be bitter that Nasataa had come into my life. After all, his presence had thrown me into danger and chaos. But I wasn't sorry. If he hadn't arrived on my beach, I probably would never have known Vyvera, or Octon, or Hubric, or Kyrowat. I would never have learned that it's better to give love and affection to others than to keep it for yourself because I never would have felt that kind of protective selfless love that I felt for that little dragon. I probably wouldn't have realized how much Heron meant to me. That I ... that I loved him.

I felt tears forming. But they weren't tears of despair or regret. They were deep thankfulness. If I died now, at least I'd really lived first. Maybe all that nonsense of Hubric's actually made sense. Maybe all of this really was *for* something that would come after us.

Maybe.

At least these last moments of mine were blessedly free of Atura. That was something to be grateful for, too. That mudfeeder was going to kill me in the cruelest way she could, but I would never give her my knowledge and skills. Not even if I was in a rock.

A roar from the other side of the camp filled the air and then a bright flash of fire bloomed. Maybe they had some kind of weapon. Or maybe they were trying out whatever they were going to use to burn me alive.

A second roar followed by a burst of flame made me tilt my head to the side. That had sounded just a little bit dragon-like.

Something tugged at my ropes.

What?

Sela!

Chapter Twelve

I gasped.

Nasataa! He was alive!

Sela! Sela!

The tugging continued and then a tiny flare of light seared the edges of my vision. The ropes fell free.

I snatched up the Dragon Staff, ready to defend myself, but there was no one there, just a small dragon flaming wildly and rubbing his face all over my belly.

"Nasataa," I breathed, caressing his excited face as relief filled me. He was okay! From the light of his flares, I could see he was unharmed. But where had he been?

He was trying to show me a picture in my mind, but it was broken and blurry, flashing from one thing to another too quickly for me to make out the details.

"Calm down, little blue. We need to get out of here while we can!"

He was tugging me behind the rock before I could complete my sentence.

"But first we have to free Kyrowat!"

I owed him that. I looked uncomfortably at Hubric, slumped against the ropes. We were in a hurry. There was no time to tend to him.

"One minute, little guy."

I sprinted back to Hubric, gently reaching out to shut his eyes. There's something wrong about an empty body where a friend should be, as if life isn't really meant to end at all and death is just a horrible ruse. I hated it.

"I'm sorry," I breathed. "I'm so sorry. This isn't the death you deserved."

But what was a death you deserved? How was any death a 'good' death when it was an end?

I hated endings. I just wanted more beginnings forever.

Maybe in whatever life came after – and I was really hoping there was some life after this one that didn't involve being a rock in Atura's belly – there was a reason for all of this like Hubric had hoped. Maybe there was a great reason for reason. I wanted to hope like he did. I wanted that kind of certainty.

Nasataa hissed, pulling me away from Hubric. He was right. There wasn't time to honor him the way we should. We'd just have to honor him in our hearts.

I followed my little dragon through the rocks as we crept around the camp. If that was a dragon making all that noise, then I sure hoped it wasn't Kyrowat. We'd never get him free if he was flaring and flaming like that!

The way around the rocks was slow as we tried to hurry without light or attracting attention. Nasataa found my progress frustrating. He would flutter a little way and then wait for me. Flutter and then wait. Flutter and then wait.

And all the time I was trying to tell him how happy I was to see him again, sending him images of cuddles and his happy face, letting him know that he was precious to me.

"Thanks for saving me, little guy," I said as we emerged around the last standing rock to see Kyrowat bound, his angry snorts loud in the night. I thought they weren't going to tie him down? They must have changed their minds.

Flares and shouts continued closer to the Bubbler's camp and the snarls and ground-shaking roars of the Manticores made me jumpy, but they weren't centered around Kyrowat like I'd feared. Whatever was happening over there, was happening with a different dragon – or dragons.

"Hurry!" I whispered to Nasataa. Hopefully, if we could free Kyrowat that he would be able to fly.

I can fly.

Hope flared in me at the sound of his voice. He was alive! It was hard to believe. I could smell the blood pooling under him. It turned my stomach as

I used the staff blade to free his mouth first. They'd twined rope around it to keep him from opening it and flaming them.

Next, I moved to the huge cables, keeping him pinned between four big rocks. Fortunately, the blade at the end of the staff was sharp and the ropes sliced with only a bit of effort from me.

He stood gingerly when his bonds were finally shed, shaking his head with only enough effort to send the last scraps of rope tumbling from his neck. He swayed on trembling legs as his wings slowly unfurled. They hadn't removed the saddle or bags from his back though the saddle had slid slightly to the side of his back.

He was in no condition to carry me. I wasn't even sure if he could carry his saddle.

Get on.

Not a chance. I'd already watched Hubric die. I wasn't watching Kyrowat die, too.

"Go," I said gently. "Flee and take Nasataa with you. You can both fly faster without me and I want ... I *need* you to get as far away as you can. Head to the Dawn's Gate. Flee this land."

I just needed them both to be safe.

Wait in this exact spot. I will send help.

Yeah, that would be a winning strategy.

"Sure," I said, but I was humoring him. There was no way I'd wait here.

Right here. Promise.

That would be promising my own death.

Promise or I won't go.

"I promise," I said with a heavy heart. I needed him to go. Now. Before that disruption on the other side of camp was done and the Bubblers all came back to get us.

He ducked his head in a bow and then he launched awkwardly into the air. Nasataa launched himself into my arms and after a brief cuddle, he shot up into the air, hugging close to Kyrowat's underbelly.

Fly free, little friend, I thought. Get somewhere safe.

Sela.

Nasataa.

At least he wouldn't die here with me.

Chapter Thirteen

I felt strange just watching them go and standing in one place. Maybe I should go and see what was happening among all the screams and flares of fire on the other side of camp. But I'd promised to wait here. I gritted my teeth, eyes narrowing as I looked toward the sounds in the dark. I couldn't see anything. It was too dark and too chaotic. If only I could see!

If I hadn't been looking right at that spot, I wouldn't have seen the figure hurtling through the dark in time to dodge. I jumped back as far as I could, just in time. One of the Manticores skidded across the dark rock, landing in a heap right where I'd been standing. His massive paws were larger than my head and if he hadn't been completely still, I would have panicked.

Was he ... was he dead?

I prodded a paw with the butt of my staff, but he didn't move. I couldn't even make out his features in the darkness, only hints of fur and wings from the distant fires.

It was looking like a worse and worse idea to wait right here.

The screams in the distance grew louder and the earth began to shake and then suddenly the fire flared brighter and I could see. The Manticore beside me was definitely dead, his face and shoulders marred by nasty burns.

But worse, there were Bubblers rushing toward me, those bubbling rods brandished in their hands. It was too late to do anything but fight, too late to run or hide. I gripped my staff in both hands, ready to be as grateful as I could be and shove fear aside, but as if by its own will, my body suddenly shifted the staff to the side and leapt forward, chopping with the staff faster than I thought I could. The Bubbler running toward me stumbled as my staff slashed into his shoulder but my arms wrenched the staff blade from his body and spun it to plunge into his back as he fell past me – quicker than I could have imagined.

What was I doing? I wasn't a killer!

And yet, I was killing.

They killed us. They stacked us up like wood for the fire.

That thought was not mine! And the sound of it reminded me of Octon.

Before I could gasp at it, the next Bubbler was rushing toward me, my hands were up and ready before I was. Throwing him over my hip as I used his own momentum against him, I spun around to pin him to the rocks with the Dragon Staff.

This was crazy! This wasn't me!

But I was the one who swallowed the stone – and this was definitely Octon. He'd been a warrior. And he'd fought with his hands. And he knew Rock Eater culture inside and out.

I was just glad I had an ally inside me, not an enemy. But I wanted this to stop. It wasn't right to have part of another person inside your mind and controlling your hands. But was he controlling them or was I controlling them and just drawing on his skills and memories as I did it? Maybe I was just looking for someone else to blame so I didn't' have to admit that I was a killer.

I was still thinking that when my body spun to block a blow I hadn't even expected, grabbing the attacked by the forearm and pulling him as I ducked, using my back to spin him over me so he smacked onto the hard rock on the other side.

Whew! Octon was quite the fighter!

A spurt of bubbles rippled through the air toward me and I leapt – higher than I should have been able to go.

Something grabbed the back of my shirt at the same time wind struck me, trying to push me down. My feet left the ground and my belly lurched as I rushed up into the air with nothing to hold onto. For a perilous moment, I dangled in the air, helpless, and then I was flying, hoping that whatever had caught me wouldn't let go.

Chapter Fourteen

"Gotcha," Heron said and his voice was triumphant as his dragon spurted fire, illuminating the ground below and the Bubblers scattered in every direction. Manticores and dragons lay sprawled on the ground bleeding but a group of about six Manticores were regrouping.

"You're alive!" I gasped. Pure joy shot through me, eliminating for just a moment the guilt and pain I felt at leaving Hubric behind. Heron was alive! And Nasataa, too. And somehow we were going to escape.

Hopefully, Heron's dragon was fast. I saw Atura leaping onto the back of the biggest Manticore with her baby Felroc in her arms. If we didn't get free fast, we'd lose our chance.

"You didn't think I'd leave you, did you?" he asked tightly, but there was a lot of emotion behind his words that he was failing to disguise with his light tone.

"I thought you were dead," I said. "I hoped you weren't. I tried not to think about it. And Nasataa, too. And all those dragons."

He yanked me up to sit on the dragon, tucking me in close in front of him.

"It was a near miss. Olfijum is hurting. But we're alive. Where's Hubric?"

Olfijum was fast despite being hurt. The Manticores were shrinking in the distance as he raced away from their camp.

"Dead," I choked, all the emotion I'd been forcing back spilling out in that one word. "Dead and gone. Atura sucked out his soul and put it in her rock and then ate it."

"I'm not fond of Atura," Heron said, blackly. As if 'not fond' could encompass volcanic levels of hatred. He drew me in close, one of his thick arms wrapping tightly around me as if he wanted to hold me forever.

"I had a bad night," he admitted.

"Did you watch someone's soul get sucked form their body?" I asked dryly.

"Worse." Heartache leaked into his voice.

"Did you almost get burned alive?"

"Worse." His tone was devastating.

"Did you kill people – people you don't know, who were attacking you?"

"Yes. But that's not why it was worse." His voice was thick with something. Those weren't tears, were they?

"What happened to you?"

"I spent all these hours thinking you were dead, little honey. Spent all this time imagining what life would be without you. Just thinking about it made me so hard to be around that Olfijum agreed to come after you despite the odds."

Olfijum made a keening sound.

"He sounds sad," I said, not sure how to reply to the rest.

"He lost friends. Friends he's had since he was a hatchling."

"I'm so sorry," I said pressing a palm to his back. And now my tears were coming as hot and fast as the guilt that seared me. "I'm so sorry for everything."

"Seleska," Heron breathed into my hair. "You're alive. You're alive and safe and that's all that matters to me."

"Really?" I twisted around to look up at him. I couldn't see much in the dark, but this time I wasn't teasing him. This time I wasn't trying to make him think something or do something. This time I wasn't just playing around. This time was as honest as I could get. "Because that's how I feel about you."

When he kissed me, hot, teary kisses, I let myself melt into how I felt as if these tears could wash me clean of everything I'd done and everything I'd seen. As if just being treasured by him could make me a treasure – even if it was just for a few short hours.

"Don't leave me again, Heron," I said, but it was more like begging.

"I won't. Not ever."

I closed my eyes and held him and let myself relax for the short moments we had. They'd be gone again soon – far too soon – but for just these moments I wanted to add one more thing to my list of gratitude. I wanted to add a shared love with my best friend.

Chapter Fifteen

"I'm worried about Nasataa," I said as the night wore on and we left the Manticores far behind.

Olfijum had climbed steadily upward until he was almost floating on a strong wind high above the earth.

"We sure are high up," I added nervously.

Heron sounded affectionate as he said, "Olfijum likes flying high. The speed up here doesn't worry him."

And he didn't seem worried at all. He seemed to require minimal effort to soar here and considering that he had bite marks in his tail and wings and some dark bruising around his neck, that was probably for the best.

"Don't worry about Nasataa," Heron said. "Olfijum says that Kyrowat is just ahead with the little guy under his wing. They are riding the same current we are, headed for the Dawn Gate. The only downside is that the Manticores could be riding this current, too. But I think it will take them longer to get organized. They aren't the ones fleeing for their lives."

I looked behind us out of instinct, but in the black of the night, I couldn't see a thing. If only there was a moon out or even stars, but the sky was thick with clouds and our visibility was so poor that I felt like I was drifting through infinity. Hubric had been right about the new moon tonight.

"Olfijum says that Kyrowat thinks we'll get to the gate by dawn if we stay up on this fast current. He says that it's the only way in or out of the Lands of Haz'drazen – at least the only way into the Dominion or the lands to the north. Everything else is blocked off by magical currents impossible to pass."

"Okay," I said rallying. "Then we go through the gate and we find this Purple dragon Raolcan. And we'll be okay. Olfijum and Kyrowat will heal up.

Little Nasataa will have a chance to rest. Raolcan will know where the key we're looking for is."

I felt hope as I said it. We had a plan. We had a chance to succeed still. I wound a hand around the scarf Hubric had given me. It smelled of tea and peppermint and it made me think of him – and of my promise. I needed to make all of this worth it somehow.

Eventually, I drifted off to sleep, leaning against Heron. His strong chest and arms welcomed me like home. I dreamed island dreams of campfires and my parents, of feasts with the village, of sneaking off onto dark sandy beaches with Heron and kissing him again just for the joy of it.

I woke when his arms tightened around me.

"Seleska?" he whispered, though who needed to whisper up here? "Seleska, are you awake?"

"Mmmm," I agreed, savoring the warmth of him in contrast to the cold air blowing around us.

"We're here," he said, but there was no triumph in his tone. Instead, it sounded grim.

I pulled out of his arms to look. The first light of dawn was barely tinting the land, crawling across the surface of the ground like a curtain being drawn. Olfijum soared down from his height, head stretched forward into the wind and wings back, giving us a clear view of what was below.

The rocky, jagged mountains were dominated by a round white gate – a portal of sorts decorated with a carved dragon eating its tail. It felt oddly familiar. But it wasn't that dragon gate's carving that had my attention. It wasn't even the large heaps littering the ground and leaving long shadows behind them as the curtain pulled back.

It was the emptiness.

There was not a living creature to be seen. Not guarding the gate. Not on the road that wound out from the gate. Not anywhere.

All around us, littering the ground and spilling across the rocks, was nothing but death. The pervasive scent of death swirled in the air, growing worse as the heat of the sun rolled back over the carnage.

Not all of them were dragons. There were plenty of Manticores. And humans, too.

But all of the twisted figures below were very, very dead.

I made a sound like a whimper in the back of my throat. Nothing in my lifetime – not even the violent deaths of my own family – had prepared me for this. I felt heat in my belly as Octon's memories flashed over my eyes. He had been prepared. He had seen this before. Only last time, it was his loved ones lying tangled in each other's deaths.

Sadness stabbed through me like a dagger. All the hope we'd felt at the thought of reaching the Dawn Gate was erased in a single sight, a single realization that all was not what it seemed and never would be again. How could a culture recover from this? How could a species survive?

I wished we'd saved Jeriath when we fled. Maybe he would have had some insight into why the Ileriocs had helped bring an end to all that they knew. I wished I could understand this. But understanding escaped me as surely as the dawn.

In grim silence, we flew to the gate, not even pausing as we dove through to the other side.

Maybe Nasataa would be there. And that would, at least, be one small triumph.

The gate shimmered and a feeling of coldness washed over me – and then we were on the other side.

I bit my lip to keep from gasping again as fresh horror hit me.

Why had I thought this side would be any different? People, dragons and Manticores littered the earth here, too, as if a wind made of knives had torn through the gate and killed them all. It was all I could do not to vomit.

"What are we going to do?" I asked aloud, stunned by the silence.

"I don't know," Heron admitted, shaking his head. It felt worse when he'd admitted that. Like if he'd pretended to know it somehow would have made everything better. But I didn't know, either.

We were racing an enemy so heartless, so numb from pain, that nothing would deter them. And we were losing. Slowly, but surely, we were losing.

There just had to be some way to turn this all around. If only I could find it.

Chapter Sixteen

We followed the road, looking often over our shoulders as if we expected ravening Manticores to burst from the door at any moment. Maybe we did.

When we finally caught up to them, they were curled up together in the shadow of a jutting rock. I leapt from Olfijum's back, scrambling over the rocky ground to get to them.

Nasataa raised his little head for a moment before letting it fall again. No wonder he was exhausted. His first day flying and he hadn't had a break in twenty-four hours.

Water in the saddlebags. Kyrowat said in my mind.

"There's water in the saddlebags," I told Heron as I checked Nasataa over. A few nicks and scratches dotted his scales, but he seemed fine besides the exhaustion.

Heron busied himself watering the dragons and offering me a waterskin. I drank gratefully. After hours with nothing to drink, I'd been ignoring my burning throat for far too long. I drank deeply, grateful for the cold water.

Salves, bandages, too. Kyrowat's voice was still faint, but Heron was already pulling salves from his saddlebags and hurrying to Olfijum who snarled in pain as his wounds were tended.

I left Nasataa to sleep on Kyrowat's haunches and scurried around to Kyrowat's head. His big eyes were glazed over with pain.

"I'm so sorry, Kyrowat. So sorry," I said beginning to cry again at the thought of the big dragon all alone now, his companion gone forever.

You have his book?

"Yes. Right here." I pulled it out to show him.

And the scarf?

"Yes," tears muddied my voice as I tugged at the scarf around my neck.

Then you follow through with what he wanted. Find Raolcan. Find the keys. Get Nasataa to the Haroc.

I nodded. "You make it sound like you won't be going with me."

My saddle and tack I gift to Olfijum. Instruct your young buck there that the reins are purely for decoration. Riders of Purple dragons do not use them. He's been given a great gift in the opportunity to ride a dragon. He should not abuse it.

Behind me, Olfijum whined.

No, you aren't going to suffer my fate, you young fool! You aren't bonded to the boy, just doing him a favor. Young dragons! You'd be lucky to be bonded to a man like Hubric. The things we saw! The places we went. Every day an adventure.

He sounded like he was rambling now. I looked him over. He was battered and bruised. How had he made it this far on such ragged wings?

You do what you must, girl. I always have. And I did last night, too. But it's not the same without Hubric. I feel my lifeforce leaking away with his death.

I took the bond with Hubric many decades ago. He was a young fool then. But I could see he was going to live an exciting life. Never one to stop trying, Hubric. Solid. A true believer in the Lightbringer causes and prophecies. And look at what he did. He installed two rulers in place. He shaped them into people worth ruling. He'll be remembered. And maybe someone will even remember old Kyro, too.

"Of course, they will," I said, caressing his snout as I sniffed back the inevitable tears.

No sniveling. It's a waste of time. Won't change the future and you have a lot to do. He left his book to you. Read it. That's important to him. Tor never read his enough. He should have. Then things might not have come as such a surprise.

He coughed a big gob of black out, spitting it hard toward Olfijum who barely dodged it with an angry snap of his jaws.

Listen, girl, the prophecies in it are true. Hard to understand, but true. I've watched them fulfilled with these old eyes. Not all, but some. And there are more. Ancient ones yet unfulfilled, and more added by Zin the prophet of the Ka'vai people.

"I don't even know who that is!"

Doesn't matter. What matters is that you read it. If Hubric had lived, he would have insisted on that. Do you understand?

"Yes," I said through thick lips. The tears were coming hot and fast as I felt his voice fading.

Leave me here under these rocks. It's as good a place as any for an old dragon's bones.

"But you're not dead yet," I protested. "Maybe you can recover!"

Can't. He flamed – barely a spurt. *Won't. My bond with Hubric was too strong. I'll be lucky to last the hour. I feel myself fade. Keep that baby dragon safe.*

"Don't go, Kyrowat," I said through a broken voice. "We need you. Please."

He closed his big eyes as Heron gently removed his tack, putting it on Olfijum instead. The young dragon danced irritably, his eyes constantly focused on Kyrowat as if he were waiting for orders.

Long minutes passed, but Kyrowat was still breathing and I just couldn't go.

I've done what I can. Called ahead as far as I could reach. If anyone was listening – any allies – they'll come to help. Trust the Lightbringers. Watch out for the Dusk Covenant.

"Who?"

Read the book! He growled.

"I will."

There was a sound behind me like ripping cloth. I turned back to see Manticores plunging through the Dawn Gate. Heron scrambled from where he was tightening Olfijum's saddle. He scooped up Nasataa like he was still a baby and ran with him to the other dragon.

"Can you carry him?" he was asking his dragon. "Even for a little while?"

My eyes were back on Kyrowat.

"Goodbye, Kyrowat," I said gently stroking his nose. I didn't want to let him go.

You must. Hurry now. While there is time.

Heaving with sobs, I kissed his nose as Heron grabbed my shoulders and steered me toward his dragon. In silence, we mounted and found our seats as Olfijum sprang painfully into the air.

There was a cry of discovery from behind us, but my eyes were still fixed on Kyrowat. His chest wasn't moving anymore.

And as we flew away, I felt as though I had left a part of my heart behind.

Chapter Seventeen

It was barely midday when Olfijum first stumbled, his wings not catching the air quite right.

Another minute until he stumbled again.

"He's too tired," Heron said, his voice tight.

Of course, he was. He'd been flying with the three of us on his back after a full day and night awake and moving. No one could do that.

I snapped shut the book of prophecies I'd been diligently reading, preparing to answer, but then opened it quickly back to the end. There were hand-drawn maps at the back of the tiny book with places and notations. Not cities, I didn't think. Maybe they were places special to Hubric.

I searched them, looking for some place we could take shelter in. Surely, there would be somewhere.

The closest one I could find to the Dawn Gate was a mountain with an X at the base. The notation read, "Shelter, Food, 3 days maximum and a way out for those who dare." It wasn't much of a note. Most of the other places had more written along with dates he had last been there. This had no date, either. Was it only a place he'd heard of and not a place he'd been?

I showed it to Heron.

"This looks close. Do you think we could reach it?"

Both of us turned to stare at the nearby mountain as Olfijum sank in the air.

"He can get there. Hold on, buddy!" Heron said. His palms were pressed to Olfijum's neck.

I nearly screamed when Nasataa dove off his back, but the little dragon spread his wings, sailing beside Olfijum. Smart dragon! Maybe that little bit of extra weight removed would be enough to get him inside the – well, whatever it was.

I gritted my teeth and looked behind me. The Manticores were still behind us. I didn't know if that was because they were following us or because we were headed in the direction of Raolcan or the key or both and they knew that, but I did know one thing: if Atura saw us fall from the sky she would swoop in to kill us all and suck out our souls faster than breathing.

We didn't dare show weakness near her.

Olfijum dropped lower clearly wearing out of strength, but we were getting close to the mountain now.

"Is that it?" I asked Heron, pointing at a dark spot on the side of the rock.

He shook his head. "Just a dead tree."

A creek flowed past the mountain and we dropped beside it, Olfijum and Nasataa sticking their heads into the water while Heron leapt off to fill the waterskins.

"We don't have time for drinking," I protested despite my dry throat.

"We'll die if we don't drink," he said shortly, his mind focused on the task.

I pulled out the map and studied the mountain. Whatever this place was had to be close. By the look of the map, we should be almost right on it. I squinted at the rock, trying to see a cave or a hole or something. Anything.

But I couldn't see a thing. Frustrated, I tried to think, letting my eyes go out of focus as I turned my thoughts inward. If I had a secret place to hide, where would I put it? Near water, obviously. Heron was right about the drinking thing. People and dragons needed to drink.

I frowned but as my eyes stayed unfocused, suddenly a pattern jumped out at me. Wait.

Was that a door?

"Heron!" I called excitedly. "Look!"

I didn't want to look away from it in case it disappeared again.

"I don't see it."

I leapt from Olfijum's back, striding through the rocks and trees, keeping my eyes on the outline of the door. I didn't dare check to see if they were following me. I didn't want to lose sight of the edge of the door. It blended in with the rocks perfectly, moss and lichen growing on the side of it and across the edges in a way that suggested it hadn't been opened in a few seasons.

If it really was a door ... if we really had a chance ...

I barely dared to hope.

The rock face was further away than I had guessed and by the time I reached it, I was out of breath.

Here it was. I felt for the crack on the edge of the door and there it was. My fingers followed the uniform cut in the rock – perfectly straight and only as wide as the tip of my finger.

So, how did you open a door like this?

"I don't see a handle," Heron said from behind me. "And it's huge. Too big to push or pull open."

"What's the point of a door that doesn't push or pull open?" I asked feeling a small thrill as he came up behind me and stood so close I could feel his warmth.

"Maybe it pivots. Take your finger out of that crack."

Once I'd obeyed, he leaned his shoulder against the rock. Nothing happened.

"It was a nice try," I said encouragingly.

But he wasn't done yet. He looked over his shoulder sharply. "Olfijum?"

His dragon shuffled through the trees to join him as Nasataa's snout found my hand.

"Hungry?" I asked. "I'm afraid I don't have anything for you."

And that would be a problem, because at the rate Nasataa was growing, he could use more to eat! He was already tearing berries from bushes and eating leaves when Olfijum leaned his shoulder against the rock. With the sound of stone on stone, the wall shifted, sending little pebbles, pieces of shale, and chunks of rock raining down on us.

I gasped.

The wall pivoted on a central point, spinning from the middle to open, as the door turned in the center of the doorway. Without hesitating, Heron stepped inside. There was the sound of flint and steel and some blowing and then a dragon laugh from Olfijum.

He spat flame and a torch flared to life as he disappeared into the doorway.

"I guess we're next," I said, looking at Nasataa, but the little dragon was already rushing forward, fearless in the face of the unknown.

"You wanted adventure, Seleska," I told myself as I tried to block out images of the rock wall crumbling and falling on me or of the darkness being filled with bats. "Now you have it!"

Chapter Eighteen

Olfijum collapsed almost as soon as he passed the doorway, his eyes closing in exhaustion. I felt tense as I stepped around his body. The last dragon I'd seen lying like that was Kyrowat. We were fighting a losing battle when all our allies were spent or dying.

Fear was a new thing for me. I'd been trying all my life to be positive and hopeful and to embrace adventure and fun. But in the last two days, all my happy visions of what the world could be had seemed to shatter one by one. Though I'd known Hubric and Kyrowat for only a couple of days, their deaths shattered something in me, leaving me edgy and broken.

And now here we were, hiding in a cave.

Heron handed me a torch as Nasataa curled up against Olfijum's flank and promptly went to sleep. They were both worn past exhaustion.

The room in front of the door was carved out of rock, with a wide shelf around the edge and a stairway carved into the rock leading further back into the cave.

"There's something here," Heron said, studying a pedestal beside the stairs. "Ah ha!"

He pressed down on a wide carving and the door spun, once again grinding stone on stone before it shut.

I had the awful sensation of being locked in my own tomb.

"I don't like the dark," I said aloud, feeling silly even as I said it, but hadn't I just fled Manticores and a soul-sucking band of Bubblers in the dark? Hadn't Atura stolen Hubric's soul in the dark? It wasn't that crazy to hate the dark.

"Let's find out what we're dealing with here," Heron said. "The dragons will be fine for now."

"Unless the Manticores find this place and Atura opens the door."

Heron took my free hand. "Don't get so grim on me, now, sweet honey. Where's your sense of adventure?"

"Maybe Atura swallowed that, too," I muttered as we found the first rooms – a small sleeping quarters with three bunks, a small room with a hole in the center of it – for waste, obviously – a small storeroom with a few meager supplies. Hubric's notes had been right. Enough room for three. Enough for a few days.

"Look," Heron said as he pulled back a curtain at the back of the cave. A dark cavern led further into the mountain.

"A way out if you're brave enough for it," I breathed. "Do you think Hubric was ever here?"

"No."

"You sound awful certain," I said as he leaned back against a wall, pulling me to him and leaning his forehead against mine.

"The food was rotten. Did you see that? No one has been here in years. If he was here before, it hasn't been for a really long time. Maybe lichen and moss grow differently here. Maybe. But I'd guess no one has been here in a decade."

"Is that supposed to cheer me up?"

He kissed my forehead. "No."

His lips trailed down to kiss my cheek and I felt little thrills run down my spine.

"What are you doing?"

"Distracting you."

"Why?"

"So you don't realize that we're going to have to go into that cavern. And because I can now. Do you know how long I've been waiting to kiss you like this?"

I didn't like the sound of going into that cavern at all – though the rest of that sounded good. "Maybe they won't find us here."

"We can wedge the door and that will hold for a while. Long enough to get a head start, maybe. But Seleska, I think we have to go into that cavern.

And I know that you're trying to be brave, but you're actually scared. I know that you have someone you want to protect more than your own life. I just want to give you one moment to forget about it all before you have to call on your courage and pick up that burden again."

I liked the sound of that and as his lips trailed down to mine, I let myself melt into the warmth of his kiss, leaning against him as if he was a wall holding my world up.

The extra weight of me leaning against him must have triggered it. That was the only conclusion I could come to later on.

There was a shifting sound and then another door pivoted open and we tumbled through it to the other side.

I gasped at what I saw. Faint light trickled in from a narrow crack in the rock high up. But the torchlight was more than enough to show that this wasn't just any room.

Hundreds of keys hung on hooks on the wall. Maybe even thousands. There were iron keys and gold, silver and bronze. Keys big as the bone in my upper leg and small as my pinky finger. Some glowed with an inner magic. Some looked as common as the locks I'd seen in Abergande on shop doors.

"Well, you *were* looking for a key," Heron said with a strangled laugh at the same moment that I heard a scraping sound from the room outside. "They've found us!"

He leapt up, rushing back the way we'd come, but my eyes were glued on the keys in front of me.

I had the most terrible sensation that one of these keys had to be the one. But without having talked to Raolcan, I didn't know which one it was. And I couldn't take all of them. We couldn't carry even a tenth of them with us. Not even if Olfijum wasn't exhausted and worn.

Who hides keys in an old cave where just anyone can find them? What crazy person thinks this is a good way to protect something valuable.

Maybe they weren't valuable at all. Maybe they were just decoration. In a cave hidden by a secret door. Where no one had been in ten years.

My theory sounded flat even to me.

I stared at the wall, swallowing. Atura could carry all these keys with those Manticores of hers. If I didn't pick one and she got here, she could just take them all and choose later.

I could only choose one. And I needed to do it now.

There was a yell from outside the room.

"Seleska! Is there anything in there that can help wedge the door? I'm running out of wood!"

"No!" I called back, distracted.

There was a scurry of feet and then Nasataa stood beside me. He made a whining sound in the back of his throat as he looked at all the keys.

"Yeah, little buddy. You and me both."

I propped the torch in a holder and opened the book, flipping through the pages, trying to find the word 'key.'

Key. Key. Key.

Was there anything?

A pounding sound from outside didn't sound very good.

"It won't hold for long!" Heron called. "Come on, Olfijum. Let's see if you fit in the caverns."

There! The word key!

"The light brightens and grows

Crown to toes

But fragile lies

Our key to the skies

And only the arrow

Shot from the bow

Can steel us for

Coming war. "

Steel. Arrow. Was there a key like that? I held the torch high, tucking the book back into my belt pouch as I looked. Arrow. Arrow. Arrow. I only looked at steel keys.

"Seleska!" Heron called. "Come on!"

My fingers closed around a steel key with an arrow carved into the top of it. This had to be it, right? It didn't glow. It didn't seem special. It was only as long as my finger. Simple. Plain.

How could this be right?

There was a crash from outside in the main room and Heron grabbed me from behind, dragging me away from the keys.

"Hurry!" he whispered to me as he ran, dragging me along with him and slamming the secret door shut behind us. Nasataa's tail wrapped around my feet and I stumbled, catching myself at the last moment.

The key was still in my hand. I shoved it into my belt pouch as the sounds of cracking and snarls of Manticores filled the air behind us.

READ MORE OF SELESKA'S story in Dragon Tide: Episodes 6-10

Behind the Scenes:

USA Today bestselling author, Sarah K. L. Wilson loves spinning a yarn and if it paints a magical new world, twists something old into something reborn, or makes your heart pound with excitement ... all the better! Sarah hails from the rocky Canadian Shield in Northern Ontario -

learning patience and tenacity from the long months of icy cold - where she lives with her husband and two small boys. You might find her building fires in her woodstove and wishing she had a dragon handy to light them for her

Sarah would like to thank **Harold Trammel** and **Eugenia Kollia** for their incredible work in beta reading and proofreading this book. Without their big hearts and passion for stories, this book would not be the same.

www.sarahklwilson.com

INSTAGRAM[1] | AMAZON[2] | NEWSLETTER[3]

---

1. https://www.instagram.com/sarahklwilson

2. https://www.amazon.com/Sarah-K-L-Wilson/e/B0064MSJRE/

3. https://www.subscribepage.com/brandawareness